The Miracle

Quintus was passing through a pottery shop in London one morning when he stopped before a table displaying vases. The sight of them brought back sharply the memory of the pottery yard in Jerusalem where he had first seen his wife, Veronica. For a moment the pain was almost beyond bearing.

Suddenly his body went rigid as he turned one of the small vases slowly in his hand. The scene he was looking at was familiar—a hillside green with thorn bushes, with a burst of red where one portion was in blossom.

He had last seen this identical scene, painted with the same exquisite artistry by Veronica's own hand, in the pottery yard in Jerusalem!

VERONICA WAS ALIVE!

Books by Frank G. Slaughter

Published by POCKET BOOKS

*Are there paperbound books you want
but cannot find in your retail stores?*

The
Thorn
of
Arimathea

by

FRANK G.
SLAUGHTER

A KANGAROO BOOK

PUBLISHED BY POCKET BOOKS NEW YORK

THE THORN OF ARIMATHEA

Doubleday edition published 1959

POCKET BOOK edition published February, 1977

This POCKET BOOK edition includes every word contained in
the original, higher-priced edition. It is printed from brand-
new plates made from completely reset, clear, easy-to-read type.
POCKET BOOK editions are published by
POCKET BOOKS,
a division of Simon & Schuster, Inc.,
A GULF+WESTERN COMPANY
630 Fifth Avenue,
New York, N.Y. 10020.
Trademarks registered in the United States
and other countries.

Contents

Author's Note

Readers familiar with the so-called apocryphal books of the New Testament will recognize in this novel the story of Veronica and the miracle-working veil, very much as described in the *Acta Pilati*. Less familiar, but even more beautiful, is the legendary account of how Joseph of Arimathea founded the church at Glastonbury, in England, upon the Isle of Avalon made famous by Tennyson. Most moving of all is the legend of the winter thorn at Glastonbury, said to have been planted on the grave of Joseph of Arimathea, blooming ever after at Christmastime as a living symbol of the Resurrection.

No novelist could hope to express these legends so beautifully as did Alfred Lord Tennyson:

> This from the blessed land of Aramat,
> After the day of darkness, when the dead
> Went wandering over Moriah—the good saint
> Arimathaean Joseph, journeying brought
> To Glastonbury, where the winter thorn
> Blossoms at Christmas, mindful of our Lord.
>
> To the Island-valley of Avilion;
> Where falls not hail or rain or any snow,
> Nor even wind blows loudly; but it lies
> Deep-meadow'd, happy, fair with orchard lawns
> And bowery hollows crowned with summer sea.

FRANK G. SLAUGHTER, M.D.

Jacksonville, Florida

BOOK 1

Jerusalem

The sun was sinking toward the western hills when Quintus Volusianus brought his mule to a stop where the road from Joppa rounded a crest overlooking the city of Jerusalem. The day was hot, for spring was already well advanced. Below him the hillside was green with thornbushes, save for an occasional area which—perhaps better watered than the rest or in the more direct rays of the sun—had already burst into bloom with the odd tiny blossoms that looked like drops of blood.

With a sigh of weariness Quintus sank to a boulder and allowed the mule to crop the grass near the rocky path. His temper was none too good, for it had been a long ride and walk—mainly the latter—from Joppa. If Pontius Pilate, procurator of Judea, had remained as he should in his Roman city of Caesarea to the north, Quintus thought resentfully, he would not have been forced to journey to this hot hillside in the mountains of Judea. His business could just as well have been transacted in the cool of Pilate's courtyard in Caesarea, while soldiers were sent to bring in the man he sought. His mission completed, he would have been able to embark on the next ship for Rome without having to visit this mean city which no people in their right minds would have chosen for a capital anyway.

In truth, Quintus had little taste for the errand upon which he had been sent from Rome by the Emperor Tiberius. He had nevertheless stifled his objections and sailed as soon as the royal commission had been placed in his hands. Tiberius had never shown much patience

1

with those who opposed his imperial will and, since his illness had been so prolonged and severe, what little patience he'd had at any time was long since gone.

The passage from Caesarea to Joppa, although short in terms of Roman miles, had been complicated by a storm which kept the ship at sea for three days while covering less than a day's ordinary sail. Besides, the vessel had been cluttered with pilgrims going to Jerusalem for some sort of religious ceremony, landsmen who had called on their god in continuous prayer to save them from what was at its most an ordinary storm— between trips to the side for a more utilitarian purpose. To an experienced sailor like Quintus, who had accompanied the legions to the far corners of the world, it had been a weary and disgusting affair, certainly not in conformity with the dignity of one who bore an imperial commission.

At Joppa he had paused for the night at an inn, not realizing that the pilgrims hurrying to Jerusalem for their religious celebration would hire all the horses, carriages, and even carts. When he had ordered a horse brought around the next morning for the ride to Jerusalem, he had been able to hire nothing better than the mule now cropping grass beside the road. And that unfortunate creature had gone lame today before the sun had reached its height, forcing him to trudge into Jerusalem, leading his mule, like any other pilgrim.

Had the countryside been particularly inspiring, this in itself might not have been much of a hardship, for Quintus was a seasoned campaigner, with a hard, muscular body and a clear eye sharpened in a dozen campaigns wherever people had been foolish enough to rebel against the might of Rome and its emperor. But the narrow path had wound through a region of bare rocky hillside, with only here and there a small patch of fertile valley land where the inhabitants pastured their cattle and grew the small stores of grain necessary to keep them alive.

A few miles to the north the road had joined another leading southward from the central portion of this hilly district where Pontius Pilate ruled as governor in the name of Rome. The junction had doubled the traffic on the road; now, as Quintus moved on, carts jolted past him every few minutes and occasionally a horseman or a chariot pushed him off the highway altogether, causing him to bruise his feet on the rocks. Had he known he'd be forced thus to trudge on mountain roads he would have worn the tough leather half boots of the Roman legionnaires, but he had expected to step ashore on the quay at Caesarea and be escorted to the palace of the procurator of Judea with the ceremony due an agent of the emperor, and hence was but lightly shod.

From the small plateau or tableland where he had halted the mule Quintus could look down upon Jerusalem. The central part of the city was very impressive, where a great temple and a mighty fortress-palace with four towers stood, surrounded by less important buildings. The temple and palace were connected, he could see, by several stairways, along one of which a file of Roman legionnaires was marching in full military gear.

The temple had walls of highly polished granite that shone brightly in the setting sun. Three broad terraces were surrounded by colonnaded archways, and the rays of the sun reflected from their fluted sides turned them into what he thought at first was gold—until he remembered seeing just such columns in the Greek city of Corinth and recognized the bronze which was characteristic of that metropolis. Around the colonnaded terraces the pure white marble of the gates and courtyard gave majestic splendor to the structure.

"Look!" a youth running ahead of his family on the path cried excitedly. "Look at the temple!"

And indeed it was an impressive sight, far more so than anything Quintus had yet seen in this benighted land except the Roman splendor of Pilate's capital at Caesarea.

2

Many of the pilgrims had already camped on the hillside overlooking Jerusalem, but Quintus joined the crowd pouring through a gate in the northern wall, identified by a legend chiseled into the stone in Greek as the "Gate of Samaria." Two burly soldiers in uniforms he did not recognize scrutinized the passers-by carefully, pausing every now and then to drag one roughly from the crowd for questioning. Watching them, Quintus did not notice a Roman centurion standing on the other side of the gate until he spoke.

"Quintus Volusianus!" the centurion cried. "By all the gods, is it you?"

"Sixtus Porcius!"

"They told me Tiberius had recalled you to Rome to serve as his lackey," Sixtus said as Quintus led his mule out of the stream of traffic.

"I'm lackey to no man, as you well know," Quintus growled.

"I do know, brave Quintus," said Sixtus. "And I have this in proof." He drew back the short sleeve of his tunic to show a broad scar extending across his shoulder. "What brings you to Jerusalem, man?"

"I have come to see Pontius Pilate. They told me at Caesarea he would be here."

"Better you had stayed at the city of the Caesars. Jerusalem always puts Pilate in a black mood—and rightly so."

"Why?"

"Our governor has a rare penchant for making mistakes, and none are worse than those he makes in Jerusalem. My advice is not to let him know you are here until the Jewish feast is over. If nothing happens this time, he may be in a better mood."

"I'd hoped to finish my business and be on my way in a couple of days."

"I take it you don't like what you've seen of this land of Judea?"

"It isn't Rome—by a good margin."

Sixtus' laugh boomed out. "You've seen the best of it so far—unless you journey northeast to the lake called Tiberias, where Pilate has a villa. There's a land of wine and honey—and beautiful women. The Galileans are a spirited people, not oppressed by the yoke of the priests like those here in Jerusalem."

"I have no time for lakes—or Galileans. Tiberius is dying."

"We heard you were his favorite physician, but take my advice and don't be in a hurry. Avoid the palace of Antonia and Pontius Pilate until the celebration is over. Go to an inn and tell them you are a rich man from Alexandria or Athens. Jewish moneylenders and merchants from all over the world come here to sacrifice in the temple and be cheated by the moneychangers. Rattle your purse loud enough and the landlord will turn someone out and make room for you." His laugh boomed out again. "But don't tell him you're a Roman."

"Since when has that been a cause for shame?"

"Shame? No. Prudence? Yes. There are men among these Jews—sicarii they call themselves—who will murder anyone for a fee. Romans they kill just for the pleasure it gives them."

"You were ever one for telling tales, Sixtus. But if Pontius Pilate is in the temper you say he is, mayhap I'll wait a day or two."

"Read the signs before you enter any building," Sixtus warned. "These Jews have strange ideas about their god—and are quick to take affront at the presence of an unbeliever."

"Now I know you are cozening me. But I will watch out and settle with you later."

Still leading his mule, Quintus followed a teeming street down a narrow and steadily sinking valley that seemed to divide the city into two parts. Now that he thought about it, Sixtus' warning seemed foolish. The bearer of a royal commission must be treated as if he were a direct representative of the emperor, which in truth he was. There was no reason why he should foreswear the comfort of a sunken bath tonight and the wine of the procurator's table for such mean accommodations as the buildings he saw along the streets here must afford.

This seemed to be the business part of the city. Bazaars lined the streets, with here and there the courtyard of an artisan set back a little so his wares could be displayed in the open, under the shade of a tree or a richly woven canopy. Shortly Quintus passed beneath a magnificent viaduct leading from the palace on the western hill directly to the outer courts of the temple itself. Just beyond the viaduct he found a stairway leading upward apparently to the temple area, for people were passing up and down it in a steady stream.

Across from the stairway, at the corner of a street, was an open court shaded by a great tree. At the back of the court he could see the walls of a building and against them, protected by an extension of the room as a shed, the wheels and bake ovens of a group of potters. Some were busy turning clay on the wheels into varied graceful shapes; a young boy was tending the oven whose fires were fed by what appeared to be dried thornbushes, such as Quintus had seen on the hillside today.

Wearily wiping away the sweat from his dusty forehead with his sleeve, Quintus' gaze fell upon the inviting shade of the potter's yard and the girl who sat there, painting delicate figures and scenes on the finished vases in bright-colored enamel. Beside her was a cool-looking water jar, and when she saw his eyes fixed upon it she smiled and said, in Greek, "If you are thirsty, sir, the stranger is always welcome at the house of Abijah, the potter."

Quintus looped the donkey's lead rope over a post at the edge of the potter's yard and made his way between rows of earthenware displayed for sale to where the girl sat. She was already pouring him a cup from the water jar, and as he lifted it and swallowed the water, he was sure no wine had ever tasted better.

"Ah-h-h." He sighed with satisfaction and reached for the purse that hung at his belt.

"Water is furnished by the Most High," the girl said quietly in Greek, as had been her first greeting. "It would be a sin to take pay for it."

"The Most High?" Quintus frowned over the phrase; even in Greek it had an odd sound.

6

"That is the name we give our god," she explained. "He is so holy that not even a priest may speak his real name, so we call him Lord, or the Most High."

She was in her early twenties, Quintus judged, a slender, graceful girl with the long symmetrical fingers of an artist. Her features were delicately formed, almost patrician, like the faces seen on Greek coins. Her hair was like gold and her eyes brown and warm.

"Why did you speak Greek to me?" he asked.

"You do not have the face of a Jew."

"Neither do you."

"My mother was a Greek, of Tarsus," she explained. "My father is a Jew, but after Mother died we came to Jerusalem and he married the sister of Joseph of Arimathea."

The name meant nothing to Quintus, but she had been right about his nationality. His father had been a Greek freedman and his mother a girl of Corinth. Quintus had long since stopped considering himself anything except a Roman, however, his father having obtained Roman citizenship and passed it on to him at birth.

His eyes fell now upon the exquisite vase the girl had half finished painting. The scene was one of great beauty, a hillside green with thornbushes—just such a one as he had seen overlooking Jerusalem—with a burst of red where one small area was in blossom.

"You have great skill," he complimented her.

The color in her cheeks heightened a little. "I paint only scenes that have meaning for me," she explained. "Perhaps what they mean shows in them."

He picked up another vase from a shelf attached to the tree under which she sat. The scene was identical, the same green hillside, the same bright spray of scarlet blossoms. "What does this mean, save its own beauty?"

She hesitated momentarily. "Are you a Roman soldier?"

"Yes."

A shadow seemed to pass over her face and a look

7

of wariness came into her eyes. "It is nothing that would interest you," she said. "Only something concerned with our religion."

He sensed that his being a Roman had somehow created an atmosphere of distrust where before had been warm welcome, and he remembered Sixtus' warning about the Jews having no love for Romans.

"I am a physician, by name Quintus Volusianus," he explained. "My work is healing the sick, not persecuting anyone."

Her eyes lost the look of wariness. "Had you come two Passovers ago, sir, I would have sought your help for myself."

"You look healthy enough now."

"For ten years all Jerusalem pitied Veronica, the painter of vases. I sat here because I could not walk and tried to smile, although the pain was great when the pieces of bone were working themselves out of my leg."

"Have you been cured?" he asked, startled.

"Completely."

"Rarely does anyone recover, once the bone begins to be extruded. I would like to discuss this with your physician."

Gently Veronica shook her head. "He was not a physician but a great healer."

"And his name?"

"Jesus of Nazareth."

Quintus stared at the girl called Veronica, wondering if he could really have heard aright. For she had spoken the name written on the royal commission he bore, the name of the very healer he had been sent from Rome to find in the hope that the Jew called Jesus might help the dying emperor.

"Is something wrong, sir?" The girl's voice broke into Quintus' thoughts.

"No." He recovered his composure. "It's just that I came from Rome to find the man you named."

She looked startled. "Then you do not know?"

"Know what?"

"Two years ago—at the Passover season—Pontius Pilate condemned Jesus to death, at the behest of the High Priest Caiaphas and his followers. The Roman soldiers crucified him."

This was shocking news indeed, and yet believable. The report Tiberius had received concerning the miraculous powers of healing said to be possessed by a man called Jesus of Nazareth had been hearsay only. And, considering the distance between Palestine and Rome, two years was not an overlong time for such word to travel.

Nevertheless the realization that he had made the journey for nothing was disconcerting to Quintus. "If Jesus was crucified, how did he heal you?" he asked.

"Through the veil with the print of his face upon it."

"Save your tales for the credulous, girl," Quintus said sharply, and turned back toward the mule.

"Wait!" she cried. "Here is the proof." From the folds of her robe she took a small case such as women use to hold jewels. It was made of a rare wood—sandalwood, he judged—with a golden clasp of delicate workmanship.

"You can see for yourself," she said, holding it out to him.

"What is it?"

"The veil. The veil that healed me."

"What healing power could a veil have?" he asked, but not as harshly as before.

"The power Jesus gave it. Look." She opened the case gently and drew out a piece of cloth. It was of the fine woolen fabric woven mostly in the city of Byblos on the coast of the Great Sea between Tyre and Antioch, some miles to the north of Joppa. Soft, lustrous, and so thin as to be almost completely transparent, the fabric was prized by women everywhere for making head veils.

When she held the cloth out to him, Quintus took it and held it up to the light. To his surprise he saw that it was mottled with light brown stains.

"I see nothing but a soiled cloth."

"Look closely at the pattern of the stain," she urged.

When he examined it carefully the stain did take on a pattern, although whether real or only a figment of his imagination he could not be certain. Vaguely it seemed to have the appearance of a man's features, outlined in brown stains upon the white fabric.

"Do you see it?" Veronica asked eagerly.

"Perhaps the print of a man's face," he said, giving it back to her. "Nothing more."

Her eyes were shining as she folded the cloth reverently and put it back into the small case. "It is the print of Jesus' own face stained into the cloth by sweat and dust as he was taken to the cross."

"And it healed you?" he asked incredulously.

"I was made whole the moment I took the cloth from him. Many others have been cured by it since then."

Logic argued that this was nothing but a fairy tale. And yet it was undoubtedly his duty to overlook nothing that might help the dying emperor. "Will you tell me the story, Veronica?" he asked. "And grant me your forgiveness for being so short-tempered?"

"Of course," she said. "Come sit here in the shade beside me, and pour yourself water from the jug if you are still thirsty."

Quintus sat on the ground beside the girl with his back against the great tree. The light was already darkening in the potter's yard, and the air was growing cooler with the approach of night. It was an oddly restful place in spite of the constant whir of potters' wheels in the background and the blast of heat that touched him occasionally when the boy firing the kiln opened the door.

"Before I was healed, I would sometimes lie in the

10

house for weeks when the fever was upon me," Veronica began, "hardly knowing where I was or what was happening. The pain was like iron spikes being driven into my leg below the knee while the bone was working loose. Then for a while after the splinters would come out there was no pain and no fever and I could sit here in the shade of the tree, painting the vases we sell mainly to the crowds that come to the temple on feast days. My father hired many physicians, but none of them could help me, not even Joseph of Galilee."

"Is this Joseph a famous physician?"

She nodded. "He studied in Alexandria and learned the medicines and treatments favored by the Greeks before he became the *medicus viscerus* of the temple."

"I, too, studied at Alexandria," Quintus said. "And at Cnidus and Pergamum."

"Then you must be famous too."

Quintus shook his head. "To become well known a physician must work in the cities, treating the rich and those in high places. I dress the wounds of soldiers in battle and treat those stricken by disease in camp."

"When Joseph of Galilee could not help me, I gave up hope," Veronica continued. "Even when Jesus of Nazareth came to Jerusalem and they said he could raise the dead, I held back from going to him."

"Why?"

"My hopes had been raised so many times and most of the profits from the pottery yard had gone to pay physicians who failed to help me. I dared not hope the Galilean healer could heal me, lest I be disappointed again."

"That is understandable."

"There was great excitement during the week Jesus was in Jerusalem. The priests and Pharisees sought ways to trap him because he preached that they were corrupt and no longer gave their lives to the service of the Most High. They planned to bring charges of blasphemy against him but were afraid to arrest Jesus because of the crowds that followed him. Then came the night before the Passover feast—we eat it at this season in remembrance of the time when our God passed over

11

the children of Israel in answer to the prayers of Moses and killed the first-born in every Egyptian household as a sign that Pharaoh should let our people go. That night one of Jesus' own disciples—a man named Judas —told the temple guards he had gone to pray in the garden called Gethsemane on the Mount of Olives. The soldiers took him there and he was brought before the Sanhedrin."

Quintus frowned. "I never heard of a Roman court with that name."

"The Sanhedrin is the high court of Israel," Veronica explained. "Only a few of its members were present that night; those who were quickly judged Jesus guilty of blasphemy because he said he could destroy the temple if he wished. They sent him to Pontius Pilate, but at first the procurator found no wrong in him. Then the servants of the High Priest Caiaphas stirred up the crowds to demand that Jesus be crucified, and Pilate sentenced him to death."

"It doesn't sound legal."

"There have been many arguments about that. The Romans claim that Jesus named himself King of the Jews, so they had no choice. But Pontius Pilate himself called Jesus a just man and washed his hands before the crowd to show he had nothing to do with condemning him."

"Yet Pilate did order Jesus crucified?"

"Yes. My brother Jonathan put me on the mule he uses to bring clay for the wheels, but the crowd was so thick we could not get near the hill where they were going to crucify him."

"Then you didn't actually see Jesus of Nazareth yourself?"

"I saw him," she said, her eyes aglow. "He passed right by us as he carried the *patibulum* to the hill of crucifixion. The cross was heavy, and he fell in the street right before me. They put the beam on another man then, and when Jesus stood up I took the veil from my head and handed it to him to wipe away the dirt and sweat. He pressed his face against it, making the print you saw there, before he handed it back to me. When I took the cloth from his hands I was healed."

"As suddenly as that?"

"Yes. I found myself on my feet, although I had not stood for several years. And I walked away—walked and carried the cloth, even through the storm."

"You said nothing about a storm."

"It came up after they nailed Jesus to the cross, as if the very elements were angry at the way he had been treated. I was terrified and ran through the streets until I got home."

"Have you been well since?"

"I have felt no pain to this day."

It was a strange story, but as she told it, a convincing one. Nor did he doubt that, to her at least, it had seemed to happen as she had described it.

"Thank you for telling me your story, Veronica," he said.

"You do not believe it?"

"I can see that you are well."

"But you do not believe the healing power of Jesus cured me?"

"I am a physician," he explained gently. "I mix medicines and sometimes they cure the sick, though not so often as I would like. I splint broken bones and they often heal. I dress wounds, and if there is no corruption they, too, usually become well. But I find it hard to believe that merely the touch of a piece of cloth stained with dust and sweat in the outline of a man's face could heal disease when the efforts of skilled physicians had failed."

She nodded soberly. "I suppose it would be hard for you to understand, if you did not know Jesus."

Quintus got to his feet. "What you have told me completes my mission in Jerusalem," he said. "I shall return to Joppa tomorrow."

Her eyes widened. "But I only told you how Jesus died—and how I was healed."

"I came here in search of Jesus of Nazareth," he explained, "with instructions to take him to Rome—to

13

heal the Emperor Tiberius. But now that he is dead——"

"Jesus is not dead!" she cried. "He rose from the dead on the third day after they crucified him!"

4

Quintus stared at the girl's transfigured face. Veronica obviously believed the story she had told him. And yet as a physician he could not admit that those truly dead ever return to life.

A deep voice spoke beside him. "My daughter speaks truth, sir—though perhaps indiscreetly. Jesus of Nazareth does live."

The man who had spoken was tall, with a majestic beard and deep-set eyes in which goodness and warmth of conviction shone. "I am Abijah, Veronica's father," he said. "Welcome to our household, noble sir."

Quintus was taller than the average, but he was still shorter than Abijah. "My name is Quintus Volusianus," he said courteously. "And I have no right to be called noble. My father was a freedman in the household of the Emperor Tiberius."

"Nobility is in a man's heart and in his countenance," Abijah said simply, "not in the trappings he wears. You are a Roman then?"

"A Roman by birth, a Greek by inheritance; I am physician to the Praetorian Guard, assigned to the royal household."

"I could not help overhearing your conversation with my daughter," Abijah said. "Are you an agent of the procurator, Pontius Pilate, too—or the Legate Vitellius in Antioch?"

As legate of Syria, with his seat at the city of Antioch to the north, Vitellius was actually governor of the entire territory. Pontius Pilate, as procurator of Judea, was subject to him, as were the other rulers in this area, including Herod Antipas, tetrarch of Galilee and Peraea.

"I hold a commission directly from the emperor him-

14

self," Quintus explained. "He heard stories concerning a healer named Jesus of Nazareth and sent me to bring him to Rome."

Abijah bent his head a little and looked into Quintus' eyes. "Will you swear to that, on your honor as a Roman?"

"Why should I?" Quintus demanded, a little irked that a mere potter of Jerusalem with clay from the wheel still on his hands should question his honor.

"Pilate says we lie when we claim that Jesus rose from the dead," Abijah explained. "He paid the soldiers who watched beside the tomb to say that Jesus' disciples came in the night and stole his body away. It is not entirely safe to be known as a follower of Jesus of Nazareth, especially when the procurator is in residence."

"Then why tell me?"

"My daughter rarely mistakes what is in a man's heart, Quintus Volusianus. And since I have looked in your eyes, I see that I need require no oath from you."

"In that case, Abijah," Quintus said, "I willingly give assurance that no harm will ever come to your household because of me—on my honor as a Roman and my physician's oath as well."

"The day grows old," said Abijah. "We will be honored if you will deign to share our humble lodging."

"I had intended going to an inn," Quintus protested.

"They have been filled long since. With the commission you bear you could no doubt force someone out, but it would cause a considerable commotion."

"I have seen too many of the so-called nobles use such tactics," Quintus agreed. "If you will have me, Abijah, I shall be honored to rest in your house."

"Go, daughter," Abijah said in the same gentle voice. "Set another place for the evening meal."

Veronica got quickly to her feet and disappeared into the house at the back of the yard. "Jonathan," Abijah called to the youth tending the ovens, "come take our guest's mule to the stable and see that it is watered and fed."

"Yes, Father." Jonathan was a fine strapping lad of

15

perhaps fifteen. He had a more Jewish cast to his features than Veronica who, Quintus remembered, had told him she was half Greek.

"Put our guest's roll beside your sleeping place, my son," Abijah directed. "He rests with us this night."

The boy's face lit up at once and Abijah smiled. "Jonathan is young, with a youth's curiosity. Tell him some stories of Rome and Alexandria, and he will be your slave.

"We are a family of potters," Abijah explained as they walked through the yard. "Members of the guild who specialize in fine work—mainly vases and such. Because of my daughter's skill with enamel, our product is much in demand."

"Your craftsmanship is very superior," said Quintus. "I have seen none better, not even in Egypt."

"That indeed is a compliment," Abijah said. "The potters of Egypt have been skilled for thousands of years, long even before our people were brought out of slavery in Egypt by Moses." They stopped before a wheel, a wooden disc on a vertical spindle, so arranged that it could be turned by kicking the feet against another disc at its base, leaving both hands of the potter free to mold the clay. While the wheel spun he shaped it with skilled fingers into a delicate vase.

"Jonathan brings in the clay with his mule every morning," Abijah explained, "before he goes to the school where he is studying to be a scribe. When his lessons for the day are finished, he comes back to fire the ovens and glaze the work of the day. After it is fired and the glaze is set by the heat, Veronica paints on the colors. Then our work goes into the oven for the final heating before the product is ready to be displayed in the yard."

"Your daughter is a skilled artist."

"Everyone here is an artisan," Abijah said with quiet pride. "The potter's is one of the oldest arts, going back to the very beginnings of man on earth." Then he changed the subject abruptly. "What will you do now, Quintus Volusianus? I heard you say your mission was to bring Jesus to Rome."

16

"I don't know," Quintus admitted. "I suppose I shall go back and report to the emperor that I came too late—by two years."

"Why not tell him that the Most High God sent his son to dwell among us and show us in his own life and by his teachings how we should live?"

"Romans have many gods," Quintus reminded him. "Even the emperors believe themselves divine."

"Jesus of Nazareth is the Christ, the Saviour our people have been expecting for more than a thousand years, Quintus, sent by his father, the only true God. He lives today even though Pontius Pilate had him nailed to the cross."

5

Veronica announced the evening meal, and Quintus was not able to pursue further the amazing statement of Abijah that the healer called Jesus was also the earthly son of the Jewish god. The meal was simple but well prepared, cakes of bread baked in the family oven, goat's milk, and a dish of goat flesh prepared with spices and herbs in a pleasing manner. A sweetish wine was also served which he found very pleasant. Veronica, as in all Jewish households, did not eat with the men who made up the family, including several brothers besides the young Jonathan and various other relatives who also worked in the pottery yard.

Jonathan questioned Quintus shyly at first, but when the physician answered freely, he launched into a veritable flood of queries about Rome and the other cities of the empire. When the meal was finished, Abijah said, "If you would learn more of the men you came here to seek, Quintus, I can take you to a kinsman of mine named Joseph of Arimathea. He knew Jesus well."

"I would like to talk to him," Quintus said. "The emperor will insist upon knowing everything that happened."

The streets were still thronged with people as they

17

made their way across the city to the slope of the western hill in what was known as the "Upper City." Around them Greek was heard as often as the Aramaic tongue favored by the Jews. Abijah explained that there was also another language, Hebrew. It was used largely now in religious ceremonies, however, having been replaced by the Aramaic tongue which was understood and spoken by most of the people in this area at the eastern end of the Great Sea.

"The Passover is one of our holiest seasons," the potter added. "It is a ritual meal which begins what we call the 'Week of Unleavened Bread.' After the meal is eaten on the morrow, we can have no leavening in our bread for a week."

"Why are so many Greeks and other nationalities here when this is a strictly Jewish religious ceremonial?" Quintus asked.

"We Jews have been dispersed many times," Abijah explained. "You will find our people in the far cities of the Roman Empire; in fact, the Jewish colony at Alexandria is larger than the city of Jerusalem. Yet each one, no matter where he happens to be, looks to Jerusalem and the temple always. As often as he can he makes a pilgrimage to the city of our God to sacrifice in the temple."

"That should bring much business to the city."

Abijah nodded. "Of late too, many Jews have been concerned with the profit they gain instead of the real reason for the feast days. Only the shekel coined here can be used as money in the temple; every other coin must be changed, and the money-changers often bilk the pilgrims. Because the priests in the temple approved their actions, no one had the courage to name them thieves until Jesus of Nazareth came here. That was another reason why the priests and the scribes conspired to put him to death."

"If he was the son of your god, as you say," Quintus protested, "why was he killed?"

"I do not say that I understand it entirely myself," Abijah admitted. "But I believe it was so all could see

18

that Jesus is truly the Messiah and that he was able to triumph over death."

They were climbing the streets of the Upper City now. Below them lights winked here and there as torches were carried along the streets and a muted hum arose, the sound of people settling down for the night. Abijah turned in through a gate leading by a path through an enclosed garden to a rambling house of earth-plastered walls, surrounding a smaller garden court. Here was a well and the coolness of a shaded enclosure.

A bent and gnarled old man, greeted by Abijah as "Jonas," conducted them to a chamber inside the house. Here an elderly man in the long robe and gold chain of a well-to-do merchant was working at a table with a lamp burning beside him. "Abijah!" he cried warmly, getting to his feet and embracing the potter. "It is good to be visited by a kinsman at the time of a holiday."

"I have brought a physician from Rome, Quintus Volusianus, to see you, Joseph," Abijah said.

The old man bowed courteously. "Welcome to my household, Quintus of Rome," he said. "I would have named you a soldier instead of a physician."

"My father was a freedman and a soldier in the Praetorian Guard," Quintus explained. "I was brought up in the house of the emperor and became a soldier before studying the science of medicine at Alexandria, Cnidus, and Pergamum."

Joseph of Arimathea called for wine and sweet cakes. When they were brought, he served the others himself. "How is your lovely daughter, Abijah?" he asked.

"Whole in body and happy in spirit," the potter said. "I brought Quintus to see you because he is on a peculiar mission."

"The emperor sent me to bring a man called Jesus of Nazareth to Rome," Quintus explained. "Tiberius badly needs the healing power the Nazarene was reputed to possess."

19

"Not *was*, Quintus," Joseph corrected him gently. "Jesus heals every day."

"I have heard of the veil and the miraculous way it is said to have cured Veronica."

"I speak of the powers given his disciples by Jesus, especially him who leads them now."

"Who is this man?" Quintus asked quickly. Since the healer was dead, it might be that the leader of his followers could serve the purpose for which Quintus had come to Jerusalem—if by chance any of the magical powers said to have been possessed by Jesus had descended upon the disciple.

"His name is Simon Peter."

"Can you tell me where he can be found?"

"No. For one reason, I do not know; for another, you are a Roman."

"Is Peter a fugitive?"

"Much of the time. Both Herod and Pontius Pilate would like to see him caught and executed because he goes about telling how Jesus rose from the dead."

"I still find that hard to believe, sir."

"I saw Jesus crucified," Joseph said. "And with my own hands I helped take his body down from the cross and lay it in my own tomb hewn from a great stone outcrop at the corner of my garden. My servants rolled a great boulder before the tomb, and from this very room I could see the torches of the guards as they watched before it."

"How can you say he is not dead then?"

The merchant's voice took on a deeper quality, a note of deep reverence. "On the morning of the third day Mary of Magdala went to the tomb and found the stone rolled away—though not by the hands of men. She looked inside and found it empty."

"Someone could have taken the body."

"The high priest and his lackeys made that very claim," Joseph admitted. "But they could produce no one who saw it happen. The stone could not have been rolled away by less than a half dozen men. And that many would surely have been seen or heard by the guards."

"Unless they were asleep."

"The rumble of the stone would surely have awakened them."

"They might have been bribed."

"Many people saw Jesus alive after I laid him in the tomb." The merchant went to the door. "Jonas!" he called. "Come here, please. We would speak with you."

The gnarled hunchback who had ushered them into the house came and stood peering at them with rheumy eyes.

"Sit down here with us, Jonas." Joseph poured a cup of wine and gave it to the old servant. "I want you to tell my guest the story of how you gathered the crown of thorns."

6

Jonas cleared his throat with wine. "It was several years ago," he began in a quavering voice. "At the Passover season, just as it is now. I was on the hillside gathering thornbushes to fire the ovens of the potters. I sold them then," he explained, turning to Quintus, "before my joints stiffened and the noble merchant here took me as his servant so I would not starve."

He took another gulp of the wine. "That day a great procession of people was on the road to the city, ushering the Master into Jerusalem."

"We who love Jesus call him by that name," Joseph explained.

"I was angry with the Galilean that afternoon," Jonas continued, "and I blamed him because I was late selling the wood and lost a day's work. A few days later the captain of the temple guard came to my hut outside the wall and offered me a shekel to bring him a green thornbush from the hillside. I told him a green thorn was of no use, but he said he wanted it to make a crown—for a king. It sounded like a joke, but I gathered it and he gave me two shekels. Jesus was

arrested that very night, and I saw him in the courtyard of the high priest as a prisoner, wearing a crown
made from the thorns I had picked. His face was
bruised and bleeding where they had tortured him."

Jonas' voice broke and for a moment he could not
go on. Finally he blew his nose loudly and continued.
"I tried to get to the Master and tell him I did not
know the crown of thorns was for him, but the crowd
was too great. After the governor condemned him and
he was on the way to the cross, I tried to reach him
again and beg his forgiveness, but the crowd was pushing me and he could not hear."

"You saw him crucified then?" Quintus asked.

Jonas shook his head. "I felt so guilty and ashamed
that I hid in my hut for two days. On the third day
there was no more food for me or the mule, so early
in the morning I started for the hillside to gather dead
thornbushes to sell the potters for their ovens. I could
not forget how Jesus had looked with blood from the
thorns dripping down his face, but I couldn't let my
mule starve because of my grief and guilt. At the gate
the soldiers told me there was a rumor that Jesus'
disciples had stolen his body. Then on the road the
stranger appeared beside me."

"What do you mean by appeared?" Quintus asked.

"That was the way it happened, sir. One moment I
was walking along the road with the mule ahead of me
—he had been to the hill where I gathered thornbushes so often that he knew the way. The next moment the stranger was walking beside me. I don't know
where he came from."

"And you recognized him?"

"Not right away. He was wearing a long robe with
loose sleeves and a hood covering his head and hiding
his face. I somehow knew he would understand, so I
told him I was sorrowful because I had gathered the
thorns that had been used to torture the good man who
had been crucified. The stranger seemed to be sure
Jesus would forgive me, but I was not content. I kept
saying that only a sign from the Galilean himself could

ease my guilt. 'You will see the sign, Jonas,' a voice seemed to say in my heart. It was then that I saw the print of the nails."

"You saw what?" Quintus asked, startled by the matter-of-fact statement.

"The wounds where the nails had been driven through his hands when they put him on the cross. But when I looked up he suddenly disappeared."

"What did you do?"

"I stood for a moment trembling with fear; it is not every day someone like me sees a dead man come to life. When I was sure he was gone, I went up the path after the mule, and as I came around a rock beside the road I saw the sign he promised me. It was still early for the thorns to be in bloom. But in one spot, where I had pulled up the ones they used for the crown, the bushes were in full bloom, like the drops of blood I saw on the Master's face in the courtyard of the high priest. I knew then that Jesus had risen from the dead and had spoken to me on the road."

Quintus did not have the heart to remind the old wood seller that none of the evidence he'd heard so far would carry any weight in a court of law. Joseph of Arimathea had helped to put the Nazarene into the tomb and had found it empty two days later, but had not seen the body after the tomb was closed. Jonas, a childish old man whose rheumy eyes could not possess very clear vision, had talked to a stranger with scars on his hand on the road outside the city and had immediately assumed that he was the man who had been crucified. As for the blossoming of the thorns, Quintus himself had seen a dozen spots on the hillsides that afternoon where one or more bushes had bloomed prematurely.

When the old man left the room, Joseph of Arimathea turned to Quintus. "You do not believe Jonas' story?"

"As a physician I believe only what I see and understand," Quintus said. "But if Jesus of Nazareth really does live as you claim, I must find him wherever he is and take him to Rome."

23

The Jewish Passover season was scheduled to begin at sunset the day after Quintus' visit to Joseph of Arimathea. Veronica and Jonathan had invited him to accompany them early that morning to the temple where they would make the sacrifice required of every devout family at the Passover season. And since it would give him a chance to learn more about the Jews and their god, he had agreed. Shortly after sunrise Quintus ate a few dates and drank some goat's milk with them before starting out.

"The animals for the sacrifice must be ceremonially clean," Veronica explained as they ascended the staircase that had its foot almost in front of Abijah's pottery yard. "Even if we brought a lamb ourselves, the priests would never allow it. All animals must be bought from the vendors in the temple."

"At a considerable profit, no doubt."

"It is no secret that the priests share with the vendors. Jesus spoke against that too."

At the top of the steps they found themselves in the midst of a throng of people jostling each other as they moved toward the outer court of the temple. The constant roar of conversation was exceeded only by the voices of the vendors, crying their wares shrilly.

"We have been favored by the Most High this year," Veronica told him. "My vases have sold well and Jonathan is the brightest pupil in the Scribes' School, so we are sacrificing a small lamb ourselves, besides the regular sacrifice my father makes. I must go on to the Court of the Women—you can see it there through what they call the 'Beautiful Gate,' the one that shines like gold."

Veronica left them, and Quintus stood watching her slender and graceful figure as she moved through the crowd toward the Beautiful Gate. It was hard to believe she had ever been crippled, but he did not doubt her story. He was recalled to the present by Jonathan's impatient tugging at his sleeve.

"I promised to show you the sights of the temple," the youth reminded him. "This is the Outer Court. The space between the walls and the platform reached by the steps there in the center is open to anyone, whether Jew or Gentile."

"Including Romans?"

"Yes."

Around the court stretched a row of white pillared columns hewn from marble and polished until they shone. They formed a shaded cloister against the outer walls and were roofed over with timbers of cedar in a beautiful grained pattern. A section of the roof was visible from here, and Quintus could see Roman soldiers pacing back and forth upon it. Pontius Pilate, he decided, was taking no chances with the religious excitement that gripped so many of the Jews at this season—a wise precaution with the city as crowded as it was.

Jonathan had followed his gaze. "The soldiers reach the roof from the stairways leading across to the fortress called Antonia," he explained. "The governor is always in residence there at Passover season, and for the past two years they have doubled the guards."

Moving around the Outer Court, they came to the portico on the southern side of the temple area. "This is sometimes called the 'Royal Porch,'" Jonathan said. The architecture was familiar to Quintus, being in the form of a Roman basilica with a central nave and a lower aisle. In Greek cities similar structures were used as courts of law and as places of trade. Here the latter purpose was being served, for the porch was lined with booths in rows running the full length of the southern side. Pigeons in cages clucked and cooed in one section.

"Pigeons are for the poor," Jonathan explained a little contemptuously, for after all he and his sister were sacrificing a lamb today.

"Where will you buy your lamb?"

"At one of the booths. They give you a piece of parchment with your purchase written on it, and you claim it where the animals are given over to be sacrificed."

25

It was all very efficient, Quintus saw while Jonathan was bargaining importantly with a bearded Jew who ran one of the booths. When he came back, the youth carried a piece of parchment with writing on it and his purse was notably lighter. As they moved on around the Court of the Gentiles, they came upon a group of men sitting beside heavy chests. These chests had short legs and were propped up on small wooden boxes.

"The money-changers will exchange any coin for temple shekels," Jonathan said. "Only those can be used as gifts or in buying animals for the sacrifice."

"Who determines the rate of exchange?"

"They do. Jesus accused them of making the temple into a den of thieves."

Moving with the crowd that swirled through the court, they passed to the east portico. "This is called 'Solomon's Court,'" Jonathan told him. "The teachers sit here and expound questions of law."

"Surely not Roman law."

Jonathan shook his head. "Our own religious law. If we break it, we sin against the Most High."

The east portico was dotted with small platforms, each placed against one of the pillars. On these sat the teachers who, Jonathan explained, were called rabbis. A circle of people surrounded each of the rabbis, listening intently while he answered questions put to him by the crowd.

"Over there"—Jonathan pointed to a group—"is my teacher, the Rabbi Emanuel. See the young men before him? They are students with questions to ask him so the crowds can hear his wisdom."

"Is that exactly fair?"

Jonathan shrugged. "You couldn't expect ordinary people to ask intelligent questions about the law. Most of them break it ten times a day. I will come after the noonday meal to sit with the questioners."

"What is he describing now?" Quintus asked. The talk was in Aramaic, since many of the people—he had learned—no longer knew how to speak the ritual Hebrew.

"The coming of the Messiah." Jonathan lowered his

voice. "Only a few of us believe Jesus of Nazareth was the 'Expected One.' The rest still await his coming to free us from foreign rule by establishing his kingdom and exalting the Jews above all nations of the earth."

"Is that really the purpose of the Messiah?" Quintus asked, startled.

"Most Jews believe he will establish an earthly kingdom," Jonathan confided. "But my father says Jesus taught that the Kingdom of God is in a man's heart." He shrugged. "It is hard to know what is right. In the Scribes' School I am taught one thing, at home another."

"Which do you believe?"

Jonathan looked troubled. "Jesus healed my sister with the veil; I saw that myself. But if he was truly the Messiah, why did he allow the Romans to crucify him?"

"I don't know," Quintus admitted. "Even your father admits he cannot answer that question."

"Jesus' disciples believe he let himself be crucified so he could rise from the dead and show that he had triumphed over death. They think he will soon take his rightful position as the Messiah and King."

"King of what, Jonathan?"

"Of the world," the youth said confidently. "He will be above all the rulers of the earth, even the emperor of Rome."

Quintus put his hand on Jonathan's strong young shoulders. "Be careful how you say such things in a public place," he warned. "Informers are everywhere, and such talk could be called treason."

Somewhere within the temple a gong sounded. "That means the morning sacrifice is about to begin," Jonathan said excitedly. "I must claim my lamb and give it to the priests."

Quintus followed him as he threaded his way through the crowd that now filled the so-called Court of the Gentiles, until they reached the steps leading up to the second level. Here Jonathan stopped and held Quintus back.

27

"You can go no further," he said. "Read what it says on the blocks."

On the low wall separating the terrace itself from the inner court had been graven in Greek:

Let no Gentile enter within the limit and enclosure of the sanctuary. He who is caught will carry the guilt on himself, because death will follow.

Jonathan ran up the steps, the parchment ticket that entitled him to the lamb clutched in his hand. Quintus made his way to the lower court and the area where the teachers were expounding questions of the law. Some were obviously more popular than others, for the crowds around them were much larger.

While he waited for Jonathan to return and for Veronica to come from the Court of the Women, Quintus looked idly over the crowd. Every degree of wealth —indicated by richness of dress—could be seen from cripples begging alms on the steps to rich merchants in luxurious robes and gold chains talking loudly and importantly together. Varied in dress, manners, and even in appearance, as the Jews obviously were, they all seemed to be drawn to this one holy spot by the common heritage of their single god.

Quintus' musings were disturbed by a sudden commotion on the southern side of the temple court and the sound of vigorous shouting. Above the clamor of the crowds he could distinguish cries of: "Thief! Murderer! Stop the killer!"

8

Like the waters of a pool roiled by an unseen force erupting from its depths, the crowd was suddenly in a frenzy of motion. Many sought to push their way through the press of people toward the stairways leading to the upper terraces from which the outcry had come. Others tried to escape from the area before the commotion could spread to become a full-scale riot.

A heavy pigeon crate had been left against a pillar near where Quintus was standing, and he climbed upon it in order to see above the heads of the crowd. Before him was a small sea of head coverings, bobbing and weaving, rising and falling. Meanwhile the cries of "Thief" and "Murderer" had been taken up by hundreds of voices until the sound, interspersed with the shoutings of the guards, poured down the narrow nave like a torrent.

At the end of the southern portico a tall man with dark skin and a white headdress seemed to be fighting his way through the press. He was strong and, by laying about him vigorously, moved rapidly toward the very spot where Quintus stood, hardly three steps away from the stairway leading from the temple area down to the city below. The crowd seemed of two minds, some trying to evade the tall man, others to attack him. The reason was apparent when a sudden eddy formed around the fugitive, revealing that he carried a bloody dagger in one hand and a cudgel in the other.

The fleeing man was only a few paces from Quintus when a concentrated effort by his attackers brought him down. Immediately he was up again, slashing about him strongly with the cudgel, his face distorted as he shouted curses at the crowd. The very fury of his defense pushed them back, forming another eddy with him in the center, and seizing the opportunity for escape afforded by this temporary retreat of the crowd, he lunged toward the stairway beside which Quintus was standing.

The fugitive might have escaped that way, had not a beggar wearing a dingy and patched robe darted at him as a terrier worries a mastiff and wrapped his skinny arms around the tall man's legs, bringing him down. His head struck one of the outer pillars as he fell and, momentarily stunned, he crashed to the stone floor, striking his head a second time with a thump that was clearly audible. Unconscious, at least temporarily, the fugitive lay almost at Quintus' feet, while the bloodstained dagger and cudgel dropped from his hands and went skittering across the floor.

29

For a moment there was silence, then someone cried, "He is dead! The fall killed him!"

Instantly the crowd gave ground as if the prostrate man were a poisonous serpent, forming a circle around him.

"Touch him not!" a man from the crowd warned. "The law forbids touching a corpse."

Without thinking what interpretation might be put upon his action, remembering only that he was a physician and that the man before him was injured, Quintus stepped down from his pigeon crate and knelt beside the body. A glance told him the fugitive was not dead but probably only stunned by the twin blows against his head.

With skilled fingers Quintus examined the fallen man's skull, seeking the crunching feeling that would have indicated a break in the bone itself. He felt none, however, and as he removed his fingers, saw the other's eyes flutter open. For an instant they were dazed and uncertain, but they cleared quickly and his gaze swept the open area around him and the edges of the crowd now drawn away several paces in a circle, exposing the open stairway.

"He lives!" someone in the crowd shouted. "The sicarius has been raised from the dead!" Immediately others took up the cry, and the crowd surged around Quintus. Meanwhile the dagger man—for that was the literal interpretation of the term sicarius—took advantage of the confusion and turmoil to leap to his feet and plunge down the stairway to safety.

The crowd had already forgotten the murderer, however. They thronged about Quintus, some seeking to touch his garments, others trying to strike him. Backing against the pillars, he tried to fend them off, but he had put aside even the small dagger he usually wore—this morning it seemed an inappropriate ornament for a visit to a religious ceremony—and was unarmed.

To resist could mean an instant melee and his own death at the hands of the excited people, Quintus realized, so he waited as quietly as he could. Meanwhile cries of "The Nazarene has returned!" "He is one of the sicarii!" and the like sounded as the crowd ebbed and flowed about him. The most welcome sight to Quintus' eyes at that moment would have been the trappings of Roman soldiers, but they all seemed occupied elsewhere. Then, just when he was sure the balance in the sentiments of the crowd was swinging against him, help came from an unexpected source. Around the edge of the court, moving between the pillars and driving back the crowd with drawn swords, raced a party of temple guards, distinguished from the Romans by their colorful uniforms and dark skins. In what was obviously a well-practiced maneuver they surrounded him and marched him toward the stairway leading into the inner sections of the temple.

The captain of the guards was a burly man with a scarred face. As they moved along—the pace was so fast that Quintus almost had to run to keep up—he swept the crowd alertly with his eyes, obviously wary of further disturbance. The crowd had been cowed by the swords in the hands of the guards, however, and the little party made its way up the steps and into the inner recesses of the temple without further incident.

Quintus was taken directly to a sumptuously furnished room across one end of which was a polished wooden table and two chairs. A stack of parchment scrolls lay on the table, and an oil lamp burning on the wall gave illumination to the room. The captain of the guards sent the other men from the room and waited with Quintus. Shortly a door in the far wall opened and a tall man with hawklike features came in. He was dressed in a richly brocaded robe with tassels upon the hem and wore on his forehead one of the odd, boxlike ornaments called phylacteries which, Jonathan had told Quintus, contained sacred writings of the Jewish people.

"Kneel before the High Priest Caiaphas," the captain of the guard ordered. When Quintus did not obey immediately, he buffeted him on the temple with his fist, almost knocking him to the floor.

Quintus got to his feet and faced the high priest. "I

am a Roman, not a Jew," he said angrily. "Romans kneel to no Jewish priest."

"Liar!" the captain snarled. "You are one of the sicarii; you killed a money-changer and stole from him." He struck at Quintus again and thereby made a mistake. Before he had studied medicine Quintus had been a legionnaire and had grown up in the quarters of the Praetorian Guard where readiness for physical combat was almost a religion. As the captain's fist descended, he seized it and, twisting his body quickly, put his shoulder and hip against the man's burly form and catapulted him over his head easily, sending him to the floor with a crash. While the officer lay half stunned on the floor, Quintus jerked his short sword from the scabbard and laid it on the table before the priest, who had as yet not spoken.

"Tell your lackey to show a Roman the respect he is entitled to!" he snapped.

Caiaphas glanced at the captain who was painfully getting to his feet. "Why did you kill the money-changer?" he asked in Greek.

"Ask any of the crowd," Quintus said. "They will tell you the real thief was knocked to the floor in front of me and they thought him dead. While I was examining him to see what were his injuries, he regained consciousness and ran down the steps."

"Then you did not raise him from the dead?"

"Of course not. He was no more dead than you or me." He grinned. "And not half so dead as your captain there."

The officer was on his feet now, glowering. He strode to the table and reached for his sword, but the high priest put his hand on it. "Compose yourself, Malchus," he said. "It seems you have been even more stupid than usual."

Malchus drew himself up angrily. "I heard the crowd shouting the name of the Nazarene. Obviously he was trying to stir them up and cause trouble!"

The high priest turned back to Quintus. "Who are you?"

"Quintus Volusianus, physician to Tiberius, Emperor of Rome."

Some of the haughtiness went out of Caiaphas' manner. "Why are you in Jerusalem?" he asked.

"I bear an imperial commission, with orders to bring to Rome the healer called Jesus of Nazareth, that he may attend the emperor."

For a moment the high priest seemed stunned, as if he could not believe what he had heard, but he quickly regained control. "Your mission has ended then," he said. "The man you seek was condemned to death two years ago by Pontius Pilate—and crucified."

Quintus let the room fill with silence before he answered. "I have already learned that," he said. "But I have also been told that Jesus of Nazareth rose from the dead."

"A lie!" the high priest snapped. "His disciples stole the body from the tomb."

"Many claim to have seen the Galilean since he was taken down from the cross."

"They lie too! He is dead, I tell you! Go back to Rome and report that to the emperor."

"His followers say Jesus will come again—as the Messiah," Quintus insisted.

"The man was a charlatan, an impostor." Caiaphas' voice rose shrilly. "He deserved to be crucified."

"I can be no judge of that," Quintus said quietly. "But I have heard differently."

The captain called Malchus spoke. "Who told you of the Galilean?" he demanded.

Quintus shrugged. "Everywhere I go people speak of him. You saw how quickly the crowd sought to touch me when they thought I had raised the thief from the dead."

"The Nazarene pretended to be the 'Expected One' and claimed to be King of the Jews," Caiaphas said sharply. "Pontius Pilate judged him according to the laws of Rome, and he was crucified like a common criminal. He is dead and all his disciples cannot raise him up."

33

"If you are so sure of that," Quintus said softly, "why does his very name strike fear in your heart?"

The haughty countenance of Caiaphas grew white with anger. He stepped forward as if to strike Quintus, then seemed to think better of it when he saw the Roman tense himself. The way Quintus had handled Malchus was a potent reminder that he was not a man to be trifled with.

"You Romans crucified Jesus of Nazareth," Caiaphas said finally. "The responsibility is not mine."

"I am told you bribed a man called Judas to betray him so you could take him in the night and condemn him. That is not the Roman way of administering justice."

"The procurator approved what was done," Caiaphas snapped. "Protest to him."

"I intend to do that," Quintus said gravely. "If Pontius Pilate put to death a man who could have healed the emperor of a grave illness, he must answer to Tiberius himself."

Caiaphas leaned back in his chair and studied Quintus for a moment. "What will you do now?" he asked.

"If Jesus of Nazareth rose from the dead and still lives, I will find him and take him to Rome. If he does possess power over death, that power must not be denied to the emperor."

"You will only make a fool of yourself by running over Judea looking for a dead man," Caiaphas sneered. Then he turned to Malchus. "Hold him here while I talk to the governor about him."

At least a half hour passed before Caiaphas reentered the room. "Where is the commission of which you spoke?" he demanded of Quintus.

"I left it with my belongings," Quintus said, wishing now that he had taken the precaution of bringing the commission with him this morning. But it had never occurred to him that an innocent visit to the temple with Jonathan and Veronica could possibly result in any situation where he would need to produce his credentials.

"Where are you staying?"

Something in Caiaphas' manner warned Quintus that the question was not nearly so offhand as it might seem.

"At the home of some people I met when I arrived."

"Where do they live?"

"I am not familiar with your streets, but if you will release me, I will bring my commission and present it to Pontius Pilate."

Caiaphas shrugged. "It is of no matter. The procurator wants you brought before him at once." He turned to Malchus. "Escort the prisoner to the Antonia at once."

The word "prisoner" did not have a pleasant sound, but Quintus did not argue about it. He was hustled over one of the stairways connecting the palace of Antonia with the temple through a massive gate where a burly legionnaire stood guard. Here a servant guided him and his captor down a long passageway to a room looking out over the city. It was large and sunny, obviously an audience chamber, with a broad table at one end and a long couch across one wall.

A heavy-set man with brooding eyes and full lips lounged on the couch, the Roman official complete with all the appurtenances of his office. Recognizing Pontius Pilate, Quintus was sorry now that he had chosen to travel as a civilian rather than as a Roman officer, to which position he was entitled by his rank of *tribunas laticlavus* or "tribune of the broad stripe." Somewhat more of a civil office than the strictly military position of tribune, it was equally honored.

Before Pilate, Quintus came to a stop and brought his right arm and clenched fist smartly across his breast in the military salute.

"How dare you give the salute of a Roman soldier?" the procurator demanded coldly without returning the salute.

Quintus understood at once what had happened during the time the high priest had been absent from the room where he had first been interrogated. Caiaphas and Pilate had evidently decided to refuse him

35

recognition as an imperial representative. And without his commission they might well succeed.

"I hold the commission of *tribunas laticlavus* in the Praetorian Guard," Quintus said proudly.

"The high priest tells me you have been stirring up trouble in the temple, pretending to be a malefactor I crucified several years ago."

"If the priest told you that, he lied, noble Pilate," Quintus said quietly. "I was in the temple as a visitor when an altercation occurred over a thief. He fell at my feet, and when I attended him the crowd thought I had raised the man from the dead."

Pilate leaned forward, his face suddenly distorted with anger. "The dead do not rise!" he almost screamed. "Do you hear me?"

"As a physician, I agree," Quintus said evenly. "But many Jews seem to believe differently."

Pilate snatched a cup of wine from the table before him and drank, gulping it down and spilling it on the rich cloth of his tunic.

"Who are you?" he demanded, putting down the cup.

"Caiaphas must have told you. My name is Quintus Volusianus, and I am physician to the emperor."

"If you are the envoy of Rome you pretend to be, why did you stir up these people who only wait to defy us?"

"I searched for you at Caesarea to present my credentials," Quintus explained. "They told me you were in Jerusalem, so I went on to Joppa by ship and came here overland."

Pilate shrugged. "At this season of the year every troublemaker who is caught pretends to be a Roman. If you are really what you claim, you would have reported to me at once."

"I was warned at the gate that your temper is short at this season," Quintus explained, "so I decided to present my commission later. Since my arrival, I have been questioning people in the city concerning the healer called Jesus of Nazareth."

Pilate stiffened and Quintus expected another outburst, but the governor finished the cup of wine and lay back on the cushions. "I know you now. You are another of the cursed Zealots who use the Nazarene's name to cause trouble among the Jews."

"I first learned of Jesus two months ago when the emperor commanded me to come to Judea and seek him," Quintus said quietly. "We had heard that he healed all who came to him—even the dead."

Once again Pilate went rigid with anger, but this time the pallor of fear was plainly visible through the lividity of anger on his face. And his eyes were now like those of a hunted animal, instead of a proud Roman.

"The Galilean was crucified as a traitor," he said. "He died on the cross, with two thieves, and his body was laid in the tomb of Joseph of Arimathea. If he could save others, why didn't he save himself?"

"I am told that on the third day the stone was rolled away by no man's hand. And the tomb was found to be empty."

Pilate shrugged. "The Nazarene's disciples bribed the soldiers and stole his body so they could say he rose from the dead. The guards confessed."

"And were executed?"

"Of course. You claim to be a Roman, so you should know Roman law."

"I only know that my orders are to bring the Galilean to Rome to heal the emperor," Quintus said. "Many people claim to have seen him after he was crucified, and I intend to question some of them and find out whether Jesus is in hiding to keep you from crucifying him again."

"The Nazarene is dead," Pilate said stonily. "And you will not be able to question anyone for a long time. We do not go easy with those who stir up the people of Jerusalem to revolt."

"Would you arrest the bearer of a royal commission?" Quintus asked incredulously.

"I will arrest any troublemaker who falsely claims to be a Roman." Pilate turned to Malchus. "Tell Caiaphas I will see that this fellow causes no more trouble."

Quintus started to protest, but Pilate cut him short. "Take the prisoner away," he ordered the Roman guards who stood on either side of the door. "Lock him in the lowest dungeon."

"I demand that you notify the Legate Vitellius in Antioch," Quintus shouted, as the guards seized him and started to drag him from the room. But his words only echoed back mockingly in the large chamber. Caiaphas and Pilate had obviously joined forces—as they must have done in the case of the Galilean healer —to see that he did not carry out the mission for which he had come to Jerusalem or return to report what they had done. Nor did he doubt his eventual fate. Locked in the deepest dungeon—a cold damp place from which there was no escape—no one would ever hear of Quintus Volusianus again, imperial physician or not.

9

The guards, with Quintus held firmly between them, were almost at the door leading from the chamber when it opened and a woman entered. More than ten years had passed since Quintus had last seen the Lady Claudia Procula, Pontius Pilate's wife, but he recognized her at once. She still possessed the same regal beauty and the same proud carriage that spoke her Claudian heritage, one of the noblest blood lines in the Roman Empire.

Procula had grown up in the household of Tiberius. As a member of the emperor's own Praetorian Guard before he had studied medicine, Quintus had known her then as a young girl. Now he saw that the promised beauty of girlhood had more than been fulfilled in the loveliness of maturity as a woman. Something else, too, distinguished Claudia Procula, a calmness of spirit and a deep inner dignity strangely like—he realized with a start—what he had seen in the face of the merchant, Joseph of Arimathea, the potter Abijah, Veronica, and others who were followers of the healer called Jesus of Nazareth.

"Forgive me, my lord," Procula said. "I did not know you were occupied." Then she saw Quintus and frowned as if uncertain whether she recognized him or not. Quintus was not taking any chances that she might have forgotten him, however. Although held on either side by a burly soldier, he still managed to bow courteously.

"The years have been kind to the Lady Claudia Procula since I last saw her in the emperor's household," he said.

Procula took a quick step toward him, a smile of welcome breaking over her face. "Quintus Volusianus!" she cried. "I had heard in letters from Rome that you were now physician to the emperor. How is my kinsman, Tiberius?"

"He is gravely ill, my lady," Quintus said. "That is why I came to Jerusalem."

By now Claudia Procula had noticed the guards and her eyes kindled angrily. "Is this how you treat a tribune of the Praetorian Guard and the trusted physician of the Emperor Tiberius?" she demanded.

The soldiers looked toward Pilate questioningly. "Release the prisoner," he ordered in a choked voice.

Procula approached the couch where Pilate sat. "Is anything wrong, my lord?" she asked. "Why was Quintus under guard?"

Pilate shook his head but his eyes were still angry. "A Zealot troublemaker was at work in the temple. The physician was mistaken for him."

"Why must we always have trouble at this season in Jerusalem?" Procula said sadly. "They seem determined not to give you any rest."

"This was only a minor affair," Pilate assured her. "Nothing to trouble yourself about."

"I hope not. Crucifixions disturb me so much, after—"

"I hope you will accept my apology, tribune." Pilate's heavy voice drowned out whatever she had been going to say, but Quintus was sure it was something concerning Jesus of Nazareth.

"No harm has been done," Quintus said quietly. Only the timely entrance of Claudia Procula had saved him from the dungeons, he knew quite well. As to whether the temporary armistice—so to speak—resulting from the presence of Claudia Procula would continue, he could not yet be sure.

Pilate got to his feet. "I must speak to Caiaphas," he said. "You may take up quarters here in the palace if you wish, tribune."

"I am very well situated where I am, sir." He had no desire to be under the thumb of Pontius Pilate, with no way of knowing what evil the procurator and the high priest would be plotting. One thing at least was certain, if the Galilean healer was still alive, neither of them wanted Quintus to find him and take him to Rome.

"Stay here awhile with me, Quintus," Claudia Procula begged. "I am dying to hear the news from Rome and the emperor's court."

"I am no longer on duty with the Praetorians, my lady," he told her. "But a court physician does hear a little gossip."

"Leave word with my wife where you can be found," Pilate said as he left the room. "As soon as this religious holiday of the Jews is over, we will entertain you at a small dinner."

When Pilate was gone, Claudia Procula drew Quintus out on a little terrace overlooking the city. It was sunny, and a servant brought them cool wine and spiced cakes. He had not eaten since the early-morning meal at the house of Abijah and was hungry and thirsty. Claudia Procula watched him silently while he refreshed himself. Her eyes were thoughtful, and when she spoke, it was not of gossip from Rome.

"What was really happening when I came in just now, Quintus?" she asked.

"I'm afraid I was on my way to the dungeon," he told her. "The lowest one."

She shuddered. "I was down there once—crucifixion might be preferable." Her eyes were troubled

40

with something, he was sure now, more than just concern for him. "But why?"

"The governor says it was a case of mistaken identity."

"Who arrested you?"

"The temple guards."

"Were you taken before Caiaphas?"

"Yes. He sent me to your husband."

She shivered again, although it was not cold. "Caiaphas is a bad influence for Pontius; they are closer than ever since——"

She stopped, and Quintus finished the sentence for her.

"Since Jesus of Nazareth was crucified?"

She caught her breath. "How did you know?"

"I am here because of the healer. The emperor heard of him and sent me to bring him to Rome."

The color drained from her cheeks, and for a moment he thought she was going to faint. Quickly he poured some wine into a cup and gave it to her. "Drink this," he commanded.

She obeyed like a frightened child, but the color came back slowly. "We've had nothing but trouble since it happened," she said finally, the words barely audible. "Pontius has nightmares; sometimes he doesn't sleep all night. And he drinks more than ever before."

"Your husband was always considered an excellent administrator in Rome, my lady," Quintus told her. "He was probably acting within Roman law when he ordered the Galilean crucified; I am told Jesus claimed to be King of the Jews."

She shook her head. "Caiaphas tricked him, Quintus. Pontius found no fault in Jesus and sent him to Herod, since he was a Galilean. But Herod would not judge him, and the priests insisted that Jesus had set himself up as a king. Caiaphas hired people to stir up the crowd so they would demand that he be executed. It was then that Pontius washed his hands of Jesus' blood and turned him over to them."

"The guilt is not really your husband's, if the Galilean really did set himself up as a king."

41

"Jesus was not speaking of an earthly kingdom, Quintus. I sent word to Pontius to have nothing to do with the case the priests were making against him. He had never tried to stir up an insurrection as they claimed. And now"—she stopped and her voice broke in a sob—"now I suppose Pontius will be punished. You know how the emperor is when people go against him."

Quintus had witnessed the wrath of Tiberius more than once and was only too happy that it had never been directed against him. In this instance, however, it did seem that Pontius Pilate had acted according to Roman law.

"Pontius has paid for what he did," Procula went on. "If you only knew how he has paid. Sometimes he washes his hands hundreds of times a day. Worst of all it has driven him closer to Caiaphas." She shivered. "You don't know how evil that man is."

"I was before him only a few hours ago," Quintus reminded her.

"He will lead Pontius on to more evil things, like today." She turned to face him. "Did Pontius really make a mistake of identity in your case?"

"So he said."

"Didn't you tell him who you are?"

"He did not believe me."

"He didn't want to believe you," she cried. "Because he's afraid of what will happen when the emperor learns that he crucified Jesus. But for me he would have let you rot in that dungeon." Then her face brightened. "Still you could always have pleaded your rights as a citizen of Rome and demanded a fair trial."

"I did plead them—with no effect."

Claudia Procula nodded slowly, her eyes black with pain. "It has gone farther than I realized then. We must free Pontius from the influence of Caiaphas somehow, or the high priest will convince him they must stand together."

"I bear a royal commission," Quintus reminded her.

"It gives me the authority to take your husband to Rome where he could explain his actions to Tiberius."

"That would kill him," she said quickly. "Pontius is a proud man—proud and unrelenting. Anyone can make a mistake in dealing with the people of Judea; none of the procurators before him lasted very long, but he has been here almost ten years, so he has been a good governor—in most ways." She put her hand on his arm with a pleading gesture. "When you get back to Rome, speak to Tiberius and ask him to give Pontius another assignment—anywhere else, just to get him away from here."

"I may not go back for some time," Quintus told her. "Jesus of Nazareth reportedly rose from the dead and is still living. I must find him if I can."

And then she said something that startled him. "He did rise."

"Did you see him?" Quintus asked eagerly.

Procula shook her head, a little sadly, he thought. "No. He appeared only to those who believed in him. I suppose my own faith was not strong enough. But he was seen by Mary of Magdala, a friend of mine."

"Where is she?"

"In Galilee, I believe, at Magdala, on the Lake of Tiberias. Her husband, Joseph, is a physician and once lived here in Jerusalem. Mary and many others saw Jesus after he rose from the dead."

"Then I must talk to them."

"When you do return to Rome, will you intercede for Pontius?"

"Of course."

"He is a sick man, Quintus; you must have seen that already. The Jews say he has been seized by a demon, but I know the real answer. He is being punished by remorse and fear for crucifying the Son of God."

10

Veronica was not painting in her accustomed position beneath the spreading tree when Quintus returned to Abijah's house. The potters were busy at their wheels, however, and a hot fire of dried thornbushes burned in the great oven where row on row of delicately beautiful vases and other ware were baking. Jonathan had explained that the thorn wood was particularly selected to fire the kilns because it gave the hottest fires and the smallest amount of ash. When the youth looked up from the fires and saw Quintus, a smile broke over his face.

"Quintus is safe! Quintus is safe!" he shouted happily.

Veronica came from inside the house. She had been baking and her cheeks were red from the heat, her forehead damp with perspiration. "We were worried about you when we finished the sacrifices and could not find you," she told him.

"One of the students with Rabbi Emanuel saw us together in the Court of the Gentiles," Jonathan explained. "He told me the guards arrested you and took you away."

"Your friend has good eyes," Quintus said. "It happened just as he said."

"Why did they arrest you?"

"The guards thought I was trying to make trouble—a case of mistaken identity."

"Did you see the high priest?"

"And the procurator." There seemed to be no point in troubling them now with an account of what had actually happened. "When Pilate discovered who I really am, he let me go."

"Then you are going to the palace?" Veronica asked with a note of disappointment in her voice.

"I told them I had promised to eat the Passover feast in the house of a friend," Quintus said. So far today everyone else seemed to be busy not wanting him; it was good to feel that the welcome he'd found here in the home of Abijah still existed, as warm as ever. "Unless being arrested this morning has made me unwelcome."

Abijah left the wheel where he had been molding a vase. "The Passover is a time of gladness and thanks-

44

giving to our God for saving our first-born," he said. "At such a time the guest in our house is doubly welcome. Unless it will cause trouble with the procurator if you ignore his hospitality."

Quintus grinned. "Pilate's hospitality left much to be desired." He gave Abijah a quick summary of what had happened. When he finished, the potter's face was grave.

"Caiaphas is the evil force there, although the governor grows more cruel as the months pass. Do you intend to go on to Galilee?"

"As soon as I can be sure Jesus is not still in Jerusalem."

"He is not here," Abijah said. "I would know it if he were, through Joseph of Arimathea. Perhaps it will be best for you to go to Galilee, but for your own safety. And you can learn much about the Nazarene."

"Now that he knows who I am, Pilate wouldn't dare harm me."

"Perhaps not, but it is another matter with Caiaphas. He would be content for things to remain exactly as they are, but Jesus overturned the tables of the money-changers and told them they had turned the temple of the Most High into a den of thieves. He even said a Samaritan was as good as a Jew."

"That doesn't sound like the rebel against Roman authority they claimed him to be."

"I heard the Master speak many times from Solomon's Porch. Not once did he ever utter treason against Rome."

"Then Pilate had him crucified unjustly! No wonder he is troubled by guilt."

"The governor could have saved Jesus," Abijah agreed. "The common people loved the Galilean, but the rabble was stirred up against him by troublemakers hired by Caiaphas and the priests. When Pontius Pilate left the decision to the crowd, these people shouted for him to be crucified and the rabble took it up."

"You spoke of Samaritans," Quintus reminded him. "Is this another Jewish sect, like the Pharisees I've heard of?"

"Samaria is a section lying to the north here," Abijah explained. "Its border extends southward very near to Jerusalem itself. Many hundreds of years ago there were two kingdoms of our people, Israel in the north and Judah to the south. Then Israel fell to invaders. Thousands of Jews were taken away, and foreigners from the east were brought into the area of Samaria to take their place. That region was soon filled with people who are not pure Jews as most of us are here in Jerusalem. Actually their city of Samaria is more Greek and Roman than Jewish, and they have a temple of their own on Mount Gerizim."

"But it is all under Rome?"

"Yes. Samaria is governed by Pontius Pilate too."

"Why do you Jews hate the Samaritans?"

"A strict Jew will have nothing to do with a Samaritan," Abijah explained. "But Jesus taught that all who worship the Most High are one family, so we no longer hate the Samaritans."

Quintus frowned. "I don't exactly understand what you mean by 'we,' Abijah."

"Those who worship Jesus as the Son of God," the potter explained, and Quintus was reminded of what Claudia Procula had said only a little earlier. "Each year our number grows larger and we reach new areas. Soon we will be everywhere, even in Rome."

Quintus gave him a startled look. "Do you claim that the Son of God is above all earthly rulers?"

"He is above everything," Abijah said simply. "Kings and emperors will one day bow down and worship him."

"I prefer to forget what I have just heard, my friend," Quintus said earnestly. "Each country naturally believes its own god to be the most powerful and above every other, but I am a Roman. I look about me and see that for the first time in the history of mankind nearly all peoples are joined together under one government. It may not always be a just government since it must be served by men, but it brings much good to those it rules."

He paused, then continued: "It is true that Pilate has

done evil, especially by crucifying the Galilean; his soul is in torment because of it. But he has also done good. There is no rebellion in your land. Many of your cities do not have walls any more, and a man can journey from one place to another in safety. The water you drink is sweet because Pontius Pilate took money from greedy priests and built an aqueduct. I can see that these things given by Rome to your people and to others all over the world have been good for you, so I cannot hold my tongue when you would throw the world into chaos again so another man who calls himself the Son of God can rule."

"Like so many people, you fail to understand," Abijah said. "Jesus will rule only in the hearts of men, not by sword and spear and by conquest. Kings and emperors will govern in his name, for their power will be given by him."

Quintus shrugged. "What is the difference? In the end he would be served by men."

"I am not learned," Abijah said. "I was not even a follower of Jesus until Veronica was healed. Some of his disciples are in Galilee, and Joseph of Arimathea frequently sends caravans there, so I will ask him to take you with the next one. You will be safe in Galilee and there you may talk to those who were closest to Jesus."

"And perhaps to the healer himself," Quintus suggested.

"Jesus was last seen there and he loved the region beside the lake. When he returns as he promised, he will surely go to Galilee."

"I will leave as soon as your feast is over," Quintus decided. "But I need no escort. A Roman officer is safe in any territory ruled by Rome itself."

But there, as it happened, he was wrong.

11

Darkness had fallen over the pottery yard of Abijah in Jerusalem. In one corner the lamb brought from the

47

temple by Jonathan after the sacrifice of that morning had been spitted upon a freshly cut wooden stick. A hole had been dug, and since the sun had started its descent a fire had been burning briskly in it. Now the hole was almost filled by a thick bed of embers and over this the lamb had been placed several hours before. It had been handled carefully by Jonathan and Veronica, to whom it belonged, for the flesh must not be damaged in any way and no bones broken, else it would not be suitable for the ceremonial feast.

As the sky grew dark with the coming of night, Quintus stood at the edge of the pottery yard looking up at the hillside beyond the city. A thousand fires, it seemed, had begun to wink into being as the families camped there prepared to eat the ceremonial meal and celebrate the occasion of the Passover.

Quintus had not realized that Veronica had come out of the house, where she had been supervising the final preparations for the feast, until he saw a movement in the shadows of the big tree and turned to find her there. She was dressed somewhat more richly than during the working day. Her robe of finely woven wool was embroidered in gold thread, no doubt by her own skilled fingers. The sash about her waist emphasized its slenderness and she wore little jewelry, for her beauty was healthy and natural, needing little embellishment.

"Is your work finished?" he asked, as she came out of the shadows into the light of a cresset burning on a post in the yard.

"Almost. We can begin the feast very soon now."

"It was kind of your family to take a stranger into your midst, especially when I am not of your own faith."

"Jesus taught that every man is our neighbor," she said. "We try to observe that as nearly as we can."

"Until today I might have said the same."

"My father believes they will try to harm you again."

"I suppose Caiaphas might seek to make further trouble for me," he conceded. "But he will have to be very careful what he does."

48

She shivered. "He is evil, we know that. And what happened to you this morning proves that he has the governor under his thumb."

Obeying a sudden impulse, Quintus asked, "Will you keep the imperial commission for me, if I place it in your care?"

"Of course. But why give it to me?"

"They may try to steal it, as the first step in getting rid of me. But I hardly think they would expect you to have it."

He went to his baggage roll and removed the small scroll sealed with the imperial seal. "Keep it safe," he told her. "If I am taken prisoner, go to the Legate Vitellius in Antioch. He knows why I am in Jerusalem and will see that I am released."

Jonathan came to examine the lamb roasting on its spit. "I believe it is nearly ready," he called. "Remember the flesh must all be eaten before midnight."

In honor of Veronica's and Jonathan's first sacrifice of a lamb at the Passover, a number of relatives and friends had gathered for the ceremonial feast at Abijah's home, among them the merchant, Joseph of Arimathea. In spite of his wealth, which Quintus had heard was great, Joseph was no more richly dressed than the others. Nor was there any sign of ostentatiousness about him. At a call from Abijah they gathered around a long low table in the main room.

First the potter, as head of the household, took wine and blessed it, giving each a cup in turn. When this had been drunk solemnly, Veronica poured a bowl of water and each washed his hands while Joseph of Arimathea repeated a prayer. Next came a bowl of bitter herbs mixed with dates and raisins and a little vinegar from which everyone took a small portion.

"The vinegar and bitter herbs are a symbol of the clay with which our forefathers made bricks in Egypt when they were slaves," Joseph explained to Quintus as the ceremony proceeded. "The Passover sacrifice celebrates the occasion when the angel of death passed over the houses of our people but struck down the first-born in every Egyptian household as a sign to Pharaoh that he should free us from slavery."

It was a solemn and yet a happy occasion, with the ring of people sitting around the long low table in the light of two oil lamps burning there. From the pit outside rose the savory smell of the roasting lamb.

When the solemn preliminary ceremonies were over, the celebration took on a less somber hue. The lamb was now brought in, crisp and savory, on a great platter of fired earthenware. With it were unleavened cakes and fruit, with wine to drink. The real feasting began then and continued until the lamb was eaten.

About an hour before midnight, when the dishes had been taken away and the final ceremonial cup of wine drunk, Veronica brought out a harp which she strummed skillfully.

"We will sing together the 'Hallel,'" Abijah announced, and they lifted their voices in the ancient Jewish psalm of thanksgiving, a song of adoration to their god, ending with the joyous cry:

"O give thanks to the Lord for he is good
For his steadfast love endures forever."

Filled with a sudden loneliness, Quintus stepped out of the house while they were singing. He could not distinguish the words for they were in the ancient language of the Hebrews, but no one could fail to sense the exaltation and joy in the voices of the singers as they gave thanks to their god for his kindnesses during the past year.

Outside voices were being raised everywhere in the music of thanksgiving. From the hillsides songs poured down upon the city from the glowing coals of hundreds of fires where the Passover lambs had been cooked and eaten. On its commanding hilltop the temple glittered like silver in the light of the moon, and from it came the sound of trumpets celebrating once again the triumph over death which the Passover symbolized.

Only the black fortress of Antonia with its great

towers looming above the temple seemed out of keeping with the scene, a grim shadow of military power that had no place here at a time when the chief concern of men should be to reconcile themselves to their god.

The door of the house opened and Joseph of Arimathea joined Quintus at the edge of the pottery yard.

"I saw you leave the room," he said. "Are you troubled?"

"It seemed wrong for me to intrude upon the song of thanksgiving to your god."

"He sent his son to let the world know he is everyone's god. You need only to believe in him, Quintus, and he will be yours too."

"I cannot believe in something I cannot see."

The merchant smiled. "Do you see the fever that you relieve with your drugs?"

"No, but I can see its effects."

"So can you see God's effects everywhere about you —in the blossom of the thornbushes on the hillside, even the fires that burn in the camps. He gives us everything we have; therefore we and all we possess belong to him."

"Does he ask nothing of you except to believe that— and sacrifice to him once a year?"

"He asks much more," Joseph said. "Long ago, in the time of Moses, the Most High gave us commandments, the laws that govern the relationships of men to each other over most of the world are based upon them. Lately, through Jesus, he gave us a new commandment, that we should love one another, even as he loved us."

"That is a strange rule for a merchant. Can you love a man and make a profit at the same time?"

"I asked myself that question," Joseph admitted, "and God showed me the answer. Abijah produces fine vases and other ware in his pottery yard. Another man weaves cloth on a loom, and still another prepares leather and makes shoes. They cannot sell all they produce here in Jerusalem, so I buy what they make at a fair price and sell it in other cities where men have need of such things. The profit I make is my own reward for the service I have rendered to both the seller and the buyer. Can you censure me for it?"

"No," Quintus admitted, "since no one is any the worse for what you do."

"Have you ever denied your services as a physician to anyone because you thought he could not pay you?"

"Of course not. I would be untrue to the oath we all swear if I did."

"Then you are only doing what Jesus commanded us to do before he left us. You are giving your services because you love your fellow man."

"I never thought of it that way," Quintus admitted.

"Neither did I, until I heard him teach. Before that I was as grasping, I suppose, as any other merchant. But now that I follow the teachings of the Nazarene, I find that I am rewarded even more than before. I have agents representing me in Antioch and in Corinth, in Rome and Alexandria, even in Cyrene. My goods move to all these places and many others; in return I buy the products of those who work in those cities and sell them elsewhere. And as I go about the world attending to my business, I tell others what I have learned from the Galilean."

"Do you think Jesus is still in Galilee?"

"Some say he was taken up into heaven forty days after he was raised from the dead. Others insist that he has gone away for a little while but will soon return. I do know that he was seen by Peter and some others on the lake at Galilee, for I had it from their own lips. Were I in your place, I would go there and talk to Peter."

"Has Abijah spoken to you about my joining one of your caravans?"

Joseph nodded. "One will leave Jerusalem the day after tomorrow. You are welcome to accompany it."

"Suppose I find Jesus in Galilee and take him to Rome. The wrath of Tiberius is a formidable thing. If the Nazarene fails to heal the emperor, he might even be put to death."

Joseph smiled. "Jesus has already triumphed over death, Quintus. I am sure that even the power of Tiberius could not harm him now."

12

Abijah, the potter, was a stubborn man and a wise one, with a shrewd knowledge of his fellows. For that shrewdness Quintus had reason to be thankful before the night was over. Weary after the long and eventful day, he retired to Jonathan's couch as soon as the Passover celebration was finished. Had he troubled to look around him, he would have noticed that a number of Abijah's kinsmen and fellow potters who had attended the feast remained in the house. They slept with stout cudgels at their sides, and some of their number kept watch throughout the night.

The attack they were expecting came a little before dawn, with a silent rush upon the pottery yard and the house from several quarters by perhaps a half dozen men wearing dark robes and hoods that hid their faces, the typical costumes of the professional dagger men called sicarii.

They had obviously counted on finding the household of Abijah asleep and defenseless. Instead they were met with heavy cudgels in the hands of determined and angry men.

Quintus knew nothing of the preparations Abijah had made and was slow in arousing from sleep when the cry of warning came. In the darkness and confusion of early dawn he found himself attacked by a lithe figure in a dark robe with a long dagger in his hand and might have lost his life then and there, had not his training as a Roman soldier come to his succor. Half awake, he instinctively rolled aside when he saw the dark figure lunge toward him and so eluded the blade that was aimed at his heart.

Wide awake now, Quintus grappled with the man who had attacked him, seizing a wrist that was like a band of iron and thereby managing to keep the dagger

53

away from his own body. Silently the two wrestled in the darkness, the attacker seeking to free his right hand which held the blade and deliver a fatal thrust. Quintus, on the other hand, was trying to disarm the dagger wielder and capture him, so he could learn the identity of those who had hired the sicarius. Whoever it was— even Pontius Pilate or the High Priest Caiaphas—the authority of Quintus' commission from the Emperor Tiberius was sufficient for him to place the culprit under arrest and have him taken to Rome for punishment.

The fact that he was more desirous of taking his attacker prisoner than killing him placed Quintus at a slight disadvantage. Outside the room the battle was raging swiftly and efficiently as the kinsmen and employees of Abijah beat off the attackers with their heavy cudgels. Of the whole group, only the one with whom Quintus was struggling seemed to have gotten into the house. And since he had managed it without the knowledge of those outside, Quintus was left alone to defend himself.

Struggling for an advantage in the darkness, Quintus stumbled over the cloak he had thrown about himself against the early-morning chill which came at this elevation. He went to his knees but managed to hold on grimly to his assailant's wrists and thus keep the hand with the knife away from his body. By now the men outside had finally realized that one of the sicarii was inside the house and came rushing in.

The sandaled foot of a would-be rescuer struck Quintus on the elbow in the darkness, and the sudden pain lancing through his arm paralyzed it long enough for his fingers to loosen their grip. Unhindered now, the man in the dark cloak was able to jerk his hand and dagger free. Quintus felt a sharp stab of agony when the blade penetrated the skin over his upper chest and went home to the hilt, then a second as it was withdrawn. In the light of a torch carried by one of his rescuers he saw Abijah raise a cudgel and bring it down upon the skull of the man who had stabbed him.

The veil of blackness was already enveloping Quintus, however. He had only a momentary glimpse of Veronica's pale face and her eyes, wide and dark with concern, before he lost consciousness.

BOOK 2

Samaria

Quintus awakened in a bright and cheerful room to the sound of birds chirping outside an open window through which the sun was streaming to reproduce on the white wall a dappled pattern from the leaves of a tree growing outside. The air had a freshness and coolness, which he did not remember of Jerusalem, nor was anything familiar about the room itself. The last thing he was able to remember clearly was the fight following the Passover supper and the sudden stab of pain as the knife of the attacker had plunged into his body. Obviously then, he thought, he must be in Abijah's house in Jerusalem; and yet the vague memory of other scenes kept forcing themselves into his mind, the swing of a litter between the mules, a twinge of exquisite pain as the animals' hoofs stumbled upon a stone, strange faces staring at him, and many other fragmentary pictures.

The weakness that assailed him with even the exertion of trying to recollect the immediate past was hard to explain too. He felt no pain from the dagger thrust in his chest, which seemed strange. In fact, from the stab of agony he'd experienced when the weapon had entered his body, it hardly seemed possible that he could be alive at all. And yet he undoubtedly was, as the testimony of his own eyes and ears assured him.

A new sound reached Quintus' ears now, the murmur of a woman's voice, rich and full even in its low tones, speaking in what he recognized as the everyday language of the Jews, but with an odd sort of an intonation that did not sound like the dialect spoken in Jerusalem. The only women he could remember in his recent past were Veronica, the daughter of Abijah the potter, and Claudia Procula, wife of Pontius Pilate. Yet this voice sounded like neither of them.

The sound seemed to come from a corner of the room, and by moving his head a little he was able to see a graceful woman with dark red hair, wearing a robe of soft material that clung to her lovely body. She was praying, her eyes uplifted to the window through which the sun was streaming. She was in her early thirties, he judged, with the full beauty of maturity, and made an extraordinarily lovely picture kneeling there with the sunlight bright upon her hair.

The prayer finished, the woman turned toward him. When she saw his eyes upon her, her face glowed with a look of gladness. Getting quickly to her feet, she came across the room to where he lay, moving with an innate grace that made him wonder whether she had not been a dancer in her youth.

"Our prayers have been answered, Quintus Volusianus," she said in her rich voice, but speaking now in faultless Greek.

He tried to speak and found it almost beyond his strength. "Where am I?" he finally managed to ask.

"In Magdala. I am Mary, the wife of Joseph, the physician."

The names seemed vaguely familiar in themselves, as if he had heard them independently and should remember them. But in their present relationship the connection eluded him. Magdala—he decided—must be some suburb of Jerusalem to which Abijah had taken him after the attack by the dagger men, perhaps to the care of the physician who was her husband.

The woman called Mary left the room, returning a few moments later with a cup. She put her arm beneath Quintus' head and raised him gently, placing the rim of the cup against his lips. "Drink this," she said. "It will give you strength and help you to rest."

The drink was pleasant to taste, with a flavor of wine and something else, a touch of fragrant spices and herbs. He drank it gratefully and lay back on the couch, shutting his eyes because the walls of the room had begun to waver and sway with even that small exertion. Almost immediately a pleasant drowsiness claimed him and, with no strength to resist, he yielded himself up to it.

When he awakened again, he felt much stronger and the room was now lit by an oil lamp.

A man sat beside the couch. His face was lean and his features clean-cut, his eyes deep-set and kind. "Welcome back to the realms of the living, Quintus Volusianus," he said with a smile. Then he turned to the doorway and called in a cheerful voice, "Bring the broth you have been preparing, Mary. Our guest is awake again."

"What happened to me?" Quintus asked, but the man only shook his head. "We will talk of that later, when you have taken nourishment." His fingers went to Quintus' wrist and rested there with the practiced touch of a physician. "A little rapid yet," he commented, "but slowing. And your fever is gone, an excellent sign."

Mary brought a bowl of steaming broth on a platter. "You look much better," she said warmly. "Much better indeed." She spoke Greek almost like a native of that land, with little of the somewhat stilted phrasing marking those not accustomed to the language. Seating herself beside the couch, she began to feed him the savory broth with a spoon.

"Are you a physician?" Quintus asked the man.

"My name is Joseph of Galilee," he said. "A physician lately of Jerusalem but now living here in Magdala. This is my wife, Mary."

"Mary of Magdala," Quintus repeated. "Where have I heard that name?"

"Probably from Joseph of Arimathea, or perhaps Veronica," she said. "Drink the broth; you need it to give you strength."

The broth was tasty and warm. Quintus drank it gratefully, even chewing on a crust of bread that Mary soaked in the liquid.

59

"You were wounded in the fight at Abijah's house," Joseph explained. "A band of sicarii hired by the High Priest Caiaphas tried to kill you."

"Was Pontius Pilate involved?"

"Neither Abijah nor Joseph of Arimathea thinks so," the physician said. "It would be very dangerous for the procurator of Judea to hire dagger men to kill an envoy of the emperor."

"My commission!" Quintus exclaimed. "Was it stolen?"

"We have it here," Mary assured him. "Safe whenever you need it again."

"In the fight," Joseph continued, "you were stabbed in the chest. I did not see the wound at first, but from the location it would seem that only a miracle saved you from death then and there. The dagger entered the spongy tissue of the lung, and I believe the pressure of air escaping helped control the bleeding. But you had lost much blood and they despaired of your life for several days. Then the fever came and it was even worse."

Quintus frowned. "Is this place near Jerusalem?"

"Magdala is a city overlooking the Sea of Galilee. The Romans call it the Lake of Tiberias."

"How did I get here?" The warmth of the broth was spreading through Quintus' body. He could even feel the strength of it seeping into his sinews.

"Abijah was afraid Caiaphas might try to kill you again. Only the fact that he was expecting the attack saved you the first time, and even then one of the sicarii got into the room where you lay."

"I remember struggling with him."

"A caravan belonging to Joseph of Arimathea was leaving Jerusalem the next day, so they brought you here on a litter slung between two mules. I had been in Jerusalem for the Passover and came with you."

"Then I must owe you my life," Quintus said gratefully.

Joseph of Galilee shook his head. "No, Quintus," he said. "You became steadily worse on the way here in spite of everything I could do. Even after we reached

Magdala, the fever continued to wrack your body. I despaired of your life and sent for Peter, hoping he could cure you—"

"Peter?" Quintus frowned. "Another physician?"

"Not a physician—as you and I understand the term —but one who has power to heal beyond anything you or I could ever hope to possess. He is the leader of those who follow Jesus of Nazareth."

"Then Jesus is still alive?" Quintus asked eagerly.

Joseph smiled and looked at Mary. And as Quintus had noticed before in followers of the Galilean, their faces seemed to glow for a moment with an inner light, as if they were transfigured by some power he could not see or comprehend.

"Jesus lives, Quintus," Joseph of Galilee said. "You can be certain of that."

2

The conviction in Joseph's voice was such that Quintus did not doubt for a moment that he was speaking the truth.

"Can you tell me where he can be found?" he asked quickly.

Joseph shook his head and said a strange thing. "No one can tell another where Jesus can be found, Quintus. It is something each man must learn for himself."

Quintus curbed his irritation at the seemingly evasive answer. After what Rome, through the authority of Pontius Pilate, had done to the Galilean healer, he could hardly blame them for not revealing his true whereabouts to one who was—potentially at least— an enemy. And yet their reticence could only hamper him in accomplishing the purpose for which he had journeyed so many miles.

"Where is Peter then?" he inquired. "Maybe he will tell me how to find the Nazarene when he realizes I mean him no harm."

"I think Peter might lead you to the Master," Joseph said, "but we were not able to find him immediately.

61

After Herod put Peter into prison, he was forced to hide for a while. Even now there are those who would do him harm if they could."

"But I thought you said you sent for him—to heal me."

"We did—when I realized that no skill of mine could save you. When we could not find Peter quickly, Mary thought of another way. A week ago we sent to Jerusalem for Veronica and the veil."

"The veil?" Quintus frowned. "You mean the cloth—the one with the print of the Galilean's face upon it?"

"The same," Joseph confirmed. "Veronica came on a swift camel furnished by Joseph of Arimathea, but by the time she reached Magdala I had given up all hope of your recovery. In fact, I told her when she arrived that you were dying."

"When did you say that was?"

"She arrived the day before yesterday, as the sun was setting."

Quintus frowned. "If I were as ill then as you say, I could never be as well as I am now in this short a time."

Joseph of Galilee nodded soberly. "As a physician, I would say the same thing. Actually I could not count your pulse, and your back was arched like a bent bow from the spread of the inflammation to the spine. Your body was shaking with a rigor, and for a while before Veronica arrived I was forced to hold a mirror before your face even to determine that you were breathing."

It was utterly unbelievable. The signs described by the other physician were those of impending death; never had Quintus seen a patient go that far and be saved. Only a mistake in evaluating his condition could possibly explain the fact that no more than two days later he was well on the way to recovery, able to eat, drink, and talk, with only a remnant of the weakness he'd noticed so much when he first awakened a few hours ago to remind him that he had been gravely ill. And yet there was conviction in everything Joseph of Galilee said, a conviction that he found it hard not to believe.

"As soon as Veronica came," Joseph continued, "we put the veil upon your body."

"Was there an immediate effect?"

"You did not die—although just before she arrived I could not even be certain that you were alive at all."

"And then?"

"Your condition improved perceptibly as the hours passed. We were all praying here beside your couch, and with my finger on your wrist I could feel the pulse beat return, although I had not been able to detect it for several hours. It grew stronger, and by midnight I was fairly certain that you were out of danger."

"How do you explain it? Or can you?"

"Jesus possessed the power to heal, even to raise from the dead, as he did Lazarus, who had been in the grave for three days. When he put Veronica's veil to his face on the way to the cross and left the print of his features upon it, some of that power was transferred to the cloth."

"But that is impossible," Quintus protested. "You say you studied medicine in Alexandria, so you know ours is a rational science, not explainable by the whims of gods and goddesses."

"Five years ago I would have agreed with you," Joseph said gravely. "Until I met Jesus."

"And you really believe this piece of cloth brought me back from the very brink of death?"

"You are not the first to be healed by the veil," Joseph told him. "I had told Veronica she would always be a cripple with a leg that could only grow worse and worse from inflammation of the bone. Yet the moment she took the cloth from Jesus' hands, she was made as whole as any other."

Quintus shook his head slowly. "My mind and my senses tell me what you say is impossible. And yet you speak with a conviction I find it hard to resist."

Joseph smiled. "Don't try to resist, my friend. Once you have learned for yourself the truth brought to earth by Jesus of Nazareth, it is simpler to give yourself to him and resist no longer."

Quintus finished the broth and lay back on the

cushions of the couch while Mary took the bowl to the kitchen. What Joseph had told him was disturbing, because it violated everything he believed. In the Museum of Alexandria—actually a university built around the great collection of tablets and papyri located there first by Alexander the Great and later by the Ptolemies who had followed him on the throne of Egypt—medicine was taught as a rational science, based upon observable truths, like mathematics, which had also flourished there.

He knew from his brief period of service in the Temple of Asklepios on the island of Cnidus—one of the centers of the strictly ritual practice of the healing art—that the cures attributed to Asklepios were really the result of a shrewd combination of ordinary medical measures—such as diet and purging—with so-called suggestions by the gods, conveyed to the sufferer during a trance induced partly by drugs and partly by the priests themselves. In this rite of *incubatio* the sufferer was advised of his condition and measures were suggested for its cure—not by an earthly priest or physician, it seemed, but by the god himself, actually a priest wearing a mask to represent the divine Asklepios, god of healing.

Quintus had remained at Cnidus and at nearby Pergamum, another great center of the worship of Asklepios, only long enough to convince himself that such quackery could not compare in value as far as healing the sick was concerned with the rational teachings which he had learned at Alexandria. He had moved on to Rome and completed his studies under the great Celsus who, more than any other teacher of the period, exemplified the rational method of approaching disease as a natural phenomenon with a describable cause and an effect.

And yet Quintus himself was alive because of a power he could neither understand nor even believe—except that he could feel its effects in the strength which was increasing steadily within his body. To do so, he must acknowledge the existence of a god who controlled all things—a rational enough credo in itself, because men instinctively believed in some higher power than themselves. But he must also accept that this same god had sent his son to earth in human form as an obscure Jewish teacher from a town called Nazareth, which Quintus himself could not even remember seeing on a Roman map.

Most incredible of all, he must believe that this same all-powerful god had then allowed his son to be crucified by unscrupulous men who sought to maintain their own political hold upon the minds and fortunes of a people. And having let his son be killed in the most ignominious of fashions—through the crucifixion ordinarily reserved by the Roman authorities for only the most dastardly of crimes—this all-powerful god had then raised him from the dead. And now this man, whom they believed to be the Son of God, was hiding somewhere, apparently because Herod and Caiaphas still sought his destruction.

"I can read your thoughts," Joseph of Galilee said quietly. "And because I have known all these doubts myself, I can understand them. But trouble yourself no more, Quintus. We heard yesterday that Peter will soon be in the lake region again. After you have talked to him and heard from his own lips the story of Jesus, I think you will better understand what happened here last night."

"Is Peter a leader here in Galilee?" Quintus asked.

Joseph shook his head. "He was only a fisherman called Simon before he followed Jesus. But to those who knew and loved him even then he was a veritable tower of strength. Jesus named him Peter and called him the rock upon which his church would be built."

"In Greek the words have the same root," Quintus reminded him.

"I think Jesus chose the name Peter for that reason," Joseph agreed. "And he chose well. Herod and Caiaphas could not keep Peter in prison when they tried to stamp out those who followed Jesus. They put him in chains, but the fetters dropped off and the doors of the prison opened although no man had unlocked them." Joseph got to his feet. "You have exerted yourself enough for now, Quintus. Try to sleep, and we will talk again when you have rested."

"Where is Veronica?" Quintus asked. "I should thank her for saving my life."

"Word that she was here with the veil spread quickly, and she has been busy ministering to the sick. She will return later tonight and you can see her tomorrow."

3

Quintus did not awaken again until morning. By then, except for some soreness in his upper chest where the dagger had penetrated, he felt almost as strong as ever. From the kitchen near by came the muted voices of women talking, and outside the birds were in full song. Lying there, in the period of relaxation between sleeping and waking when one is loath to put forth the exertion required to face the day, he thought that he could not remember a more peaceful or more pleasant scene.

The soft step of a sandaled foot made him turn his head. Veronica stood in the doorway leading to the kitchen. With the sunlight from the high window in the wall falling upon her slender body and lovely head she made a picture of beauty that even a sick man could appreciate.

"Shalom, Quintus Volusianus," she said softly.

"Shalom?" He frowned over the unfamiliar word.

"It is our greeting between friends."

"From what the physician, Joseph, says, you were a true friend to me, Veronica. He insists that you saved my life."

The girl shook her head. "The Master saved you through the veil. I deserve no credit."

"But you had faith that I could be saved."

"I knew you could," she said simply, "if it was the will of God."

"Do you have any idea how this cloth—this veil of yours—really accomplishes such miracles?"

"Jesus works through it," she explained. "I felt it

that first day when I was healed, but you were too sick when I placed the veil upon your body to feel the power. If Joseph had not told me you were alive, I would have believed you to be dead."

"You simply laid the veil upon me?"

"And prayed, with the others, that you would be healed."

Quintus shook his head slowly. "I wish I could believe as you do."

"You will. Whenever God wills it."

"I think you know how grateful I am," he said. "That will have to do until I can repay you."

"I cannot gain from what the veil does," she protested quickly. "It would not be right."

He looked at her keenly. "Are you afraid the veil would lose its power if you did?"

"Perhaps, I don't know. But Jesus took nothing himself and neither can I."

Joseph of Galilee came in from the kitchen just then. "If I did not know better," he said warmly, "I would say you had never been ill."

"I feel almost that well myself," Quintus admitted. "May I go outside and sit in the sun?"

Joseph nodded to Veronica. "There is the physician who healed you. Ask her."

Veronica brought a robe for him and helped him put it on. Then she took his arm and drew it across her shoulder. Thus supported, Quintus was able to walk through the door and out upon a small terrace shaded from the direct rays of the sun by the leafy branches of a green fig tree. A bench stood beneath the tree and he sank down upon it, leaning back against the tree itself.

The house, he saw now, was built on a steep hillside leading down to the white sandy shore and blue waters of the lake far below. It was a spot of unparalleled beauty, with the white walls of the house at the back and the shaded terrace protected on either side by flowering trees and shrubs which filled the air with fragrance. The roof of the house below was barely visible through the leafy foliage of the tree at the next level.

On the shore of the lake Quintus could see a fishing boat about to set out. Two men were pushing it off the shore while a third in the bow raised the gaily colored sail upon its single mast. Farther away, toward the north end of the lake, he could distinguish a group of fishing boats at their work.

"What a beautiful place!" he exclaimed.

"I think it must be the loveliest spot in the whole world," Veronica agreed. She pointed to the northeast where he could see the white buildings of a town along the shore. "I was in Bethsaida yesterday, healing the sick."

"Why do the boats all seem to gather at that end of the lake?"

"Peter says the cold water from the river Jordan drops into the lake there and for some reason the fish gather at that point. I saw them hauling in the nets yesterday as I went along the shore. Sometimes it seemed that the boats would sink from the weight of the fish."

"Why does your father live in Jerusalem, when such a beautiful place as this is near?"

"We make fine pottery—vases, jewel boxes, and such things," she explained. "The people of Galilee are not rich and could not buy them—except perhaps the Tetrarch Herod at Tiberias and the Roman officials who live there and in the cities of the Decapolis on the other side of the lake. Our market is better in Jerusalem, where rich people come from other countries to worship at the temple."

"Wouldn't you like to visit other cities, Veronica?"

Her eyes brightened. "I have always wanted to see Rome. They say the paintings on the walls there are very beautiful."

"No more so than the scenes you paint upon the vases."

The warm color flooded her cheeks at the compliment. "I would like to paint other things," she admitted. "But there are many vases, and it takes gold to send Jonathan to the Scribes' School."

"I hope he was not hurt in the fight."

"Father was waiting for the sicarii and so were the workmen. It didn't last long."

"I was a fool not to listen to your father's warning, but I am glad none of you suffered because of my folly."

"They say in Jerusalem that the governor was furious with Caiaphas."

"He should have been. Tiberius could remove Pilate as procurator for letting it happen."

Mary came out on the terrace bringing a tray upon which was cold goat's milk, bread, dates, and a sliver of cheese. "It is time you had some real food," she told Quintus. "Broth and soaked bread are for babies; cheese is for men. Tonight we will have meat." She bustled about, putting down the tray on the bench beside him. "Peter is coming; we will have a feast in his honor."

"Good!" Quintus said. "I have been lazy too long."

"Lazy?" Her eyebrows rose. "If you had seen what strength it took for four of us to hold you down in your delirium, you would never judge yourself lazy."

"Did I babble all my secrets?" Quintus asked with a smile.

"Secrets are for people who have things to hide." She looked at Veronica, who stood to one side. "Has our young friend here managed to hide from you how happy she is that you are whole again?"

Quintus glanced at Veronica and saw her cheeks suddenly flame into color. Then—to his amazement— she turned quickly and went into the house.

"You are a handsome man, Quintus," Mary said. "I don't blame Veronica for falling in love with you."

"But that is absurd! I am thirty years old."

"And Veronica is about twenty-two. Remember she was an invalid for many years."

"You must be mistaken—about her feeling for me," Quintus protested, even as he wondered why the suggestion that Veronica might love him filled him with something very close to a soaring ecstasy. "We are worlds apart—in thought, background, everything."

"Everything except that you are a man and she is a woman. Once I ran away from Magdala, although I loved Joseph and knew he loved me. But he came to Alexandria seeking me and almost lost his life to save mine. That is what love means, Quintus—not whether you are a Roman and she a Jew, or you an aristocrat and she the daughter of a potter."

"I am the son of a freedman," Quintus said soberly. "My father worked with his hands, as Abijah does, and my mother was a slave. Everything I am I owe to the favor of the emperor. That is why I must let nothing keep me from finding Jesus of Nazareth and taking him back to Rome with me."

Mary had been straightening the terrace while they talked. "Peter will be here tonight," she said. "He can tell you how to find Jesus—for yourself, if not for the emperor."

4

The guest of the evening arrived shortly after dark, a big man with a massive head and a full beard. He radiated vitality, strength, and the sense of inner confidence and serenity which seemed to characterize those who had known intimately the man called Jesus of Nazareth. With him was a slender youth with dark hair and eyes who was introduced as Mark. Quintus judged from the conversation that Mark served as companion and secretary to Peter; Joseph told him later that the youth was writing down the story of Jesus and his teachings as Peter remembered them.

The big man greeted Quintus gravely, his deep-set eyes penetrating—the Roman physician felt—into his very soul and laying bare his thoughts. "The hand of Rome was lifted against me at one time," Peter said, "and it may be still. The whims of your governor, Pontius Pilate, and Herod, who rules here in Galilee for Rome, are not always predictable."

"Pilate all but had me imprisoned," Quintus said. "Fortunately I knew the Lady Claudia Procula when she was a young woman in the household of Tiberius. She recognized me and saved me from the dungeon."

"Procula is a good woman. She pleaded with Pilate not to crucify Jesus. The governor of Judea is a guilty and unhappy man. He sees rebellion when none exists and uses the sword where kindness would suffice."

Listening to Peter's deep, confident voice, Quintus found it hard to believe that this man had ever been a fisherman here on the Sea of Galilee. For now he radiated the authority of a natural leader of men and spoke with wisdom and consideration.

Peter put his arm across Veronica's slender shoulders. "Joseph tells me you were saved by the cloth our daughter here cherishes, Quintus," he said. "Then you already know the power of the Master."

"I'm afraid I was too near to death to experience anything," Quintus admitted.

"It was impressed on your soul nevertheless," Peter assured him. "Later, when we have eaten and had fellowship with our friends here, you and I will talk of the reason why you have come."

The feast was an informal time of happy companionship over good food and an excellent wine which, Mary said, was produced from the vines of a rich and fertile region called the Plain of Gennesaret, somewhat to the northward along the shore of the lake. The followers of Jesus were like neither the severe and withdrawn men Quintus had seen fulfilling the functions of priests in the Temple of Jerusalem nor the Pharisees of somber mien he had heard teaching on what Jonathan had called Solomon's Porch. These people were busy and gay, obviously loving each other and joyful in fellowship.

When the food was eaten, Mary brought out a small harp from which Veronica drew a pleasant melody and they sang the old songs of Israel, Mary leading them with her beautiful voice which—Quintus had learned by now—once held the great theater of Alexandria spellbound. While the singing was in progress, Peter nodded to Quintus and they left the room for the terrace outside. It was pleasant there with the fragrance of the flowers and the vines.

Peter stood at the edge of the terrace and breathed deeply of the cool air. "I have journeyed the length and breadth of this land," he said, almost to himself. "Soon I must go to Antioch and perhaps even to Rome, but I yearn always for the lake." He turned to Quintus. "Joseph and Mary tell me you have come from Rome with a commission from the emperor seeking Jesus."

"Tiberius is dying slowly of an incurable disease," Quintus explained. "He had heard rumors concerning a healer called Jesus of Nazareth and sent me to bring him to Rome. But in Jerusalem I discovered that Pontius Pilate had crucified the healer two years ago."

"Had the emperor received no report of it?"

"Only a rumor that the Nazarene could heal the sick. Pilate made no mention of having crucified him in the official reports."

Peter nodded. "Pontius Pilate knows he killed the Son of God. He cannot admit it, for that would damn him forever, so he tried to hide his guilt."

"But if Jesus is the son of your god, as you say, is Pilate not damned already?"

Peter sat down on the bench and motioned for Quintus to join him. "The Most High is not my God alone, Quintus, nor does he belong only to the Jews. He is the god of every man, wherever he lives and whatever the color of his skin."

Quintus gave him a startled look. "I thought you Jews shunned all contact with Gentiles. In your temple I could go no farther than the Outer Court, under penalty of death."

"So our people have always believed," Peter admitted, "because we were burdened with a fierce pride and a desire to think ourselves better than others. Jesus took away the rich garment of pride we wore to hide our inner unworthiness and made the mercy of God free to all who seek him."

"Then if Pontius Pilate were truly repentant, even he would be forgiven."

"Jesus did forgive him," Peter said. "From the cross he forgave even those who crucified him."

"When did you last see Jesus?"

"He appeared to some in Jerusalem and to several of us here on the lake when we were fishing."

"Then he is still in Galilee?"

Peter smiled. "Jesus is everywhere, Quintus—in the hearts of those who love and follow his teachings. But his physical presence was taken up into heaven two years ago."

Quintus could not hide his disappointment; Peter's words meant that his mission was ended.

"But you can always find him for yourself," the big man said, "by accepting him in your heart."

Quintus shook his head. "I am not even sure there is a god," he said. "Most of what I see about me can be explained without one. And even if there was, I cannot conceive of his being cruel enough to let his son die in such a shameful death."

"You will know the truth when Jesus wills you to know it," Peter said cheerfully. "Then you will have no trouble understanding."

"I do appreciate your coming here," Quintus said gratefully. "Especially when you must be weary from your journey."

"I have eaten and drunk with friends," Peter said simply. "And I have prayed with them. Nothing more is needed to refresh me and make me ready for another journey."

"Are you leaving soon?"

"Tomorrow I must visit those who witness for Jesus in Capernaum and Bethsaida and along the lake. Then I must go to Samaria. One calling himself the Messiah has appeared there; he claims to know the hiding place of the sacred vessels which the Samaritans believe were buried on Mount Gerizim by order of Moses."

"I don't understand," Quintus admitted.

"When the first temple was built in Jerusalem, the holy vessels used in the ritual worship of God were placed there. They were made in the time of Moses over a thousand years ago and have been kept by our

73

people ever since. The Samaritans quarreled with our priests, however, and built themselves a temple on Mount Gerizim. They claim the vessels in the temple at Jerusalem are not the true ones, and this so-called Messiah is trying to make them think he knows where the real vessels are hidden."

"Who is he?"

"A magician named Simon Magus. He pretended to follow Jesus for a while, but now he is trying to delude the Samaritans into believing he possesses divine power."

"Does he heal the sick?"

"Some claim to have been healed by him, but I suspect their souls were sick instead of their bodies."

"Perhaps I should see him just the same," Quintus said. "I owe it to the emperor to leave no stone unturned."

"Simon is an impostor. If you really seek to heal the emperor, take Veronica and the veil with you to Rome."

Quintus wondered why the thought had not come to him before. If the veil had indeed saved him from death—as all evidence seemed to prove that it had—then it might help Tiberius also. And yet he hesitated to expose Veronica to the long voyage and—more important—to the dangers that threatened a beautiful young woman in Rome.

"Perhaps I could take only the veil," he suggested.

Peter shook his head. "The veil is Veronica's; it was Jesus' particular gift to her. If anyone is to heal the emperor with it, she should be the one."

"You are probably right," Quintus conceded. "The reward should be hers, if she succeeds."

"Veronica would ask no reward except the privilege of showing the emperor the power of Jesus to save men."

"But would she go?"

"I will speak to her," Peter said. "You may be sure that she will."

Another thought struck Quintus. "They tell me you heal also. If you cured Tiberius, many would believe in your god. In Rome people eagerly take up anything favored by the emperor."

But Peter only shook his head. "My time for going to Rome has not yet come, Quintus," he said. "First I must keep the Samaritans from acting foolishly, if I can. Then I must minister to Jews scattered about over the world. Later I will come to Rome—when the cause I serve needs me there."

5

True to his promise, Peter talked to Veronica and she willingly agreed to accompany Quintus to Rome, bearing the veil. Quintus gained strength rapidly and was soon anxious to be away. He still planned to stop in the city of Samaria and see the man called Simon Magus, who, Peter had told him, claimed to be the divine leader called the Messiah for whom these troubled people seemed constantly to yearn. Mary of Magdala agreed to go with them as chaperon as far as the city of Shechem, where a friend of Simon Peter named Philip had his home.

The most direct route between Galilee and Jerusalem lay through the district of Samaria. There was a traditional enmity between the Samaritans and the Jews, who considered the former to be a mixed race. And indeed they were, being composed of descendants of the original Israelites who had remained after Sargon II, King of Assyria, had carried off some twenty-seven thousand of their people into captivity, replacing them with men from the east. The Samaritans hated the Jews particularly because John Hyrcanus over a hundred and fifty years before had attacked Samaria and destroyed the temple on Mount Gerizim. Later, in the time of Archelaus, who had been one of the heirs of Herod the Great, Samaritans had degraded the temple at Jerusalem in reprisal by throwing the bodies of dead men into it overnight. More recently, however, there had been relative peace between the Jews and the

Samaritans, particularly since the strong hand of Pontius Pilate had ruled over both areas as procurator.

Leaving the beautiful lake region, Quintus' party entered the mountainous district that lay to the west. Here a narrow cleft gave access to what was called the "Valley of the Doves," where thousands of the cooing birds nested in the trees and in crevices among the rocks. Dove catchers were at work with their traps and nets, catching birds to be sold in the markets of the teeming cities surrounding the lake, so the place was a constant clamor of shouting men and screaming birds.

Beyond the valley lay a tortuous region of steep hills and narrow valleys through which the road, a well-worn track, led southwestward. At the moment they were traveling the so-called "Way of the Sea," an ancient caravan route between Damascus and the cities of the east and Egypt far to the south. It wound about the northern end of the Sea of Galilee and, cutting through a cleft in the mountains back of Magdala, turned southeastward.

Having departed early from Magdala, the travelers passed Nazareth shortly after noon and continued on their way. Westward an elevation of mountains loomed between them and the distant sea. To the south lay a great plain called Esdraelon, and in the east a mountain called Tabor rose above the surrounding hills. Far to the north was a snow-capped crest which Veronica named Mount Hermon and from which she said the headwaters of the Jordan River that formed the Sea of Galilee took their origin.

"Sepphoris lies to the north," she said. "The Roman garrison for Galilee is quartered there."

As Quintus studied the impressive-looking city shining in the sunlight, a flash of something metallic caught his eyes. And as he squinted to make out the details, he recognized a marching column of soldiers. They were heading southeast on a road that wound along the hills from Sepphoris to Nazareth and the so-called central highway leading southward across the mountaintops toward Jerusalem.

Long before Quintus, Mary, and Veronica stopped

for the night at an inn on the edge of a village called Ginaea, the Roman party had overtaken and passed them, marching at a steady pace with full military equipment. The train of wagons which would normally have followed such a large group of men to bear their equipment and other supplies was not with this party. By this Quintus, from his long familiarity with the legions, judged that the soldiers were making a forced march because of some sort of an emergency.

As a big legionnaire swung by at the end of the column, Quintus called to him in Greek, "Where do the Romans march so fast?"

"To Sebaste," the soldier replied. "The Samaritans are in revolt in that region."

Quintus remembered what Peter had said about trouble at the Samaritan city called by the Romans Sebaste, the name with which Herod the Great had christened it when he had rebuilt it along with a massive temple dedicated to the Emperor Augustus. If Pontius Pilate had ordered part of the Galilee garrison into the region of Samaria, he evidently meant to see that things did not get out of hand.

At the inn where they spent the night there was much talk about the feats of Simon Magus whose followers were reported to be naming him openly as the Messiah, the political-religious leader whom both Jews and Samaritans expected to free them from Roman rule. Excited tales were told of the marvels worked by the magician, and he was said to have promised to set the Samaritans over the hated Jews, whose center of worship was at Jerusalem.

Anxious to get on and find the new healer about whom such lurid tales were told, Quintus roused Veronica and Mary at dawn and they set out along the road leading across the tops of the hills southward. Many people were on the road, hurrying toward the Samaritan cities. One of these informed Quintus that the so-called Messiah was at Shechem, the Samaritan town at the foot of Mount Gerizim, rather than at Sebaste itself.

Philip, of whom Peter had spoken to Quintus, was

the leader of those who followed Jesus in Samaria, according to Mary and Veronica. As they approached Shechem in the afternoon they found the roads seething with people, many of them tremendously excited, some almost to the extent of a religious frenzy. Daggers, short swords, and large clubs were everywhere in evidence, and, wanting no trouble while Veronica and Mary were his responsibility, Quintus gave them a wide berth. He could not help wondering how Pontius Pilate was going to handle the excited crowds, though, if it became necessary to exert the authority of Rome.

Located in a narrow glen, hardly a Roman mile in width, Shechem lay between two mountain heights boldly facing each other. The peak to the north, Veronica told him, was Mount Ebal. To the south and somewhat lower lay Mount Gerizim, where the people on the road said the magician Simon Magus claimed to have found the sacred vessels so revered by the Samaritans, who had long considered themselves shamed by the alleged presence of the holy relics in the temple at Jerusalem.

The hillsides around Shechem were green and appeared to be well watered. As they walked along the road entering the city, Quintus identified groves of walnut trees, almonds, pomegranates, olives, pears, and plums. From the slope small torrents of water tumbled down the mountainside to cross the road, their banks ablaze with colorful flowers. As they came down from the hills into the glen where Shechem lay, they could see that the city itself was half covered by groves and gardens and over the warm summer air seemed to hang a bluish haze or canopy.

"It's almost as beautiful as Galilee," Quintus said.

"Our forefather Abraham thought so," Mary said with a smile. "He settled in this region when he came here from Ur of the Chaldees. They say he pitched his tent in this very glen where the city now stands."

"How long ago was that?"

"Even the teachers in the School of the Scribes where Jonathan goes do not know," Veronica told him. "Some think it was as much as three thousand years ago—long before our people were taken into bondage in Egypt."

Quintus made a mental calculation and was startled to realize that the Jews had been in this region almost five times as long as there had been people who could call themselves Romans, even long before the appearance of his own ancestors, the Greeks. Before he had reached Jerusalem, he had thought of the Jews as no more than an unimportant people at the very edge of the Roman Empire, known mainly for their quarrels, not so much with Rome as with each other. Now he was seeing them in a different light.

6

The house of Philip in Shechem was small and not luxuriously furnished. He was not one of the original of Jesus' disciples, Mary had said, but belonged to another group called deacons who had been selected to help them. But as Quintus had found true with all followers of the Galilean, the warm welcome given them in the house of Philip more than outweighed the lack of luxury. Philip himself was a sturdy man with a broad, patient face and the same look in his deep-set eyes that seemed to characterize all the people who had known and loved Jesus of Nazareth. Quintus liked him at once.

Philip's buxom daughters were friends of Veronica and Mary. They bustled about, setting out cold meat, dates, and figs, goat's milk, and a wine which, while not as palatable as the delicious product of Galilee's Plain of Gennesaret, was still pleasant. When Philip and Quintus had eaten, being served by the women as was the custom, they moved to the shady court outside where a spring bubbled from the rocks and gave the whole area a cool and pleasant atmosphere.

"I'm glad you arrived here before nightfall," Philip said soberly. "The situation becomes more dangerous all the time."

"A Roman column passed us on the road," Quintus

79

told him. "The men were marching with full equipment, and one of them said they were going to put down a revolt in Samaria."

"It has not come to that yet. And I don't think it will—if Pilate does not use force."

"He will be forced to—in case of revolt."

"Simon Magus is a charlatan," Philip explained. "His pride was hurt when Peter would not let him lead the followers of Jesus in Samaria. And he is seeking to salve it by setting himself up as the Messiah. But when he cannot produce the sacred vessels he claims are buried on Mount Gerizim, the people will desert him and go home."

"Are you sure he does not have the vessels?"

"They are in Jerusalem, in the temple. How could they be here in Samaria too?"

"I am not a Jew so I don't know the meaning of such things," Quintus said. "In fact, I still can't be sure I understand the difference between a Jew and a Samaritan."

"There is no difference; Jesus taught us that with a parable. He told of a man—a Jew—going from Jerusalem to Jericho who was robbed and beaten and left half dead by the road. A priest came by but passed him on the other side, and a Levite did the same. Then a Samaritan stopped, and he took the man to an inn and bound up his wounds and paid the innkeeper for his care. 'Which of these three,' Jesus asked, 'do you think proved neighbor to the man who fell among the robbers?' "

"The Samaritan, of course," Quintus said.

Philip nodded. "Jesus taught often with parables. The Samaritans had not heard much of him until I came, but they listened when I spoke. Simon Magus had a great reputation here as a magician and pretended to believe in Jesus himself, because many were healed and turned from their ways."

"He could have been sincere."

"I hoped he was, but when John and Peter came here from Jerusalem, they laid hands upon those who had believed and the Holy Spirit came upon them——"

"What is this Holy Spirit?" Quintus asked.

"The unseen presence a man feels in his heart when he gives himself up to God's will. When it did not come to Simon Magus because he had not really yielded, he offered Peter silver to give him the power to bring it to others. But Peter was stern and said, 'Your silver perish with you, because you thought you could obtain the gift of the Holy Spirit with money.' Simon has hated Peter ever since. Now he claims he has found the sacred vessels on Mount Gerizim and that, because they were revealed to him, he is the Messiah."

"Why would the vessels be so important?"

"When the Assyrian king took away the Jews from Samaria hundreds of years ago, he populated this area with people from beyond the Jordan, even as far as Damascus," Philip explained. "After these people settled here, they decided to adopt our God, thinking that he ruled in this region. Then, as some of the Jews came back from captivity, they began to marry with those already here, and soon the people we call Samaritans filled this region. The priests at the temple at Jerusalem would not let them worship there because their blood was mixed, so they built themselves a temple on Mount Gerizim. Now Simon claims God has revealed to them the sacred vessels of Moses and has sent him as their own Messiah. As a result, thousands may suffer."

"For one man?"

"There was another like him called Judas, the Galilean or Gaulonite, at the time of the Procurator Quirinius, when I was a young man. He set himself up as a Messiah and many followed him. When the Romans attacked them, two thousand Jews were crucified, but the Zealots who followed Judas were not destroyed even then. In fact, they are stronger now than they were then."

"What do they seek?"

"For the Jews to rule themselves."

"And eventually the world?"

"The most rabid among the Zealots believe so. They think a leader will be sent from God with divine powers to overcome armies and earthly kingdoms. They could not understand the mission of the real Messiah when he came, because he only gave men the power to save themselves and become immortal."

"Do these Zealots support Simon Magus?"

Philip shook his head. "The Messiah—to the Zealots —must be a Jew; Simon is a Samaritan. They had trouble believing even a Galilean could be the 'Expected One,' so they would never accept a Samaritan."

"And because they do not support Simon, you think he will fail?"

"Simon appeals only to simple and credulous people who are amazed by feats of magic, like children."

"But he heals, doesn't he?"

"He pretends to, at least. I hear that he has promised to raise a man from the dead tomorrow."

Here was something concrete at last. "Where will this take place?" Quintus asked eagerly.

"On the slopes of Mount Gerizim, at the steps of the Samaritan temple. Simon is a very clever man. He will appear to do what he claims, but you can be sure it will be a trick."

"It may be a trick, as you say," Quintus said. "But if this Simon can really heal, I must take him with me to the emperor. In fact, I might be doing you a favor," he added, "by removing a source of trouble from this region."

Philip shook his head. "There will always be trouble so long as men are driven by false pride and envy. The magician envies Peter the power given him by Jesus, so he claims to be as great as Jesus himself. Let us hope this will not be like the affair of Judas the Gaulonite."

7

Only the ghostly half-light of dawn illumined the city of Shechem when Quintus and Philip left the house the following morning. Even at this hour, however, the streets were already packed with excited people, moving toward the lower slopes of the mountain they called Gerizim. On the hillsides around the city hundreds of campfires showed where others, unable to find lodging inside Shechem itself, had made their camps for the night. The babel of voices mingled with the shouts of hawkers who, shrewdly seizing the opportunity to make a profit, offered for sale bread, olives, dates, and even the small skins of wine which were often sold at Roman theaters and games. Actually the mood of the people seemed to be more like a political rally than a religious occasion. Many, Quintus noted, carried daggers or clubs, in itself an ominous sign.

At the west corner of Shechem a narrow valley or gorge ascended the slope of Mount Gerizim gradually and veered toward the south. Here he and Philip stopped at a copious spring—as many of the early pilgrims moving toward the Samaritan temple were doing—to drink the cold clear water.

Beyond the spring the slope grew steeper. Quintus and Philip climbed for more than half an hour, gaining altitude steadily as the path wound upward from the depths of the gorge. At the head of the gorge they came out on a broad plateau or plain which seemed to be a halfway point or resting place. A number of people had pitched their tents there the day before so as to gain a march on those who had still to toil their way upward from the city below, clearly visible now in the rays of the early-morning sun.

Quintus' service with the legions had accustomed him to walking long distances, but Philip was older and more portly, so he had to pause for the other man to catch his breath. While they sat on a rock, Quintus studied the countryside. To the northeast the whole length of the valley between Mount Ebal and Mount Gerizim could be seen, with green fields and orchards, olive groves, and turbulent mountain brooks. Above the trees rose the white roofs of a town; he could even see women standing on the roof tops of some dwellings, looking toward the mountain where exciting events were reputedly about to take place.

Leaving the plateau where they had stopped to rest,

Philip and Quintus followed the crowd moving toward the temple which stood just beyond the summit of the hill. The plateau was narrow here as it sloped upward, and the press of people struggling to find a favorable spot was considerable. With his broad shoulders and strong body Quintus was able to push a way through the crowd, and Philip followed closely in his wake. In this way they soon reached the temple which stood at the eastward end of a ridge forming the top of the mountain itself, almost at the very peak. A section had been roped off at the foot of the temple steps in preparation for the appearance of the self-styled Messiah, and they pushed their way close to it so as to have a good view of whatever took place there.

The view from the top of Mount Gerizim was worth the effort, Quintus decided, whether or not anything else came of the venture. To the north, across the narrow valley in which the city of Shechem lay, the slope of Mount Ebal was clearly delineated in the morning sunlight, bare and desolate, in sharp contrast to the northern slope of Mount Gerizim upon which they stood. Here and there terraces had been dug out of the lower slopes of Mount Ebal, and Quintus could see large cisterns from which the gardens growing on the mountainside were watered.

"The springs on Mount Ebal are on the north side," Philip explained. "That is why you do not see much growing on the southern slope of the mountain."

In the valley itself a village Philip called Sychar was plainly visible beyond Shechem. Near it was what he called the Plain of Makhnah, with fields of rich brown soil. Far to the west a vague white irregularity on the horizon was identified by Philip as the city of Joppa, the nearest seaport to Jerusalem.

"This hilltop is sacred to our own people, as well as to the Samaritans," he explained. "Here our forefather Abraham was ordered by God to sacrifice his son Isaac."

"His own son?" Quintus asked in amazement.

"Yes, as a token of true obedience."

Quintus shook his head. "I have heard of such things

in the worship of Baal and Moloch, but not by a civilized people. It is as hard to understand as the fact that your god let his son die on the cross."

"Abraham would have sacrificed Isaac because he obeyed the Most High in everything," Philip explained. "But his hand was stayed and Isaac lived to become the father of our nation. Here Joshua raised a tabernacle when he took the land from the Canaanites after our people were led out of Egypt by Moses. And on Mount Ebal, across the valley there, Joshua wrote out the whole law of our people on stone tablets. The Samaritans believe the twelve stones containing the law are still hidden on that mountain."

"To be found by Simon Magus, I suppose, as he claims to have found your sacred vessels."

Philip shrugged. "Perhaps. No one can tell what he will try next—if he succeeds today."

Having surveyed the valley and the mountainous slopes rising from it, Quintus turned his attention to the Samaritan temple but found it disappointing after the magnificence of the one in Jerusalem. It was built in much the same way with rising terraces, one above the other, but the walls were of rather roughly hewn blocks of stone, and there was none of the brave show of Corinthian bronze which made much of the structure at Jerusalem appear to have been fashioned of pure gold. The lower terrace of the Samaritan temple was reached by a flight of steps leading upward. It was upon these that the newly proclaimed Messiah had elected to perform his miracles.

From the temple Quintus turned his gaze toward the valley and the slopes below them. Suddenly he rose and pointed downward. "Look down there, Philip," he directed. "Isn't that a group of Roman soldiers marching on the lower slopes of the mountain?"

Philip shaded his eyes with his hand and studied the area Quintus indicated. The morning sun was fairly high above the eastern slopes of the mountains now, high enough to be reflected from the polished helmets and metal-studded harnesses of the legionnaires moving into place all along the lower slopes.

"Troops must have come here from Caesarea as well as those who passed you from Galilee," he said, his face grave. "I can see them moving into position along the roads leading upward to the temple here. Do you suppose Pilate plans to use drastic measures in order to show his authority and discourage an uprising?"

Quintus shook his head. "No Roman governor would attack a peaceful assemblage. He would have to answer to the emperor for his action."

"I hope you are right," Philip said. Then his voice changed. "Look over there! Simon is coming to the temple!"

8

A party of men was approaching the lower terrace of the temple. Most were priests, judging by their white flowing garments, but the man in the center stood out above all of them with a presence that was somehow magnificent and evil at the same time.

He was tall, fully a head taller than those around him. His skin was swarthy, even for a Samaritan, and his teeth were white and flashing as he smiled at the people who pressed against his bodyguards, seeking to touch him. His eyes were deep-set, and his face was set off with a prominent nose and a jutting cleft chin.

Simon Magus would have stood out in any assemblage, however dressed, but his raiment was also calculated to attract attention. His long robe of spotless white was embroidered heavily in gold with striking symbols which Quintus remembered having seen on the gowns of magicians in Far Eastern lands. Simon's head was wrapped in a white cloth after the fashion of the men of India, and in the middle of it, centered above his commanding beak of a nose, was a single flaming jewel, as large as a pigeon's egg and as red as blood itself.

"I can see how such a man could stir up the common people," Quintus admitted. "But even his apparel marks him as a charlatan."

"To you, yes," Philip agreed. "But most of those here today are common folk, without your intelligence and knowledge of the world. To them such magnificence fully befits the coming of the Expected One."

Simon Magus and his party were being escorted into the roped-off area by a priest. Once inside it, he continued up the steps until he was well above the crowd that covered the entire ridge. From this commanding elevation they could see him and he could easily be heard. At his appearance a great roar of approval went up.

The magician was a consummate showman, Quintus decided. He did not speak at once but let the waves of sound swell and echo out across the valley for a long moment before raising his hand for silence. While he waited for the crowd to become quiet, two of the white-robed men with him carried a small table up the steps to a position before him. Upon it they placed two small bottles of blown glass and a single drinking glass. One of the bottles was empty; the other appeared to contain clear water.

"Believers in the one true God." Simon's voice rolled out across the crowd and echoed down the hillside. He was speaking in the Samaritan dialect, but Philip translated for Quintus. "We are gathered today in this holy place where our father Abraham would have sacrificed his dearly beloved son to prove himself always subject to the voice of the Most High."

A roar of approval went up from the crowd and Simon waited for it to subside. "That same voice came to me not long since and spoke to me, saying, 'I am the Lord, Simon; it is time you listened only to me. Go now and tell the people of Samaria and all the world that I have given you power over all men and over all priests and Levites—yea, even the power to raise the dead.' "

Again a thunderous roar shook the very mountain-top. The man was more than simply a rabble rouser haranguing a mob, Quintus realized now. He was something far more dangerous, a skilled orator, able to sway the emotions of a crowd and play upon them as a musician plays upon the strings of a lyre.

"Not only did the Most High speak to me and give me power over death," Simon continued when the noise of the crowd died away, "he also showed me the hiding place of the sacred vessels of Moses, brought here and hidden by our great leader, Joshua, when he led our people across the Jordan against Jericho and took this land of Canaan to be our home. This very day will I bring them out and place them in the care of the priests, as proof that this is indeed the true temple of the Most High God and not some structure built by a Roman lackey on a hilltop in the country of the Jebusites."

This reference to Herod the Great, who had been as much Roman as Jew—and the fact that Jerusalem itself had been located neither in the southern kingdom of Judah nor the northern kingdom of Israel, but in a Jebusite city between the two—fell upon willing ears. The roar of the crowd was like a giant wave rolling up the mountainside from the paths and terraces below where people by the thousands were packed in a solid mass. It beat upon the stone walls of the temple and went echoing and re-echoing off across the valley toward the bare rocky face of Mount Ebal to the north.

Quintus looked down from the second step of the temple terrace to which he and Philip had been pushed by the great crowd. A sea of excited faces surrounded them—except on the one side where the temple stood —thousands of eyes already burning with the fires of fanaticism. There could be trouble here, he realized, serious trouble, if Simon chose to proclaim himself a leader in what could easily become a holy war. And any such war, it was obvious, could only be directed against the Jews in Judea, whose border lay only a little distance to the south, or against Roman authority. Actually these were one and the same thing, for Judea was ruled directly from Rome by the Procurator Pontius Pilate as an agent of the legate, or president, of Syria, Vitellius.

"Soon I will bring the sacred vessels from their hiding places," Simon continued. "But first I must prove to you that I am indeed the Expected One who will lead you to the place you deserve in the world."

With a sweeping gesture he took up a flask from the small table before him and held it up so everyone could see that it was empty, even turning it upside down in final proof. Next he took the partially filled bottle and held it aloft, shaking the clear fluid and letting the sun show through it.

"I have here water taken from the spring at the foot of the mountain," he proclaimed. "By the power given me in the name of the Most High it will be turned into wine." With a quick movement he poured part of the contents of the full bottle into the empty one. And even as the clear liquid touched the interior of the bottle it was changed into a red solution the color of wine.

Amid the thunder of applause that beat across the hilltop Simon took up the glass and poured some of the wine-colored liquid into it, drinking it down with evident relish.

"You can see how clever he is," Philip said soberly. "Watching him, I find it hard to believe myself that he did not actually turn water into wine."

"That is an old magician's trick," Quintus assured him. "I have seen it performed at least a dozen times."

"He is doing it this time for a particular purpose," Philip explained. "One of the first miracles performed by Jesus was turning water into wine—during a wedding feast in Cana of Galilee."

Simon Magus engaged in some common feats of magic, making objects appear and disappear with what, to the credulous, must have seemed startling rapidity. When the crowd began to grow a little restive under these more familiar feats of trickery, he paused dramatically and shouted, "Spirit of the Most High, come to us, I pray, to prove thy presence here."

An expectant hush fell over the crowd. In the midst of it a white dove suddenly appeared in the magician's hand and went fluttering up to the very topmost stone of the temple, where it settled into place.

With this dramatic act Simon had once more riveted the attention of the people upon himself; he took no chances of losing it again. While the dove was yet settling down on the temple roof, a small funeral cortege began to push through the crowd toward the temple steps. First came the mourners, clad in black, wailing and beating themselves with thyrsi cut from green branches. Behind them the body was borne on an open bier. It was that of a young man lying on a platform carried on the shoulders of four strong men and seemed absolutely immobile in death. In the wake of the bier plodded the family: the father, the mother, and the young wife bearing a baby in her arms. The wailing, and the shouts of those who carried the bier for others to make way, caused a considerable din. Every eye was instantly upon it as, Quintus judged, Simon had intended them to be.

The crowd parted for the sad procession, and two of the white-robed priests who had ushered Simon into the roped-off area on the temple steps quickly opened the ropes. The men carrying the body on the bier lowered it to the steps of the temple, almost at Quintus' feet where he stood upon the third step from the bottom. He took advantage of the confusion to study the corpse as carefully as he could from a distance of some two arms' length but could not see any sign that the young man was alive. His face was marble pale, the eyes closed, and Quintus could detect no sign of any movement of breathing.

He did not realize that Simon had noticed his study of the body until the magician's voice said, "You seem very curious, my friend. May I ask why?"

Quintus looked at him evenly. "I am a physician. Naturally I wish to know if this man is really dead or in some sort of a trance."

"A physician?" Simon's brilliant eyes mocked him. "From Jerusalem?"

"From Rome," Quintus said and then added with some pride, "The imperial physician to the Emperor Tiberius."

He saw a sudden gleam in Simon's eyes, a gleam of interest and something more, perhaps of calculation.

"What could bring the emperor's physician to Samaria?"

"I came seeking a healer called Jesus of Nazareth."

"But you found him crucified."

"And risen from the dead, I am assured."

Simon's manner changed quickly. There was real anger in his face now and in his voice when he spoke. "It is a lie told by his followers; they bribed the guards and stole the body from the tomb."

Quintus shrugged. "I will not debate that with you, no more than I will debate whether this man is dead or lies in a trance such as Egyptian magicians are able to produce, to be raised at the proper time by a trick of magic."

He was sure that a look of apprehension showed in the magician's eyes, but it lasted only a moment. Then Simon Magus smiled and said with great courtesy, "Examine the body, O Physician, and tell me whether the breath of life remains within it."

Quintus would rather not have become involved, for he recognized that Simon had shrewdly seized the opportunity of using him to impress the crowd. But he was trapped and could not very well decline the invitation, so he stepped forward and knelt beside the young man on the bier. His examination was quick but thorough. Only a mirror would have revealed whether any breath entered or left the body, and that Quintus did not have at the moment. In every other respect, save the fact that the skin was still somewhat warm, the body fulfilled the criteria of death.

"What is your decision?" Simon inquired.

"His skin is warm."

"Would it not be if he had just died?"

"Yes."

Simon turned to the young woman who seemed to be the victim's wife. "How long has he been dead?"

The girl took a quick breath and Quintus saw her look down at her husband and then up at the magician as if for instructions. "Hardly two hours," she said, and her eyes filled with tears. "You will save him, O Expected One. Tell me that you will."

"*I* cannot save your husband," Simon said pontifically. "But the power given me by the Most High will breathe the breath of life into his nostrils, if it be the will of God." He turned to Quintus. "You pronounce him dead then, physician?"

"I find no sign of life save the warmth of his skin," Quintus admitted reluctantly.

"A great and noble physician from Rome itself has certified that this man lies dead before you," Simon assured the crowd in louder tones. "I will now seek to determine whether the Most High wills that he shall be raised." Kneeling, he put his mouth to the apparently dead man's mouth and breathed into it, closing off the nostrils at the same time with thumb and forefinger.

Quintus saw the victim's chest rise and fall several times as air was forced into his lungs, but that in itself could indicate either that the man was not actually dead or had been dead only a very short time, not long enough for the stiffness of death to settle upon his body.

Simon rose now and passed his hands over the apparent corpse rapidly several times. "Justus of Sychar," he intoned, "arise and walk."

Even though he was thoroughly convinced that the whole thing was a cleverly concocted trick by a master magician, Quintus could hardly repress the feeling of awe, almost of fear, that came over him when the man called Justus started to come alive under his very eyes. First color began to come back into his cheeks, cheeks that seconds before had been marble-pale. Next his eyelids fluttered open. When they did, his wife uttered a shrill shriek and threw herself down beside him, sobbing. If it were a rehearsed act, Quintus decided, it was a tremendously impressive one.

Simon bent and took Justus by the hand. "Arise, Justus of Sychar," he said. "The power of the Most High manifested in me has given you life once more. Rise now from the bier of death and walk."

As if he were awaking from a deep sleep, the man who only moments before had appeared to be dead got slowly to his feet and faced the crowd. There was an instant of awed silence, then, as if in concert, a great pent-up sigh arose from the crowd.

"Examine him, O Physician!" Simon shouted exultantly in his deep, rolling voice. "Examine him and tell us whether he lives again."

"He lives," Quintus said. "Anyone can see that."

"The Most High God has chosen to give you once again the breath of life through me, Justus of Sychar," Simon said. "Go now and testify to that which has been done."

Somewhere in the crowd a voice suddenly bellowed, "The Christ of God! Simon is the Christ of God!" And as if this were the signal they had been awaiting, thousands of voices took up the cry in unison. The noise spread over the top of the mountain and, passing from one to another, poured down its side like a stream of water overflowing a dam. Those below took up the cry, passing it down from terrace to terrace and path to path, until the whole mountainside echoed to the applauding shouts of the Samaritans.

Simon moved up a few steps to the very edge of the temple terrace. There he stood, his arms upraised, receiving the acclaim of the people who had named him the Expected One, the Messiah they were confident would free them both from the oppression of Rome and from the haughty contempt of the Jews in Jerusalem.

This was the period of greatest danger, Quintus recognized, the time when—if the religious enthusiasm now sweeping the vast crowd were to be turned into revolt—Simon Magus would need only to sway the crowd in that direction with a few words. He waited, watching the tall man with arms outstretched as he stood on the top step of the temple. Finally, as the roar of the crowd began to subside, Simon spoke once more.

"God has revealed himself to me and shown where the sacred vessels are hidden," he announced. "I will go now and bring them to the temple. Let every man stand where he is until I return."

He was turning away when a sudden outcry came welling up from the people on the lower slopes of the mountain, a cry of fear, pain, and anger that was passed up from voice to voice, creating terror in its wake. Quintus did not need to hear Philip's translation, or to see his shocked face, to understand its meaning.

"The Romans are attacking!" fear-crazed voices were shouting. "They are putting the people to death!"

9

For a moment Quintus could not believe what he had heard. It was true that the people gathered on the slopes of Mount Gerizim were in the throes of a religious frenzy at the apparent proof that their god had sent the long-promised Expected One or Messiah, but Simon himself had done nothing as yet to stir them up into anything resembling a rebellion against Rome. Having seen the man, Quintus rather doubted that the magician wished to take such a chance at this time. His intended course of action would more probably be to cement thoroughly his hold upon the Samaritans by letting them proclaim him the Messiah and then allowing himself to be exhibited in all parts of the region so the entire populace would be behind him. After that only Simon knew what his plans would be. Actually, Quintus was forced to admit, nothing in either his speech or actions could be considered as even the beginning of a rebellion against Roman authority.

"Pontius Pilate must have loosed the soldiers upon the people," Philip cried in horror. "We will all be killed."

Everywhere there was fear and confusion where a moment before only exaltation had prevailed. Armed, as so many of the people were, and gathered together in numbers which must exceed many times the total number of Roman troops Pontius Pilate could possibly muster, Quintus was sure that a concerted attack by the Samaritans could turn the tables on the soldiers and, trampling them down in a human wave, destroy them along with all Roman authority in this area. In fact, Simon Magus could, if he wished, still accomplish just that if he acted quickly. But the magician showed no sign of assuming such leadership. He stood on the temple steps, a picture of complete bewilderment. Obviously what was happening on the slopes below was the very farthest thing from his mind.

At the moment Quintus was much more concerned with finding a way by which he and Philip could escape from the mountaintop than with either the fate of Simon Magus or the motives of Pontius Pilate in ordering the attack. The crowd gathered before the Samaritan temple milled around frantically, trying to reach the paths leading downward to the plateau where they had rested that morning. Against them was an upcurrent as those on the lower levels sought to climb higher and escape the attacking Romans. At any moment fighting could break out among the fear-crazed Samaritans, Quintus realized. And that would be the beginning of the end.

In the midst of the confusion he felt a hand pluck at his sleeve and looked around to see a man in the white robe of a temple priest, one of the group who had ushered Simon Magus through the crowd.

"Are you the Roman physician?" the priest asked in Greek.

"Yes."

"Simon bids you come with us."

"Where?"

"Into the temple." He lowered his voice to a whisper. "A way of escape leads to the other side of the mountain."

Quintus wasted no time in questions. Seizing Philip's hand, he followed the priest who had already started up the steps toward the lower terraces of the temple itself. Simon Magus was just ahead of them, Quintus saw, surrounded by the four brawny fellows who had carried the bier of Justus of Sychar. They were battering a path through a small swell of the crowd that was already surging up the temple steps, driven by the pressure of people moving up the hillside. Quintus, half dragging Philip with him, plowed after the priest, who stayed close behind the magician.

There was a dangerous moment at the very doors of the temple when a group of men ranged around Simon. "If you are truly the Christ of God, Simon," one of them shouted, "strike the Romans dead before they destroy us!"

Simon paid no attention to the plea. Protected by his four bodyguards, he moved into the temple, with Quintus and Philip following closely. The press of people was already filling the lower terrace and surging up the stairs to the one above it, but the resolute action of Simon's party gained them the second terrace without incident. Here one of the priests opened a great door with hinges of bronze. When they had all passed inside, he pushed it shut again in the very faces of the crowd that surged after them, barring it from the inside.

They were in one of the rooms of the temple, Quintus saw. The sudden change from the shouting outside to the silence inside was startling. Two of the bodyguards seized torches from wall brackets on either side of the door and Simon's party plunged on, through another door which a priest again shut and barred and down a flight of steps built from blocks of stone. Farther down the blocks changed to a rough winding stairway hewn from the solid rock of the mountain. It wound downward for some distance, then leveled out into a natural passage or cave deep within the bowels of the mountain.

A little farther on they came into a great room like a natural amphitheater wth long formations of rock hanging from the ceiling. Moisture dripped from the rock formations, and the huge chamber was cool and damp. At one side a stream ran for some distance before tumbling into what appeared to be a bottomless pit, for they could not even hear the splash of water when it struck far below.

Philip was almost exhausted and Quintus was panting. When the others stopped, they sank down upon a rocky shelf that projected from the wall of the cavern.

Simon Magus came over to Quintus and Philip. The

magician's eyes were blazing with anger, and his cheeks were suffused in spite of the coolness of the cavern. "Pontius Pilate is a fool!" he snapped. "By what authority did he loose troops upon the crowds?"

Quintus shrugged. "He must have thought you intended to start a rebellion."

"The time is not right." Realizing that he had said more than he intended, Simon caught himself up. "With my power over the people I could have controlled them. Pilate should have realized that I want no rebellion."

"Do you mean now—or later?"

Simon ignored the question. His anger had already begun to subside and the blaze in his eyes was changing, being replaced by a thoughtful look. "Did you speak truly when you said you were the imperial physician?" he demanded.

"Of course. My commission is with my baggage at the house of Philip."

"Why are you in Samaria?"

"I am taking a girl named Veronica to Jerusalem and then to Joppa, to embark there for Rome."

"The girl with the miraculous veil? Do you seek to heal the emperor with it?"

"That is my hope."

Simon shook his head. "You would be better advised to bring Tiberius a physician who can raise him from the dead."

Quintus saw the drift of the other's thoughts. "By name Simon Magus?"

"Why not? Emperors are as loath to die as other people."

"I might agree with you, if I were sure you can do as you say."

"You examined Justus of Sychar and pronounced him dead. Yet you saw him rise."

"I examined him but I did not say he was dead," Quintus corrected. "I still have grave doubts about a warm corpse."

"You heard the wife. He had been dead only a little while and was not yet cold."

"When you blew into the body, you had no trouble in expanding his chest," Quintus pointed out.

"The rigor of death had not yet set in," Simon said, but Quintus saw a look of respect—and a wariness too—in the magician's eyes. "That is a simple enough explanation."

"Perhaps. I also know the magicians of Egypt are able to induce a stupor that closely resembles death. Such could have been the case with Justus of Sychar."

Simon studied him for a moment. "You are clever and a learned man."

"As you are," Quintus conceded.

"We can have respect for each other's intelligence then," the magician said. "That is why I shall ask you a question. Can you be so certain Justus of Sychar was not dead that you would refuse to take me to Rome so I can try to heal the emperor?"

Quintus already knew the answer. He had decided it at the very beginning of the conversation. "I am planning to take you to Rome, if we escape from the crowd."

"And if I refuse?"

"I can place you under arrest; an imperial commission demands obedience from any Roman officer or soldier. But I don't think it will be necessary for me to use it."

A ghost of a smile appeared fleetingly on Simon's lips. "Why do you say that?"

"As you say, we are both men of intelligence. In addition, you are ambitious and also scoundrel enough to realize that whatever you might gain by being called to heal the emperor—even if you should fail—will more than outweigh the loss."

"The Samaritans have acclaimed me the Messiah," Simon reminded him.

"Will they still call you that when it becomes known that you ran away and hid inside the mountain here instead of striking down the Romans with a word—as the real Messiah could have done if he wished?"

"You are overly bold for one who is at my mercy."

"Not bold," Quintus told him with a grin. "Just—

as you say—intelligent. Your need for me far outweighs any impulse you might have to destroy me."

Simon did not argue the point, since it was self-evident. "When do you plan to leave for Rome?"

"When I can get a ship."

"Pontius Pilate seeks to destroy me, as he did Jesus of Nazareth. He will have people looking for me at every port."

"Not if you are traveling with me to Rome."

"I cannot chance it," Simon said. "Pilate is obsessed by fear of a rebellion and sometimes acts impulsively, as he did today. Do you know the Port of Accho that the Romans call Ptolemais?"

"Only that it is on the coast north of Caesarea, but not as far as Tyre."

"Accho is in territory ruled directly by the Legate Vitellius in Antioch and outside the jurisdiction of Pontius Pilate," Simon said. "Once there, we can hire a fishing boat to take us up the coast to Antioch, where we can easily get a ship to Rome."

"What makes you think you would be any safer in the hands of Vitellius than Pilate?"

"Vitellius is a prudent man, anxious to keep the peace. I have been in Antioch and I know of him. Will you go to Accho and wait for me?"

"How long?"

"I should be there within a week at most."

"Done," said Quintus. "But see that you come; I will have no trickery."

Simon shrugged. "Why should I be foolish enough to fail you when I have everything to gain?"

The cave was not uncomfortable, although damp and cool. The priests had stored food and wine against some such emergency as this, and there were woven blankets in a chest. Quintus was hungry and ate well of dates, figs, bread, and wine. Simon had said they would not leave the subterranean hiding place until it was dark outside, so he wrapped one of the blankets around him and was soon asleep.

He was awakened by a hand shaking his shoulder

and looked up to see Philip standing beside him. Around him the others were rising, too, and one of the priests was putting the blankets back in the chest. "Simon says it is time to go," Philip told him. "It is getting dark outside."

"How can he tell? This place is like a tomb."

"One of the priests has been stationed farther down in the cavern near the opening. He just came to report that the daylight is about gone."

They joined Simon and his slaves who followed a priest serving as a guide. The way led downward steadily through several slanting-floored passageways and a number of vast rooms with vaulted ceilings like the one where they had spent most of the day. The dirt floor underfoot was wet in spots from the moisture that dripped constantly from the ceiling, but by walking carefully they were able to avoid an accident. After threading their way through room after room in the bowels of the mountain they finally came to a narrow passage where they were forced to walk in single file. Shortly it opened out on a hillside through a narrow crevice in the rock. Once outside, Quintus looked back but in the darkness could not tell where they had emerged.

"The opening is equally well hidden by daylight," Simon's voice said beside him. "You are on the south side of Mount Gerizim. A path passes just below here; it will take you into the town."

"What about you?"

"The Romans will be seeking me for a few days, but I will be safe here. Remember—Accho in a week."

"How shall I find you there?"

"At the inn called the Blind Camel. It is well known to the caravan drivers."

"At the Inn of the Blind Camel, in a week," Quintus agreed.

The magician turned and almost immediately melted into the underbrush.

"What a strange man," Quintus said thoughtfully. "If he were a Roman he might one day be emperor."

Philip snorted indignantly. "A scoundrel emperor of Rome? Don't be absurd."

Quintus grinned. "It has happened before, my friend, and will no doubt happen again. The royal palace has no monopoly on integrity; I grew up there, so I know."

10

The city of Shechem was still in an uproar over the sudden attack by the Romans upon what had been up until then a peaceful religious assembly. Indignation against Pontius Pilate ran high everywhere, but the town was full of grim-faced soldiers whose swords were still red with the blood of those who had died on the mountain that morning, so there was little active fighting.

Quintus and Philip made their way through back streets to Philip's house. There they found a scene of intense activity, for it had been turned by Philip's daughters and the other followers of Jesus in Shechem into an improvised hospital where the wounded were being cared for. There also, to his surprise, Quintus found the merchant from Jerusalem, Joseph of Arimathea. He was on his knees beside a pallet upon which lay a dying Samaritan boy, telling him the story of Jesus. When Joseph described how the Nazarene had risen from the dead, the boy's pain-dulled eyes, already filmed over with the approach of death, brightened.

"Will he raise me?" he asked eagerly. "If I die?"

"You have only to believe in Jesus to have eternal life," Joseph told him.

"I believe," the boy said with the rattle of death already in his throat. "I believe." Suddenly he raised himself from the pallet on his elbows and his eyes took on the look which Quintus had seen before in the followers of Jesus of Nazareth, a transfiguring light in which their very souls seemed to shine through.

"I can see him now!" the boy cried. "On the right hand of God! He is reaching downward to me, asking me to come to him."

The unearthly glow in the boy's eyes burned only a moment, then suddenly was extinguished as he fell back, limp in death, upon the pallet. Quintus knelt beside him and felt for the pulse, but he already knew it would not be there.

"He has gone to be with Jesus," Joseph said, rising to his feet. "But he went in happiness, not in fear. What brings you here, Quintus Volusianus?"

"I might ask you that."

"Philip sent word to Jerusalem of trouble brewing in Samaria because of Simon Magus. I came to see if I could persuade Pontius Pilate not to do anything rash. He has listened to me before on several occasions."

"But not on this one?"

"I arrived just as the soldiers were attacking. One of the officers told me they were putting down a rebellion of the Samaritans, but I saw no fighting until the Romans struck first."

Quintus gave him a rapid account of the reason for his own presence in Shechem, as well as what had happened on the mountainside that day. When he came to his escape from the caverns within the mountain itself, Joseph said, "Pilate has grown more and more unreasonable since you came to Jerusalem. If Simon Magus will testify to Vitellius about what happened here today, we may be able to have Pilate replaced before he kills more innocent people. Vitellius is the only man who can stop him, short of the emperor himself."

"Come with me to Antioch," Quintus urged. "I promised Simon to meet him at Accho in a week. I was going to Jerusalem, but I think I can do more good here as a physician."

"I will go with you," Joseph agreed. "Veronica and Philip's daughters have done what they could for the wounded, but many are still untreated."

Quintus found Veronica working in the midst of the wounded who filled the courtyard and spilled out into the street before the house. She was pale with fatigue and her eyes were dark-shadowed with weariness. Yet even then—he thought as he stood watching her for a moment before she realized he was there—she was more lovely than any woman he had seen in all his travels.

Veronica was giving water to a wounded Roman soldier; there were a few of them among the Samaritans, which surprised Quintus. He would have thought that both Jews and Samaritans would have shunned Romans after what had happened. She saw him when she turned to put down the cup, and for a moment he thought she was going to faint. She took hold of the branch of an olive tree under which the wounded had been placed to support herself.

"Veronica!" He took a step toward her and, dropping the cup, she ran to meet him with a glad cry, her eyes shining with happiness. Without hesitation she threw herself into his arms and seized him in her own embrace. His arms went about her as she clung to him, pressing her face against his chest while she alternately sobbed and laughed hysterically.

"I thought you were killed!" He managed to distinguish the words in the midst of her sobs. "I started to go to the mountain to seek you, but the soldiers drove me back."

"It's all right, my darling." He used the endearment instinctively, from the sudden surge of emotion welling up in his heart. "Simon Magus saved me."

She raised her head, and at what he saw revealed in her eyes, he obeyed an impulse that seemed the most natural thing in the world and kissed her softly parted lips. They were a little salty from her tears but clung to his with the eager trust of a child for someone it loves very much. And suddenly he knew why she had looked so lovely to him, even with her hair in disorder, her cheeks smudged with dirt, and her eyes big with fatigue. He loved her, not with the casual sort of affection he had given more than one woman, but with the kind of love a man reserves for the one who will share the innermost experiences of his life and bring him warmth, understanding, and a constant adoration, the kind of love a man gives to the wife he selects to be the mother of his children.

Not caring who was watching, they clung thus for a long sweet moment, then he held her off by the shoulders gently. "You have overtaxed your strength," he said reprovingly.

"But there is so much work to be done, darling." The endearment came as naturally to her lips as it had to his. Both of them accepted this thing that had happened to them as something which had been growing between them for a long time. In fact, he realized now, it had begun that first day when he had seen her sitting under the spreading branches of the tree that shaded Abijah's pottery yard painting the graceful small vases and she had offered him a cool drink from the water jar beside her.

"We will work together," he told her. "You can point out those who are the most seriously wounded."

"I tried the veil," she said, "but most of these people do not believe in Jesus. I think it does not help those who do not have faith in him."

"It cured me," he reminded her.

Veronica smiled in the strange way women have when they know something men do not know. "I loved you even then," she said, "so it was as if you were a part of me."

11

All through the night Quintus worked in the courtyard of Philip's home, giving his knowledge and skill untiringly to the wounded. He carried only the barest minimum of medical supplies in his baggage roll, but Philip knew the city of Shechem well so Quintus sent him out to find the shop of an apothecary. His instructions were to purchase whatever he could find to relieve pain, preferably the powdered leaves of the poppy plant which, when stirred up in a little wine, had an amazing power to relieve pain and bring on sleep. Failing to locate an apothecary, Philip was instructed to seek what the Greeks called a *circumforaneus*, a traveling dispenser of medicine who, though actually no more than a quack, might possess poppy leaves and other pain-relieving plants.

The wounds themselves Quintus treated in the approved manner of the surgeons who accompanied the legions even into battle. First the bleeding was stopped by applying a tightly bandaged dressing where possible. If the hemorrhage was so severe that it could not be controlled in this way, he probed the wound with the slender forceps of Damascus steel he carried in his pack and sought to grasp the open end of any spurting blood vessel with jaws. This he next tied shut with a tough cord.

With the major bleeding stopped, Quintus next washed out the wound with water and with wine, the latter being well known to exert a healing effect if used early enough. With his limited equipment he could not do much toward closing wounds with sutures, but he could apply a clean dressing from strips of cloth torn at his direction by the daughters of Philip, folding them expertly into pads to cover the wounds themselves and then bandaging them into place.

The wounds were for the most part sword thrusts and therefore relatively clean, a fact which he knew from experience made them much more liable to heal than if they had occurred from bludgeons and other instruments. A few heads had been broken by being slapped with the flat of a sword in the hands of the soldiers, but scalp wounds always healed well. The broken bones he splinted as best he could, using pieces of firewood and sections of saplings cut in the woods back of Philip's house.

As with most battles, fully half of the wounded had died where they fell, and of those who had been carried to Philip's house, hardly half survived the night. Roman and Samaritan were cared for together here, and neither was treated better than the other. Toward morning Quintus finally looked up from where he was working and saw that no one else awaited his care. Veronica had worked beside him all night, and now she brought a bowl of water and clean cloths so he could wash his hands and arms which were red with blood up to the elbows. After that she brought spiced wine, warm and fragrant, with bread and meat. They ate sitting together under the olive tree where Quintus had been working upon an improvised table.

Around them the wounded were for the most part asleep, for Philip had been lucky enough to find a traveling apothecary among those who had come to Shechem for the ceremony on Mount Gerizim. The man had been carrying a fair supply of poppy leaves, and Joseph of Arimathea had purchased his entire supply of the medication. A few of the wounded were groaning in pain, but all had been done for them that could be done. Some others were babbling in the delirium of impending death under the watchful eyes of Philip's daughters and some women of the surrounding area who had volunteered to help. Remembering how these people had brought cloths to be torn up into bandages, wine for the washing and food, and had then remained to help even the wounded Romans, Quintus found himself understanding why Jesus had used the Samaritan in the parable about which Philip had told him earlier. For although the Samaritans were despised by the Jews, he knew them now to be a people of rare generosity and kindness.

"I watched Jesus lay his hand on those who were sick and heal them," Veronica said as they sat eating. "Your touch is like his—gentle and kind and wise."

Quintus shook his head. "From what I have heard of your Nazarene, I don't deserve to be compared with him."

"But you do," she protested quickly. "You are like him in many ways."

"You believe he is the Son of God," he reminded her.

"That is what makes Jews so easy to know and to understand and love—the fact that he chose to become one of us, to be happy and sad as we are, suffer pain, and even to die. When he rose from the dead, it was a sign to us that, if we believe in him and what he taught us, we too can live eternally."

"I was never attracted much by the prospect of immortality," he admitted. "Until today."

"Why today?"

He turned her slender hand over in his palm and kissed it. "Because I have at last found someone I want to live with forever—as my wife—if she feels the same way."

She leaned forward and kissed him. "You must have seen the answer to that in my eyes when I looked up and saw you were alive, after believing you had been killed on the mountain."

"But why should you love me? I am a rough soldier—"

"With hands more gentle than a woman's."

"And not even of your own people."

"Jesus said a Samaritan in a parable he taught us once was more of a neighbor to a man who fell among thieves than his own people. Besides, my mother was a Greek, and Father has always said I am very much like her."

"Would you go with me to Rome, Veronica? Not just to try and heal Tiberius, but as my wife?"

For a moment she did not speak, and he sensed that she was considering what marriage with him would mean, leaving her father, Jonathan, the pottery yard, and all the good life they had in Jerusalem, to enter a new world that would be completely alien to her. But there was never any doubt in her eyes, and when, in a moment, she turned and put her hands in his, her voice was firm and sure.

"A woman of Moab once spoke a creed that has served for every one who must give up home and family to be with one she loves," she said. "Her name was Ruth and these were her words:

"Entreat me not to leave thee, or to return from following after thee: for whither thou goest, I will go; and where thou lodgest, I will lodge: thy people shall be my people, and thy God my God: where thou diest, will I die, and there will I be buried: the Lord do so to me, and more also, if aught but death part thee and me."

"I never heard words more beautiful or knew one more worthy of a man's whole love," Quintus said huskily, drawing her close. "We will be married by the Legate Vitellius in Antioch. Only a Roman official can give permission for a soldier to marry, but I hear that he is a just man and we should have no trouble."

12

Quintus and Veronica discussed their love and their plan to marry with Joseph of Arimathea, who was her uncle by the marriage of Abijah with Joseph's sister, after Veronica's own mother had died. The Jews in general frowned upon marriages between Jew and Gentile, but in this case Veronica was half Greek and in both appearance and thought considerably more Greek than Jew. Joseph gave them his blessing, and a courier was sent hurriedly to Jerusalem for her father's permission. A letter of approval from Abijah arrived on the very day Quintus, Veronica, and Joseph were to start for Accho to meet Simon Magus.

Accho, an ancient town of the Phoenicians, lay at the northern end of the bay of the same name in the shadow of Mount Carmel. It had been rebuilt during the rule of the Ptolemies, after the death of Alexander the Great, and given the Greek designation of Ptolemais. A seaport of only minor importance, it could not be approached by large vessels except by anchoring offshore and communicating with the land by means of boats and lighters.

Mount Carmel was a commanding height and heavily wooded, Quintus saw, as they approached it on the afternoon of the last day of the week that Simon had specified he would wait for them in Accho. They had journeyed north to Cinaea on the same route by which they had come to Shechem, choosing this direct highway because it took them more quickly beyond the domain of Pontius Pilate, which ended less than ten miles north of Ginaea.

From Nazareth they had turned northwestward to Sepphoris. For many years one of the largest cities in Galilee, it had been the site of a royal palace during the time of Herod the Great, father of the present ruler, but had been burned by the Roman commander Varus during the insurrection led by Judas the Galilean, or Gaulonite. Herod Antipas had rebuilt Sepphoris with a magnificent palace and the usual amphitheater for the games. He had also built there quarters for the Roman soldiers making up the garrison of Galilee, which now made Sepphoris their headquarters. Herod, however, had quickly forsaken the city for the more pleasant climate of Tiberias on the Sea of Galilee.

Mount Carmel, Joseph told Quintus, had once been the site of a sanctuary devoted to the worship of Baal, the god who had prevailed in this area before the Jews had taken it from the inhabitants more than a thousand years before, when they had escaped from bondage in Egypt. It was separated from the main part of the country by a mountain chain through which passes led in several places, particularly in the southwest corner where the road from Nazareth entered.

Through one of these passes Quintus, Joseph, and Veronica—with several of Joseph's servants who made up the remainder of the party and a number of mules to carry their baggage—came down to the protected area of the Bay of Accho late one afternoon. No large ships were anchored there, however, and only a few mean-looking fishing boats were drawn up on the shore.

At the edge of the town they inquired about the Inn of the Blind Camel and were directed to it, an unprepossessing-looking structure on the water front smelling of fish and drying nets. Quintus went inside to talk to the proprietor, leaving the others outside where the air was more pleasant, with the breeze sweeping across the broad reaches of the blue Mediterranean to the west.

The proprietor was a plump man who seemed anxious to please, his demeanor making up somewhat for the character of his establishment.

"I am seeking Simon Magus, who was to meet me here," Quintus told him.

"Do you mean Simon, the magician of Samaria?"

"Yes."

"He left yesterday, after staying only one day."

"But I was supposed to meet him here," Quintus protested.

The innkeeper shrugged. "The magician seemed to be in a hurry; he hired a fishing boat."

"Do you know where he went?"

The man looked blank until Quintus tossed him a coin, then his memory seemed to improve. "I heard him bargaining with a fisherman for a boat," he confided. "He spoke of going to Antioch."

Quintus frowned. It did not seem likely that Simon would have gone off without him—unless he was being pursued.

"Was anyone following him?" he asked the innkeeper.

The man shook his head. "No one that I saw. Simon's party came here alone."

"How many were there?"

"Five. No—six. A young man and several slaves, I think."

A thought suddenly came into Quintus' mind. "Was there a woman with them? A young woman with a small baby?"

"Yes." The innkeeper grinned. "I remember now; she was very pretty."

One thing was clear at least. The alleged miracle on Mount Gerizim had been nothing but a trick. The man called Justus of Sychar was obviously a confederate of Simon's, placed in some kind of a stupor that resembled death so closely as to be almost indistinguishable from it—until the magician chose to end the deception with what was apparently a true miracle.

"Did Simon leave any message for me?" Quintus asked.

The innkeeper shook his head. "He seemed in a great hurry. The boatman did not want to sail until today, but the magician gave him extra money, saying they could put in for the night at one of the fishing villages between here and Tyre."

Quintus tossed the man another coin and went outside to where Veronica and Joseph waited. "Simon has made a fool of me," he admitted to them. "I could not be sure his raising the man Justus was not a trick so I agreed to take him to Rome. Now it appears that he was just using me as a means of getting there."

"Why wouldn't he wait for you?" Veronica asked.

"Perhaps he decided not to try and fool you any longer and went on his way," Joseph suggested.

"I'd wager he's embarked on another scheme to gain power and money for himself," Quintus said. "He knew I'd recognize Justus of Sychar as his confederate and denounce him as an impostor, so he left ahead of us."

"We'll catch him in Antioch anyway," Joseph said.

Quintus picked up the lead rope of one of the mules. "I doubt that too. Anyone who could convince the Samaritans he was the Messiah will not settle for anything small. I think we will see and hear much more of our friend Simon."

"What do we do next?" Veronica asked.

"Get to Antioch," Quintus told her. "By the quickest possible route."

Joseph looked doubtfully at the meanness of the inn and the fishing boats dragged up on the shore. "I don't like the idea of trusting ourselves to one of those," he said, nodding toward one of the boats. "Tyre lies less than two days' journey to the north. Why not camp in the hills tonight and wait there?"

"Can you walk that far?" Quintus asked Veronica.

"I am the daughter of a potter," she reminded him. "Not a princess. I will walk all the way to Antioch if you choose it."

They left Accho with no regrets and spent the night camped beside a bubbling spring along the road to Tyre. There was little traffic on the road, for this was mainly a seafaring country with rugged hills coming down to the sea, leaving only small areas of level land here and there suitable for growing crops or pasturing sheep. It was, in fact, the ancient land of the Phoenicians who had constructed their city-states like Tyre and Sidon on the shore and engaged almost entirely in seafaring. From these vantage points they had built up a vast mercantile empire which had at one time included Carthage and even Tartessus in far-off Spain. Phoenician seamen had sailed the ships of King Solomon and fought the Greeks for the Mediterranean trade.

Tyre itself, a bustling seaport and commercial center, was built on an island. It had resisted attack from many would-be conquerors, until Alexander the Great had subdued it by building a giant causeway from the mainland, a task that took him all of seven months. As they went about the city seeking a ship to take them to Antioch, Veronica's eyes glowed at the sight of the famous rich purple dye extracted from a kind of shellfish, the exquisitely carved ivory which had been famous in this part of the world for nearly a thousand years, and many other wonderful things made here in Phoenicia or brought by the ships that still traveled to all parts of the world from this port.

There were followers of Jesus in Tyre and Sidon, for the Nazarene had withdrawn here for a while at the height of his ministry in Galilee, before going on to Jerusalem and his tragic end there. Joseph knew many of them, and the travelers were welcomed while Quintus sought a ship to take them to Antioch. A great storm arose, however, on the day of their arrival and lasted nearly a week. All in all, it was more than ten days before they were able to find a small coastal sailing vessel that would take them to Antioch, ordinarily only about three days' sail away.

Of the three only Veronica was not a seasoned traveler, but she proved quite adaptable to the hazards of voyaging along the rugged shore in often stormy seas. The route between Antioch, Tyre, and the other cities of the empire was a regular highway of the sea.

A constant stream of vessels moved to and from the cities of Egypt and Rome by way of Antioch, Ephesus, and the other great population centers which had been built by the Roman emperors so they would have powerful cities under their direct control in case the constant struggle for power with the Roman Senate ever went against them. A vast labyrinth of shipping cluttered the seaport of Seleucia, port city for Antioch, as their boat was warped to its mooring a few days later.

Quintus showed his commission to the captain of the port and they were immediately given a carriage to take them into Antioch, some eight miles away. The palace of the legate was located on the *insula,* an island in almost the center of Antioch formed by a division of the river Orontes, which split the city into two parts and, with its broad mouth, formed the harbor at Seleucia. The *insula* housed the administrative center of the entire province of Syria, including the former domains of Herod the Great to the south as well as the essentially Greek cities of Decapolis to the west of the river Jordan.

The day was warm and bright as they were driven rapidly through the stone-paved streets of the great metropolis of Syria. To reach the bridge leading to the *insula* and the legate's palace they had first to travel by way of the Via Caesarea, a broad street that cut the city in half and ended at the foot of Mount Silphius. Quintus had been stationed in Antioch years before when, as a soldier of the legions, he had helped subdue an attack by the Parthians to the east. He found pleasure in pointing out the places of interest to Veronica, while she stared in wide-eyed wonder at this great city in which Jerusalem itself could easily have been lost.

He showed her on the summit of Mount Silphius the grim walls of the fortress built by the Romans both to guard the city from invasion and to keep it constantly under military control. On yet another crag was the great Temple of Jupiter Capitolinus, and eastward shone the gleaming white walls of the luxurious baths built by Julius Caesar after his defeat of Pompey. To the east, located in the famous grove of bay trees, stood the white shining walls of the Temple of Diana, scene of an annual saturnalia whose details he judged much too orgiastic for Veronica's tender ears.

Veronica's cheeks were pink with excitement and pleasure when the carriage rumbled across the bridge leading to the *insula* and the palace of the legate. With his imperial commission Quintus had no difficulty in obtaining an audience. Vitellius welcomed them into a small chamber where he was receiving informally.

The present legate of Syria had been a commander of the legions and still looked the part, a stocky man with deep-set dark eyes, a broad face scarred by many campaigns, and graying hair. Quintus gave him the Roman military salute with the clenched right fist brought across the chest and resting over the heart.

"Quintus Volusianus, with the rank of *tribunas laticlavus,*" he said, "bearing a commission from the emperor."

"I recognize you from the Parthian campaign," Vitellius said cordially. "Your father was once an officer under my command; I respected him greatly."

"As he did you, sir."

"Why are you not wearing the uniform?"

"I am now a physician," Quintus explained. "I only wear the uniform when I am on duty with the legions. Besides, the nature of my mission made it seem best not to flaunt the authority of Rome."

Vitellius smiled wryly. "To flaunt the authority of Rome, as you put it, in Judea and Galilee is to invite a dagger in the back."

"I learned that, sir," Quintus said. "My life was saved by my betrothed here, Veronica, daughter of Abijah of Jerusalem."

"May I compliment you on your choice in women, if not in dress?" Vitellius lifted the small parchment roll and read it carefully. " 'To seek out the healer called Jesus of Nazareth and bring him to Rome.' " He frowned. "From the last reports I had concerning Tiberius, I fear he is beyond all human help."

"So I told him before leaving Rome, sir," Quintus

said. "But he had heard of the Galilean and sent me to bring him."

"Is this the man Pontius Pilate crucified over two years ago—for stirring up an insurrection in Judea and Galilee?"

"Jesus was crucified by Pilate," Quintus confirmed. "I only learned it after I reached Jerusalem."

"Then your mission has been a failure."

"Unless the emperor is helped by a miracle-working veil possessed by Veronica. It seems to have some of the power that Jesus of Nazareth possessed."

"So?" Vitellius turned to her. "May I see it, my dear?"

Veronica came forward and laid the cloth in Vitellius' hand. "You can see the print of Jesus' features on the cloth," she explained. "I gave it to him on the way to the cross, and he held it to his face before handing it back to me. I myself had been an invalid for more than ten years, but I was completely healed at that moment."

Vitellius studied the cloth for a moment, then handed it back to her. "You believe this cloth can heal then?"

"I know it, noble sir," Veronica said quietly. "It has already healed many who believed besides myself."

Vitellius nodded thoughtfully. "I am no physician, but I suspect that believing they will be healed has cured almost as many people as physicians have—at least the kind of physicians I see preying upon the ills of the rich people of Antioch. What of the man called Simon Magus, who also claims to heal, Quintus? They tell me he has even raised the dead."

"Have you seen him, sir?" Quintus asked eagerly.

"He arrived here less than a week ago, claiming you had sent him ahead to minister to the emperor."

The picture was clear now. Simon had evidently decided he could accomplish more for his own fortunes by going immediately to Rome. And since he claimed to have been sent by Quintus as a healer, he would no doubt be given an immediate audience by the emperor.

Accomplished scoundrel that he was, the magician needed no more of an advantage than that.

"You seem disturbed by the news," Vitellius said. "Did you not send the magician to Rome?"

"I was taking him there," Quintus explained, "to see if he actually possesses the power to heal. We were to meet at Ptolemais and hire a boat to bring us to Antioch. Evidently Simon plans to go on to Rome alone."

"He left over a week ago," Vitellius confirmed. "On a swift military vessel of war that happened to be in the harbor when he arrived, ready to take dispatches directly to Rome. I arranged his passage since he bore a letter from you, asking that he be sent by the most direct route."

"It was a forgery!" Quintus exclaimed.

"Then the man must be a charlatan."

"Of the worst sort," Quintus confirmed. "Somewhere—probably in Egypt—he has learned how to bring about a deep trance that can only be distinguished from death itself by the warmth of the body. When he brings his confederate out of the trance, he seems to be raising the dead."

"And yet you say you were taking him to Rome."

"I was taken in by him at first," Quintus admitted ruefully. "Only at Ptolemais did I learn that the man he seemed to bring back to life is actually a confederate."

"I suppose you will want to follow him then?"

"As soon as I can, sir."

"A vessel of war has gone to Caesarea on official business. It should return in a few days and will sail for Rome immediately. You may have passage on it." Vitellius turned to his nomenclator, the freedman who stood at his elbow. "Meanwhile Plautus here will see that you are made comfortable."

"I have one other favor to ask," Quintus said.

"Name it."

"Your permission to wed Veronica. Her father and her uncle Joseph here have already approved."

"And what does the young lady say?"

"I love Quintus, noble Vitellius," Veronica said simply, her cheeks pink and her eyes glowing. "I would follow him to the very ends of the earth."

"I see no reason to withhold permission then," Vitellius said, but the nomenclator standing beside him spoke.

"Our law prohibits marriages between Roman officers and women of another country, noble Vitellius," he said. "Unless the woman is also a citizen of Rome."

"I had forgotten that provision," Vitellius admitted. "Plautus is right; only the emperor himself can give you the right to marry one who is not a Roman citizen."

In the excitement of his betrothal to Veronica, Quintus had forgotten the rule. But he knew how strict Roman law was in this matter. The provision was designed to keep the men of the legions from making casual marriages with women in the countries where they were stationed, and thus possibly dilute the purity of their Roman blood by giving citizenship through paternity to the offspring of such marriages. The Emperor Augustus had been responsible for what were called the *Lex Iulia de Maritandias Ordinbus,* part of the *Lex Iulia de Pudicitia et de Coercendis Adulteriis*— the Julian law of chastity and repressing adultery. Though honored largely in the breach by the Roman populace, these Julian laws were strictly enforced where the soldiers and officers of the legions were concerned.

"Is it my understanding that Veronica could marry Quintus if she were a Roman citizen, Excellency?" Joseph of Arimathea inquired.

"That is correct," Vitellius assured him.

"She was born in Tarsus of Cilicia. Her father is a citizen of Rome and so was her mother."

"Then that gives her citizenship by birth," Quintus said eagerly.

Vitellius turned to the nomenclator. "What say you, Plautus?"

"If what the merchant says is true, the girl is a

citizen," Plautus agreed. "She can be married to the tribune with your permission."

"I will make a certificate to that effect," Joseph offered.

"Then the obstruction has been removed from the path of love," Vitellius said. "May you be blessed with long life and many children."

13

The marriage between Quintus Volusianus and Ve-ronica of Jerusalem was simple yet beautiful. Had they been in Judea, it would have been celebrated in the ancient Jewish fashion. First Quintus would have visited Abijah, bringing the bride price called the *mohar,* symbol of his purchase of the bride. Abijah would then give Veronica most of the bride price as her dowry. Next would come the wedding procession, in which the bridegroom was escorted to the house of Abijah by young people singing and dancing to show everyone— including the demons that waited always to cause trouble at times like this—that the procession was not a funeral. At the house of Abijah, Quintus would next claim his bride and the wedding feast would follow with much eating and drinking, music and dancing, and great gaiety. At a late hour he would carry his bride over the threshold of the bedchamber while the gay crowd beat upon drums and shook rattles outside.

Quintus and Veronica had decided to be married with a simple Roman ceremony, however. And since marriage under Roman custom was firmly *liberum quaerendorum causa*—for the sake of getting children —it was much less complicated than the Jewish ritual.

As to the method of marriage, they had several choices. Marriage *cum manu* meant what it said, the handing over of the bride and all her possessions to the authority of her husband—or to his father. It could be either by *usus,* through living together for a year before the actual ceremony, or by *coemptio,* meaning actual purchase. Marriages *sine manu* dispensed with any religious ceremony but were easily dissolved. Actually they were little more than casual unions frowned upon by both the state and more serious-minded citizens.

A third form of marriage—and the one which they selected—was by *confarreatio,* which meant literally "eating a cake." For the ceremony Vitellius insisted upon providing the wedding feast, during which he pronounced them man and wife under Roman law when they broke the ceremonial cake together. A happy celebration followed before they marched through the palace to the garland-surrounded door of the luxurious chamber Vitellius had placed at their disposal. At the door Quintus, following the traditional ceremonial, turned to his bride and asked formally, "Who art thou?"

Veronica answered with a simple avowal, much as she had answered him that day in Shechem when he had asked her to be his wife: "Where thou art, Quintus, there am I, Veronica."

He lifted her over the threshold then and gave her the keys to the chamber, as he would have given her the keys to his own home had they been in Rome. As the wedding party gathered around them holding a flower-decked yoke such as oxen used when pulling a plow or cart, Quintus put his neck with Veronica's beneath it to signify their common duty to each other. With this ceremony of *coniuqum*—yoking together— the formal marriage ritual was completed and he closed the door of the chamber upon the guests, leaving the pair alone for the first time as man and wife.

The days passed in a haze of bliss for the newly wedded lovers. There were long walks in the gardens of the *insula,* rapturous days for Veronica visiting the shops that lined the streets of Antioch, where anything could be purchased that had been fashioned by the hand of man in the far-flung corners of an empire which extended from the tin mines of Britain to the weaving looms and forges of Damascus.

As the wife of a Roman official who was the friend and confidant of high persons, including both the legate of Syria and the emperor, Veronica chose to adopt Roman dress. This meant that inside the house she put away the heavy homespun robes of dark color affected by Jewish women in favor of the Roman stola, a simple straight tunic of silk, linen, or less expensive cloth, usually leaving the arms bare but sometimes gathered with a jeweled pin across only one shoulder. From the shoulders it fell straight or in single folds and was bound with a girdle of a differently colored cloth or an embroidered strip beneath the breasts. On her feet she wore sandals laced with slender strips of leather, tied or buckled together. Her fair hair, like a golden aureole about her face, was secured usually with a bright ribbon or, when she and Quintus were alone together, allowed to fall about her shoulders in a golden cloud.

Outside Veronica wore a palla or cloak of a heavier material over the stola, with a hood attached which she could draw up over her head for protection. With her clear skin, delicate coloring, and the warmth that rose to her cheeks when she was stirred or excited, she had no need for what the poet Ovid had called *medicamina faciei feminineae*—the cosmetics with which women of faulty complexion sought to hide their blemishes. So lovely was she at all times that the thoroughly enchanted Quintus was certain he would never need the same poet's somewhat cynical advice called *remedia amoris*—ways of getting rid of love— the principal one being to "surprise your lady in the morning, before she has completed her toilette."

Now that he was back in direct contact with Roman authority again, Quintus had once more adopted the uniform of the legions. His tunic was of fine wool, the skirts pleated and reaching almost to his knees. Over it he wore a leather jerkin or harness, reinforced with bands and strips of metal around the torso and over the shoulders. His close-fitting metal helmet bore the

120

proud crest of a tribune in the Praetorian Guard, the elite corps that constituted the personal troops of the emperor. Heavy sandals, laced up the calves with leather strips, were upon his feet. And over the tunic he wore a brown woolen cloak secured at the shoulders so it hung free when not wrapped about him.

He and Veronica made a handsome pair as they went about the *insula* and the streets of Antioch. Joseph of Arimathea had moved from the palace shortly after the wedding, taking up quarters in a mercantile establishment in which he owned an interest in Antioch, as he did in various other parts of the world. Quintus thought the merchant was engaged solely in commerce until Veronica came to him one afternoon and asked shyly if he would go with her to a gathering in the city which Joseph had arranged.

North of the Orontes lay the richer section of Antioch containing the homes of well-to-do merchants and officials who did not live on the *insula* itself, professional men such as doctors, lawyers, and the richer *apothecarii*. In the shops of the latter could be found drugs and medicaments from all parts of the world, dried seaweed from India for the treatment of goiter— the swelling of the neck that was considerably prevalent in this region—and needles of finest steel for treating the blindness caused by cataracts, according to the technique of needling or couching described by Greek surgeons. In addition, of course, there were the more common medicaments, like oil of asses' hoofs, fat of Abyssinian greyhounds, toads, and vipers, and the universal theriac—for treating poisoning—whose ingredients were almost beyond counting.

All kinds of special shops were located in the Upper City too. In them one could buy exquisite figurines of the goddess Artemis fashioned in Ephesus, purple dye from Tyre, amber of the northern countries, stibium —the white metallic paste for ornamenting women's cheeks—precious stones and jewels from the mines of Africa, gold from the region of Sinai, and hundreds of other exotic things.

When they came off the bridge leading to the *insula* today, however, Veronica turned along the south bank of the Orontes where the old well of the city was located and beyond which teeming suburbs had long since sprawled outward. There were no great houses here, and the streets, though stone paved, were full of holes in which stagnant water still stood from the last rain. Emaciated children stared at them with lackluster eyes, and from the shops even after dark came the whir of potters' wheels and the pounding of black-smiths' hammers as the artisans worked into the night to eke out enough to keep themselves and their families from starving.

The Jews, Quintus knew, were scattered all over the world. He had seen their synagogues—as their meet-ing places were called—in every city he had visited. In Alexandria they occupied a complete section of the city with a certain degree of their own government, and he had been told that there were actually more Jews in the city of Alexandria than in Jerusalem. Many of these Hellenized Jews—so called because of the Greek influences which they had adopted—no longer adhered strictly to the traditions of the law or the strict ritual of worship that prevailed in Jerusalem.

Veronica led the way to a dingy-looking building that backed up on the river. Inside a number of people had gathered and the structure was nearly filled. She left Quintus at the entrance to the synagogue and went to one side where a sort of raised platform or gallery was set off by a latticing behind which a number of women were already seated. Quintus took a seat on a bench near the back of the building and looked around him. A raised pulpit stood in the center so as to be visible from all sides. Several older men, each wearing an embroidered scarf across his shoulders, sat on some benches elevated upon a lower platform than the gallery where the women sat. Joseph of Arimathea was among these.

The service began with the reciting of what seemed to be a set of prayers by one of the older men, in a

122

language which Quintus recognized as Hebrew. Following this, the leader brought some large scrolls from a cabinet located on the south side of the synagogue building. From one of these another of the men read, first in Hebrew and then in Greek, a simple but moving story from the early history of the Jewish people, telling how they had been freed from bondage in Egypt by Moses and brought into what they called the promised land of Canaan. Finally, at the end of a long reading, the scrolls were rolled up and put back in the cabinet.

The leader now rose and said in Greek, which seemed to be used largely by this congregation: "The distinguished merchant of Jerusalem, Joseph of Arimathea, is with us tonight and will speak to us."

Joseph rose and went to the pulpit. Before he had spoken more than a few sentences, Quintus realized that here was another man entirely from the gracious merchant in whose house he had been entertained the first night he had come to Jerusalem or the tired, elderly man who had plodded beside him with never a word of complaint on the road to Accho and Tyre. Joseph's normally quiet voice had taken on a timbre and a warmth of conviction that were strangely moving, even though he was telling a story that had become very familiar, at least in several parts, to Quintus during the past several months.

It began with a discussion concerning the promised Messiah whom Jews everywhere seemed to believe would one day be sent from heaven by their god to lead them. Joseph quoted from the writings of their prophets and other writers down through the ages to show that the coming of this great leader had been foretold, including—to Quintus' surprise—the manner of his death and resurrection.

The introductory part of his discourse completed, Joseph now launched into the story of how Jesus, a carpenter of Nazareth, had begun to teach and had been acclaimed as the Expected One by a man named John who had apparently called himself the Fore-

123

runner. John, Quintus had already learned, had been beheaded several years before on the order of Herod Antipas, as a whim to please his wife's daughter by another marriage.

After the death of John, known also as the Baptist, Jesus of Nazareth had called twelve men, mostly of Galilee, as his disciples. These had begun to teach and heal in the teeming cities surrounding the lake. At one time the press of those seeking to listen and be healed and the disturbance engendered by the huge crowds had forced the Nazarene to go into seclusion in the region around Tyre and Sidon. Finally, after many miraculous feats, he had come to Jerusalem. The conflicts with the Pharisees and priests had followed, ending with the sentence of death by Pontius Pilate.

Joseph's voice grew deeper as he told how Jesus had taught men to love one another, to treat each other kindly, and be generous and forgiving. It rose on a triumphant note when he gave his personal account of how he had come into his garden after the crucifixion and seen the stone rolled away from the empty tomb. When he told of Jesus' appearance after death to various people and at last to Peter and the others on the lake, an audible sigh went up from the audience.

For a long moment after Joseph finished there was no sound from the congregation save the softly muffled sobbing of a woman. Then the people began to move around and shuffle their feet, as if in reaction to the grip of a strong emotion which had held them for, Quintus realized with a start, more than an hour. The leader rose to his feet and spoke a prayer in Hebrew, ending the service.

Quintus made his way outside and waited for Veronica. He was still strongly moved by what he had heard and could tell by the comments of the people leaving the building that they, too, had been gripped by it. Then he heard a soft footfall beside him and a familiar small hand crept into his.

"Uncle Joseph says to wait and he will walk back

to the Upper City with us," Veronica told him. "I never heard him speak so well before."

"Nor I," Quintus agreed. "I did not know he was so eloquent."

"Jesus gives men eloquence to spread his teachings. Peter was an ordinary fisherman, yet I have heard him move thousands with the story you heard tonight."

"Peter may have been a fisherman," Quintus said, drawing her arm through his against his body, "but he was never ordinary. Some men are born to be leaders; Peter is one of them."

Joseph came up then, and they started to walk back toward the *insula* and the Upper City beyond the bridge across the Orontes. "They listened intently tonight," the merchant said happily, "and many of them believed. Soon we will have people telling the story of Jesus in Antioch as they are in other cities. And with so much going and coming, other parts of the world will hear of it too."

"Your address was very moving," Quintus complimented him.

"The Holy Spirit was upon me tonight," Joseph said simply.

"How could you know?"

"It is something you feel, as you feel happy or sad. When it comes, you will know it."

"I am a Roman," Quintus protested. "How could such a thing happen to me?"

"Romans have heard Jesus and believed," Joseph told him. "The servant of a centurion was healed because of his master's faith."

"I was tempted to believe tonight," Quintus admitted. "Then reason and logic assured me there are other explanations for the miraculous things you describe, like the way Simon Magus appeared to raise a man from the dead."

"The real proof that Jesus is our Saviour does not lie in miracles," Joseph said quietly. "Nor even in his resurrection. It is in what believing in him can do to a man's heart and soul. One day you will know what I mean, Quintus. When that day comes, you, too, will

125

feel the Holy Spirit take possession of you completely and you will be happy to yield yourself up to it."

"What sign will I have?"

"Sometimes God does send signs, like the blooming of the thorn on the hillside for the wood seller Jonas, or a boatload of fish that Peter and some others caught one night on Galilee. The fact that Veronica loves you and became your wife is in itself a sign that you are closer to becoming one of us than you yourself admit. Later you may realize that her love and yours are in themselves the only sign you will ever need."

That night, with the moon shining through the window of their chamber and Veronica asleep in his arms, Quintus wondered if Joseph had been right. For he was sure that the god all men worship in their hearts—whatever name they give him—had blessed him beyond anything he could ever do to deserve having her as his own.

On the morrow all other thoughts were driven from Quintus' mind when Vitellius summoned him to the palace early in the day.

"The ship we have been waiting for has now come from Caesarea," the legate said. "I have a charge for you, Quintus."

"I am under your orders."

Vitellius took a parchment roll from the table before him. "This is your commission of authority from me," he said. "You and your companions are to journey at once to Seleucia. There you will board the ship of war *Olympia* and take charge of a prisoner being sent to Rome for trial before the emperor."

Quintus took the roll. It was sealed with the seal of the empire and the private insignia of the legate of Syria.

"The prisoner's name is not unknown to you," Vitellius added. "He is Pontius Pilate, formerly procurator of Judea."

14

"Pilate has ruled well in Judea over a period of ten years." The grave voice of Vitellius stirred Quintus out of his state of shock at what he had just heard. "It is no light thing to be forced to remove him from office now and send him to Rome."

"Is it on account of Jesus of Nazareth?"

The legate shook his head. "I have heard many stories of the Galilean and the reasons for his death. If a rebellion was intended in Jerusalem that day, he does not seem to have been the leader of it. However, some of those who followed him were undoubtedly in league with the Zealots who are always seeking to make trouble. They may even have intended to set him up as King of Judea."

"I don't believe so from what I have seen of them," Quintus said.

"That may well be," Vitellius admitted. "It has always been the policy of Rome in Judea to carry out the verdict of the Sanhedrin, however. Pilate acted within his rights in ordering a crucifixion when the Jewish court condemned the man on religious grounds."

"Then it must be the Samaritan affair," Quintus said.

"That and what Joseph of Arimathea has reported to me," Vitellius agreed. "Actually envoys from the Samaritans reached Antioch a week before you did, protesting against the way Pilate ordered the soldiers to attack the people on Mount Gerizim that day. I spoke to Simon Magus, and he assured me that no revolt was intended, even though some of the people were armed."

"Did he admit that he had managed to have himself acclaimed the Messiah by trickery?"

"He was much too clever for that," Vitellius said. "Had I known it, I would have arrested him and sent him to Rome under guard."

"But you must have known from the things I said that I was also in Samaria."

"I was sure you were, but I purposely didn't ask you

details," Vitellius told him. "You have a right to know why." He paused, then went on. "It is not easy to govern foreign lands in the name of Rome, Quintus. We think we bring peace and prosperity to them by stopping them from fighting among themselves, but in the years I have been here in Antioch I have often wondered whether that is really true."

"No one could deny that these people are better off under Roman rule," Quintus protested.

"We Romans would not deny it—no. But I try to put myself in the place of the people themselves. Knowing how I love Rome and how fiercely proud I am of being a Roman, I can see why a Jew loves Judea and Galilee and how fiercely proud he would also be of being a Jew. So long as a man can see both sides, he is a good governor; when he fails, he needs to be removed."

"And you think Pontius Pilate has failed?"

"The evidence would seem so, but it is not my province to judge a procurator of Rome. Therefore I did not ask you your story but chose instead that you should go with Pilate to Rome where the whole question can be heard impartially."

"I wonder just when Pilate did begin to fail," Quintus said thoughtfully.

"I suspect it was after he crucified the man called Jesus," Vitellius said. "Herod wants to rule Judea again, as well as Galilee and Peraea. It has always irked him that when Archelaus proved incapable of ruling Judea, it was made into a Roman province. The Tetrarch Philip didn't mind; he was content to govern his own domain of Peraea. But Herod is ambitious; he would like to be called 'Great,' as his father was. I think he has stirred up as much trouble as he could for Pilate during the past several years, but Pilate has also been a troubled man."

"I could see that when I was before the procurator in Jerusalem," Quintus said. "He and Caiaphas conspired then to kill me."

Vitellius looked relieved. "Now I am sure that I am making no mistake in sending Pilate to Rome." He got to his feet. "May the gods of the sea—if such there are—speed you on your way." He tapped the parchment roll that Quintus carried. "This gives you complete authority. Don't hesitate to use it—if you have trouble."

Quintus and Veronica had been packed for several days, since the arrival of the ship from Caesarea had been expected at almost any time. They sent their baggage to Seleucia in a chariot and were driven in the private coach or *raeda* of the legate himself to the mercantile establishment where Joseph of Arimathea was staying.

The old merchant greeted them with a smile. "I am all packed and ready," he said. "Word from Seleucia comes as quickly into the houses of business as it does to the *insula*."

"Are you sure the trip will not be too wearying for you?" Quintus asked.

"Jesus will give me the strength I need for whatever comes," Joseph assured him. "I have planted seeds here in Antioch and now I find myself eager to sow them elsewhere."

"Rome is hardly fertile ground," Quintus warned him.

"God sends rain and the sun's warmth to make seeds grow even in crevices among the rocks," Joseph said confidently. "Some will always fall on barren ground, but if only one plant survives, the wind will carry its seeds even farther and farther afield."

The galley of war, *Olympia,* was a large, swift vessel, much narrower and sleeker than the heavy-bodied "round" vessels carrying freight and grain from Egypt and the cities at the eastern end of the Mediterranean to Rome. It lay beside one of the large quays projecting into the harbor formed by the mouth of the Orontes. All around the travelers as they drew up to the quay there was a beehive of activity. In the construction docks a swarm of *fibri navales* worked on a half-finished hull. A nearly completed ship stood to one side; from it came the rhythmic tapping of hammers wielded by the *stuppatores* at their work of calking.

A completed ship stood at another quay and a long line of *sabuarii* were loading sand into it to be used as ballast.

A large merchant vessel stood beside the next quay with a host of *sacaraii* loading grain into it. The *mensores* weighed the sacks and counted them while small boys called *urinatores* busied themselves diving for objects that fell overboard in the process of loading. The *Olympia,* Quintus saw, was of medium length, perhaps seventy-five paces long, with a great furled sail forward. From his experience in sea travel with the legions he was sure the accommodations in her would be much more spartan than in the larger merchant vessels, which sometimes carried as many as six hundred persons. Also, the best cabin space in the *Olympia* would undoubtedly be given to Pontius Pilate and the Lady Claudia Procula, who was of royal blood through her kinship with the Julian line, so he and Veronica and Joseph would be forced to take only second best.

The captain, a bluff Greek mariner with weather-toughened cheeks and the clear eye of a sailor, met them at the gangplank and greeted them courteously. He escorted them to their quarters which, as Quintus had surmised, were adequate, if somewhat cramped.

"How is your passenger?" Quintus asked when they had put down their baggage.

"Hardly once did he come from his quarters on the way from Caesarea," the captain said. "Is it true that his mind has failed?"

"I do not know," Quintus said. "I last saw Pontius Pilate several months ago in Jerusalem."

"I would not change my position as captain of this ship with any governor of a Roman province," the captain said. "They are all hotbeds of trouble, and Judea is the worst."

Quintus visited the quarters of Pontius Pilate later in the day while preparations for sailing went on apace. He found his prisoner lying on a couch staring up at the ceiling, while the Lady Claudia Procula sat beside him.

"Quintus Volusianus!" she cried warmly. "I am glad an old friend is to be with us on the voyage."

Pontius Pilate spoke heavily from the couch. "You would hardly call my jailer a friend, would you, my dear?"

Procula gave Quintus a startled look. "Is this true?"

"I am traveling to Rome after completing my mission," Quintus evaded. "The Legate Vitellius asked me to be your escort."

"Not so long ago Vitellius complimented me officially on my efficient administration in Judea and Samaria," Pilate said. "Have I fallen so low in favor that he cannot even drive the few miles to Seleucia to see me?"

"The legate is very busy," Quintus explained, conscious of how lame he must sound, "and the ship is to sail soon. He sent you his greetings." The last was stretching the truth somewhat, but Quintus could see no reason to make Pilate feel any worse than he obviously felt already. The former procurator of Judea seemed to have aged years since Quintus had faced him in the fortress of Antonia on the day after his arrival in Jerusalem.

"I hope your quarters are adequate, sir," Quintus said to Pilate.

"I have been a soldier, tribune. So I am no stranger to discomfort."

In Pilate's present mood the less said the better, Quintus decided. From the door he said, "If I can do anything to increase your comfort, please let me know."

Claudia Procula followed him from the cabin to the deck outside.

"Is what Pontius said really true, Quintus?" she asked. "Are you our jailer?"

"Vitellius has placed your husband in my charge, but he has not been condemned. You may be sure he will be heard by the emperor, like any other Roman."

"Pontius will not fare well with Tiberius," Procula said. "The emperor does not tolerate those he thinks have failed him. This business of the Samaritans caused almost an insurrection in that part of Judea."

"The Samaritans were not in rebellion, my lady. A clever man named Simon Magus had duped them into proclaiming him the Messiah, but I was there and saw no sign of revolt against Rome."

"I think Pontius knows that now," she admitted. "He has not been himself since Jesus of Nazareth was crucified, Quintus. Even before the Samaritan affair Pontius was troubled. Since then he has been as you see him now."

Quintus knew no way to comfort her, for there was none. Only the emperor could decide the fate of her husband.

"What a lovely girl!" Procula's voice broke into his thoughts and he turned to see Veronica standing with Joseph in the bow of the ship, watching the lines of porters carrying supplies on board. "And isn't that the merchant, Joseph of Arimathea, from Jerusalem?"

"The girl is Veronica, my wife," Quintus said proudly. "Joseph is her uncle."

"Have they come to see you off?"

"They are going with me to Rome."

Procula turned to him, her eyes warm. "What a fortunate man you are to find such a beautiful girl! Take me to her, Quintus, I must speak to them both."

Veronica and Joseph bowed low when Claudia Procula approached, but she reached out both hands and took one of theirs in each of hers. "I am happy to see you again, Joseph," she said, speaking to the older man first as custom dictated. "I well remember being entertained in your home in Jerusalem."

"It was I who was honored, noble lady," Joseph said.

"And you are Quintus' wife!" Procula turned to Veronica. "How lovely you are, my child!"

"Thank you," Veronica said with quiet dignity. "I am honored to have been chosen by Quintus."

"He is a fine man; I knew him when I was growing up in the emperor's household before he became a physician. And how nice it is that he can take you to Rome. Most officers' wives are not allowed to travel with their husbands."

"Veronica possesses a miraculous veil, with the

print of Jesus' face upon it," Quintus explained. "We hope it may be able to heal the emperor."

"Could it heal an illness of the mind as well as of the body?" Procula asked quickly.

"For those who have faith," Veronica told her.

Quintus sensed what Procula was thinking and he saw that Joseph did too. Yet he knew he could not ask Veronica to try and heal Pilate with the veil whose power came from the very man he had crucified. Joseph, however, solved his dilemma for him.

"I am sure my niece will be happy to use the veil and try to heal your husband with it," he said quietly.

"Even after what he did to the Galilean?"

Joseph smiled. "I will repeat the words of Jesus himself: *Love your enemies, do good to them who hate you, bless those who curse you, pray for those who abuse you. To him who strikes you on the cheek, offer the other also.*"

For a moment Procula did not speak. When she did, her voice was soft. "He had so much to give the world. What a pity he was killed before he could give it."

"The spirit of Jesus of Nazareth lives in the souls of thousands who believe in him and in his teachings although they did not see him when he was on earth," Joseph said. "And he dwells now with the Most High, until he comes again."

"But is it possible he might even forgive the man who ordered him crucified?"

"He will—if your husband repents and believes in him."

"Thank you, Joseph," Procula said quietly. "I will talk with you more about the Galilean." Then she turned back to Veronica and took her hand again, reaching out to take Quintus' with her remaining hand. "I give you both my blessing. May nothing ever come between you and your love for each other."

15

The *Olympia* sailed that afternoon. By nightfall the mountainous coast line of Syria was only a dimly irregular line behind which the sun was slowly sinking. The sail was pulling strongly and the slaves at the oars were able to rest much of the time, a respite they needed badly, for when the wind failed, they would be forced to pull on the long oars for twenty hours or more at a stretch.

Like most ships in the service of Rome, the *Olympia* had been built by Greeks who had taken over the ancient Phoenician art of shipbuilding and seafaring. She was a trireme, representing the finest type of maritime construction. Long, narrow, and low, her length was perhaps seventy-five paces and her breadth no more than five. The upper deck was about the height of two tall men above the sea. Like most ships of that day she rode high in the water so that in a severe storm the hull could be driven upon a sloping shore for safety, with a chance of being gotten off later by digging around and sliding the keel along rollers toward the sea.

A tall mast with a large sail was stepped in the bow and a smaller one at the stern. Ranged some two thirds of the vessel's length on both sides were a series of seats and footrests for the galley slaves, set in three tiers, each above the other. The lowest rowers were just above the water line. So closely were they packed that, when a slave reared back upon the oar, his head settled between the feet of the next man above and behind him. Those of the second row similarly fitted in between the ankles of the ones on the third tier. Thus they were so closely intertwined that any failure on the part of one man to continue the steady rhythm of the oars when rowing could cause interlocking and confusion all along that side of the ship.

The central part of the vessel contained space for the cargo, on these ships amounting to little more than the supplies necessary to keep the vessel's complement and the passengers alive, since they carried mainly military and civil dispatches. These, however, were considerable when it was remembered that more than two hundred men were needed to speed one of the swift galleys on its way.

The days passed with good weather for the most part. Pontius Pilate remained in his quarters and Quintus did not trouble him, paying only a daily call upon the Lady Claudia Procula to see that they did not lack for anything available on the ship. The Greek captain was equally solicitous for the comfort of such high-ranking passengers, so Quintus had little to do as far as taking care of Pilate was concerned.

Both Veronica and Joseph were excellent sailors, and Quintus occupied himself by taking care of the medical needs of the crew and passengers, treating bruises and scratches and occasionally the broken scalp of a slave whose foot had slipped, dropping him low enough for the heavy handle of the oar just behind him to strike him across the temple. The overseers who had charge of the slaves treated them very considerately, using the lash only in times of danger when it was necessary to drive the boat at considerable speed in order to escape an unexpected current threatening to set the ship upon the shore or some obstruction floating in the sea, such as a log or a tree. Then they strode up and down the platform on either side of the ship, laying the long whips across the backs of the galley slaves to step up their straining upon the long oars, each turning in its leather collar inside an oarlock cut into the timbers of the hull.

Sailing between the island of Cyprus and the mainland of Cappadocia and Lycia, they came in good time to Rhodus, an island lying southeast of the city of Ephesus. Pausing there to take on water and food, the *Olympia* swung southward and skirted the fabled island of Crete, choosing the northeast route past the coast of Greece and sailing then across the Mare Ionium to Rhegium. From Rhegium northwestward they paralleled the coast of Italy with the mountainous region at the toe of the Italian boot on the right hand.

It had been all of six months now since Quintus had left Italy and many weeks since they had left Antioch. His prisoner had stayed sequestered to himself during the voyage, so Quintus was surprised when he came on deck early one morning—leaving Veronica brushing her hair and singing softly in their small cabin —to see Pontius Pilate standing in the very bow of the ship, at the highest point it afforded above the water. He gripped the low rail there with both hands and stared down at the water, and Quintus could not help wondering whether his prisoner was summoning up enough courage to jump.

Treading softly, Quintus moved along the deck until he was just behind the Roman official, so as to be ready in case Pilate started to leap over the rail. Not certain whether he should risk startling the other man by revealing his presence, he waited there for a few moments. To his relief, Pilate straightened up and turned to face him.

"I know what you are thinking, Quintus," he said, his voice quiet and controlled. "But I have no intention of throwing myself into the sea—at least not for a while."

Quintus relaxed. "Things may not be as bad as they seem, sir," he said. "The emperor might take a different view entirely from the Legate Vitellius about what happened in Samaria."

"Tiberius will take the strictest possible viewpoint," Pilate said, turning to look to the sea again. "He has always maintained his power by coddling the people of the provinces."

"The reign of Tiberius has been the most peaceful the empire has ever known."

"On the surface, perhaps. Underneath the pot of unrest is always boiling and not alone in Judea and Samaria. Britannia might as well be lost to us. The Gauls are ready to revolt and the barbarians are marshaling their strength, while the Parthians wait only for the legions to be occupied somewhere else before starting trouble again in the east. Julius Caesar would not have let such things happen, nor would Augustus.

But Tiberius is determined to have peace at any price, so long as he is undisturbed in his lechery on Capri."

Quintus made no answer, for much of what Pilate said was the truth. The amours of Tiberius were known to be as capricious as his temper.

"I made a mistake with the Samaritans," Pilate continued moodily. "But at the time how was I to know? They say I killed an innocent man when I let the Galilean named Jesus be crucified, but the Jewish court had condemned him and there were known Zealots among his followers plotting against Rome."

"I am neither prosecutor nor judge," Quintus reminded him.

Pilate turned to face him. "Perhaps I might fare better if you were either or both. At least you have been to Judea and you were in Samaria, so you know something of conditions there."

"You know I was on the mountain that day?"

"Of course. One of the soldiers from Sepphoris passed you on the road to Shechem and recognized you. I knew you were at the house of Philip and that you went up the mountain to observe Simon Magus."

"Why didn't you stop me?"

Pilate shrugged. "Do you think I was responsible for the attack made by the sicarii on the house of Abijah the potter?"

"It seemed reasonable to believe that at the time."

"Then you were wrong. I will admit that I was disturbed when you appeared in the temple and I did try to keep you a prisoner—at least until I could be sure just why you were in Judea. But surely you do not believe me such a fool as to have a fellow soldier assassinated—especially when he carried a royal commission."

Pilate might or might not be telling the truth; Quintus could not say. There was more reason to believe he was lying, for should Pilate succeed in winning him over, he might be spared the testimony Quintus himself could give at the trial before the emperor concerning the attack upon the Samaritans. And yet the man seemed frank enough.

"It is no easy thing to govern a province," Pilate went on moodily. "Especially a naturally rebellious people like the Jews. I made mistakes at first, none of them very serious. But after I convinced Caiaphas that we both had one purpose, to keep the country at peace and collect the highest taxes possible, there was little trouble. The crucifixion of the Galilean was itself of no importance. Herod scattered those who followed him afterward, and that was the end of it."

"Except for your own sense of uneasiness?"

Pilate turned his head and stared at him for a moment. "Why do you say that?"

"Something has seriously disturbed you. Everyone says it, and I can see the signs myself."

Pilate's shoulders sagged. When he spoke again it was as if he were talking to himself. "I have sent many men to their deaths in battle and ordered others crucified as a judge. None of them are on my conscience, not even the Samaritans who were killed. They had weapons and there was ample evidence that they intended something more than a mere religious ceremony on Mount Gerizim. But I cannot forget the Galilean's face and his eyes. It was as if he were pitying me, even while I was sentencing him." He paused for a moment, then went on. "Why would he pity me when he was the one who was going to his death?"

"The Jews believe him to be the son of their god."

Pilate wheeled to face Quintus. "Have they convinced you of that?"

"Logic tells me it is impossible."

Pilate laughed shortly. "I exhausted reason and logic a long time ago. If the Jewish god is all-powerful and I crucified his son—as they claim—I could not possibly have escaped the wrath of their Jehovah even this long. He would have destroyed me immediately."

"Why let the Galilean's death trouble you then?"

"He pitied me! How could he do that if he were only a mortal man?" With an effort he controlled himself. "Ordinary men don't pity their executioners. They grovel before them if they are cowards; they defy them if they are brave men. But they do not pity them."

138

Quintus had no answer save what was obviously troubling Pilate, namely that Jesus was actually what his followers believed him to be. And that he was not ready to accept.

"I suppose you think I am sick in my mind," Pilate said shortly.

"It is no more shameful to have a sickness of the mind than one of the body."

"If it is really a sickness," Pilate agreed. "But if it is a cowardly fear that you have killed a god—" His shoulders slumped. "Perhaps I should admit that my soul is sick, Quintus. Sick with fear, sick with guilt, sick with loathing—sick unto death."

"You might be cured," Quintus told him. "Veronica has the veil—"

"Speak no more of it! Procula has driven me nearly out of my mind about that veil. Surely a physician does not believe such a thing."

"I did not—until it healed me."

"You know that to be true?"

"Yes."

Pilate looked thoughtful and Quintus continued. "Why do you refuse—when it cannot harm you?"

Pilate shook his head. "Have you ever known fear, Quintus? Fear that entwines itself about you like a serpent, crushing you with overpowering strength, sucking away the substance of your pride? If I let the veil your wife carries be put upon me and my sickness—if you can call it that—is healed, it would mean that the Galilean was indeed what they claim him to be—the Son of God. As I am now, I have some hope of redeeming myself, through the favor of the emperor or through my own efforts. But if the veil healed me and proved the Galilean to be what they claim, I would have no choice but to throw myself into the sea."

Pilate straightened his shoulders and for a moment his eyes were clear, clearer than Quintus remembered seeing them before. "I have not given up, tribune. And I will not. The emperor must decide my guilt or innocence." Turning on his heel, he strode to the door of his cabin, jerked it open, and stepped inside.

Veronica met Quintus as he was leaving the bow of the ship. "I saw you talking to Pontius Pilate," she said. "Will he let me use the veil?"

"No. He is afraid."

"Afraid to be cured? Why?"

"He thinks that if you healed him it would mean Jesus is actually the Son of God, as you and Joseph claim. And he is sure he could never be forgiven for crucifying him."

"But he is wrong," Veronica protested quickly.

"How can you know that even Jesus would forgive the man who had him crucified?"

"He already did—from the cross. His own words were, 'Father, forgive them; for they know not what they do.'"

"I only know Pilate will not let you use the veil."

"Then we must pray for him," she said, "as Jesus would have done."

16

With a fair wind and a calm, sunlit sea the *Olympia* plowed steadily northwestward along the seacoast of Italy. At Ostia, where the Tiber emptied into the sea, the passengers debarked for the trip overland to Rome. There Quintus presented himself to the commander of the post, an officer of the legions named Cornelius whom he had known on military campaigns.

"Quintus Volusianus, returning from an imperial mission in Judea," he announced himself formally. "With the former procurator of Judea, Pontius Pilate, and his wife Procula, ordered by the Legate Vitellius of Antioch to be judged by the Emperor Tiberius."

"You have been long at sea, tribune, else you would have heard the news," the port commander said. "Tiberius died almost a month ago."

"Died? Then who rules in his stead?"

The commander grinned. "Him we of the legions used to call Caligula, 'Little Boot.' Gaius Caesar Germanicus is Emperor of Rome."

BOOK 3

Gaul

Gaius Caesar Germanicus had been born to Agrippina while she was accompanying her husband, the popular Germanicus, on one of his campaigns. He had grown up in the camps of the legions and because of his fondness for soldier dress had been nicknamed Caligula, or "Little Boot"—from the half boot called the caliga worn by the legions. When the Emperor Tiberius, while on a tour a little over a month before, had fallen in a faint at Misenum, the courtiers had flocked about Gaius and hailed him as emperor, a title for which he had waited many years while Tiberius remained in retirement at Capri and the empire was ruled largely by freedmen. When the emperor did not die immediately, however, the followers of Caligula had solved this impasse—it was reliably reported—by smothering the feeble ruler with a pillow.

Gaius had begun his reign before the ashes of Tiberius were cold by stopping all the niggardly practices of his uncle. Ninety million sesterces were immediately distributed to the people as a legacy from Tiberius. To this Gaius himself—now known affectionately to the mob as Caligula—had added a gift of three hundred sesterces each to several hundred thousand recipients of state corn. Having thus endeared himself to the common people, and assured the allegiance of the Roman mob, he was free to give rein to the more dissolute factors in his nature. All this Quintus learned from Cornelius while a carriage was made ready to take the travelers on to Rome.

Pontius Pilate was ordered to appear before the emperor a few days after their arrival in Rome, and because of his assignment by the Legate Vitellius, Quintus was present. Veronica accompanied him, but not Joseph of Arimathea. The merchant had active business interests in Rome through the commercial houses that represented him there, as they did prominent merchants in all parts of the empire. He had rented a small house or *insula* in the Jewish section of Rome located in the region known as the Transtiberina, because it lay in the lowlands across the river from the main portion of the city. Quintus and Veronica had taken up residence there also but knew little about the activities of Joseph, whose business affairs seemed to occupy much of his time.

Before he had been sent to Jerusalem, Quintus' duties with the emperor had kept him for the most part at the magnificent villa on the island of Capri, where Tiberius had been a recluse for almost nine years before his death. He had seen Gaius only a few times, since the heir apparent had lived in Rome where he had been surrounded with the usual coterie of sycophants who toadied to his every desire, while they waited for the old emperor to die. The new emperor—Quintus was told by the Praetorians who did not hold Gaius in too great respect because of his lavish generosity to the mob —was subject to fits of near fainting. During some of them he fell to the floor and foamed at the mouth like a mad dog and afterward seemed in a daze for hours, the usual story, Quintus knew, with epilepsy. Caligula was also said to wander through the palace for hours at night waiting for sleep to come. And, since he aspired to become an actor, he passed the time practicing all sorts of fearful grimaces before every mirror he encountered. Everyone agreed, however, that he possessed a keen mind, was eloquent in oratory, and had a rapier-like wit, although obeying no rules or limits in the satisfaction of his often perverted desires.

On the morning of Pontius Pilate's hearing Caligula seemed in good humor. He was in his late twenties, Quintus saw, and quite tall in stature. His wrists and arms were hairy, but he was almost completely bald. His eyes were hollow and his temples almost cadaverous, which with the large ears and sallow look from long dissipation gave him a rather unpleasant appearance. His eyes were keen, however; they moved constantly and did not seem to miss anything of what was going on.

The emperor received them in a small audience chamber with only a few attendants, one of these the freedman Janus who, almost alone of the former servants of Tiberius, had been selected by Gaius as one of his major administrative assistants.

Pontius Pilate had changed a great deal since his arrival in Rome, Quintus saw. His carriage was now erect, his eyes clear and sure, and he was no longer the broken man Quintus had found when he came aboard the *Olympia* at Antioch. The change seemed to have begun after Quintus had come upon him standing in the bow of the vessel before they had reached Ostia and had been afraid for a moment his prisoner would leap overboard and destroy himself.

Janus lifted the parchment roll on which Vitellius had recounted the charges against Pontius Pilate and began to read them. No detail had been omitted concerning the Samaritan incident, but nothing had been added either. Whoever had investigated the affair for Vitellius had evidently been instructed to be entirely unbiased in his search for the facts.

When the freedman finished reading, Caligula turned to Pilate. "What say you in defense of yourself?" he asked. His eyes roved around the room as he spoke, and Quintus saw his gaze fix on Claudia Procula who sat near the back. She was simply but richly dressed, as befitted a member of the Claudian house and the wife of an important Roman officer.

"The noble Vitellius has been fair in the presentation of the facts," Pilate said. "You will note that he has drawn no conclusions concerning my guilt or innocence."

Caligula took his gaze from Claudia Procula with some reluctance. "I am the judge," he said simply, as if he were saying, "I am God"—a statement which Quintus had also heard attributed to him.

"I place myself in your hands," Pilate said. "And beg only to call a few witnesses in my behalf."

"Call them," Caligula ordered.

"Let the magician called Simon Magus enter."

Quintus repressed an exclamation of surprise. He had heard nothing of Simon since he had last seen the magician on the slope of Mount Gerizim the night after the slaughter of the Samaritans on Pilate's orders. Whether Simon had sought Pilate out—or the reverse—he did not know, but he rather suspected the former, knowing Simon as he did.

Even in the magnificence of the emperor's palace Simon Magus was a striking and bizarre figure. Nor had he lost any of the self-assurance he had displayed in Samaria. He strode forward now, resplendent in a robe embroidered in a cabalistic design, the white turban and the brilliant jewel topping his narrow-templed head as usual. Coming to a stop before the dais upon which Caligula sat, he knelt in an oriental salaam, bending forward until the top of his turban touched the floor and remaining there in an attitude of utter subjection.

Caligula appeared to be delighted with the man's appearance—which no doubt appealed to the actor's instinct within him—as well as by his attitude of subservience.

"You may rise," the emperor said. When Simon was standing erect, he asked, "What is the jewel you wear in your turban?"

"Pigeon's blood turned to stone by a method of magic which I alone know, O Most Exalted One." Simon's deep tones filled the room, while he expertly removed the stone and its setting from his turban and handed it to the emperor. "Accept it, please, as my tribute to a god."

Caligula's eyes kindled with pleasure as he rolled the jewel in his palm. "You see, Janus," he said almost petulantly. "Even a stranger from a far country recognizes our right to divinity."

"As all Rome does, *Dominus*," said the freedman, and Quintus understood now why Janus had been able to keep his position of responsibility under the new ruler.

"I accept your gift in the spirit with which it was given, Simon," Caligula said. "What can you tell us of the affair in Samaria?"

"Know thou, O Ruler of the World," Simon began, "that I am a Samaritan priest engaged in leading my people in the worship of their god and giving full allegiance to Rome. Once a year it is our custom to gather on the holy mountain called Gerizim. On the occasion of which I shall speak it was my good fortune to locate some sacred objects long lost but much revered by my people."

"Were they of great value?" Caligula asked.

"Only as symbols of our religion," Simon explained. "The vessels were of base metal, but they had been lost long ago and meant much to the Samaritans. The news that the sacred vessels had been found naturally attracted my people to our temple on the mountain in the hope of seeing these revered objects."

"It was a purely religious ceremony then?"

"Purely, O Divine One." Simon paused, and Quintus wondered whether Pontius Pilate had made a mistake in enlisting Simon's help, by whatever means—and bribery seemed the simplest—the feat had been accomplished. For if Simon identified the gathering on Mount Gerizim as a religious event alone, then Pilate was doubly guilty for having attacked the people. Pilate, however, seemed unconcerned by what Simon had revealed, and the magician's next words showed the reason—as well as the fact that the two were now acting in collusion.

"Unfortunately." Simon paused a moment, so the word could have its full effect on the listeners. "Unfortunately large numbers of another element were on the mountain that morning. I had no knowledge of their presence, else I would have postponed the ceremony until another time."

145

"What do you mean by another element?" Caligula inquired.

"In Samaria we call them Zealots, men with no respect and appreciation for what Roman rule has brought us, who seek only to overthrow that rule and take control for themselves. I know now that large numbers of these men had gathered there seeking to influence the emotions of the people to the point where they could have their own way. As I say, I know now, but I did not then. Unwittingly I was in a position of helping those who would flaunt Roman authority."

It was an audacious admission, quite in keeping with the tissue of half-truths and outright lies Simon was building so cleverly. Quintus could see that Caligula accepted it at full value, however, as Simon—and no doubt Pontius Pilate too—had planned.

"What happened then?"

"O Divine One, it is well known in my country of Samaria that the procurator of Judea, who stands before you unjustly accused, has always been diligent in protecting and maintaining the authority of Rome in our troubled land. Nearly three years ago he prevented a bloody rebellion by crucifying the leader of a band of Zealots who tried to stir up an insurrection at the time of the Jewish Passover. For this some Jews have sought to condemn him, most of them followers of the Galilean who was crucified. But we in Samaria know that Pontius Pilate saved the whole region then from a bloody revolt."

"Go on," commanded Caligula. "This is like a tale by a storyteller."

Quintus almost laughed aloud, for the potbellied emperor had very accurately described Simon's discourse. To Caligula, however, what Simon was saying obviously sounded like the truth.

"The noble Pilate was at the city of Shechem with his troops and knew what, as a priest in the temple on Mount Gerizim, I had no way of knowing," Simon continued. "Namely, that the Zealots at the foot of the mountain were well armed and in large numbers, in-

146

tending to hold the priests and the worshipers prisoner while they stirred up a rebellion against Rome."

"Fortunately." Here he paused again. "Fortunately the noble Pilate acted in a forthright manner and attacked the armed Zealots——"

"Are you sure they were armed?" Caligula interposed.

"Weapons were found on most of those killed or wounded," Simon said. "As I have said, the noble Pilate ordered an attack upon the rebellious elements and broke them up, destroying most of them."

"Will you swear to this?" Caligula inquired.

"Upon your own divinity as a god," the magician said promptly.

Caligula smiled with obvious satisfaction. "You are a worthy servant of Rome, O Magician," he said. "At another time you many exhibit your skills before us."

"For you, sire, I will even perform the most difficult feat of all—that of raising the dead."

Caligula gave him a startled look. "You can raise the dead?"

"Only I possess the power, although others have claimed it falsely."

"I would see this feat," Caligula said. "Arrange it soon, Janus."

The freedman nodded and the clerk sitting at the table behind him made a notation with a stylus upon a wax-covered tablet.

Caligula turned to Pilate. "Have you anything further to bring before us, noble Pilate?" His manner was distinctly more pleasant than it had been at the beginning of the hearing, and he smiled at Claudia Procula.

"The Tribune Quintus Volusianus was on Mount Gerizim when the attack was made," Pilate said. "If you will permit, I wish to ask him some questions."

"Call him then," the emperor directed.

Quintus got to his feet and came forward. Caligula's eyes raked him up and down, and a frosty glare took form in their depths. "A physician by that name treated the Emperor Tiberius. Are you related?"

"I am the one," Quintus said. "The emperor sent me on a mission to Judea, to seek a healer there."

"It is said that your skill prolonged Tiberius' life by several years."

"I served your uncle to the best of my ability," Quintus said. "Even as I will serve you if called upon."

Caligula was reputed to be somewhat of a hypochondriac, as most Roman emperors had been recently, fancying themselves the victims of all sorts of strange maladies. Quintus was hoping the emperor would realize that a physician of considerable skill whose loyalty was unquestionable might well be an asset.

"Your loyalty will be tested—at the right time," Caligula said. "At present I find myself in good health."

"A condition I hope always prevails," Quintus said with sincerity. "A true physician would rather see people healthy than sick."

Caligula laughed, a rasping sound that was not at all pleasant. "Not the physicians of Rome, I dare say."

"I am a soldier of the legions," Quintus said, "and physician to the Praetorian Guard. I know little of my profession outside the Army."

"We will talk later of where your duties may lie in the future," Caligula told him curtly. "Answer now the questions of Pontius Pilate."

The former procurator of Judea studied Quintus appraisingly for a moment before he spoke. "Why were you on Mount Gerizim at the time the events which have been related occurred?" he asked finally.

"I wished to see whether Simon Magus could indeed raise from the dead as he claims," Quintus said.

"For what reason?"

"If he possessed that power, I planned to bring him to Rome to help the Emperor Tiberius."

"But you were sent to Judea for another healer?"

"I sought Jesus of Nazareth who was crucified nearly three years ago, on your order," Quintus said evenly. He could have added that he had brought back Veronica and the miracle-working veil, but after seeing the way Caligula had been looking at Claudia Procula, and

148

from the tales he'd heard about the emperor's appetites, he had decided to keep her in the background.

Caligula leaned forward. "Is this the Galilean of whom the magician spoke?"

"The same," Quintus said.

"Was he actually able to raise the dead?"

"So his followers claimed. Jesus healed many who came to him, and his disciples believe he rose from the dead after being crucified."

Quintus swung his eyes to Pontius Pilate as he spoke. For a moment the ex-procurator's face was a wooden mask, as it had been on the ship. Then Pilate straightened his shoulders with an obvious effort and seemed to bring himself under control.

"Only a god could accomplish such a feat," Caligula said in a tone of wonder.

"Many Jews believe Jesus of Nazareth was the son of their god," Quintus explained.

"This is a passing strange thing," Caligula observed. "Do you know anyone who believes it?"

Quintus hesitated. Before he could speak a familiar voice sounded behind him. "I do, sire," Veronica said quietly.

Caligula jerked his head around. "Who spoke?" he demanded.

"My wife," Quintus said quickly. "She is from Jerusalem."

"A Jew?" Caligula's eyes were fixed on Veronica, and Quintus felt his heart grow cold at the light he saw kindling there.

"I am both Jew and Greek," Veronica said.

Caligula turned to Quintus sternly. "It is forbidden for a Roman officer to marry a foreigner."

"Veronica is a Roman citizen by birth," Quintus explained. "She was born in Tarsus of Cilicia. Her mother was a Greek."

Caligula smiled. "Come forward, child, that we may see you."

Veronica moved to the front of the room and stood beside Quintus. Her cheeks were pink, but she showed no sign of fear.

"How lovely you are, my dear," Caligula said warmly. "Beside you the women of Rome are as wilted flowers."

"You do me great honor, sir, but it is undeserved," Veronica said modestly.

"You are a lucky man, Quintus Volusianus," the emperor said. "I must see that you are assigned permanently to Rome, so this lovely creature may remain here."

Quintus looked toward Pontius Pilate, hoping the procurator would turn the emperor's attention in another direction, but Caligula was too captivated by Veronica's fresh young beauty to be easily diverted. "You say you knew this healer that Quintus was sent to bring to Rome?" he asked Veronica.

"Jesus healed me although I had been a cripple for many years."

"To look at you now, one would never know it. How did this happen?"

With a sincerity that could not fail to impress even the dissolute Emperor of Rome, Veronica told the familiar story.

"This veil you speak of," Caligula said when she had finished speaking. "Has it healed others?"

"Many."

"And raised them from the dead?"

Veronica shook her head. "I believe only Jesus could do that—or perhaps one of his disciples."

"Why did the Galilean possess that power?"

"Because he is the Son of God."

"Some say I am divine," Caligula said.

"We Jews have worshiped only one god for thousands of years," Veronica explained. "Rome has always recognized our right."

Caligula pursed his full lips. "So it has," he admitted, and turned to Quintus. "Do you believe this man Jesus possessed the power to raise from the dead, tribune?"

"I do not know," Quintus said. "Many swear they saw him do it."

"Have you seen the magician here perform the feat?"

"I saw him do a trick—in which he claimed to have power over death. But it was only a trick."

Caligula broke into his braying laugh again. "As one whose lifework is ushering people to the grave, a physician would hardly favor anyone who saved them from it." He turned to Veronica. "Do you now have this veil, my dear?"

"It is at the house where I live."

"I suffer much at times. Perhaps you could use it to heal me."

"I would try," Veronica said. "Jesus counseled us to serve others."

"Have you any more questions for the physician?" Caligula asked Pilate.

"Only a few." Pilate turned back to Quintus. "Tribune, you were on Mount Gerizim. Did you see any people there bearing arms?"

"Yes," Quintus admitted.

"Very many?"

"A large number."

"Did you think this was a religious or a political gathering?"

"Both," Quintus said. "I believe the magician intended to have himself proclaimed as the Messiah."

"A religious title, I believe," Pilate said quickly.

"A man was crucified in Jerusalem because he was said to be the Messiah," Quintus reminded him.

Pilate's lips tightened, but this time he kept rigid control of himself. "The Nazarene also claimed to be King of the Jews."

"What is this?" Caligula demanded. "The Jews have no king."

"That is exactly why I had Jesus of Nazareth crucified," Pilate explained. "He claimed to rule the Jews— who could only have one ruler, the Emperor of Rome."

"And you say Simon Magus also claimed to be this —this Messiah?" Caligula asked, his cheeks reddening with anger.

"I made no such claim, O Divine One," Simon said quickly. "No more loyal subject of Rome exists than myself."

Caligula turned his displeasure upon Quintus. "It seems you are making wild charges which you cannot support, physician."

"I make no charges," Quintus said quietly. "Simon was acclaimed as Messiah by the people on the mount. I heard it myself."

"Did you hear Simon make any such claim himself?" Pilate demanded quickly.

"No."

"Or set himself up as a king?"

"No."

"Then you will concede that there was no connection between him and the Zealots who were armed and eager to make trouble?"

"I believe there was no connection," Quintus admitted. "At least none that I can prove."

Pilate spoke to Caligula. "The physician admits that the magician here did nothing which could be considered troublemaking. The whole difficulty was caused by fanatic Zealots—the people I ordered the soldiers to attack."

Caligula pursed his lips thoughtfully. "Do you deny this?" he asked Quintus.

Quintus shook his head. "I cannot deny it or affirm it," he admitted. "It may well have happened as the procurator has described to you."

Caligula's eyes were on Claudia Procula again. "It seems that you have been unduly maligned, noble Pilate," he said finally. "I decree that the charges against you shall be dismissed. You will await my further orders."

Pilate drew himself up and gave the salute of the legions. "I am under your command, mighty Gaius," he said, his eyes glowing with satisfaction.

2

As they were leaving the audience chamber, Quintus took the magician by his flowing sleeve. "I want to talk to you, Simon," he said.

Simon was all smiles. "Of course."

"Why did you leave Accho before we arrived?"

"I had business in Antioch that could not wait."

"The business of persuading Vitellius to send you on to Rome? So you could approach the emperor in my name and entrench yourself in his favor by trickery?"

Simon smiled and his white teeth shone. "Can you blame a man for looking after himself? You are an officer of the legions with an established reputation. I have nothing but my own skills and my wits."

"As a trickster?"

"Tiberius was already dead when I got here. I had to fend for myself."

"By joining forces with Pontius Pilate to exonerate him from killing your own countrymen?"

The magician shrugged. "I had no wish for those who proclaimed me Messiah to stir up revolt against the Romans. They interfered with my own plans and forced me to flee for my life. You know that, for I saved yours in the bargain."

"For which I owe you a debt," Quintus admitted.

"You and I can work together profitably in Rome," the magician suggested.

"What could I possibly gain from an association with you?"

"Your wife is a follower of Jesus of Nazareth and so is her uncle. If I remind Caligula that she and Joseph of Arimathea openly teach adherence to a man who was crucified as a traitor to Rome, it might not go well with them."

A chill gripped Quintus at Simon's words. He remembered how suspicious Caligula had been when the question of Jesus of Nazareth being proclaimed King of the Jews had arisen. Nor had he missed the way the dissolute emperor had looked at Veronica. Her fresh, innocent beauty would undoubtedly have a strong appeal to one as depraved as Caligula was known to be. More than one woman of wealth and beauty already had received letters in the emperor's name, inviting them into his embraces if they did not want to see their spouses arrested and even executed on some trumped-up charge.

"You have no such influence with the emperor," Quintus countered.

Simon shrugged. "Caligula distrusts you already because you helped keep Tiberius alive. It would be easy to convince him that all three of you are traitors."

"Why did you clear Pilate just now? To put him in your debt?"

"Naturally. His wife is of royal blood, and Pilate ranks high as a Roman official. They can introduce me to the highest social levels."

Quintus knew that men with far less accomplishments than Simon had risen to high positions under former emperors. The magician could—and probably would—go far. Nor was his threat against Veronica an idle one. To further his own cause Simon Magus would not hestitate to sacrifice anyone who stood in his path. And Quintus himself could do nothing to deter him. Perhaps might even be forced to help, lest Veronica and Joseph suffer.

3

By order of the Emperor Caligula, Quintus resumed his post as surgeon to the Praetorian Guard quartered at Rome. In the time of Augustus only three of the nine cohorts of the emperor's personal troops had been stationed in the capital, the rest being located in various larger towns of Italy, mainly to make sure that the insurrections which had followed the assassination of Julius Caesar would never be repeated. Tiberius, however, had been more certain of the people, though perhaps less sure of Rome itself with his long absences at Capri. He had returned the Praetorians to Rome in a permanent camp just outside the Viminal Gate. And since they were known to be strongly in favor of the centralized form of government represented by an emperor—rather than the looser organization where the

Senate was in major control—Caligula had also kept them in Rome.

As the weeks passed, Quintus settled easily into the routine of his work, caring for the ills of the Praetorians and the wounds they suffered in frequent skirmishes with civilians and the swaggering gladiators who reigned briefly as popular favorites after the games and sought to prove their courage by attacking members of the elite cohort.

Even before the time of Julius Caesar the walls which had protected the inhabitants of Rome from the threat of Gallic invasion had already begun to constrict the city and limit its very life. The first zone of expansion had been in the region between the capital and the Tiber. When Caesar had moved the official limits of Rome a mile outward, he was only making legal a condition which had been in existence for a long time.

Augustus—first to call himself divine—had divided the city into fourteen regions, thirteen on the left bank of the Tiber and the fourteenth—called the *Regio Transtiberina*—on the right bank. Here the Jews had early begun to settle in line with their established policy of living together, as they did in all the great cities of the empire. In Alexandria they occupied one whole quarter of the city with almost an autonomous government, and in the other great population centers such as Ephesus and Corinth a similar situation existed.

The *insula* which Joseph of Arimathea had rented was located in some high ground overlooking the river and the sprawling city beyond. It was not pretentious, being only a little more elaborate than the *casa,* or cottage of a prosperous farmer, and not nearly so fine as the *domus,* or palace, of a rich noble. The *insula* fronted upon the street in the form of an open-ended rectangle with a small court in the center where a fountain tinkled. Windows opened both to the outside and the inside, making it pleasurably cool in summer and allowing the sun free access in winter.

Within the building each floor was a separate *cenacula* or apartment. Joseph had taken the ground floor for his own, and the second, reached by an outside stairway, had been assigned to Quintus and Veronica. Quintus' pay as a Roman officer was adequate and he insisted upon paying rent. Here in the Transtiberina the height of the buildings had attained no such dizzy levels as in the major portion of the city across the river, largely because the Jewish population had been concentrating there and did not favor the tall houses of central Rome.

The ground floor of the *insula* Joseph had arranged —as was common in many such structures—as a shop or *taberna,* opening directly on the street by an archway. Here he had installed clerks to buy and sell goods from all parts of the world. Veronica helped her uncle in the shop by day and also painted small vases which she purchased from a nearby potter, who set the colors for her in his oven after she had finished the painting.

By day the narrow streets of Rome teemed with humanity—nobility and commoner alike—bent on every sort of errand, and the hum of their conversation was a constant roar. By order of Julius Caesar all vehicles, except a very few special means of transport, had been barred from the streets between sunrise and dusk. Only by this means had the people themselves been able to move about freely. With the coming of darkness they stayed off the streets for two cogent reasons. One was the danger of being run down by the wagons and carts which thronged nightly into the city, bringing produce and other food and supplies to the shops and markets. A second reason was the army of thieves, footpads, and roisterers—many of them from among the nobility—who prowled the streets at night. If a rich man had reason to go abroad after dark, he was accompanied by slaves bearing lights and by the heavily armed night watchmen called *sebaciarii,* who patrolled in squads with torches.

By virtue of being an officer in the Roman army, Quintus—and his wife, by right of marriage—belonged to the upper social order called the *honestiores,* as distinguished from the *humiliores,* sometimes called *plebeii.* As a foreigner, Joseph of Arimathea was not immediately entitled to social recognition. In practical use, however, his wealth easily made up the difference, since his business dealings brought him into contact almost daily with the leading merchants of the city.

In addition to Joseph's activities as a merchant, he was busy in another field, that of bringing the story of Jesus of Nazareth to the people in the teeming Transtiberina. Perhaps because they were far from the orthodox worship of the temple at Jerusalem, as well as the more Greek character of their religious ceremonies in the great cities of the empire, he found large numbers of converts here among the Jews. Many Gentiles also espoused this new doctrine that all men were equal before God.

The teachings of the Nazarene formed a particularly acceptable philosophy to the *humiliores* or plebes, whose position in the Roman world was at best a very humiliating one. Actually they never knew when, because of a small infraction of the law, they might be sent *ad metella* (to the mines), thrown to the beasts in the arena for the pleasure of the mob, or even crucified publicly.

Quintus purposely did not bring himself or Veronica to the attention of Caligula in the months following their arrival in Rome. The emperor had already acquired a reputation for profligacy and sexual license beyond that of any former ruler. The full treasury left by the frugal government of Tiberius was being steadily depleted, and it was common gossip that Caligula had begun to take his baths in perfume instead of water and to spend as many as a million sesterces on one banquet.

The shipyards along the Tiber were busy now building pleasure barges with gardens, trees in tubs, and adornments of precious jewels, instead of constructing ships of war or the even more important round vessels that carried on the vast trade of the empire and kept Rome supplied with grain. Caligula was reported to have given a favorite charioteer a million sesterces as a reward for winning a race, and from the roof of the Basilica Julia he often scattered gold and silver coins to the crowd. The nobles who did not fawn upon him for their own advancement feared and hated him for the monster he undoubtedly was, but the rabble who spent his gold and lived without working on his gifts of state corn adored him.

As the days grew into months, Veronica was busily occupied performing miracles of healing with the veil among the poor who thronged the Transtiberina. Soon her fame spread even farther and the miserable plebes of the *subura*—a district of brothels and filthy *insulae* packed with people located between the Viminal and the Esquiline—began to seek her out. Women brought children almost blind with inflammation of the eyes. Old people stumbled to her with the aftermath of paralytic strokes. And young women from the brothels, their bodies burning with the fires of inflammation, sought her help. To all, in the tradition of the man she followed, she gave her services unstintingly.

Quintus, however, could only watch what was happening with apprehension. For as Veronica's—and Joseph's—fame spread, the chances of their coming to the notice of Caligula also rapidly increased. He could do nothing, however, for he would not forbid his wife to carry on the work that brought her such happiness, and she would not give it up even to save her life. Nor did he have any control over the activities of Joseph of Arimathea.

If Quintus had his troubles, Simon Magus, it seemed, had none. As the center of the civilized world, Rome teemed with all sorts of people. Charlatans of every type came there to prey on the rich and noble. Fortune-tellers, soothsayers, magicians, oracles, scoundrels of every sort and variety were everywhere, from the topmost social level down to the most miserable *cenaculum* in the often block-long *insulae* of the *Nova Via,* the *Olibus Victoria* (victory hill) of the Palatine, and the *subura* itself. There were pickings aplenty for such scavengers at all levels, from the palace of Caligula down through the homes of the senators and the nobles, even to the longshoremen who inhabited the Emporium, the sellers of fish in the Forum Piscatorium, the butchers who thronged the Forum Boarium, and elsewhere.

As clever as Simon Magus undoubtedly was, he had an added advantage over his competitors. Not only had he appeared before the emperor immediately after his arrival in Rome and made an excellent impression, but he also enjoyed the sponsorship of Pontius Pilate, who had been vindicated by Caligula and restored to his position as former governor of a province, awaiting a new assignment. Simon's rise in popularity was rapid, and soon all of Rome rang with the name of the magician who was not only scheduled to perform the feat of raising the dead before the emperor, but had also announced that at the time of the annual Saturnalia—which took place late in December—he would fly through the air with wings of his own making.

Quintus was surprised one day while at work in the Praetorian camp to receive a call to the commander's office. Lucius Stulla was a friend of long standing, but it was not the commander who wanted to see him today. A handsomely dressed and bejeweled woman awaited him there—Claudia Procula, the wife of Pontius Pilate.

4

Quintus had not seen Claudia Procula or her husband since the day of their joint appearance before Caligula. That affair had turned out in their favor, but Claudia Procula did not seem to be happy now. She acknowledged Quintus' bow graciously, but her eyes, he saw, were troubled.

"You honor me greatly, my lady," Quintus said warmly. "I am sorry Veronica is not here."

"Is she well?"

"Well—and very busy helping the people of the Transtiberina and the *subura*."

"Is Joseph of Arimathea still in Rome?"

"Yes. And he, too, is occupied."

"Teaching about Jesus?"

Quintus hesitated and Procula said quickly, "You need have no fear of me, Quintus."

"Those who believe in Jesus wish everyone to know his story."

"I know. Sometimes the memory of what he taught is the only thing that gives me strength to go on."

"Why are you troubled, my lady? The emperor has cleared your husband."

"Pontius is a man of action, Quintus. In Judea he was busy constructing the aqueduct at Jerusalem, repairing the roads, and rebuilding the city of Caesarea. Now he has nothing to do and the added worry of not knowing what assignment he will eventually receive."

"Surely it will be an important one—after his years of loyal service."

Procula went to the window and looked out at the city and the Viminal Gate, through which a stream of people—as always in the daylight hours—was pouring. "I grew up here in Rome, Quintus," she said, "in the time of Tiberius. Whatever they say about him, he kept the empire at peace and Rome in a state of calmness. But under Gaius the whole situation has changed. Once a man could rise to a position of honor and trust because of his ability and his devotion to the empire and its welfare. Now his whole future is dependent upon the whim of—a madman."

"My lady—"

"You can see how I trust you. If I said that to some people, I might lose my head tomorrow."

"You can be sure of my loyalty."

"I know it." She came across the room to stand before him. "That's why I have come to you for advice —as a physician and as a friend."

"I will help in either way, or both."

"I must get my husband away from Rome—and Simon Magus."

"Why should the magician trouble you?"

"Simon came to Pontius as soon as we reached Rome and proposed that he tell the story of what happened in Samaria in such a way as to justify the attack. In return, my husband was to sponsor him here in the city."

160

"Surely Simon has risen fast enough to satisfy even him."

"He is insatiable, Quintus. Pontius helped him by recommending that high officials consult him for advice. But Simon has used the information he got from them to make a considerable profit in buying and selling goods."

"It is not the first time a soothsayer profited by his own advice," Quintus reminded her.

"No, but Simon wants to be recommended to more and more important people. I think this tower from which he plans to fly is costing a great deal of money."

"He will be the talk of the town if he succeeds."

"Do you think he will?"

"I would put nothing past anyone as clever as Simon Magus," Quintus admitted. "The trick of apparently bringing a dead man back to life seems to have come from Egypt, but I hear that he performs feats of magic that the Persian magicians learned from tricksters in India. It may be that in his travels he has learned a way of appearing to fly."

"If the men Pontius has sent to Simon ever find out how the magician has been using them, they will blame my husband," Procula said. "You know how a scandal can ruin the career of a public servant, Quintus. We escaped it once; I don't want that to happen again. Besides"—she turned to the window again—"there are other things."

Quintus did not question her. Pontius Pilate was a handsome man in the prime of his life. Never in the history of Rome had a more dissolute or lascivious court been maintained than during the last months of the reign of Tiberius—when Rome had been governed *in absentia,* so to speak—and in the early months of Caligula's reign. He had no doubt that many women among the nobility would welcome an affair with Pontius Pilate. And in his troubled condition the ex-governor of Judea might easily be drawn into such a complication, in spite of the fact that so far he had appeared to be entirely faithful to Procula.

"What would you like me to do?" Quintus asked.

"Pontius must never know I spoke of this to you," she warned.

"Of course."

"Janus was a freedman in our household long before he became a trusted adviser to Tiberius and Gaius. The governor of Lugdunum in Gaul is being recalled to Rome because of illness. Gaius is not satisfied with Lentulus Gaeticulus, who acts as consul and commands the Roman troops in that area, because he has not held the Germani in subjection. I am sure Janus will recommend that Pontius be sent to Lugdunum."

"It is an important post—and far away from Rome."

"That is what troubles me. My husband is still sick, Quintus. He was better while he was fighting for his life and his career when we first came to Rome. But now that he has nothing to do, the black moods have become more and more frequent. A few more months of waiting and I'm afraid he might go mad."

"And you think I can help?"

"You and Veronica. I would welcome the Gallic post if you and she were there with the veil in case Pontius is ill again. I have no right to ask you to give up what you have here, merely as a favor to me," she added. "But I know of no other way."

"We are not nearly so secure as you think, my lady." Quintus told her of the bargain he had entered into with Simon Magus. "Simon is ruthless; the way he has used your husband is proof of that. Whenever he thinks he can profit by telling Caligula lies about Veronica and Joseph—or even about me—he will not hesitate."

"I know Caligula has been inquiring into the affairs of the Jews," Procula said. "He fancies himself more and more of a god and has even begun to set up images of himself here in Rome so the people can at least pretend to worship him. He asked Pontius what would happen if he put his own statue in the holy place of the temple at Jerusalem."

"The whole area would rise up in arms!" Quintus exclaimed in horror.

"Pontius told him that, but Caligula is so drunk with

162

power I think he would welcome a blood bath in Judea to demonstrate it."

Quintus nodded thoughtfully. "Simon Magus is probably encouraging him, hoping the Jews will destroy themselves so the Samaritans can move into Judea and take control."

"Pontius thinks Simon is the one who put the idea into Caligula's mind," Procula agreed.

Here was troubling news indeed, and trickery in its most venal state. Yet the whole scheme was quite in keeping with the grandiose ideas which the magician had already demonstrated.

"Would you be willing to go to Gaul with us, if I can arrange it?" Procula asked.

"I must talk to Veronica and Joseph first."

"Do it quickly then," Procula begged. "I want to make the final plans with Janus."

5

Quintus told Veronica and Joseph about the interview with Claudia Procula when they gathered for the evening meal that night. "Veronica and I must decide what to do at once," he told the merchant. "What do you advise?"

Joseph smiled. "I understand that Gaul is a fair land and a lovely one. We should enjoy it there."

"We!" Quintus exclaimed in surprise. "I thought—"

"That I am too old to travel so far? I will tell you a secret, Quintus. The spirit of the wanderer has always been within me." Then his face grew sober. "But I think something besides the mere desire to travel is at work here, something higher even than Claudia Procula's device to keep her husband from going mad with guilt for what he did."

"What do you mean?"

"Jesus commanded his disciples to go abroad and tell others what he had taught them," Veronica said. "What Uncle Joseph means is that all of us who know that Jesus is the Son of God sent to show us the way to

163

eternal life must tell the story too, wherever he sends us."

"Surely you don't think we would be sent to Gaul for that reason."

"Nothing is impossible to the Most High God," Joseph said. "Who knows what may come of our going to Lugdunum? It will be like sowing seeds in fresh soil where no crop has ever grown before."

"The Gauls are an unruly people," Quintus warned.

"Do you fear them?" Veronica asked.

"No. But it is different with you."

She smiled. "Whither thou goest I will go," she said. Her fingers closed about his. "I pray daily that it will never be otherwise with us."

6

Quintus called on Claudia Procula the next day, at the small but expensive villa where she and her husband were living. He stayed at the villa only long enough to tell Claudia Procula that he, Veronica, and Joseph would accept the transfer to Gaul without protest. Actually, as a Roman officer, he would not have been able to transport Veronica with him officially to a distant post such as Gaul, but Joseph could take her as his niece. And since there was a great deal of commerce between Rome, Lugdunum, and other cities in Gaul now, there was no reason whatsoever why Joseph should not go or why Veronica could not accompany him.

As he was leaving the villa, Quintus met Pontius Pilate on the street outside. The ex-procurator of Judea was a little drunk although it was not yet noon, an ominous sign of the character degeneration which had so disturbed his wife. Quintus gave Pilate the salute of the legions and would have gone on, but the procurator stopped him with a command.

"Is business so bad for physicians that you must solicit patients?" he demanded truculently.

"I was calling on your wife," Quintus explained.

"Procula seemed well when I left this morning for the baths."

"A trifling indisposition," Quintus assured him. "Nothing of any importance." It seemed better to let it go at that rather than reveal the real reason for his visit to Claudia Procula.

"You seem to keep busy," Pilate said a little more civilly.

"I have the Praetorians to keep healthy."

"At least you have something to do then," Pilate said morosely. "Here I am, a soldier and a governor who has served the empire faithfully for thirty years, jerked out of my position because a few provincials chose to lie about me and forced to cool my heels in Rome without money enough to live decently."

"Surely the emperor will give you another assignment soon."

"Legates live well and seem to be remarkably healthy," Pilate grumbled. "I could grow old here waiting for one of them to die—or be caught stealing from the treasury."

It was a measure of Pilate's ambition and self-confidence that, in spite of his removal from his previous post, he expected one of the most important offices in the empire outside of Rome itself, that of a legate who was, in a sense, ruler of an entire country and responsible only to the emperor, a monarch in everything save the name.

Quintus could understand now why Claudia Procula hoped to obtain for her husband the governorship of Gaul with headquarters at Lugdunum. In spite of its relative quiet since the time of the Caesars, Gaul was one of the frontiers of the empire. There Pilate would be less subject to the whims of the emperor and Claudia Procula herself would be beyond the range of Caligula's roving eye. Knowing Pilate, Quintus suspected that the opportunities for personal gain in Gaul would be considerable and that perhaps—if the position were offered to him—he would recognize how these tended to offset the fact that a mere governorship was not quite so high a position as he had·expected.

"Do your wife and Joseph still believe in the Nazarene healer?" Pilate asked.

Quintus could not lie. "Yes."

"You know the emperor is interested in the religion of the Jews?"

"I heard that Simon Magus was stirring him up."

"The Jews are rich. If they ever rebelled, the army and the emperor would gain much booty in putting them down."

It was a chilling thought, that a ruler would deliberately incite one of his own provinces to revolt in order to take their possessions for himself. But Quintus did not for a moment put it beyond the evil genius of Caligula.

"Many soldiers would be killed," Quintus reminded him.

"The Jews are a mob," Pilate said contemptuously. "They cannot even work together."

"They worked together once." Quintus was nettled at Pilate's tone. "When they came to Caesarea because the eagles of Rome had been taken into Jerusalem."

The shot went home, as Quintus had intended it to do. The incident of the eagles, occurring when Pontius Pilate had first become procurator of Judea, had been a defeat for the Roman governor. When thousands of Jews had come to Caesarea unarmed to protest the desecration of the Holy City, Pilate had been forced to give in and order the imperial standards removed, or butcher thousands of unarmed people, an act that would have sent him to Rome in disgrace.

"They would not defy Caligula," Pilate said with a shrug. "He is of different stuff from Tiberius."

"I agree," Quintus said shortly. "The treasury is empty. No man's wife is safe. The people spy upon each other to see which can carry the worst tale to him, and Simon Magus is the worst of all."

"What have I to do with the magician?" Pilate demanded.

"Only you can say that," Quintus said evenly. "But

Simon would sell his own mother into slavery if it worked to his advantage."

"Save your warnings for cravens," Pilate said contemptuously. "Simon knows I can destroy him when I wish, merely by revealing his real intentions in the affair on Mount Gerizim."

Quintus brought his fist up across his chest in the military salute. "I bid you good day then," he said.

He was several steps away when Pilate said, "I did not mean to be ungracious, Quintus. Thank you for visiting my wife."

Quintus nodded and went on. Save for his admiration of Claudia Procula, he would cheerfully have consigned Pontius Pilate to the regions presided over by Pluto.

7

The order assigning Pontius Pilate to Lugdunum in Gaul as governor was signed only a few days later. It was a prize assignment—although not the position of legate that Pilate had wished—one of the most treasured governorships available to the emperor's noblemen administrators. Quintus' own assignment as physician to the troops of the governor was less ceremonious but equally as definite. He was ordered to proceed immediately to Lugdunum in the company of Pontius Pilate.

The vessel upon which they traveled stopped at Nicaea, Antipolis, and Forum Iulii before coming to the metropolis of Massilia. This flourishing seaport city on the warm shores of the Mare Nostrum proved a veritable treasure house of surprises for the travelers. Quintus had never been in Gaul but, like all Roman officers, he was familiar with the military history of the empire. He had heard in Alexandria of the schools of medicine and law in the Gallic center of Massilia, world famous as one of the large and busy Greek settlements along the Mediterranean coast long before Julius Caesar had conquered the territory with his legions.

Caesar had wisely maintained much of the tribal government of the canons, and Roman citizenship had been given to important Gauls who chose allegiance to Rome, thus cementing the ties between the prosperous province and the empire.

Under the Pax Romana Gaul had quickly become one of the most prosperous parts of the Roman Empire. Forests were cleared and fields sowed with grain to be sold in the markets of Rome. A reaping machine that did much of the work by mechanical means was even in use, having been invented by the canny Greeks who always throve wherever Roman might brought peace and economic security. Potters, workers in metal, glass blowers, weavers, and many other artisans prospered in Massilia, selling part of their products to the lords of the rich estates that sprang up everywhere and the rest in Rome itself. A steady stream of shipping connected Massilia, Narbo, and other cities along the eastern coast of Hispania with Rome and the other great cities of the empire. Many thousands of miles of typical Roman roads had been built, aqueducts brought water to the cities, and the typically Roman *cloacae*, or sewers, gave the benefits of sanitation.

Gallia Narbonensis, the province that included Massilia and the mouth of the river Rhodanus—also called the Rhone—was one of the richest jewels in Rome's necklace of great cities. Already an ancient center of population in the time of the Phoenicians long before a conquering Caesar had been born, Massilia had remained essentially a Greek city, even under Roman government. Near by at the town of Arelate the great river near whose mouth Massilia stood emptied its waters, draining the southern and central portions of Gaul and forming the joint port of this rich land, in a sense bridging two worlds.

Roman and Greek cultures, spreading up the river and through its branches into the very heart of Gaul itself, had borne with the stream the products of Gallic artisans in this predominantly Celtic region. In fact, so important was Massilia as the central point for the entire commerce of the area by way of the great river

168

that it had been allowed to maintain the status of a free city, independent of the provincial governor.

Quintus would have enjoyed exploring this great educational and cultural center with Veronica and Joseph. But since Massilia was not under the jurisdiction of Pontius Pilate's new post as governor of Gallia Lugdunensis, he was anxious to journey on to his new site of government. At nearby Arelate, where the mighty river actually entered the sea, they turned northward into the current of the Rhodanus and sailed up the broad, south-flowing stream, pausing for one day to visit Nemausus, a short distance to the west of the river mouth, where Augustus had raised a beautiful edifice in memory of his grandsons Lucius and Caius Caesar, with lovely Corinthian columns equal in beauty to any in Rome itself.

Sailing on upriver, they passed Avenio and came to Arausio, where a powerful arch had been erected by the Emperor Augustus and a great Roman theater had also been built. Soon they approached Lugdunum, capital of the province and situated where the rivers Rhone and Arar had their confluence. The coming-together point of the great highways built by Agrippa, Lugdunum had naturally become a center of both commerce and culture. At this time it contained more than a hundred thousand people and ranked as one of the most important secondary cities of the entire empire.

Quintus and Veronica stood on the foredeck of the ship watching Lugdunum come into view ahead of them on the shores of the river as the slaves strained at the oars to drive the vessel upstream. It was a lovely prospect with rolling hills, green fields, and the roofs of the city in the distance.

"It is as beautiful as Italy!" Veronica cried.

Her words made Quintus happy, for after the rocky hillsides that made up her own country for the most part—except in the fertile region around the Sea of Galilee—Veronica had been entranced with Italy. He knew she had been a little reluctant to leave it for a distant land which only a short while ago had been conquered by the Romans. But now, with loveliness and peace everywhere and the warm sun of a climate almost as mild as that of Italy shining upon them, he could understand her pleasure.

He squeezed her hand where it lay on the rail beside his. "Perhaps we'll find a permanent home here. I know they have a university, and skillful physicians are sure to be in demand."

"Would you leave the legions?" She knew how proud he was of the Praetorians, the elite group to which he belonged.

Quintus did not answer for a moment. He had never asked himself that question before, until the sight of this beautiful land had put the idea in his mind. And yet—when he thought about it—the prospect was not at all unpleasant. Rome—at least in the time of Caligula—was no place for a lovely and innocent girl like Veronica. And of all the far-flung regions where he had served, Lugdunum and the surrounding country certainly seemed from the first view to be the most pleasant.

"I would leave it for you," he told her, "if I were sure we could be happy here."

"I can be happy anywhere," Veronica said, "anywhere at all with you." Her hand was still in his and her fingers tight about his own, but he sensed that she had not finished voicing the thought that was in her mind. "But I have a strange feeling about all this." He felt her shiver where her shoulder touched his, and the pressure of her fingers about his tightened suddenly with an almost desperate urgency.

"What is it, my dear?" he asked.

"Somehow it seems that this is only the beginning—of something dangerous for all of us."

"And for Pilate?"

"For him too. Don't ask me why. It is something I feel—for no reason at all."

It was absurd, of course, to believe that such a presentiment actually could mean anything, and yet Quintus could not help experiencing some of her anxiety. He put his arm around her and for a moment they clung together. Then Veronica stopped trembling and straightened her shoulders resolutely. "Jesus was not afraid, even when they drove him to the hill of Golgotha with whips and the burden of the *patibulum* upon his back," she said. "I will not let myself be either."

"Do you still persist in following a dead rabble rouser?" a cold voice asked behind them. They had not heard Pontius Pilate approach, but when they turned he was standing behind them. The new governor was in full uniform, his cloak lined with purple as befitted a representative of the emperor, his polished metal helmet with its brilliant purple-plumed crest set proudly on his head.

Veronica did not quail but curtsied before Pilate. "Jews take their god with them wherever they go, sir," she said gently. "Both Emperor Augustus and Emperor Tiberius granted us that right."

"Caligula will soon take it from you," Pilate said shortly. "When he does it will be my duty to enforce the edict."

Veronica did not answer for there was nothing to say. The right of the Jews to worship their own god seemed to be much on Pilate's mind lately, and Quintus thought he understood why. Tortured by the fear that he had crucified the son of a god, the governor's distorted mind could find comfort in the fact that the emperor—madman that he was—planned to outlaw that god and his worship. Then if the one the Jews called the Most High did not summarily punish Caligula with death, it could only mean that the Jewish god was a myth without power and without a divine son. Thus Pilate was, in a sense, letting Caligula be a stalking horse for him.

"We were remarking upon the beauty of this land," Quintus said, hoping to draw Pilate's attention away from the subject of Veronica's religion.

"It is a pleasant region," Pilate agreed, "and a rich one. Gallia Lugdunensis extends to the shore of the Western Sea opposite Britannia." Pilate's eyes kindled, as if he were seeing something to the westward other

171

than the rolling Gallic countryside along the river. Veronica took the opportunity to move away.

"Cunobelinus, king of the Britanni, has not been remitting his taxes to Rome lately," Pilate continued, almost as if speaking to himself. "With a strong hand in control here, enough troops can be concentrated on the shore opposite Britannia to make a raid across the channel between it and Gaul to subdue the Britanni."

"Isn't Lentulus Gaeticulus still general of the armies in this region?" Quintus asked. "I thought he held the rank of consul under Tiberius." Roman generals in the field were sometimes given the temporary rank of consul in order to place them above the provincial governors and avoid controversy over rank.

"Lentulus long ago relaxed the discipline of his troops so he could draw allegiance to himself instead of to the emperor," Pilate said. "Tiberius let him do it, but Caligula will not make that mistake."

"Does the emperor know of this?" Quintus asked quickly.

"Of course. But Lentulus is the son-in-law of Sejanus and has powerful friends in Rome." Sejanus, an archplotter, had been executed by Tiberius for treason in the latter years of his reign. But with characteristic leniency the aging emperor had not destroyed ruthlessly all those who might have had a part in the intended insurrection. "For this reason it was better not to speak too much of this in Rome," Pilate added.

"But I thought——"

"That my wife arranged all this to get me out of town?" Pilate laughed. "That was Janus' idea—to cloak the real reason for sending me to Gallia Lugdunensis."

"I served under Lentulus once," Quintus said. "He is strong-minded—and ruthless."

Pilate shrugged. "Lentulus is on the upper Rhine where the Germani have been in revolt. By the time he knows what is happening here, the attack upon Britannia will be finished and he will be in disgrace for allowing Cunobelinus to go unpunished."

"And the emperor will have the proof he needs to remove him from his post and have him executed?"

"Naturally. As commander of all the Gallic legions then, I will be the direct representative of Gaius in Gaul and superior to all provincial governors in this region. From there it is only a step to being named legate."

It was an audacious scheme. And it probably would succeed, if carried out with the kind of thoroughness and efficiency Pontius Pilate would bring to it, since the plan offered such a tremendous opportunity for advancement on his own part. The whole scheme was quite in accord, too, with the roundabout way Caligula had adopted in carrying out some of his more fantastic plans. No doubt when Pilate rose to the eminence he desired as virtual ruler of Gaul with all of its fabulous riches he would reward the freedman Janus liberally for his part in it. Empires had been run that way since time immemorial; there was no reason to expect a change now.

"Of course you will say nothing about this," Pilate was saying, his voice cold once again. "I should have to execute you at once if you did."

"I will not speak of it," Quintus promised. "But I hope for your sake no one in Rome already has."

"Janus and I saw to that," Pilate said confidently. "Nothing will go wrong."

The city of Lugdunum was an intriguing sight as their ship was rowed toward a pier that extended into the stream. The sun was warm and pleasant, although it was late winter, and the aroma of spring seemed to be in the air already. Not so solidly built as Rome, Lugdunum still had a surprising air of permanence and age—until one remembered that the Gauls had been in control here for hundreds of years and the city at the confluence of the two great rivers had been a large commercial and governmental center all the while.

The rivers themselves gave credence to Pontius Pilate's daring plan, for it was only a short overland trip from the headwaters of the Rhodanus and the Arar to any one of several large waterways flowing westward to the coast of Gaul opposite Britannia. Thus, by a combination of land and water routes, a small

173

but highly mobile force could move swiftly and accomplish its mission before word could reach Lentulus in the regions of the upper Rhine.

As the ship neared the dock, Quintus was surprised to see a large number of Roman troops drawn up in military formation upon the quay, pennons flying and the eagles of Rome gleaming in the afternoon sunlight. Pilate stood at the side of the ship near where the gangplank would be lowered, resplendent in uniform, with Claudia Procula at his side. As the ship grated against the pier and the gangplank was swung across to settle upon the deck, the captain stood aside for Pontius Pilate to march down it first as befitted his rank.

The new governor was a handsome military figure dressed in the full splendor of a high Roman official as he stepped from the plank to the deck and turned to face the troops drawn up at attention. Quintus recognized the tribune who commanded them as an old comrade in arms, by name Cato Gaetinus, and a trusted lieutenant of Lentulus Gaeticulus. The sight of Cato's craggy, grim-featured face gave him a sense of foreboding.

While Pilate waited to receive the salute of the troops, Cato stepped forward and drew his sword. "Are you Pontius Pilate?" he demanded. His tone was icy and showed none of the respect due a governor arriving to take his post.

"I am," Pilate said stiffly, obviously incensed at the manner of his reception.

"I arrest you upon the order of Lentulus Gaeticulus, general of the armies of Gaul," Cato said in a loud voice.

8

Pilate remained as rigid as a statue, the color slowly ebbing from his cheeks. Only a strangled sob from Claudia Procula broke the shocked silence.

"Betrayed!" she cried. "We have been betrayed."

Pilate finally found his voice. "What is the meaning of this?" he demanded in choked tones.

Cato stepped forward and handed him a small roll of parchment. "Here is the order for your arrest, signed by Lentulus Gaeticulus himself."

Pilate did not even read the parchment. "Where is the general?" he demanded.

"At Vindobona. I was sent ahead with the order for your arrest. He will follow in a few days."

"What is the charge?" Claudia Procula asked in a subdued voice.

"Treason," said Cato. "Treason against the Roman commander in charge of this area. Word of it came from Rome to Lentulus even before you sailed."

"It must have been Simon," Pilate said stonily then. "Simon Magus betrayed me."

Pilate made no further objection to his arrest. He seemed stunned, very much as he had been when Quintus had come aboard the *Olympia* in Antioch.

Cato included in the arrest everyone identified by the captain as belonging to the party of Pontius Pilate, which meant Quintus, Veronica, and Joseph also. The women were separated from the men. Veronica went with Claudia Procula, Pilate was alone, and Quintus shared a cell with Joseph of Arimathea. Their prison was actually a villa with comfortable accommodations, but eight soldiers were posted around it constantly to insure that Pilate did not escape.

Cato visited Quintus after the guards had been posted for the night. The two men greeted each other warmly, and the tribune removed his plumed helmet and sat on the couch in the room. "The order included Pilate's entire party," he explained to Quintus. "I had no choice except to place you under guard too."

"No one can blame you for carrying out your orders," Quintus told him. "What is the real charge against Pilate?"

Cato went to the door and looked out in the corridor. When he saw that the guard was at the other end, he came back and spoke in a low voice. "I am not supposed to know, but Lentulus was raving with anger

175

while his clerk wrote out the order for Pilate's arrest, so I learned the whole plot. He had received word from Rome that Pilate planned to mount a swift attack immediately against King Cunobelinus in Britannia. Lentulus has not gone against Cunobelinus because his hands have been filled with the Germani."

"Is the King of Britannia in open rebellion?"

Cato shrugged. "Who knows? It is true that he has not paid his taxes, but he has not attacked any Roman soldiers."

"How did Lentulus get word of this?"

"His wife is Sejanus' daughter, remember? Many in Rome did not like Tiberius, and I understand that even more hate Caligula."

"If you saw the emperor you would understand."

"I knew Gaius when he was a mere child, strutting in soldier's boots in the camp of Germanicus. He must have planned this thing with Pilate, to discredit Lentulus and provide a reason to recall him. Do you mean you didn't know about it?" he added.

"Only today, a few hours before we debarked."

"Then how are you involved?"

Quintus told him of his first contact with Pilate and the events that had followed, including Claudia Procula's asking him to accompany them to Gaul.

"Say nothing of what Pontius Pilate told you today," Cato advised. "All you know is that you were ordered here from Rome as a physician. Lentulus is raving mad; if he thinks you are part of the plot, your head may roll too. But if you only obeyed orders, you are safe."

"He couldn't have Pilate executed; even a general lacks that authority."

"Legally Lentulus can only hold Pilate under arrest and return him to Rome for trial," Cato agreed. "Maybe Caligula would execute Pilate, rather than have his part in the affair become known. Or again he might free him, to spite Lentulus. The general has to be absolutely sure Pilate will be destroyed, so an accident will happen conveniently." He stood up. "I will do what I can to

176

keep you out of it, Quintus, but I can't vouch for the temper of Lentulus."

"What of my wife?"

"She will not be harmed; you can be sure of that. Roman soldiers don't make war on women—at least not yet." He grinned. "Except these Gauls and Germani. Their women fight as fiercely as the men."

Joseph of Arimathea had been sitting quietly on a stool, listening to what was said but taking no part in the conversation. "I am sorry you are involved in this, Joseph," Quintus told him when Cato was gone. "It seems nothing but trouble has come to you because of me."

The merchant shook his head. "This is all part of a plan, Quintus. None of us can control it."

"Surely you don't think we are being moved about like pieces on a chessboard?"

"Something like that, but to a more important purpose."

"And what is that?"

"Spreading the teachings of Jesus to all men."

"Do you think Pontius Pilate is being punished for killing the Galilean?"

"I prefer to think he is being brought to the place where he may repent and save himself."

Quintus shook his head. "I find that hard to believe."

Joseph smiled. "Who can know the purposes of God? We can only go where he directs us."

9

Lentulus Gaeticulus arrived several days later, and Quintus, Veronica, and Joseph of Arimathea were brought before him. The general's face was set and cold, but he listened attentively while Quintus told him of being assigned to accompany Pilate to Lugdunum. Under the questioning of Lentulus he also told of his previous experience with Pilate. When he finished, the general took a small parchment roll from the table beside him.

"Your story agrees in every detail with a statement made by the Lady Claudia Procula," he said. "It seems none of you had any knowledge of the plot that brought Pontius Pilate here."

Quintus kept silent, as Cato had advised. He had taken no part in the actual plot, and the fact that Pilate had revealed it to him just before he was arrested did not involve him in any way.

"You three are absolved from blame in this affair," Lentulus told him. "Your record as a soldier and a physician are well known to me, Quintus. For the time being you will be assigned to the garrison here at Lugdunum as a physician."

"Thank you, sir," Quintus said. "May I say something?"

"Does it concern this matter?"

"Yes."

"Speak then."

"I am sure the Lady Claudia Procula knew nothing of this affair."

"How do you know this?"

"She was anxious to get her husband away from Rome and spoke to me of it more than once. I know she was happy about the assignment to Lugdunum because it would take him away."

"She should have gotten him out sooner," Lentulus growled. "But I will consider what you have said when it is time to decide what to do with her." He rubbed his square chin, scarred from years of battle. "After all, she is of the Claudian line and has royal blood." He made a gesture of dismissal. "Report to Tribune Cato and he will see that you get your pay."

Cato helped Quintus find a small *casa* for rent near the military headquarters. Lugdunum was no longer a frontier post since what frontier there was now existed in the upper Rhine area—unless the indeterminate rebellion of the Britanni under King Cunobelinus became important.

Britannia had not been wholly conquered by Julius Caesar, Quintus knew, and little attention had been paid to it since. Actually Caesar's legions had done little more than skirmish there and confirm the fact that the tribes of Britannia, who constantly fought each other, were not capable of joining together for effective resistance against invasion. Equally important was the observation that crops grown in the fertile land would be sufficient to feed an army of invaders, should it be necessary to conquer Britannia. Thus it would not be necessary to carry large amounts of food across the narrow channel called the Fretum Gallicum between it and the coast of Gaul.

Pilate's planned invasion of Britannia—had it succeeded—would have been little more than a reconnaissance raid, designed to frighten the king of the Britannic tribes facing toward Gaul into obedience to Rome. No large expedition could have been mounted with the relatively small number of troops Pilate would have been able to raise in this area independent of the army commanded by Lentulus Gaeticulus. Such a raid would have had to be spectacularly successful, but the known inability of the Britanni to mount a joint action had seemed to augur its success. Now, of course, the whole plan had collapsed like an emptied wineskin.

The villa Quintus and Veronica selected with the help of Cato was small, located on a bluff overlooking the river Rhodanus with its constant movement of shipping. In the courtyard fruit trees and vines grew in riotous profusion and birds sang everywhere. There was water in plenty from a well in the courtyard.

"This must be the loveliest place on earth!" Veronica cried when she first saw it.

"Lugdunum is a fine city," Cato agreed. "I will be glad when we get back here from fighting the Germani."

"Will that be soon?" Quintus asked.

"Sooner than was our plan. Until now Lentulus preferred to be in the upper Rhine region with headquarters at Vindobona, where he could move quickly to Rome if the occasion demanded."

"Why?"

The tribune lowered his voice. "Didn't you hear

of the ambitions of Aemilius Lepidus toward the throne?"

Quintus shook his head. "I never trouble myself with political gossip."

"You would do well to listen more closely. A man must know what horse to bet on or he will never win."

"Does Lentulus support Lepidus?"

Cato was suddenly closemouthed. "Let us say he thinks Caligula will not last long."

"I hope he is right. You cannot know what Rome has become."

"After Augustus and Tiberius it could do with a little excitement," Cato said. "But Caligula may have gone too far."

"What will Lentulus do now? Attack Britannia?"

Cato shook his head. "First he must get rid of Pontius Pilate. Then the Germani will have to be contained." He got to his feet. "You need not report for duty for a few days. Take time to see something of the city."

Veronica, Quintus, and Joseph were busy during the next several days getting their house in order and exploring the teeming Gallic center of Lugdunum. Veronica exclaimed with pleasure over the skill of the glass blowers and the exquisite workmanship of their product. Joseph was interested in the opportunities for trade here and in the surrounding cities. He had brought letters of credit on Roman bankers and, since these were acceptable in even this farthest corner of the empire, they did not lack for any necessities. In addition Quintus was able to draw his military pay.

The second day after their release a message arrived asking him to attend Lady Claudia Procula in the villa where she and Pontius Pilate were under guard. With the message was permission from the Tribune Cato commanding the troops guarding Pilate for him to attend the prisoner. The guards passed him into the villa and Claudia Procula came to greet him. Her eyes were red from weeping and her face was lined with worry.

"Thank you for coming, Quintus," she said, taking

his hand and drawing him into the room where she had been sitting. "You are all unharmed?"

"Lentulus did not hold us after you assured him I was not involved in the affair."

"I am glad I could do that much," she said. "Are Veronica and Joseph well?"

"Yes. Cato helped us find a villa. Are you ill, my lady?"

"Only in my heart. But Pontius is worse even than when he was removed from his post in Judea. Unless he gets to Rome where Caligula and Janus will give him a fair trial, I fear he may go mad."

For a moment Quintus thought she was going to break down into sobs, but she straightened her shoulders and controlled herself with an effort. "Please help him, Quintus."

"He has never sought aid from me, my lady."

"I know. But you could tell Lentulus that unless Pilate is returned to Rome at once he will go mad."

"I doubt if that will have any effect."

"Roman law requires that a person of Pontius' rank be sent to Rome for trial. Even a general cannot change that."

Quintus hated to be blunt, but there seemed to be no point in allowing her to have hopes that weren't justified. "It is true that your husband cannot be tried here, my lady," he said. "But I doubt if he will ever reach Rome."

She caught her breath. Evidently the thought that Pilate might somehow be killed had not yet occurred to her. "If you tell them he is going mad, they will have to send him to Rome. Even Lentulus would not kill a madman."

"I will do what I can. May I see him now?"

"He is in the next room. And, Quintus———"

"Yes, my lady?"

"Even if my husband did crucify a good man—surely he has already been punished enough."

10

Pontius Pilate was standing before a large window at one side of the room watching the ships moving up and down the river on the way to and from the sea. He turned when Quintus entered but did not speak. His eyes were filmed over, as if a curtain had been drawn over his thoughts, and his face was set and bleak.

"Your wife asked me to visit you, sir," Quintus told him. "She thinks you are ill."

"My sickness cannot be cured. The gods themselves are against me."

"The philosophers say a man is master of his fate."

"They are fools. I am loyal to my emperor and to the empire I serve, yet you see me in prison." Pilate came closer, his eyes burning with a strange light. "Or do you think I am being punished for crucifying the Galilean?"

Quintus shook his head. "I do not judge."

"Perhaps you think I am sick in my mind then, as you did on the *Olympia?*" Pilate turned back to the window. "You are right at that, I suppose. I have suffered blows heavy enough to drive a sane man out of his mind."

"Perhaps I can help you," Quintus suggested.

"How?" Pilate demanded savagely. "By putting a veil over me and praying? Don't be a fool, Quintus! You know me better than that."

"Others have been healed by it."

"Because they were afraid and let fear drive them out of their senses. I am too strong for that."

"Yet you yourself say you are sick in your mind."

Pilate's shoulders sagged and he seemed to collapse. In that instant he became no longer a strong and arrogant Roman but a tired and broken man. "Yes, I am sick," he admitted. "Sick unto death, Quintus. And not long removed from it."

"Sickness of the mind does not often kill," Quintus reminded him.

Pilate laughed then, the harsh, grating cry of a man in pain. "Do you think I don't know what is in the mind of Lentulus? He is a strong man, as I am—and a ruthless one. You warned me of that once. Lentulus will do with me as I would with him, in similar circumstances. I may start for Rome—although I doubt even that—but I will never get there alive."

"Your wife has asked me to tell the general you are mad."

Pilate's eyes kindled. "In the hope that his conscience will not let even him kill a madman in cold blood?"

"Something like that."

"She gives Lentulus too much credit, but it may be the only chance at that." He moved about the room like a caged beast, then stopped before Quintus. "I know how much you pride yourself upon your honesty. Would you certify that I am sick in my mind?"

"You have been sick in your soul ever since you crucified Jesus of Nazareth," Quintus told him bluntly.

"But I washed my hands! I left it up to the people. They chose Barabbas and crucified Jesus. The crowd heard me say I found no fault in him and saw me wash my hands."

"But you could not wash away your guilt," Quintus reminded him.

"No," Pilate said slowly. "I could not wash it away— then or since. It has followed me to this day." He straightened his shoulders with an obvious effort and stood erect. "But I can still fight; after all, I am a Roman. By all means tell Lentulus I am mad. I will not deny it—I cannot."

Quintus went immediately to the headquarters of Lentulus Gaeticulus and requested permission to speak to the general. Lentulus was surrounded by maps and looked up impatiently. "What is it, tribune?" he asked.

"I have just come from examining Pontius Pilate, sir."

"So?" The general leaned back in his seat. "Is he ill?"

"Pilate has been sick in his mind for a long time.

183

On the voyage between Antioch and Rome I feared he might throw himself into the sea."

"Too bad he didn't," Lentulus growled. "So you think he is mad?"

"I am sure of it."

"I suppose that means you want him sent to Rome at once?"

"His wife hopes that will be your decision."

"And you?"

"Only a miracle can cure Pilate, sir—and he refused that."

Lentulus frowned. "Cato assures me that your integrity is absolutely without question, Quintus, or I would doubt what you say. Will you certify as a physician that Pontius Pilate is a madman?"

"Yes," Quintus said without hesitation. "I am convinced of it."

"Your certificate will give me a logical reason to remove him from the governorship and send him back to Rome." The general toyed with a map on the table. "And the fact that he is mad will certainly keep Caligula from appointing him to another position of responsibility." He laughed harshly. "Even a madman would hardly employ another madman. Write a certificate for Quintus Volusianus to sign, stating that Pontius Pilate is mad," he directed a clerk sitting at the end of the table. "A vessel will be leaving Avenio in a week. Pilate will be sent there by carriage in due time and will take ship for Rome."

"May I tell the Lady Claudia Procula that, sir?"

"Of course. Tell Pilate too, if you wish. Even madmen don't want to die." Lentulus laughed suddenly. "This is working out much better than I thought. By all means tell Pilate he is going to Rome—and his friends."

11

Pontius Pilate left Lugdunum for Avenio one morning about a week later. Claudia Procula traveled in a carriage with their baggage, but Pilate rode a horse,

184

fully uniformed and holding himself as erect as if he had been the real governor of Lugdunum instead of a prisoner returning to Rome in disgrace. Only a small guard accompanied them, surprisingly small, Quintus thought as he watched. Then he remembered that Pilate was, in a sense, going of his own free will and therefore would not be likely to try an escape.

Quintus was busy patching up the wounds resulting from one of the frequent fracases between the soldiers of the garrison and the riffraff of Lugdunum, who were not above attacking even a member of the legion in the hope of stealing his valuable weapons and equipment. This particular street brawl had been a bloody one, resulting in two cracked heads, a broken leg, and an assortment of minor wounds. It was mid-morning before Quintus finished his work; the broken bones had been splinted and the scalp wounds closed by sewing them together with a tough thread, since such injuries healed well with that treatment in his experience. He was regaling himself with a cup of wine and a piece of bread in the quarters of the officers when Cato came in and tossed his plumed helmet on a chair.

"I thought I heard troops riding out just now," Quintus said. "More trouble in the city?"

Cato filled a cup and drank it down. "Just a party going to take care of your friend Pontius Pilate."

"What do you mean?" Quintus asked, suddenly alert.

"You knew he left for Avenio this morning, didn't you?"

"I saw him go. But that was several hours ago."

"Lentulus is a crafty one," Cato said. "Today will be the end of Pilate, you can wager on that."

"But how? He is supposed to take ship at Avenio for Rome. Lentulus told me that when I signed the certificate certifying Pilate as being mad."

"The ship is waiting at Avenio, but when Pilate doesn't arrive tomorrow, the captain will undoubtedly get tired of waiting and sail without him."

"Don't talk riddles," Quintus said. "Why shouldn't he arrive there?"

185

Cato shrugged. "We kept it from you on Lentulus' order—for fear you might warn him."

"Kept what from me?"

"The scheme Lentulus fixed to get rid of Pilate." Cato looked at the water clock. "But enough time has passed now; there's no reason to keep it from you any longer."

"What are you talking about?"

"Pilate's jailer intimated last night to his prisoner that he had information of value and allowed himself to be bribed. He then revealed to Pilate that he is to be killed near the town of Vienne, lying between here and Avenio. Pilate knew his only chance of escaping death was to get away from the guards and somehow find a boat on the river and reach Massilia, so the jailer agreed to arrange everything for a price. The governor of Massilia takes orders directly from Rome, so Pilate could be sure of being safe—if he reached the sea."

"When Pilate tries to escape, I suppose the guards will cut him down?"

Cato shook his head. "That might appear too obvious. Pilate was allowed to ride a horse, and the jailer promised to have a boat ready for him on the river just below Vienne."

"With such a small guard he might actually get away."

"That's where Lentulus showed real genius," Cato said admiringly. "We want Pilate to escape. The second party that left just now is supposed to be hunting for a band of Gauls that has been robbing in the region of Vienne."

Quintus saw the whole plot now. It was crystal clear and practically certain to succeed. "I suppose the second party will just happen to be scouting around Vienne when Pilate makes his escape," he said.

"Of course." Cato filled his wine cup again. "It's hilly country, and at a distance Pilate could easily be taken for a Gallic robber. By the time the mistake is discovered he will be dead."

It was certainly no more nefarious a scheme than happened frequently in Rome, Quintus was forced to admit—especially under the rule of Caligula. But although he'd had no actual part in it, he could not escape the conviction that in certifying Pilate as mad to Lentulus he had helped send him to his death.

Quintus had finished eating. Now he put down his cup casually. "I'm tired," he said. "May I go home for a while?"

"Go wherever you please," Cato said. "We'll have another crop of broken heads before morning, but things should be quiet until then."

Quintus left the headquarters, being careful not to give any impression of haste. Once away from it, however, he hurried to his own villa. Veronica and Joseph were at the noonday meal. He told them of the plot by which Lentulus planned to get rid of Pilate and of how he had unwittingly been made a part of it.

"Lentulus would almost certainly have murdered Pilate in any event," Joseph said. "But I can see how you would feel guilty."

"What can you do?" Veronica asked.

"You have been exploring the country looking for artisans, Joseph," Quintus said. "Doesn't the river take a great bend between here and Vienne?"

"Yes. But the road follows the river."

"If I ride across country I may be able to overtake the party with Pilate and warn him against trying to escape."

"Won't they kill him anyway?" Veronica asked.

"Roman soldiers obey orders," Quintus said. "If Pilate does not try to escape, those guarding him will have no reason to harm him. The second party is supposed to hunt him down, but they would not attack an official escort and its prisoner."

"It will be a hard ride, but I have a good horse," said Joseph. "Go with God, my son."

"And take this—to protect you." Veronica took the veil from its sandalwood box on a nearby table and thrust it into the bosom of his tunic as she kissed him good-by.

Riding the swift horse Joseph had bought for his own travels in and around Lugdunum, cutting across

187

country by whatever paths he could find and over open fields when there were none, Quintus headed in the direction of the small town of Vienne, lying between Avenio and the confluence of the Rhodanus and the Arar at Lugdunum. He had done his share of campaigning on horseback as an officer of the legions, but that had been years ago, and of late he had usually traveled with the wagons hauling medical supplies when the columns were on the march. It was hard going, but he felt sure he was outdistancing the second group of soldiers whose job it was to pretend they were hunting Gallic thieves in the hills, while managing to kill the fugitive Pilate at the same time.

As he approached Vienne, the terrain became more and more hilly, with almost mountainous crags overlooking narrow valleys. In this country, he thought, it might take the soldiers a long time to find a fugitive if he got very far away from the road. Actually Pilate might even be able to make his way to the river and bribe a fisherman or boatman to carry him down it by night, if he could manage to elude those sent to kill him.

Upon the crest of a hill not far from Vienne, Quintus stopped and studied the landscape below him. He could see the town in the distance to the south. The major part of its buildings were on the hilly side of the river, with only a few flat fields on the opposite bank. The road wound below him, and when he could not detect either party upon it, he dared to hope that Pilate's group, traveling slowly as they would be with the carriage, had not yet come this far. Then he heard shouts below and saw the second Roman detail riding up a hillside some distance away. The pace they were going, as well as their shouting, told him he was too late. While he watched, a smaller figure on horseback appeared higher up in the hills on the crest of a rock well above him.

Pilate had already escaped from the first party, Quintus realized. By now he had no doubt seen the second Roman party and realized just how Lentulus planned to kill him. His only alternative then was to try and reach the town of Vienne to the south in advance of the pursuers. There, with people thronging the town, he could at least hope not to be hunted down and killed like a mad dog before he could give himself up. But the soldiers following him were equally determined not to let him reach Vienne, lest they earn the displeasure of Lentulus Gaeticulus for letting so important a quarry elude them.

Rooted at the lower level and unable to help, Quintus could only watch the macabre drama being played out. Pilate's strategy was obvious. If he could get his mount over the particular craggy hilltop he was climbing, he would be ahead of the Roman soldiers sent to kill him, with an excellent chance of making the town and perhaps even hiding along the riverbank or finding a boat. To accomplish this, however, he must traverse the narrow and winding path that made its way across the face of the craggy hillside, overlooking a deep valley hundreds of feet below.

Again and again Quintus lost sight of both horse and rider when the road wound behind a craggy outcrop, only to see them appear again at a higher level. Once the path seemed to lead along the very edge of a crag and Quintus held his breath until horse and man were safely past. Pilate obviously could not leave the horse behind, because once he reached the other side and a more accessible road he would need it to outdistance his pursuers. From where Quintus stood, however, it seemed that at any moment both horse and man might go tumbling out into thin air.

For what seemed hours—actually only minutes—Quintus watched the desperate climb of horse and man. Pilate was a superb horseman, but both rider and mount must be well nigh exhausted by now, Quintus realized. The path disappeared again and he dared hope Pilate had reached the top of the hill and was now galloping down to safety on the other side. Then horse and rider appeared just under the crest of the hill and Quintus drew a long breath of relief. Having

189

reached the crest, with probably a much more easily negotiable road leading down on the other side, it seemed that Pilate had made good his escape.

As to just what happened at that instant, Quintus could only speculate. At the very crest of the hill the animal shied away from something—perhaps a snake or a stone dislodged as they ascended. Or again Pilate might have intentionally or unintentionally goaded the exhausted animal with his spurs. Horrified, Quintus saw the horse shy off the level area toward the edge of the crag and the abyss yawning below. At the last moment it set its hoofs desperately to keep from sliding over the rim of the precipice and stumbled to its knees.

Like a small figure in a puppet show, Pilate's body turned in a lazy somersault out of the saddle and over the horse's head. Falling clear of the cliff edge, the tiny human figure turned like a feather caught in a current and plummeted downward. Halfway down the mountainside the body struck an outjutting rock, and Quintus, already spurring his horse toward the deep part of the valley below where it seemed the crumpled form would strike, expected to see it hang there.

But the momentum of the fall carried it over the craggy outcrop and, unimpeded now, Pilate's body fell like a diving hawk toward the valley below.

Perhaps half an hour later Quintus came upon what was left of the former procurator of Judea, a crumpled figure lying in an oddly bizarre posture like a doll made of rags, a position which could only mean that his spine and a number of other bones were broken. Quintus tethered his horse and knelt beside the body of Pilate merely as a last courtesy to the dead; obviously no one could have survived a fall like that.

And yet when he took Pilate's wrist between his fingers with the instinctive touch of the physician to feel the pulse—which stilled would indicate death as surely as its rhythmic pounding indicated life—Quintus realized that the terribly broken body was still alive. The pulse was no more than a flutter beneath his fingers, hardly enough to be called a beat at all, but it told him that death had not yet claimed its victim entirely.

Just then Pilate opened his eyes. They were already filmed by approaching death but cleared a little with the light of recognition.

"Quintus." It was the barest of whispers.

"I had nothing to do with this plot," Quintus assured him.

"I know." Pilate gasped for breath and grimaced with pain. "Lentulus has won."

"Maybe not yet." Quintus reached into his tunic for Veronica's veil. It was unbelievable that even the veil could help a man who should already have been dead. And yet he could not withhold its miracle-working properties—even from Pontius Pilate.

The veil was halfway out of his tunic when Pilate saw it.

"No!" It was a cry of terror and pain. "No!" His eyes closed and his mouth suddenly went slack. Quintus thought he was dead, but in a moment the bruised and torn lips moved again, although the words were barely audible.

"If the Galilean—heals me now—I will have lost everything. Promise—not—to use the veil."

"I promise." It had been a desperate expediency anyway, with little, if any, hope of success. Even before he finished speaking, Pontius Pilate was dead.

12

The party sent to hunt down Pontius Pilate became his funeral cortege instead. It arrived in Vienne just before dark with the badly broken body wrapped in the purple lined cloak. Claudia Procula had waited there and, having accomplished his purpose in the destruction of Pilate, Lentulus was properly magnanimous. He agreed to Procula's wishes that the funeral be conducted at Vienne, the lovely little city on the banks of the river Rhodanus toward which Pilate had been desperately striving when he had fallen to his death.

Quintus worked all night with an embalmer of the city, restoring Pilate's broken body to some semblance of its former self. The next day the dead man was carried through the streets of Vienne upon an open bier borne by Roman soldiers, with his wife, Veronica, Joseph, and Quintus in the funeral procession, and the garrison at Lugdunum marching behind in martial array.

The funeral pyre at the edge of the town blazed brightly in the warm air of early spring, consuming the remains of a man whose destiny had cast him in difficult roles indeed. When only the ashes remained, Claudia Procula ordered them interred in Vienne. The next day she continued on to Avenio to join the ship that would take her to Rome.

"What really happened?" Veronica asked as they were returning to Lugdunum in the carriage that had brought Joseph and Veronica to Vienne. "Was Pilate dead when you got there?"

"He lived only a few moments," Quintus told her. "I wanted to use the veil but he would not let me."

"Why?"

"Pilate's last words were, 'If the Galilean heals me now, I will have lost everything.' "

Veronica frowned. "What did that mean?"

"Pilate was a proud man," Joseph explained. "Proud men must believe they are always right, else they lose their pride in themselves and suddenly become nothing."

"But what pride could he take in having crucified Jesus?" Veronica asked.

"Pilate was a servant of the empire," Quintus said. "He was profoundly certain that he was doing his duty when he crucified the Galilean. Even if he had made a mistake and admitted it—as he did when he removed the standards from Jerusalem—he would have lost only a little face. But to admit that he had crucified a god was to condemn himself forever."

"But if he had asked forgiveness——"

"The ability to forgive others, even when they take your life, is a gift that comes to men only from God," Joseph said gently. "Pontius Pilate refused to seek that gift, so he never received it."

BOOK 4

Camulodunum

Before Lentulus Gaeticulus could launch a punitive raid against the Britanni and King Cunobelinus, he needed to be certain that he would not be committing the military blunder of leaving his rear in danger of attack by the Germani on the upper Rhine, who were always watching for an advantage. It was therefore necessary to continue his campaign against the rebellious Germani, and he embarked upon this project again shortly after the death of Pontius Pilate, expecting to be gone for nearly six months. Quintus had hoped to remain at Lugdunum but was not displeased when Lentulus—because of his experience and his rank of *tribunas laticlavus*—assigned him medical supervision over all the military posts in Gaul. Part of his duty was to make a survey—ostensibly of medical and sanitary facilities—but actually to visit and study the number and disposition of the several small garrisons that had held Gaul for Rome, so Lentulus would know just what strength could be depended upon when he finally looked across the narrow channel of the Fretum Gallicum toward Britannia.

Word had come from the western coast of Gaul that the Britanni had stepped up their attacks across the channel, and it was therefore important that Lentulus launch his own punitive expedition as soon as possible, lest there be more trouble from Rome such as Pontius Pilate had been sent to stir up. Some of the attacks by the Britanni had been against the Veneti, the most noted seafarers of the tribes along the Gallic coast. If these raids were for the purpose of capturing boats, then it could be that the Britanni were intending to range farther afield and attack shipping along the western coast of Gaul.

As the center of the entire region, Lugdunum enjoyed special privileges not afforded the other cities of Gaul. Only there did the inhabitants enjoy the rights of Roman citizenship as well as the privilege of coining imperial gold. Quintus and his household would have been content to remain in the fair and bustling city where the Rhodanus and the Arar had their meeting, but they were not saddened by Quintus' commission to inspect the military posts of Gaul. And since, as personal representative of Lentulus, he traveled under his own orders, he was able to take Veronica and Joseph of Arimathea with him. The latter, in spite of his age, proved an eager traveler and rarely stopped in a town that he did not somehow manage to gather a group around him to tell the story which he had been repeating with no sign of weariness across much of the civilized world of that day.

Traveling northward by easy stages, following the rivers and the fine Roman roads, they visited Cabillonum, Caesarodunum, Augustodunum and came finally to a beautiful town in the northern part of Gallia Lugdunensis called Lutetia, inhabited by a tribe known even before the conquest by Caesar as the Parisii. Lutetia was a charming place located on an island in a river that flowed to the Western Ocean. The climate was pleasant, the wine the finest they had tasted in Gaul, so they remained there a week before traveling to the coast and the towns of the Veneti, who in the time of Caesar had largely controlled this area as well as the trade with Britannia.

One of Quintus' assignments from Lentulus had been to visit the coastal towns and see what would be available in the way of water transport when the planned expedition against Britannia was launched during the spring months, the actual date depending upon how long the Germani of the upper Rhine kept the Romans occupied. For this purpose the travelers drifted down the river Sequana, upon which the city of the Parisii stood, as far as its mouth. They next visited Samara and, moving northward along the coast, came to Gesoriacum, a town looking directly across a narrow body of water to Britannia itself.

Quintus had hoped for a glimpse of the land of the Britanni, but as far as he could see in the west there was only a bank of dense fog, shrouding the mysterious region of which Julius Caesar had written and which the great conqueror had so obviously intended one day to make an important province of Rome. Only occasionally—the inhabitants of Gesoriacum told Quintus—were they able to see Britannia, and then only a glimpse of tall white cliffs shining in the sun.

Lentulus had thought that this area, so promising looking on the map, would be an excellent stepping-off point for the planned invasion. Quintus, however, was forced to decide that this was not the case. Putting troops to sea was at best a difficult procedure, as every Roman officer knew; to embark them in vessels of any size from an unprotected shore against seas whitecapped most of the year was well nigh impossible.

Even though Gesoriacum was not suitable as an embarking point, however, Quintus was able to obtain considerable information concerning the Britanni, since most of its people had been captured in the not infrequent raids from the strange land across the narrow sea and had managed to escape. The Britanni had paid the tribute first required by Caesar for many years, Quintus knew. And although it had not been paid recently, vessels from Rome still visited their ports to buy tin and other materials.

Years before—Quintus was told by the people of Gesoriacum—the tribes inhabiting the coastal areas of southern Britannia had been joined together under King Cunobelinus, who had recognized the advantage of trade with Rome, if not actually acknowledging the sovereignty of the emperor and paying heavy tribute to him. Under Cunobelinus the entire coastal area of Britannia had become strong and commercially progressive. Recently, however, with the king growing old, a new faction had arisen in his realm, particularly among his sons. Some, it was said, worked to maintain allegiance to Rome, while others called for an out-and-out break. As with so many of the more distant provinces of the empire, the peaceful reigns of Augustus and Tiberius had given the Britanni encouragement to break the somewhat tenuous bonds which attached them to distant Rome. The attacks upon the coastal Gauls were therefore for two purposes, Quintus judged, to gain booty, including slaves, women, and perhaps ships, and to see just how strong the Romans were and what likelihood there was of another military invasion such as the one carried out by Julius Caesar.

In order to interview everyone who could give him any information about Britannia, Quintus decided to remain in Gesoriacum for a few days. Besides, the weather was hot at midsummer in the inland areas and Veronica—accustomed to the cool nights that prevailed in the hilly uplands around Jerusalem where she had grown up—had been a little indisposed. The cooling breezes sweeping in from the Fretum Gallicum and the Oceanus Atlanticus had made her feel much better, and he wanted to give her time to benefit from the climate and the salt air before they pushed on. It was a pleasant region too. The fish and shellfish here were delicious, so Quintus was not adverse to a rest, nor was Joseph.

The Roman garrison of Gesoriacum consisted of only a few men whose duty it was to administer justice and maintain a watch upon the coast of Britannia to the northwest. A small *casa* was put at Quintus' disposal, and they were all pleased with this brief vacation from travel and the endless inspections he had been making during the past several months.

They had eaten an excellent meal one night of fish roasted over coals and braised with the savory herbs growing here which the Parisii and the neighboring Belgae seemed to know so well how to use in cooking. The wine had been cooled in a spring and was almost as good as that to which they had become accustomed in the lovely city of Lutetia. When they had finished eat-

198

ing and the dishes were taken away, Veronica went to talk with the women while Quintus and Joseph of Arimathea sat on a bench in the yard beneath a spreading tree.

"This is a good land, Quintus," Joseph observed. "I had to leave Jerusalem to appreciate what benefits the civilizing influence of Rome can really bring to a barbarous people in such a short time."

"I could have told you that the first time I saw you in Jerusalem," Quintus said. "But it isn't as evident everywhere as here in Gaul."

"We Jews are an ancient race and inclined to be contemptuous of others whose roots are not so deep as ours," Joseph admitted. "Do you know that we were a separate people thousands of years ago in the region of Ur of the Chaldees?"

"Veronica told me something about it."

"Actually we were probably a distinct people even in the valley of the Tigris and Euphrates. But since we built no great tombs, we are still unknown to much of your Roman Empire."

"Is that important?"

"I suppose not. Or perhaps it is, now that we have been given the task of spreading the truth abroad."

"Pontius Pilate was always seeking truth," Quintus reminded him. "I suspect he never found it though, until he tumbled from the crag that day."

"The truth of death," Joseph said thoughtfully. "And the truth that man is never more than one step away from it? Yes, I suppose Pilate did learn that truth at last. But there is one beyond it, the truth of life."

"Death takes life," Quintus objected. "So the truth of death overcomes even the truth of life."

"That is where you are wrong, my son," Joseph said earnestly. "Every man instinctively knows there is a life beyond this one. And he knows he will exist there after death, if he fulfills certain requirements."

"Perhaps we tell ourselves we will live forever because we don't want to admit that the flame of the funeral pyre destroys all of a man."

Joseph shook his head. "You have watched life

199

come into the world from the body of the mother, so you know that a man lives on forever in his children."

"Are you talking about that kind of immortality?"

"No, not exactly. Jesus called all men his children. And since he was God living on earth, we who are his children are also a part of God through him. What is more reasonable, therefore, than that we will one day live with him as he promised, if we will only believe and follow his teachings?"

"The teachings of Jesus are things I have tried to practice all my life," Quintus said. "Principles like loving your neighbors, helping even those who hate you. I have risked my life more than once to minister to the wounded on the battlefield."

"You are very near to eternal life," Joseph assured him. "Only a hair's breadth separates you."

"The admission that your Nazarene was the Son of God?"

"*Is* the Son of God," Joseph said. "Jesus lives, Quintus. I feel him in my heart every day."

Quintus shook his head a little sadly. "Your hair's breadth becomes a great chasm to me—like the Fretum Gallicum out there."

"But you expect one day to cross that—with Lentulus Gaeticulus," Joseph reminded him. "It will be even easier to surmount the barrier to the knowledge that Jesus is divine."

"Perhaps."

Joseph smiled. "You are a stubborn man, Quintus, but I suspect that your faith—when it comes—will be the stronger because of your stubbornness. Did you know that the people of Britannia also believe in a life after death?"

"How did you learn that?"

"I have talked to some men who were captured and later escaped. The religion of the Britanni is very similar to that of the ancient Gauls. They have a clan of priests called druids, who have complete control of all religious life and also act as judges in disputes between men or where a crime has been committed."

"A powerful combination," Quintus observed.

"The Gauls say the druids administer justice fairly. They teach the young men, too, so they largely control the thought of the country."

"That can be good—or bad."

Joseph nodded. "I wish we could cross the Fretum Gallicum and see what lies beyond the mist and fog."

"Not this time," Quintus told him. "I must soon report to Lentulus on my findings. Are you about ready to journey again?"

"In which direction will we go now?"

"One of the fishing boats here will take us down the coast and into the port of Caletes. A boat from there can take us along the coast to Aquitania and perhaps to Burdigala. From there we can journey overland to Lugdunum again." He turned to look out across the rolling waves of the Fretum Gallicum to the fog-shrouded coast beyond it. "It is a pity to come this close to Britannia and not visit it, but the risk is too great. Perhaps we can see it another time, when Lentulus has taught the people to respect Rome and Roman rule."

But as it happened, things turned out quite differently.

2

The surprise attack came in the early hours of the morning. Because of previous raids the Roman garrison maintained a sentry post overlooking the shore before Gesoriacum, but the Britanni had anticipated that and made their landing a little way down the coast out of sight of the town. Thus the actual attack came from the landward side and caught the garrison and the inhabitants of the town largely by surprise. Because of former raids the Roman commander had armed the men of Gesoriacum and, once the element of surprise was over, they were able to fight bravely and give a good account of themselves. By that time, however, the damage was done. The Britanni were everywhere, tall, fierce-looking men with hair growing down to their shoulders and long mustaches. They carried shields of bronze and short swords as well as spears and wore round caps of the same metal upon their heads.

During his travels Quintus usually wore the short sword of a Roman officer and carried a spear, but he had put aside his weapons when he lay down and, the night being warm, wore only a loincloth. He was awake at the first alarm but in the darkness was not able to find his plumed helmet of authority as a tribune or his armor. With his body unprotected, he fought as best he could but was quickly surrounded by Britanni who disarmed him, rounding up Veronica and Joseph as well. Quintus tried to tell them he was a Roman officer, but the attackers, either because they did not understand Latin—which seemed reasonable—or were not in the mood to listen to protests, paid no attention to him.

Along with a number of men, women, and children who had been captured in the raid, the three of them were prodded along the shore to where the boats of the Britanni had been beached. The raid had not been a very profitable one other than the haul in slaves, Quintus saw as they plodded along in the half-light of dawn with their wrists bound. Several of the Britanni wore Roman helmets, taken from soldiers killed in the raid, and a few others carried some small amount of booty. For the most part, however, they were empty-handed and apparently not very happy about it.

At another time Quintus would have been interested in studying these stalwart men, their preference for golden ornaments and their loud, fierce talk as they herded along the captives from Gesoriacum, jabbing the women, children, and old people with spears whenever they stumbled. But he was too busy now, trying to help Veronica and Joseph struggle through the soft sand of the beach. He was surprised that the Britanni had even bothered to bring the older captives who could not be expected to do much work; slave raiders often did not. Later he was to discover the reason.

The boats of the Britanni were shallow-bottomed craft so exactly like those built by the Veneti that

Quintus was sure they had been bought or captured. The captives were pushed and kicked into the boats, which were then shoved into the surf and the sails quickly raised. By now the wind that had brought the attackers to the shore of Gaul was changing and, with the sails filled, the fleet craft sped toward the still fog-shrouded coast ahead.

Because of the shallow draft of the boats they rolled a great deal and many of the captives—plus, Quintus noted, some of the Britanni themselves—were ill from the motion. Quintus was accustomed to sea travel and so were Veronica and Joseph. With the Britanni busy at the sails or prostrate in the bows, he was able to talk with Veronica and Joseph who, he was happy to see, had not suffered seriously from the attack.

"Someone on the shore of Britannia will certainly understand Latin," he told them with an assurance he was far from feeling. "We will be released as soon as they understand that I am a Roman officer."

But he was talking to drum up his courage and all of them knew it.

The Britanni had water and food but made no move to offer any to the prisoners. When a child cried out for water, a great brute of a fellow sent it sprawling with a stiff blow of his fist. Quintus started up from the floor of the boat but realized that he could not possibly help the child, since his hands were still tied together, and resumed his place.

With the hot sun and the motion of the boats, plus the lack of water and food, even Quintus was feeling ill by the time the flotilla of sailing craft entered a small river and, shortly after noon, nudged against the bank beside a large grove of trees. In the background they could see what appeared to be a small templelike structure built of stone, its walls massive and weather-stained, as if it were very old.

At one end of the grove more stones had been arranged in a circle, some standing as columns which supported others laid on top of them in the form of an elevated ring. Inside this ring was a high stone altar that was blackened by fire. The ground around it was littered with ashes, while above the strange structure towered massive oaks, their topmost branches interlaced so that even this early in the afternoon a strange and somehow frightening gloominess permeated the entire area.

The prisoners had been herded ashore roughly. Once there, however, they were given water to drink and a few crusts of bread, the remainder of the food supply which the Britanni had taken with them on the raid. Their hands were untied so they could eat and drink, but they were kept in a tight group and closely guarded by the tall men with flowing hair.

A number of the Britanni, Quintus saw, had been wounded. Some wore crude bandages, and several limped along with the help of their comrades. A few were carried ashore on planks torn from the thwarts of the boats to form improvised litters. A number of bodies were lugged ashore and laid out under one of the trees, evidently having been killed during the raid.

Among the wounded a handsome young man in his early twenties seemed to be of somewhat more importance than the rest, for those who carried him ashore showed him great deference, in spite of the fact that he was obviously unconscious. A bloody bandage almost covered the young warrior's head. If he had been able to communicate with his captors, Quintus would have offered to do what he could for the wounded, but the warriors paid no attention to his attempt to tell them by signs that he was a physician.

Some of the Britanni carried long oxhorn trumpets slung over their shoulders. Perhaps half an hour after they arrived in the grove a horn sounded, and shortly a strange procession filed into the grove.

First came four warriors even taller and fairer than those who had captured Quintus and the others. They seemed to be some kind of honor guard, for behind them walked an old man of massive build with a flowing gray beard and a shock of almost white hair. His face was like stone, and the eyes beneath heavy brows burned with a fanatic glare. Behind him were four other men, dressed as he was but obviously of lesser rank. All of them wore long flowing robes, girt about the waist with ordinary cord, and heavy sandals upon their feet.

The dress of the priest was in marked contrast to the warriors, who wore trousers of vivid colors patterned somewhat like the Eastern fashion which Quintus had noticed in Persia and among the northern Germanic tribes. Tunics of the same or different material hung almost to their knees. Their calves were bound about with strips of leather or cloth holding heavy sandals or low boots in place. The chief of the priests—for that was what he seemed to be—wore no ornament or symbols of rank, but his elevation above the others in importance was obvious, merely from his manner and the reverence paid him.

"He must be a leader of the druids," Joseph whispered to Quintus as the priest went to one side of the grove where the wounded had been placed. He stood looking down at the wounded young man whose station, judging by the deference and concern displayed by the others for him, must have been well above the level of the rest of the warriors.

"Perhaps he understands Latin," Quintus said hopefully. "If he comes near I will try to speak to him."

The chief druid had moved now and was looking down at the bodies laid out upon the ground. He paused there only a moment, however, then continued across the grove until he came to the strange stone circle and the altar. There he lifted his hands high and immediately all of the Britanni were silent, the only sound being the snuffling of the child the warrior had slapped that morning.

The druid's voice boomed out over the crowd, but the words were indistinguishable to Quintus. It seemed to be a tongue of many syllables, rippling sometimes like poetry as the old man continued to speak, now dropping to harsh notes that had a portent of doom. When he finished, the warriors who had been lounging around the grove—except a few guards surrounding the prisoners—moved briskly into the forest, apparently on some task he had set for them.

Having finished speaking, the druid finally turned his gaze toward the prisoners but did not come near. In desperation Quintus called in Latin loudly enough for him to hear.

"Sir," he said, "I would speak with you."

The old man gave no sign that he had either heard or understood, but Quintus continued to speak, hoping he understood Latin at least a little.

"I am a Roman," he said, "an officer in the army of Caesar." That word at least he judged would be familiar to the priest because of its connection with Julius Caesar, who must certainly be remembered here even if no other Roman was. "I bring greetings from the Emperor Gaius Caesar to King Cunobelinus."

The druid still gave no sign that he had either heard or understood, and in desperation Quintus pointed to the wounded men. *"Medicus!"* he shouted in Latin. "I am a physician."

One of the lesser druids seemed at least to understand the word, for he approached the massive old man and spoke quickly to him. The chief priest shook his head, but when the other continued to speak urgently he nodded finally. The younger druid then approached Quintus.

"Medicus?" he said in halting Latin, pointing to the wounded men. When Quintus nodded, he cut the thongs that bound his feet.

Quintus followed the younger priest across the grove to where the wounded had been placed. Even without instruments or medicines he was able to do a great deal for them. The young druid working with him had bright, intelligent eyes and none of the forbidding manner of the massive old chief priest who had led the procession into the grove, which Quintus judged to be some sort of a holy place. He knew only a few words of Latin, barely enough to tell Quintus that his name was Carnu. Just how much the druid understood of what he said Quintus could not be sure, but he poured out a stream of explanation while he worked, emphasizing the fact that he was a Roman officer on business for the emperor and that Veronica was his wife and

Joseph her uncle, their intention being to visit the king of the Britanni. In that way he hoped at least to get word of his identity to someone with enough authority to decide that the three of them should be released.

It took all of an hour to finish bandaging several wounds that were bleeding too freely, splint the broken bones, and apply dressings, made by tearing strips from the tunics of the wounded men, to a couple of broken heads. When he had finished, Quintus started toward the unconscious young man who had been placed away from the others. Before he could reach him, however, Carnu seized his arm.

"Non! Non!" This time the Latin was easily understandable—as was the fear in Carnu's face and his eyes when he turned to look at the chief priest. Quintus surmised that the older man was himself undertaking the care of this patient but could not see that anything had been done. The wounded man was unconscious and breathing stertorously, with no attention except a bloody bandage around his head. From the way he looked, Quintus was not at all certain that any medical skill could help the unconscious warrior, but he was anxious to remove the bandage and examine the wound.

Carnu had Quintus firmly by the elbow now and was guiding him back to where the other prisoners still huddled, waiting to see what would be their fate. *"Filius,"* he said stumblingly in Latin. *"Filius regni"*—which Quintus interpreted to mean that the unconscious warrior was the son of the king.

3

Quintus had been busy caring for the wounded and so had not noticed what was going on in the rest of the clearing. Now that he was back with the captives, he saw that the Britanni who had gone into the woods were bringing out bundles of faggots and several dead logs. These they had piled into a sort of platform before the strange circular altar with its stone ring.

Another group had brought in bundles of the tough withes that grew along the riverbank and were busy weaving them into a rectangular-shaped structure that looked like a cage.

"What about the wounded man over there?" Veronica asked. "The one by himself?"

"Carnu would not let me touch him. I gather that the old druid considers him his own special concern."

"He must be somebody important from the way they look after him."

"Carnu says he is the son of their king. From the way he looks, I'd say Britannia will soon be without a prince."

"Could you help him?"

"Carnu forbade me."

"Perhaps the veil might heal him."

"Did you bring it?"

She nodded. "I just had time to thrust it into the bosom of my stola before we left Gesoriacum."

"I'm sure they wouldn't let you use it yet," Quintus told her. "Apparently the old priest is going to carry out some sort of a ceremony."

The platform of logs was above a man's knees in height now, and the warriors were bringing in bundles of dry grass which they spread upon the top. As to the structure's ultimate function, there could not be much doubt any more. The grass and dry wood had obviously been selected because of their incendiary properties. Piled as they were in a rough platform—obviously something the Britanni had done many times before—there was no doubt about how quickly they would burn.

The wicker structure had now taken on the definite outline of a rectangular cage about three times as long as it was wide and roughly coffin shaped. It was almost complete, and the old priest spoke in a guttural voice, urging the men to hurry, for thunder was already muttering in the skies and a cloud which had been growing darker during the past hour was threatening to deluge the grove. The men worked feverishly, and in another half hour the wicker cage was finished.

At a command from the archdruid four of the Britanni next brought the litter upon which the wounded son of the king lay and placed it carefully on the altar beneath the ring of stones.

"Is he going to sacrifice the king's son?" Veronica asked incredulously.

"I think not." Quintus' eyes were upon a group of warriors who were carrying the coffin-shaped cage of withes to the platform built of dry logs and grass. Carefully they placed it upon the logs, making sure it rested solidly there. One corner of the cage had been left open so it could act as a gate, yet be tied shut easily.

Quintus heard Veronica catch her breath and knew that at last she realized the significance of the platform and the cage. That any people could be so barbarous and cruel as to burn others to death was something she could hardly believe—until she saw with her own eyes the final preparations for it. Her shoulder pressed against him, as if she sought to obtain strength from it, but he could do nothing else to reassure her.

The massive old druid had begun to pray in the strange liquid, flowing tongue that was like poetry or the tones of a group of horns of varied pitch. The warrior guards were going through the group of prisoners now, seizing first the old and wounded. One of them took Joseph of Arimathea by the shoulder, and Quintus moved to resist. Before he could reach the old merchant, however, Joseph moved a few steps away from the group of prisoners.

"For Veronica's sake don't resist, Quintus," he begged. "They are sacrificing one of us for each of those who were killed."

Quintus remembered now hearing the Gauls of Gesoriacum tell of barbaric rites presided over by the druids of Britannia in their sacred groves where prisoners captured in battle but not suitable for slaves were burned alive as an offering to the druidic gods, apparently on the theory that, were one life substituted for another, the fallen one could live again in another form.

"I am old," Joseph continued in the same urgent voice. "If they take me, you and Veronica may live."

The two Britanni who were holding the old merchant jerked him toward the wicker cage. Veronica started toward her uncle, but Quintus managed to hold her back. As Joseph had said, his sacrifice might save Veronica, and Quintus must save his own life if he could in order to protect her.

One by one the old and the wounded were separated from the little band of captives huddled in the shade of the tall oaks, led or dragged across the open space by their captors, and thrust into the wicker cage. Around it guards stood with spears ready to prod through the framework at any who tried to tear the tough withes of which it was made. Joseph had entered first, walking proudly. Now he stood within the cage, comforting the poor wretches who cringed in terror all around him.

And then a strange thing happened, for, as if Joseph's courage and his faith had communicated itself to them, the doomed Gauls grew quiet.

"I speak to you of One, the Son of God, who gave his life for you." Joseph spoke to them in Latin with his eyes shining. "Believe in him and his willingness to give you life after death and you shall dwell with him forever."

Those in the cage were quiet now—save for the sobbing of a few of the women—as they listened to his words. Even the druids were staring at Joseph perplexedly, but the chief priest, his eyes fixed upon the clouds overhead, was still intoning a ritual over the inert body of the wounded young warrior, whether praying or invoking the power of their gods to heal, Quintus had no way of knowing.

Reaching what seemed to be a point of pause in his oration, the archdruid lowered his head and fixed his eyes upon the cage. Suddenly his manner changed and his voice crackled out angrily. Quintus still could not understand the words, but the meaning was clear enough. There were not enough victims inside the wicker cage, and the reason was immediately apparent.

210

Those inside it had been selected to make up the same number as the dead Britanni lying under the trees. The old druid was demanding still another sacrifice, however, a sacrifice for the unconscious body of the king's son lying upon the altar before him.

Quintus saw the chief priest's eyes move along the group of captives and stop. He was sure the old man's burning gaze was upon him and stood firmly erect, hoping he would have the courage to go to his death as bravely as had Joseph of Arimathea, fortified by the knowledge that Veronica, at least, would be allowed to live.

But it was not Quintus the warriors seized when the old priest spoke. Instead one of them took Veronica by her hair, pulling her away before Quintus could make a move. The reason for selecting her was obvious, had Quintus thought of it. The old and the wounded among the prisoners were already in the wicker cage. There remained only men, always valuable as slaves, women, equally so because of their ability to procreate, and children who would soon grow to valuable size. Gallic women were tall and strong—it had been said that in the old days they were as fierce in battle as their husbands. Of all the women prisoners, only Veronica was slender and therefore in the eyes of the Britanni weak, compared to these tall and vigorous people. Thus she was of much less importance as a slave than the others and an obvious choice for sacrifice.

Quintus tried to thrust himself between her and the guards, but the way was blocked. As he turned upon his captors, determined to go with Veronica or die in an attempt to save her, he saw his wife march proudly with her head high toward the wicker cage. And he understood that she was choosing to give herself without resistance in order that he might live.

As Quintus struggled with his captors, one of them brought the butt of a spear down upon his temple. The first blow only stunned him, and he still kept trying to reach Veronica as she entered the wicker cage and went to stand beside Joseph.

Four men with burning torches from a fire which had been kindled to one side now thrust them into the heart of the wooden platform. They were evidently in a hurry to begin the conflagration because of the clouds that hung overhead. The dry sticks and faggots burst into flames which leaped up, shutting away from Quintus' agonized gaze the little group huddled in the midst of their own funeral pyre. He had a final glimpse of Joseph and Veronica standing in the wicker cage, eyes uplifted to the sky and praying as the flames licked about them. Then the butt of a spear struck him a second time and he sagged to the ground, unconscious.

4

Driven by the urge to help Veronica, or at least to join her in the final agony, Quintus struggled to rise. But only darkness met his gaze now, and he found that he was tied hand and foot so he could hardly move. Exhausted from struggling, he finally lay back, gasping for breath while his body dipped and swayed as if in a giant swing.

When he could think intelligently, he realized that he was lying in the bottom of a wagon or cart being driven along the road. Above him dark clouds scudded across the face of a pallid moon and jagged streaks of fire lanced back and forth across the heavens, while thunder muttered in the distance. As to how long ago the vehicle bearing him had left the grove where Veronica and Joseph had died in the flames, he had no idea. He barely remembered the last blow from the butt of the guard's spear, but he was sure he would never forget the picture of Veronica, sweet, slender, and proud, as she stood in the wicker cage with Joseph while the flames rose around them.

After a while Quintus slept. When he awoke it was dawn and the cart was moving through the narrow streets of a town. Finally it stopped, and tall men who wore no weapons lifted the board on which he lay and carried him with the others into an open courtyard, leaving them in the shade of a porch or arcade.

For a little while nothing happened, then a woman brought him water and a rich hot gruel which he ate. At the moment he still would have welcomed death if it meant any probability of joining Veronica in that eternal life in which she and Joseph believed so devoutly. But the urge to live overcame even the wish to die, and he soon began to feel strength creeping back into his bruised and battered body.

Perhaps an hour later the priest called Carnu appeared, moving among the wounded and obviously searching for someone. The druid's face lit up when he saw Quintus, and he came at once to kneel beside him.

Quintus raised himself upon one elbow, although the effort sent pain lancing through his head and made him feel dizzy. The vertigo lasted only a moment, however, by which he judged he had suffered no serious injury to his skull. In severe cases where the skull bone was cracked like an egg he had seen men stumble about half blind, or wholly so, for the rest of their lives. And he was thankful that, if he had to be spared, he was at least reasonably whole.

That his future as a slave of the cruel and barbaric Britanni would be in any degree pleasant Quintus did not for a moment believe. People who burned their captives alive for no reason, save in retaliation for their own dead in a raid where they had themselves been the aggressor, could not be very civilized and so could not be expected to treat slaves with any degree of leniency. At the moment, however, he was much more concerned with trying to find out from Carnu what had happened to Veronica and Joseph. Actually he was certain they could not be alive, but he could at least hope that death had come quickly and mercifully to them on the pyre where he had last seen them, with the flames leaping at their bodies.

Carnu's knowledge of Latin proved inadequate to the task, however. He only shook his head when Quintus made signs to him with his hands that he wished to know how Veronica and Joseph had died. The young

213

druid did help him to sit up, however, and, when the vertigo had lessened a little, get to his feet. Supported by his new friend, Quintus managed to walk a few steps into the house itself.

It was large and rambling, little more than a series of simple *casae,* such as the less wealthy Romans built, joined together by roofed passageways. The room to which Carnu took Quintus was almost monastic in its simplicity, being furnished only with a rude couch, a table on which was a water bottle and cup, and a rough chair with a frame made of wood covered with a tanned skin. Light came from a single window high up on the wall.

Quintus guessed this must be Carnu's own quarters and was happy to lie down on the couch after the exertion of moving into the building. Carnu directed him by signs to wait there and disappeared.

Quintus dozed off but awoke when the door opened, and sat up. A gaunt man with cadaverous cheeks, deep-set eyes, and snow-white hair preceded the druid into the room. He wore no regal trappings, but Quintus did not doubt for a moment that he was a person of authority. Quintus tried to get to his feet but swayed, and the gaunt man put his hand on his shoulder and gently pushed him back. He spoke in rather poor Latin, but Quintus was able to understand him without much difficulty.

"Who are you?" he inquired.

"Quintus Volusianus, tribune in the armies of Rome."

"You have the look of a Roman," the old man said. "I am Cunobelinus, king of the Britanni."

Quintus was startled to find himself in the presence of the king who was reputed to be the most powerful man in Britannia.

"Keep to your couch," Cunobelinus said when he tried to rise again. "Did you receive your wound in battle with my sons?"

"I was captured with my wife and her uncle," Quintus told him. "They were burned alive by your priests, and I was wounded when I tried to help them."

Cunobelinus glanced at Carnu who spoke rapidly in

214

his own language, apparently in confirmation of the statement. "The druids sacrifice captives in retribution for the lives of those who are killed," the king said.

"You are all a part of the Roman Empire," Quintus dared to say. "Why do the Britanni fight the Gauls when there is peace between them?"

Cunobelinus looked at him gravely. "You are a brave man—or a rash one—thus to address a king."

"Only because you seem just," Quintus said. "Would you expect me to feel grateful to those who burned my wife and her uncle alive?"

Cunobelinus nodded thoughtfully. "The druids are powerful, almost as powerful as kings, but Commius acted in good faith. He sought to save my son Adminius by giving a life in his stead."

"Is your son dead?"

"His body is warm and his heart still beats, but his soul is elsewhere."

"I am a physician," Quintus told him. "I would have attended your son, but the priest you call Commius would not let me."

"Could you help him?"

"I don't know."

"Are you willing to try now?"

"I will do what I can," Quintus said. "I could see in the grove that he was gravely wounded."

Cunobelinus nodded gravely. "Adminius has not improved. Carnu thinks he grows weaker."

"Where is your son now?" Quintus asked.

"In a room not far from here. Commius is with him."

"Send the priest away and I will attend your son."

Cunobelinus shook his head. "You do not understand, Roman. Here even a king cannot order the chief of the druids to do other than he wishes."

"Let us go to him, then."

The king's wounded son lay in a large sunny room on a couch. One glance told Quintus Adminius had not improved since he had last seen him on the stone altar in what Cunobelinus had called the Grove of the Druids. He was still in a stupor and his breathing was stertorous in character. An elderly woman sat beside the couch, her eyes red from weeping. Beside her was a younger woman. The latter he judged to be the young prince's wife or his sister.

The chief druid called Commius stood at one side of the room looking out of the window. When he turned, Quintus saw that his face held the same rock-like impassivity and his deep-set eyes burned with the same fanatic zeal which had characterized them in the Grove of the Druids.

Cunobelinus spoke respectfully to the druid in their own language. At first the old priest shook his head vigorously. As the king continued to speak, his face became even more grim and his eyes blazed with a look of anger. Finally he spoke ponderously.

The king's face was troubled when he turned back to Quintus. "Commius says Adminius will recover, if it be the will of the gods."

"Then he cannot object to my treating him," Quintus said.

Cunobelinus spoke again to Commius, and Quintus saw the druid's eyes blaze with anger. Obviously the priest had not expected to have his argument turned against him. He spoke again, this time even more fiercely.

"You may treat my son," the king said soberly at the end of what appeared to be a diatribe, "but Commius insists that your life shall be forfeit as a sacrifice if he dies."

"He murdered my wife," Quintus said angrily. "Is that not enough?"

"Commius is guided by what he believes to be the commands of the gods he serves," Cunobelinus explained. "They may not be just commands, but he must obey them."

"Ask him if there is any chance that my wife is alive?" Quintus inquired.

The king transmitted the request to the priest, but the old man only shook his massive head. "He ordered her killed to help speed the souls of the men who died to another life and to save my son."

"Promise to send Carnu to the Grove of the Druids

216

for my wife's body, or what is left of it, and I will examine Adminius," Quintus told the king. "If I believe I can help him, I will place my life in jeopardy as a forfeit."

Again Cunobelinus translated for the old druid, who nodded. "He agrees, but only to please me," the king announced. "See to Adminius, Roman, and tell me if there is any hope."

5

Quintus began his examination by removing the bloodstained bandage from the prince's head. The wound was not in itself very severe; he had sutured hundreds like it for soldiers of the legions. The bleeding had stopped, and when he separated the edges he could see the bone in the depths of the wound, indicating that the cut had gone completely through the scalp. The wound had been made, he judged, by the butt of a spear handle, driven down as a bludgeon, a weapon capable of knocking a man out with one blow—as he well knew from his experience in the Grove of the Druids.

Holding the cut edges of the scalp apart, Quintus explored the depths of the wound with his finger. Almost immediately he perceived a crack in the skull where it had been broken by the wooden spear handle. The edge toward the inner side of the half-circular pattern made by the round wooden bludgeon was depressed so as to form a small steplike area. As his finger continued to follow the crack in the bone, he discovered that the inner side of the circular pattern was more and more depressed. At the extreme portion of its depth a section of bone had been driven down upon the brain underneath for almost the entire thickness of the skull.

Quintus had seen these wounds before and the symptom pattern that resulted from them; the king's son was no exception. The pulse was always slow and full, with an almost bounding beat, the respirations were slow, and the chin and tongue relaxed from the paralysis that went with this type of wound. In the case of Adminius the injury was on the left side of the head and, characteristically, the entire right side was paralyzed, the muscles limp and flabby. The left side, by contrast, was almost stiff; even his gentle movement of Adminius' arms and legs during the examination caused them to jerk almost spasmodically, although there was no sign of returning consciousness.

When Quintus finished, he looked up to see the eyes of the king and the two women fixed upon him. Commius was staring out of the window again, the disapproving set of his massive shoulders under the gray robe eloquently proclaiming his disapproval of Quintus' presence.

"What do you think?" Cunobelinus asked eagerly.

"Your son is gravely ill. The bone of his head has been driven down upon the brain beneath it. Unless that pressure is relieved, he will not recover."

Commius spoke ponderously from the window, the syllables rolling out with a harsh, guttural quality.

"He says you lie," Cunobelinus translated with a troubled face. "Adminius has earned the displeasure of the gods." He stopped for a moment before going on, then spoke more quickly. "My youngest son favors the Romans."

"And you?" Quintus asked.

"I am an old man. My sons will soon rule here, so they must decide for themselves where their allegiance lies."

"Is Commius against Rome?"

"Yes. His grandfather was killed in the time of Julius Caesar, and his family swore eternal vengeance then against all Romans."

"Will you let your son die because of an ancient grudge?" Quintus asked.

Cunobelinus looked troubled. "I know nothing of healing. It is hard for me to understand what has happened."

Quintus looked around the room. At first he saw nothing like what he was looking for, then he noted a

218

small wooden box on a table at one side of the room, such a box as a woman might use to hold her jewels. Picking up the box, Quintus emptied the jewels it contained on the table.

"Have someone bring me a spear," he directed.

Cunobelinus spoke to a servant who stood by the door. The man returned in a moment carrying a spear with a heavy wooden handle. Putting the box on the floor, Quintus brought the butt end of the spear sharply down upon the box. As he had calculated, a semicircular piece of wood was punched out and driven downward like a flap, projecting into the interior of the box. Handing the spear back to the servant, Quintus brought the box to Cunobelinus and showed him the punched-out area. It was almost exactly the same size and shape as the depression he'd discovered in the bone of Adminius' skull. Opening the box, he showed how the section of wood that had been punched out would exert pressure upon anything inside the box.

"The bone pressing upon the brain has paralyzed your son," he explained once again, "just as anything inside this box would be pressed upon. Unless the bone is lifted up as I will lift up this piece of wood"—taking the spear from the servant, he inserted the point beneath the edge of the wood and lifted it back into place —"he cannot recover."

Commius, Quintus saw, had watched the demonstration. He said nothing, however, to indicate that he was impressed by it.

"Can you heal him?" Cunobelinus asked.

"I will try—if you will carry out your end of the agreement."

"Carnu will leave for the grove as soon as you are finished," the king assured him.

"I will need some special tools," Quintus said. "Have you an armorer and a cabinetmaker in the palace?"

"Yes. They will give you whatever you need."

Quintus looked over the armorer's tools but had trouble finding what he sought. Finally he moved on to the adjoining shop of the woodworker and there discovered a set of chisels made of bronze, a metal favored by the Britanni. These he appropriated along with a slender tool shaped like a lever with one end ground down almost like a chisel. They were poor substitutes for his own instruments, which he'd left at Gesoriacum, but they would have to serve.

"I will need help," Quintus told Cunobelinus when he came back with the instruments. "Carnu, if he will serve."

Carnu glanced quickly at Commius. When the chief druid made no objection, he stepped to the side of the couch where Adminius lay and began to roll up the sleeves of his gown. The young druid was a little pale, but his hands were steady and Quintus was sure he could depend upon him.

Deftly Quintus cut away the bandage he had replaced around Adminius' head at the end of the examination and laid it aside. He had torn a piece of clean cloth into pieces roughly the size of his hand and gave some of these to Carnu to use in sponging away the blood that tended to seep into the wound. Next he showed his assistant how to separate the edges of the skin so he could see into the depths of the wound. These preparations completed, he took up one of the chisels and, holding it almost parallel to the skull itself, began to chip and scrape against the outer surface of the bone at the edge of the half circle where it was driven downward.

It took fully a quarter of an hour for Quintus to chip a shallow opening in the bone of the skull at the edge of the semicircular depressed area. When finally he had cut completely through the bone at this level, he was able to see the membrane underneath. It was discolored and some dark bloody fluid welled up through the opening, signs which did not particularly augur well for the success of his surgery.

Next he took up the small bronze lever. On the effectiveness of this, he knew, could well depend his success or failure in elevating the depressed fragment of bone. Working carefully, he slipped the end of the narrow piece of bronze into the opening he'd made through the skull and worked it beneath the edge of the depressed section of skull. When he had obtained a firm purchase there, he began to exert pressure upon the other end as a lever. At first nothing happened, then a faint cracking sound was heard.

The young woman at the foot of the couch was sobbing with her head on the couch against her husband's feet. Cunobelinus was staring with worried eyes at the wound in his son's skull. Commius had not even turned to look, however, but stood at the window, his massive body rigid with disapproval at this tampering with what he obviously considered the will of the gods.

Steadily and slowly Quintus increased his pressure upon the slender bronze lever, moving it slowly about while he sought to find a spot where the bone could be most easily freed. The depressed fragment was being elevated under the continued pressure, but progress was very slow. Finally the edges where the bone had broken seemed to grate together and lock, for Quintus was not able to elevate it any further, even though he pressed upon the lever so heavily that he could almost feel it bend.

This was the crucial part of the whole operation, for unless he was successful in elevating the depressed bone to its normal position—or perhaps to remove it altogether, an exceedingly difficult procedure—he would have accomplished nothing.

Then just as the lever was starting to bend there was a loud crack. The semicircular section of bone split into two pieces and, with the easing of the locking effect where the broken edges of the bone met, the fragment popped up to its normal level. The surface of the skull was reasonably smooth now, save for the cracks through the bone marking the outlines where it had been driven down upon the brain and the opening he'd chipped through the skull in order to get beneath it.

Quintus steadied himself against the couch, suddenly conscious of how near he was to complete exhaustion. Sweat was pouring off his face and his head was throbbing steadily. A quantity of dark-colored fluid gushed through the place where he had scraped an opening in the skull, but there was none of the bright red flow that would have indicated a fresh source of bleeding beneath the edge of the bone wound.

He waited a moment and when there was no more bleeding motioned to Carnu to release the skin edges. Drawing them together, he applied a pad of cloth which he bandaged into place. The surgery itself was finished; what happened next was in the hands of fate.

6

The days that followed were difficult ones for Quintus. He had hoped for some immediate sign that his surgery had been effective, most logically a disappearance of the paralysis. The king's son lay unconscious, however, still breathing stertorously and apparently without any improvement whatsoever. The fact that his pulse remained steady and strong was the only encouraging sign. Even Hippocrates had recognized the importance of the state of the pulse in such conditions, and the great Celsus had stoutly maintained that it was a valuable indication of the condition of the body in general, an observation in which Quintus, drawing upon his own experience, concurred. Nevertheless he would have liked some more encouraging evidence of progress.

Quintus' depression of spirit was deepened when Carnu returned a few days later with news that a violent storm had arisen on the night when Joseph and Veronica had been burned in the wicker cage in the Grove of the Druids, washing away all trace of their ashes. The fact that cage and platform had been totally destroyed by the flames removed any faint hope he might have had that they were alive. He could only resign himself now to living alone—if indeed he were lucky enough to live at all with the sentence of death hanging over him should Adminius not recover.

While they took turns watching beside the couch upon which the king's son lay, Quintus set out to augment as much as he could the young druid's command of Latin. Carnu proved an apt pupil and learned rapidly. Soon they were able to converse fairly intelligibly in the language. Carnu in turn taught Quintus the tongue of Britannia, or at least that part of it ruled by Cunobelinus. It was not a happy period for Quintus, however, waiting to learn whether his life would be forfeit, while his grief over the loss of Veronica was still like a physical pain in his heart.

And then, when almost a week had passed, Adminius suddenly moved his right leg. Encouraged by this, Quintus dared to hope for the first time. When the next day the fingers of the sick man's right hand curled around those of his wife as she sat beside him, it seemed that a turn for the better had indeed taken place.

Shortly after the surgery the ooze of dark fluid through the opening in the skull had been rather marked and Quintus had been forced to change the dressing quite frequently. By the time Adminius flexed his right foot, however, the flow had become almost clear and had lessened considerably in quantity, showing that the wound to the deeper structures was healing. In the next few days the wounded man moved both arm and hand frequently, while at the same time the irritability of his left side decreased.

Two weeks from the occurrence of the wound Adminius opened his eyes one morning and smiled at his wife. His face was still drawn toward one side and the smile was so crooked as to be almost a grimace, but it did seem to indicate that he was near to regaining his senses. The day afterward he spoke his wife's name and late that afternoon was able to swallow broth with evident relish.

From then on Adminius' recovery was marked. In three more days he was able to sit up in the sun. His right side was still weaker than the left and at first he tended to drag his right foot when he walked, but this improved so rapidly that Quintus was fairly certain all vestige of paralysis would eventually disappear.

Now that he could speak Latin fairly well, Carnu was able to tell Quintus something of the history of Cunobelinus and the growth of his kingdom. Never really united, the Britanni had consisted of many small tribes at the time of Caesar's invasion of the island a little less than a hundred years before. Warring with each other most of the time, these tribes had not been able to make any effective resistance against the Romans and so had fallen before Caesar's legions. There had been no real conquest of the island in the actual sense of the word, however. Caesar had merely exacted tribute, and some of the kings had willingly paid it in order to obtain trade from Rome and get the Romans out of Britannia.

Over a period of years Cunobelinus had unified the warring tribes of the eastern coastal region of Britannia and from his chief city at Camulodunum—located not far inland from the coast line and a little north of the narrowest part of the Fretum Gallicum—had gradually welded the southern Britanni into one people. He had proved a wise ruler, fierce in battle but realizing that, if his subjects were to prosper and increase their strength to the point where they would not become a prey to any invader, they must learn the ways which their kinsmen of Gaul to the east had come to learn, as well as Roman colonies elsewhere. He had therefore given at least lip service to Rome, paying a small tribute and maintaining the illusion of allegiance to the empire. It had been a profitable arrangement until recently, when a number of factors had occurred to trouble his peaceful reign.

One of these had been the old king's illness, now of several years' duration and giving every evidence of causing his death before much more than another year passed. Another, and even more important, factor was the growing objections of the powerful druids to anything resembling co-operation with Rome. Among the upper class of Celts in Britannia, Quintus learned in his talks with Carnu and Adminius, the knights from whom came the rulers and the druids who made up the priesthood were held in highest respect and honor. The knights were entrusted with government and warfare, while the druids were concerned with all things spiritual and mental. As priests directing the worship of the various tribal gods of the Britanni, the druids had charge of all public and private sacrifices, interpreted sacred omens, and set down the religious laws. Even more important, they supervised the training and education of the young men and so were able to implant their own philosophies into young and impressionable minds.

The great power of the druids came from other sources too, mainly their judicial authority and freedom from all taxes. As judges they decided all disputes, whether personal or public, and even between tribes when such were not settled by the sword. When a crime was committed—even so grave a charge as murder—the druids could name the penalty, except that they could not impose a death sentence. Worse, almost, they could forbid one found guilty of a crime to take part in any religious activity. And since the druids taught eternal life for those who served the gods well, this excommunication, so to speak, could mean eternal death. Persons under the sentence of excommunication were regarded as accursed by all others and were refused the right of congress with other men, lest the contagion of their crime spread abroad.

Since the druids were free of all taxes, they had accumulated over the centuries a vast amount of property whose income went to them alone. In fact, it was widely accepted that Commius, who as leader or archdruid held all such property, was the richest man in the kingdom, his worth exceeding even that of Cunobelinus.

The lore of the druids, Quintus learned, was never set down in writing but was committed to memory by the younger priests in the process of their education. Once they had elected to follow the priesthood, all were forced to swear dire oaths not to reveal any of it save to young men studying in the druidic schools.

The reason why Veronica and Joseph had been burned to death was explained by Carnu. Disease, defeat in war, and other such unhappy events were interpreted by the priests as evidence of the displeasure of the gods. Those who died under such conditions were

225

deprived of the gift of eternal life, unless another life was sacrificed in their stead. It was customary whenever a man died of wounds, therefore, to sacrifice another person in his stead—a captive if available—so his soul would be ransomed and could live on. For this purpose the strange wicker cages were constructed, sometimes in the form of great images. Into them the victims were driven and fire set to destroy them in the druidical rite known as *holocaust*.

The hatred of the archdruid Commius for anything Roman was further explained by the fact that in Gaul, across the Fretum Gallicum to the east, the authority of Rome had all but driven out all druidical power and worship. With the druids no longer in power, their influence in Gaul had waned rapidly and their properties had been lost, much of it having been appropriated by Romans. That much the same thing would occur if Rome undertook a successful conquest of Britannia seemed a natural conclusion.

Although a member of the palace retinue and free to go and come within its confines, Quintus was still a slave. As such he did not have the freedom of the city and in fact had not yet set foot outside the king's palace. He had seen little of King Cunobelinus since the first day when he had operated upon Adminius and was surprised one day to receive a summons to wait upon the king.

Cunobelinus received him courteously. "I have not troubled you about myself, Quintus," he said, "because you were occupied with Adminius. But being a physician, you have no doubt noticed that I am far from well."

"I have noticed it," Quintus agreed. "And have been concerned."

"Thank you. Now that your skill has given my son's life back to me, I want to ask your advice concerning myself."

Quintus made an examination of the king and asked a few pointed questions. The picture was a familiar one, swelling of the ankles and belly with difficulty in breathing, especially upon any exertion. He'd seen it often enough in older men in Rome, a chronic condition that grew slowly worse and always ended in death.

"Tell me the truth," Cunobelinus said. "How long can I live?"

"Several years, if you are careful. The disease progresses very slowly."

"But it always progresses?"

"In my experience."

The old king seemed not particularly disturbed by what Quintus had told him, probably because he had arrived at the same conclusion of his own accord. "You are an honest man," he said. "You could easily have painted a brighter picture for me in the hope of gaining favor for yourself."

"As a physician I have sworn to tell the truth," Quintus reminded him.

"I am sorry about your wife and her uncle," the king continued. "Commius was acting according to our beliefs when he sacrificed your wife in an attempt to save the life of my son. Some day, if you are ever called upon to take a life to save a life, you may understand."

Quintus could not help remembering something he'd heard Joseph teach about Jesus of Nazareth. "He gave his own life that others might live through him," Joseph had said. Veronica must have felt the same way in the fire of the druids, he realized now, when she had willingly given her own life, lest he be selected as a sacrifice.

He was beginning to understand, too, why those who followed the Galilean healer were willing to make the ultimate sacrifice for others as they believed Jesus had done for them. They were motivated by the certainty that, through giving up their own lives, they would live eternally with the man they called the Master after death.

In that moment Quintus knew he was nearer to the faith of Veronica and Joseph than he had ever been before. And yet something still held him back, a feeling of resentment rather than forgiveness toward the men who had destroyed Veronica's beauty and her life with fire, plus a sense of logic which insisted there was no parallel between the cruel and depraved worship of the druids and the qualities which the Galilean had taught the world.

"I owe you the life of my son." The voice of Cunobelinus brought Quintus' thoughts back to the present. "So I have no right to demand anything of you. But as a father and a dying man, I can ask a favor."

"You forget that I am your slave and must obey."

"You are a slave in name only," Cunobelinus corrected him. "For the moment it is safer for you to remain a royal slave. But when the right time comes, I will give you your freedom and send you back to Rome if that is your wish."

"Are you protecting me from Commius?" Quintus asked.

Cunobelinus nodded. "Those in the palace here know Adminius was actually saved by your skill alone and not by any intervention from the gods who had failed already. For that reason Commius would have you killed, if I did not protect you. Even if I freed you now, I doubt if he would let you leave the city alive because you could tell the Romans I am dying and my sons are already quarreling among themselves over how my kingdom shall be divided."

This last Quintus knew to be true. Cunobelinus had three sons, with Caractacus, the eldest, chief claimant to the throne. The second son, Catarses, was generally considered weak and a braggart, following his older brother in everything. Only Adminius, the youngest, seemed to have inherited the real qualities of his father in that he thought more of the welfare of the people and of improving the kingdom than the glory of warfare and battle.

"Caractacus is strong-willed and powerful in battle as I was in my youth," Cunobelinus continued, "but who can say that these are not the best qualities for a young king? With them he can extend the boundaries of his realm and bring much wealth in the form of booty to his people. Adminius, on the other hand, is thoughtful and not inclined to battle. Such a king may wisely rule over a domain so large that it need not be expanded

228

and insure the happiness of his people. I do not know which is best and so I let my sons contend among themselves to see who will ultimately be the strongest, believing it is better for this conflict to take place while I am still alive than after my death."

The old king paused to get his breath, and Quintus went to a small inlaid taboret and poured him a cup of wine from a jug standing there.

"Drop a pinch of the leaves from the small box there into the wine," Cunobelinus directed. "The medicine was given me by an old woman from the country. She says her family has used it for generations."

Quintus did as he was bidden. The drug seemed nothing more than the dried leaves of a weed, but as a physician he was always interested in anything of this kind.

"Does it relieve the pain?" he asked when Cunobelinus had finished drinking.

The king shook his head. "I have little pain. The leaves seem to dry up the waters in my body and cause them to be expelled."

Here was a strange thing indeed, Quintus thought, one he must look into when he had an opportunity.

"Forgive an old man for talking so long," Cunobelinus said. "I was speaking of a favor you can do me."

"You need only to ask," Quintus assured him.

"Adminius is intelligent. He thinks problems out, where Caractacus and his brother rush in and try to bludgeon their way through. Your country and your armies are powerful. When your soldiers are no longer needed to put down the Germani, they will look across what you call the Fretum Gallicum. It was largely to discover whether or not they have already begun to do this that I allowed Caractacus to make the raids on Gaul."

"But you found no sign of invasion?"

"The time may not be right. My father told me how the soldiers under Julius Caesar cut down our people like grain in the field, and I hope that will not happen again. If the Romans find a wise ruler here, willing to subject himself to the authority of your emperor so we may have the tools and skills you possess, physicians to heal our sick and plows to till our soil, there will be no need to kill and lay waste the land."

"Adminius could be that king."

"If he is strong enough to take control at my death. Carnu has been my son's tutor. He has done what he can, but he lacks your knowledge of the world to the east of us. I would have you work with him and teach Adminius what he needs to know: how your emperor governs his people wisely and holds them together without war; how roads are built and ships that carry great cargoes for long distances. But most of all I would have you teach him to be a man of integrity and courage."

"Like his father?"

Cunobelinus smiled. "I am vain enough to think that, but I had in mind another."

"Who?"

"Yourself."

Quintus suddenly felt very humble and unworthy. When he spoke his voice was somewhat husky with emotion.

"I am the son of a Greek freedman who became a citizen of Rome," he told Cunobelinus. "No noble blood flows in my body."

The king shrugged. "I was only a petty chief, until I pushed myself upward. What a man really is shines in his face and is proved by his actions. Believe me, I know what I am doing when I set you up as a model for my son."

"Be sure I will not fail you then," Quintus said humbly.

"Take care that you work always with Carnu," the old king warned. "Only the druids are supposed to teach things concerning the spirit. Commius will oppose you, especially if you seek to turn Adminius from our gods."

"If I believe in any god," Quintus told him, "he is far away at the other end of what we Romans call 'Our Sea.' I do not think he will come to Britannia."

The task of training Adminius in Roman ways proved easier and more pleasant than Quintus had anticipated. The youngest son of Cunobelinus was intelligent and eager to learn, an apt pupil and a delight to any teacher. Quintus wished for textbooks, but that would have entailed teaching his pupil to read Latin, a long and involved process. Adminius learned quickly an elementary form of Latin, however, and Quintus began to speak the language used here at Camulodunum, so they soon were able to communicate freely. Actually there were almost as many dialects in the tongue of the Britanni as there were tribes scattered over the island, and only here in the kingdom of Cunobelinus was there anything resembling a common tongue.

Each day Quintus spent several hours explaining to Adminius and Carnu the mysteries of the world and its geography, the distribution of the people who inhabited different parts of it, and their customs. Since Adminius might have to lead an armed force if it came to actual conflict between himself and his brother Caractacus, Quintus also undertook to instruct him in the art of war, the training of a Roman soldier, his methods of fighting, and the strategy that had won battles and carried the golden eagles of Rome to the far corners of the world, including the coast of Aquitania to the south, the wild country of the Germani in the north, and the vast space called Arabia Deserta to the east. Adminius also possessed a considerably mechanical bent, so Quintus was able to familiarize him with the engines of war which Roman armies had long used to send terror into the hearts of savage peoples.

Between sessions on geography and the art of war Quintus also managed to impart to his pupil some of the teachings of the great philosophers among the Greeks, particularly lessons on man's obligations to man. But he was on less sure ground here since he had never spent much time in such studies. Carnu was eager to learn what he could about the art of healing and kept peppering Quintus with questions whenever they were together.

Even more than in the arts of war—where it must be admitted he proved only a moderate student—Adminius was interested in commerce and trade, the skills of the artisans who made things hardly ever dreamed of in Britannia, tools for working wood and metal, implements for farming, and new crops that might bring additional sources of food. And being naturally observant, Quintus had much to tell from his observations over the world.

As the months passed, Quintus became convinced that Cunobelinus had truly evaluated the characters of his two sons. Caractacus seemed to have inherited the belligerency, the courage, and the dynamic qualities which had made his father a great military leader and had enabled him to consolidate, conquer, and assimilate a kingdom where before there had been only warring tribesmen. But there was a pronounced streak of cruelty and savagery in the older prince which his father did not possess. Adminius, on the other hand —perhaps because he was much younger than Caractacus—had seemed to inherit the qualities which had also made Cunobelinus a great ruler—wisdom, understanding, and a deep concern for the welfare of his people in every aspect of their lives.

Just such a ruler as Adminius would be—Quintus thought—was needed by the Romans. Instead they either were given great soldiers who were poor administrators or, like Caligula, dissolute wastrels representing only the worst of human qualities.

Quintus was learning, too, for as Adminius improved he took his tutor farther and farther afield. Camulodunum near the seacoast had been chosen as his seat by Cunobelinus because it was the chief town of the Trinovantes, the strongest tribe conquered by him in his early campaign. Here he minted the coins that went far to cement his kingdom together by giving all people a common medium of exchange in the entire southern section of Britannia, encompassing what had originally been the lands of the Catauvellauni, the Trinovantes, and the Cantii.

Camulodunum was a fair-sized city including, Quintus estimated, about six legions of people. Many of the streets were paved with stone blocks in the Roman manner, and some of the houses, like the king's palace, were fairly luxurious. The capital of the kingdom, it was a busy place, and the minting of coins gave work to a fair number of people, as did keeping the tax records and the affairs of the druids who had one of their most important schools here.

Some distance to the southwest another city was growing much more rapidly than the capital and was bidding fair to exceed it in size. Located on the river Tamesis that gave it a protected harbor and still afforded access to the sea, the city of Londinium was a thriving commercial center. Here on occasion came ships from even as far as distant Alexandria in Egypt, exchanging glassware, jewelry, pottery, and other products from the entire Mediterranean coast for tin, wool, lead, and other raw materials.

Through these vessels the Britanni were afforded at least a glimpse of the teaming world outside their island fortress. But it was no more than a glimpse, and the knowledge brought with the ships rarely got much farther than the water front of Londinium itself. Much of this difficulty in speeding up communications with the Roman world, Quintus was sure, came from the opposition of the druids, particularly Commius, to anything having to do with Rome.

And so a year passed with Quintus hardly noting its passage. Busy as he was with the instruction of Adminius, his sorrow over the loss of Veronica had been gradually dulled without his becoming aware of it. He still thought of her, particularly when he had time to walk in the gardens which Cunobelinus maintained and thought how much she would have enjoyed the flowers. When this happened the pain was sometimes so great that he thought he could not bear it. But when he was physically busy training Adminius in the arts of war

233

or instructing both him and Carnu, there was little time to grieve.

Quintus saw little of Caractacus, who spent most of his time hunting or engaging in the border clashes with neighboring tribes that still went on and in raids across the channel. That the oldest son of Cunobelinus had little use for him Quintus did not for a moment doubt. His activities on behalf of Adminius could be interpreted only as what they undoubtedly were, preparing the youngest brother for the time when the final decision would be made as to who would rule the kingdom. Quintus made no motion to offend Caractacus when he was at home, giving him always the courtesy due a master by a slave, but the surly visage of the Britannic prince showed no love for him. When open conflict did finally come, it was over something that seemed far afield indeed from the demeanor of Caractacus.

Quintus had been allowed to accompany Adminius on a brief visit to Londinium in order to witness the arrival of a Roman merchant ship and purchase some of the exquisite jewelry these vessels always brought for his wife, Cymbala. The fact that Cunobelinus and Adminius trusted him made an attempt to escape unthinkable to Quintus. Besides, the Roman shipmasters were fully aware that they were allowed to visit the bustling city of Londinium on the river Tamesis only at the sufferance of King Cunobelinus. To jeopardize that sufferance in order to help an escaped slave would have been the height of folly.

Adminius not only bought the jewelry he wanted in Londinium but was also able to purchase, at Quintus' suggestion, something far more important, a sword fashioned from the fine steel of Damascus, far to the east, steel which Quintus assured him could cut through the softer bronze weapons used by the Britanni like an ax cuts through wood. In addition Quintus had recognized by his features a Phoenician slave and had urged Adminius to buy him, after determining that the man was skilled in the shipbuilders' art.

Altogether it was a pleasant group that journeyed back to Camulodunum from the port city on the

Tamesis. Their happiness turned to depression, however, when they learned that Carnu had been arrested while they were gone at the orders of Commius, charged with the grave crime of revealing druidic secrets to another—in this case, Quintus.

Adminius could not help Carnu. Reverence for the druids was deeply ingrained in him from birth, but Quintus had no such respect for the men who had killed Veronica. Carnu had been falsely convicted of betraying the secrets of the druids to him, so Quintus was himself responsible and it was his task to help the young druid if he could.

As soon as he heard the news, Quintus hurried to the luxurious palace which was both the home of Commius and the headquarters of the druids. A servant admitted him, but he was kept waiting a long time—he did not doubt by intention—before he was finally admitted into the audience chamber where the archdruid judged those accused of crimes of sufficient gravity to justify his hearing the evidence himself.

Commius sat before a massive table. He said no word while Quintus approached the table and bowed in respect to the office he filled, if not to the man himself.

"What do you want, Roman?" he demanded in a deep and menacing growl. Beneath craggy brows his eyes were burning with anger and hate.

"It is said that you have accused Carnu of revealing the secrets of the druids to me," Quintus said.

"You heard aright."

"I swear that he has not once revealed anything having to do with your secret lore."

Commius shrugged. "You would lie to save him? That, too, is breaking the law."

"He has revealed no secret to me," Quintus insisted. "Nor to anyone else in my presence."

"Carnu has already been judged," Commius said ponderously.

"With what sentence?"

"To be cast out and avoided by all men."

Quintus felt a little sick. He had come to know

235

Carnu very well this past year. The young druid was sensitive and intelligent. The ostracism that followed condemnation by the druidic judges would soon break his spirit and probably cause him to end his life—as did most of those so sentenced—by suicide.

"I myself judged him," Commius added. "There is no more to say."

"Do you refuse to hear the evidence I will gladly give of his innocence?" Quintus asked.

"You are a slave," Commius said in the same hard voice. "Slaves cannot give testimony; it is of no value."

"And you condemned Carnu with no opportunity to defend himself?"

"If he would reveal the secrets he swore to keep inviolate," said Commius heavily, "he would also lie in his own defense."

This was the rankest perversion of justice, but Quintus had already learned during the year he had been a slave here that druidic justice was often equally abrupt—and unfair.

"Is there no recourse?" he asked.

"None."

The finality of the word seemed to terminate the interview. Quintus was turning away when Commius added, "Unless someone is willing to risk his life for the condemned."

Quintus turned quickly. "Is that possible?"

"Yes, through combat."

Quintus' hopes arose. The ancient rite of trial by combat was recognized even by the most primitive of people; he was not surprised that it was allowed here in Britannia. "Then I demand the right to represent Carnu in trial by combat," he said quickly.

To his amazement Commius suddenly became almost affable. In fact, he almost seemed pleased.

"You will have that right three days hence," the druid said. "The combat will take place on the field before the gates of the city against a champion chosen by me."

"Three days from now," Quintus repeated, "in the

field before the gates of the city. May I see Carnu and tell him?"

Commius got to his feet. "I will have you taken to him."

The young druid was a prisoner in a cell-like room with a small window. He looked up when Quintus entered, but his face was set in a mask of pain and dejection. "Come no closer," he said. "It is forbidden even to touch one under sentence of banishment."

"You are sentenced unjustly," Quintus protested. "Commius told me you were not even allowed to speak in your defense."

"That is the law of the druids. One accused of betraying his vows is suspect of lying and will not be believed."

"But that is unfair."

"It is the druidic law. The sentence of Commius cannot be changed, not even by the king."

"There is one recourse."

Carnu shook his head. "You are wrong. I am doomed."

"The right of trial by combat; you forget that."

"Who would give his life for me?" Suddenly Carnu's eyes filled with horror. "Not you, Quintus."

"I have already been given permission by Commius to represent you."

"But you will be going to your death."

"A Roman soldier is the equal of anyone in the art of war," Quintus said confidently.

"But you will not be equal. You must fight unarmed against a warrior with all his weapons."

The nature of the trap Commius had so cleverly baited was apparent now. The whole thing: Carnu's arrest, the quick sentencing while Adminius and Quintus were in Londinium, his admission to the archdruid's presence—everything fitted a pattern. Commius had even suggested trial by combat, Quintus remembered now. And he had seized upon it eagerly, not realizing the nature of the prescribed conflict which doomed him from the very beginning.

"You did not understand!" Carnu cried. "The king

237

will forbid you to take part when he learns you were tricked into combat."

Quintus had recovered from the shock now and his mind was busy. "What is the nature of the trial? Do they give you no weapons at all?"

"A single sword—against a man armed with shield, spear, and sword."

"But that makes the odds even—for a Roman."

Carnu shook his head. "First you must reach the sword. It will be at one side of the field and you at the other, with the warrior you are to fight between. I have seen several such trials, but no man ever reached the sword. Go to the king, Quintus. Tell him you were tricked and he may refuse to let you be murdered. I will take my punishment."

"You are innocent, yet you are suffering because of me," Quintus said firmly. "I will represent you in combat. Whatever happens, your life will be saved."

Carnu bowed his head. "I would kill myself here in my cell but it would not help you now. Once the trial is set, it must be carried out. And you can be sure Commius will select a skilled warrior as your executioner."

"Skill does not always win over intelligence," Quintus assured him. "I will think of something. The most important thing is that you will be free."

Once away from Carnu, Quintus felt little of the optimism he had pretended in the druid's cell. An unarmed man against a fully armed warrior had next to no chance at all. He'd seen criminals pitted thus against gladiators in the arena at Rome; invariably the end had been the same.

By nightfall news of the coming trial by combat had spread like a conflagration throughout the palace and the city. Adminius' face was grave when he stopped at the end of the evening meal and spoke to Quintus. As was the custom among the Britanni, slaves ate at the distant end of the long trestle tables spanning the huge dining hall of the palace.

"Did you understand our custom of trial by combat when you volunteered today?" the prince asked.

238

"It makes no difference. I must save Carnu if I can."

"You will save him—by giving your life for him."

"He is unjustly accused because of me, so the responsibility is mine."

"Commius is only trying to be rid of you."

"I know. He has hated me since I saved you."

"And even more since you have been teaching me Roman customs and knowledge."

Quintus managed to smile. "At least I have that accomplishment to remember and be proud of. You have been an apt pupil."

"The Phoenician slave I bought in Londinium!" Adminius cried, his face brightening. "I can substitute him for you."

"Can a master order a slave to his death?"

The prince shook his head reluctantly. "I had forgotten. Our law forbids it."

"I will take my chances," Quintus said. "We Romans know a few tricks of combat."

"Then use the sword I bought in Londinium. If you do reach it, the odds will at least be much more nearly even."

It was a small hope, very small indeed. It was true that the hard steel of Damascus might enable him to split a bronze shield such as the warriors of the Britanni used and even the odds against him. But first he must reach the sword.

8

Trial by combat was enough of a novelty in Camulodunum to bring out a considerable crowd. The identity of the warrior against whom Quintus would contend was kept a secret until the very beginning of the contest. Thus he had no opportunity to study his opponent and note any possible weakness which might be turned to his own advantage.

The sentiments of the crowd were with their still unannounced champion, and Quintus could not help feeling very much alone as he waited at the edge of the field just outside the main gate of the city where the contest would be held. Adminius had given him the sword of Damascus steel but, by the rules of the combat, in order to reach the weapon he must first get past his opponent.

Quintus had carefully rubbed the blade with a mixture of soot and ashes before bringing it to the field, so its polished steel would not shine too brightly in the sun and betray the metal of which it was made. Ironworking was not practiced to any great extent in Britannia, so he doubted very much that any warrior upon the island would have so fine a blade. He did not delude himself, however, that reaching the steel sword would be anything but difficult and dangerous, if needed he were not cut down before he did reach it—a considerably more likely conclusion.

The thong of people was good-natured; not often did they have a chance to enjoy a holiday that included a battle to the death between two strong men. Hawkers went about through the crowd, selling sweetmeats and cups of the rather sour wine preferred by the Britanni. The field itself—or at least that part roped off for the contest—was about twenty paces square. The steel sword inside its scabbard lay on a table at one side of the field, while Quintus waited at the other.

Quintus had refused Adminius' offer to act as a second for fear of angering Commius. Instead the Phoenician slave, Tano, acted in his master's place.

"I have examined the weapons of these Britanni," the Phoenician said contemptuously. "The Hittites were making better swords than theirs five hundred years ago."

"Nevertheless the Britanni are strong and skilled in the use of their weapons."

"Try to make him fight at close quarters," Tano advised. "That way you may be able to grab his sword from its scabbard."

"The warriors of the Britanni are skilled with the spear. He will use that first."

"The steel of Damascus will more than make up for that."

"If I reach it."

"A Roman is the equal of two Britanni any day," Tano said confidently. "Just as a Phoenician sailor is the equal of two Romans when it comes to sailing a ship."

But he was only boasting to drum up Quintus' courage and both of them knew it.

Three blasts on a cow's-horn trumpet announced that the warrior who would fight Quintus was approaching. When he broke through the crowd and paused at the edge of the square, Quintus saw why the people had suddenly gone wild.

The champion of the druids was Caractacus, eldest son of King Cunobelinus. He wore the full armor of a warrior, including a metal cap and a shield of bronze. And he carried both sword and spear.

Quintus had known that the tall and powerful Caractacus had little use for him, but he had not realized that the prince would wish to destroy him with his own hands. And yet this was undoubtedly true, for Commius would never have singled out the eldest son of the king as champion without his permission. If by a miracle Quintus managed to win, he had every right—and indeed was expected—to kill his opponent, so Caractacus must have volunteered, supremely confident that the contest would be only a farce.

The trial itself was in charge of an elderly noble who had once been a warrior, to judge by his size and his commanding manner. He went first to Caractacus and inquired respectfully whether he was ready. Quintus saw the warrior-prince nod carelessly, as if he considered this nothing more than a practice combat. The noble then came over to Quintus.

"Are you ready, Roman?" he demanded in the tongue of the Britanni.

"I am," Quintus replied in the same language.

"Let the combat begin," he cried and stepped to one side.

Quintus faced Caractacus across the open space. Behind the prince he could see the sword Adminius had lent him, resting on the table in its scabbard. The dis-

241

tance seemed very long indeed, especially with Caractacus between him and the weapon. The eldest son of Cunobelinus held his shield before him on his left arm, the long-handled spear with its sharp bronze point gripped by his right hand in a position of readiness to throw.

"Pray to your gods while you can, Roman," he shouted contemptuously. "You have not much longer to live." Obviously he was determined to make a show of this affair and endear himself to the crowd, who loved nothing so much as a man who seemed to joy in a fight.

Caractacus was standing near the center of the square, perhaps ten paces from the sword on the table. For the desperate stratagem by which Quintus hoped to win the contest, it was important that his opponent not move closer and increase the distance to the Damascus sword. Therefore Quintus began to move toward his opponent now, stepping lightly with his weight balanced on his feet as if he were engaged in an exhibition of boxing—a sport also loved by the Romans.

The spectacle of an unarmed man carrying the fight, so to speak, to an armed one caught the attention of the crowd. A hush fell over them as Quintus moved warily toward his opponent. As for Caractacus, Quintus' action seemed to take him by surprise. A look of uncertainty momentarily showed in his eyes, then he controlled himself and laughed boisterously.

"So the hare turns on the hunter!" he shouted. "Take care, Roman, or I will run away."

The crowd roared, but Quintus did not allow himself to be distracted. In his mind he could hear again the words of an old gladiator he had treated for wounds in Rome, a doughty figure who had survived many a bloody combat in the arena.

"Always watch the eyes of your opponent," the gladiator had said. "Fix them with yours. When he is about to thrust at you, he will always blink. Catch his blow on your shield then and cut him down before he can free his sword."

Quintus had no shield to catch the blow, which he

was almost certain would be a sudden powerful lunge with the spear. Or—if Caractacus was as sure of himself as he pretended to be—he might throw it, confident that one paralyzed by the fear of death as his opponent was supposed to be could not possibly escape the heavy weapon.

Quintus moved closer while silence gripped the crowd. His eyes never left those of Caractacus, not even to note the tightening of the prince's mouth beneath his full red mustaches or the tensing of his right hand upon the handle of the spear. Since the fight had started, Quintus had not spoken once or deviated from his almost feline stalking as he moved across the open square.

By now Quintus had covered half the distance between him and Caractacus. For a moment he feared that the prince would let him come near enough to engage at close quarters with only sword and shield. But he'd seen the Britanni fight and he was counting upon his opponent to follow the usual routine. First the spear would be thrown with a powerful overhand motion of the right arm. If that failed to find the opponent's body, the next move would be a quick follow-up attack with the sword at close quarters.

When he saw Caractacus suddenly blink, Quintus changed his movement. Swinging himself sideways, he launched his body at the warrior-prince's knees in a sliding, rolling motion, thrusting out with all the power in his legs.

Quintus felt rather than saw the flash of the spear pass his body, almost touching him. Nor did he take time to note that it had buried itself in the ground to the entire length of the sharp bronze point. The jar of contact as he crashed against the sturdy knees of the taller man shook him to his very teeth, and he felt his ribs give and pain shoot through his body.

Caractacus had obviously not expected the attack. Leaning forward in the act of following through with his body after the powerful thrust upon the spear, he was momentarily off balance. When Quintus struck him just below the knees, he went down in a jarring crash.

243

Had Quintus not been so intent upon the stratagem he'd devised, the contest might have ended then and there, for his opponent was momentarily stunned by the unexpected fall. Actually there was time enough for him to jerk the sword from its scabbard at Caractacus' belt as Tano had advised and end the contest with one thrust.

Quintus did not stop to look at his opponent, however. His body was rolling when it struck Caractacus and he continued to roll for at least two full turns until he was clear of the other man. Then, clawing at the ground with his hands, he pushed himself into a half-kneeling position. In a continuing swift movement he lunged to his feet and sprinted toward the sword of Damascus steel on the table. His hand closed upon it and he jerked at the scabbard to free it.

Here occurred a mischance which no one could foresee. Some ten paces away Caractacus was in the act of rising to his feet, shaking his head like a wounded bull to clear it. Had Quintus' sword slid freely from its scabbard, he could still have crossed the ten paces of open greensward and cut down the prince before Caractacus could bring up his shield or draw his own sword.

But the blade from Damascus stuck in the scabbard and Quintus was forced to smash it against the small table to free the weapon. The table crumpled under the force of the blow, but the sword came free. Pausing only to seize the heavy scabbard which, being also of steel, could serve as something of a buffer or shield, he moved toward his opponent again, grimly intent. Caractacus had been given time to recover from the fall, however. He was on his feet again, holding the bronze shield before him on his left arm as he jerked his sword from its scabbard.

There was no overconfidence in the prince's eyes or manner now, only the wariness of a skilled fighter who knows he is pitted against an adversary worthy of his metal. The advantage was still in Caractacus' favor with the shield to protect his body, but the odds had now been evened considerably.

Now the contest took on a twofold character. Quintus sought to keep Caractacus from reaching the spear and jerking it from the ground. With it a skilled fighter would be able to hold off an opponent armed only with a sword, jabbing with the point and keeping him off balance while he searched for an opportunity to drive the long weapon home. Quintus already knew Caractacus to be skilled in the use of the larger weapon, so he could take no chances of the prince's being able to secure it again. Circling each other warily, the opponents settled down to a grim battle of wits, strength, and skill. The crowd, after the startling shock of seeing its champion thrown to the ground by an unarmed man and momentarily at his mercy, was shouting for Caractacus, keeping up a constant din of noise. Quintus was careful not to come too close to the edge of the square, lest some of the onlookers thrust out a foot to trip him or even reach over the rope that held them back to strike him.

Quintus had been an expert sword fighter during his earlier days as a soldier of the legions, before he had become an officer and later a physician. But it had been a long time since he had really fought—and even longer in a contest where his life was at stake. He knew he must soon find or make an opportunity where the superior metal of the Damascus sword could cut through the other's weapon, else his body, tiring much more rapidly than his younger and more practiced opponent, would tip the scales against him.

The opportunity came a few moments later when Caractacus launched a slashing stroke with his sword at Quintus' body. Turning to one side, Quintus swung the scabbard and managed to deflect the blade. The force of the blow knocked the scabbard from his numbed fingers, but he was able to strike directly at the round bronze shield Caractacus carried on his left arm. There was a sharp clang of metal upon metal, then the temper of the Damascus steel showed its strength. Caractacus' shield split apart and the two halves dropped to the ground as the blade went on to slash the heavy leather band holding it on the warrior-prince's arm.

A moan went up from the crowd, a cry of fear and

dismay, for now the tide of battle was definitely running out for their champion. The sword wielded by Quintus had already proved its superior quality. Caractacus was obviously startled, but he was brave and a skilled swordsman and did not let the momentary setback stop him from defending himself.

Almost in a matter of moments an uneven contest had become a tight and potentially bloody battle, for neither man could protect his body from the other's blows. Warily they circled each other. Quintus sought to end the fight as quickly as possible before his strength waned, while Caractacus tried to reach his spear which was still stuck in the ground after his first attempt to kill his opponent had failed. Determined not to let that happen, Quintus kept thrusting and slashing, forcing Caractacus to parry the strokes in order to defend himself and keeping him from launching an attack. Finally the opening Quintus had been seeking came, a chance to drive a two-handed blow with the Damascus sword upon the bronze one near the hilt. Again there was a sharp clang of metal upon metal and, as with the shield, the prince's sword snapped at the hilt, the blade severed by the tough steel of Quintus' weapon.

A cry of dismay went up as Quintus put the point of his sword to his opponent's throat. Actually he had no thought of killing the eldest son of Cunobelinus, although he knew Caractacus would have shown him no mercy had the fight turned out differently. But no one could blame him for savoring this moment of glory in victory.

Caractacus' face was pale and his chest heaved from the exertion of fighting, but he did not beg for mercy. Instead he held himself erect, waiting for the thrust that would end his life. Quintus let him wait for a long moment, so the prince would know what it meant to look death in the face, as Quintus himself had looked it only a short time before when the contest began. Then he stepped back and raised his sword upright in a salute.

246

"The contest is ended," he shouted. "I claim the rights of the victor."

The roar of the crowd gave proof that it approved his action in giving Caractacus his life. Stepping forward, Quintus thrust out his hand for the gripping of fore-arms which would have indicated that his opponent accepted his magnanimous act in the spirit in which it was carried out. But Caractacus only turned, his face flushed with rage and hurt pride, and strode from the field.

Tano rushed into the square to pummel Quintus on the body. "Why didn't you kill him?" he demanded. "Now he will hate you unto death."

"His father has been kind to me," Quintus explained. "And his brother is like my son."

"It was a fine fight anyway," said the Phoenician, wiping the sweat from Quintus' body with a towel. "If you ever tire of being a physician, you can always be a gladiator."

Quintus shook his head as he handed Tano the sword of Damascus steel. "Even with a weapon like this, I hope I never have to fight again."

9

Since the stratagem to destroy Quintus and the Roman influence he had brought into the palace of the king had failed, Commius had no choice except to release Carnu. Adminius congratulated Quintus on his exhibition of swordsmanship, but both were grave. Caractacus' manner at the end of the fight had left no doubt that Quintus' troubles were by no means over. Nor was he surprised when Cunobelinus sent for him the next morning.

The king greeted Quintus warmly. "I already owed you much for what you have taught Adminius this past year," he said. "Now I am also indebted to you for the life of my eldest son."

"I did not ask to fight him, sir."

"I know. Caractacus is much influenced by Commius. If I had known he was to oppose you I would have forbidden it." His shoulders drooped wearily. "I told you once I would give you your freedom when it was safe for you to be free, Quintus. Actually you are less safe now than you were then, but I must send you away from Camulodunum to preserve your life."

"Why do you say that, sir?"

"My eldest son is strong and brave, but there is little of greatness in him. A really great man would have acknowledged defeat by a better fighter yesterday, but he will only hold it against you. Commius is equally vindictive, and if you stay here your death will be a certainty. Tomorrow morning I am sending you to Londinium, to the care of a merchant I can trust. The first Roman ship that enters the port will take you as a passenger. Carnu will go with you."

"But he is innocent, sir. He did not betray any of the druidic secrets."

"I know that," Cunobelinus said. "But he cannot serve here any longer. There are still druids in Gaul; he will be safe there." The old king put his hand on Quintus' shoulder. "I am loath to see you leave, my friend. With the knowledge you brought I am sure my people could learn how to live in the Roman world. But I am old and sick and powerful forces are against me. Because they will not have a chance to learn it, I am afraid now my people will suffer greatly."

Quintus did not argue the point. Rome moved slowly; for nearly a hundred years it had failed to consolidate the initial gains made by Julius Caesar. But even now plans were being set into operation which must inevitably result in the subjugation of the Britanni. With Cunobelinus or Adminius as king, the transition might have been orderly. But with Caractacus in control and under the influence of Commius, a bloody conflict seemed inevitable.

"I will give you a purse of gold before you leave," Cunobelinus said. "Where do you wish to go from Londinium?"

"Rome," Quintus told him. To return to Gaul would only mean stirring up the pain of losing Veronica. She

248

had loved that fair land so much that every part of it would be a reminder of her. In Rome he might find other duties and so keep himself occupied.

"You will have much to tell your emperor about our land," Cunobelinus said. "He will surely reward you well for the knowledge you bring."

Quintus was not certain. The whims of Caligula were completely unpredictable, but it was his duty to report what he knew, particularly the fact that the kingdom of Cunobelinus was strong and such a small expedition as Lentulus Gaeticulus planned to bring to the shores of Britannia would almost certainly result in a sharp defeat for the Romans, encouraging the Britanni to further resistance.

"Tell your emperor to have patience with us," Cunobelinus said. "One day we may be worthy to be called a Roman province."

Quintus and Carnu departed for Londinium the next morning at daybreak. It was a heady feeling to be free again, but he still felt a pang at leaving the palace of Cunobelinus. Even as a slave he had found kindness and consideration there and appreciation for what he had to give. But he carried a fat purse at his belt and had found a fast friend in the young druid, Carnu, so he could hardly be downcast.

In teeming Londinium they easily found the house of the merchant to whom Cunobelinus had sent them. He greeted them pleasantly and assured them they would be safe in the bustling port city on the river Tamesis while waiting for a Roman ship to take them on their way. Carnu had elected to journey to Massilia or one of the other Gallic ports where he hoped to join other members of the small druidic cult who still practiced their strange and colorful rites among the Celts of Gaul. That he had long since been reported as dead by whatever had remained of the garrison at Gesoriacum after the raid by the Britanni, Quintus did not doubt. But he was well known in Rome and would have no trouble establishing his identity there—especially with the detailed information he possessed about the little-known island of Britannia.

No ship was expected for about a week, so Quintus occupied himself by exploring this rapidly rising commercial and business center which gave promise of soon being the largest city in Britannia. Most of the better-class homes in Londinium were of brick, often plastered over and sometimes painted with pleasant colors. The houses of the poor, however, were of wood or the mud-and-wattle construction which he had seen in Camulodunum and elsewhere.

Along the river Tamesis were many docks, warehouses for the merchants, and some shops. The roofs of the buildings were for the most part quite high pitched compared to those in Rome and the eastern countries where roof tops were often used for sleeping during hot weather. The purpose of the pitch, Quintus was told, was to shed rain and snow which sometimes fell here. The walls were cut by many windows to let in the sun, but even on clear days it was rarely seen in Londinium for more than four or five hours.

In one section of the city Quintus saw forges for the smelting of lead and tin, fired by coal. Dug from the surface of the earth in some parts of Britannia, coal was also used for heating the more luxurious houses, many of which belonged to members of the prosperous merchant class that developed quickly in a busy and prosperous seaport.

Quintus and Carnu were passing through a shop in a section of the market place devoted to the sale of pottery one morning when he stopped before a table where a number of vases were displayed. The sight of them brought back sharply the memory of the pottery yard where he had first seen Veronica when he'd come to Jerusalem seeking Jesus of Nazareth. For a moment the pain of the memory was almost beyond bearing.

The little vases were decorated in bright colors with scenes from the countryside of Britannia painted by a skilled and talented hand. Idly Quintus examined them, wondering whether it would be worth while to take some back to Rome, not only as an example of the talents of the artisans among the Britanni in the field of pottery but also because they reminded him of Veronica.

Suddenly his body went rigid as he turned one of the small vases slowly in his hand. The scene he was looking at was familiar, a hillside green with thorn-bushes, and a burst of red like drops of blood where one portion was in blossom.

He had last seen this identical scene, painted with the same exquisite artistry by Veronica's own hand, in the pottery yard of Abijah in Jerusalem!

BOOK 5

Avalon

Quintus did not doubt for a moment that Veronica's own hand had painted the scene on the vase; that particular crimson burst of blossoms among green thorn-bushes existed, he was sure, only on the hillsides around Jerusalem. This very scene, he remembered, was the one old Jonas, the wood seller, had described in the home of Joseph of Arimathea, the sign that Jesus forgave him for gathering thorns which the soldiers had put upon the Nazarene as a crown before he was crucified.

It was like seeing Veronica herself again, and for a moment he dared to hope his discovery meant she was still alive. Then the obvious explanation came to him, dashing his hopes. With the Roman Empire generally at peace, trade was free in all parts of it. No miracle was necessary to explain how a vase painted by Veronica far away across the world, at least two years ago, could turn up as an article of trade in the city of Londinium.

"Is anything wrong?" Carnu asked. "You look as if you had seen a ghost."

"Perhaps I have." Quintus held out the small vase so the druid could see it. "This was painted by my wife's hand."

"But she is dead! The ones who keep the Grove of the Druids told me all those sacrificed that night perished."

"The vase was painted a long time ago when she

253

lived in Jerusalem," Quintus explained. "It must have come here by ship."

"I did not realize trade was so general." Carnu reached into the stand of vases and picked up another, identically painted. Searching farther, they found two more and took them over to the proprietor. Quintus paid the man and was leaving the shop when the proprietor said, "We have other scenes painted by the same artist, sir, if you would like to see them."

Quintus stopped short. "Where are they?"

"Over here, on another table." He pointed across the room.

The vases in this collection were somewhat larger and the scenes different, although similar in color and stroking. Superficially, at least, they did appear to have been painted by the same artist.

The scene on the larger vases was like nothing Quintus had ever seen in Veronica's homeland, however. It showed part of a lake with lovely blue water surrounded by a grove of trees and rushes growing in the shallows near the shore. In the distance was what appeared to be a wattled hut set upon stilts.

"I have heard of places like this here in Britannia." Carnu had picked up one of the vases and was studying it.

"I, too, have seen such scenes on vases before," the proprietor agreed.

Quintus held a firm rein on his emotions. It couldn't be true, of course; there must be another explanation. And yet he could not keep down the sudden hope that surged within him.

"Are you sure?" he asked.

"I have sold many vases like this," the merchant insisted.

"But I thought they came from another part of the world, on a ship."

"All of them were made here in Britannia," the proprietor insisted. "I am sure of it."

"How did you get them?"

"They are brought to the markets in Londinium by

men who travel around buying up the wares of the potters in their villages."

"Could you tell me where this one came from?"

The merchant shook his head. "I buy from all who sell at a price I can afford."

"Would the man who sold you these know where they came from?"

"It is possible," the proprietor agreed. "But I do not know who he was."

"Think," urged Quintus. "Think hard." In his excitement he had seized the merchant's tunic.

"Sir," the man protested. "I am not a thief."

Quintus forced himself to be calm. He hardly dared to believe what his unshackled thoughts were saying— that Veronica was somehow alive here in Britannia, alive and painting vases for potters, as she had done back in Jerusalem. And yet if by some miracle, some act of intervention by her god, she had escaped the sacrificial fires of the druids, he must leave no stone unturned to find her.

"I mean you no harm," he apologized to the merchant. "My wife once painted scenes like these. I thought she was dead. But if what you say is true, she might still be alive."

"I had never seen such paintings on pottery in Britannia until about six months ago," the merchant told him. "Since then I have sold many of them."

"Then they should not be difficult to trace."

"If you can find the man who sold them to me."

"Are you sure you have no memory of him?"

He shook his head. "As I said, many such come here."

Quintus decided to try another track. "How often do the pottery sellers visit you?"

"Whenever they have a load large enough to sell— sometimes every month, sometimes only once in a season."

Quintus knew he could not leave Britannia now without solving the mystery of the vases. That would mean staying in Londinium and trying to find an itinerant merchant who remembered buying the exquisitely painted vases and where he had collected them, an almost hopeless task from the beginning, except that one thing was in his favor. The vases stood out so much from the other pottery in the shop of this particular merchant that whoever had brought them originally would be sure to remember them. The problem then was to find the merchant.

Then came a sobering thought. If he and Carnu stayed in Londinium long, Caractacus and Commius would certainly learn that they had not left the country and would seek to destroy them. That left only one alternative. If Veronica were indeed alive and here in Britannia he must try to find her quickly, before his enemies learned what he was doing. To accomplish that required a plan of action—a plan which was already beginning to take form in his mind.

"I will pay you well if you will question any who bring in pottery for sale," he told the proprietor.

The man looked doubtful. "Many traveling merchants trade in pottery."

"You need only ask whether they ever bought vases like this and where. The one who sold them to you would be sure to remember because they are of so much better workmanship than the others and no doubt bring a higher price."

"That is true."

"Find out where they come from, and I will pay you double this amount." Quintus counted out some coins into the man's pudgy hand. "Do you understand?"

"If it is possible to locate the place, I will do it," the man promised.

2

To Quintus' satisfaction, no ship of Rome visited Londinium during the next several weeks, so the question of his leaving Britannia was automatically postponed. By day he prowled the water front with Carnu, showing the vases to fishermen and those who sailed the small vessels that traveled along the coast of Britannia, inquiring whether any of them had ever seen such pottery before or knew of scenes like the lake and the stilt-supported huts.

Each day he visited the merchant in whose shop he had first found the vases as well as all who sold similar wares, but the story was always the same. A few pottery sellers came in from time to time, but none had ever seen the exquisitely painted ware which he was almost certain had been produced by Veronica's own fingers. As the days passed with no encouraging news, Quintus' spirits sank lower and lower. Had Veronica miraculously escaped the sacrificial fire, he wondered, only for him to lose her once more in the vast reaches of the island? Until that question was answered, he was determined not to leave Britannia.

Quintus and Carnu had taken a room in an inn on the water front so he could be near the going and coming of ships as well as the mercantile establishments where pottery wares were sold. To this room one night came the merchant Quintus had commissioned to learn the source of the vases.

The man scuttled in as soon as the door was opened and shut it quickly behind him. He was pallid with fear and near collapse. "I am risking my life in coming here," he panted. "But you paid me well and I had to warn you that I can serve you no longer."

"What is wrong?" Quintus asked.

"Yesterday I was visited by an agent of Prince Caractacus. If I continue to question people on your behalf, my shop will be broken into, my wares smashed, and my taxes will be raised."

It was a familiar pattern. Quintus had seen it happen many times in Rome, especially since Caligula had become emperor, and was sure the merchant was not exaggerating.

"I can't ask you to take that risk," he said. "But if one should come selling painted vases like the small vases I bought, would you ask him where he found them?"

The merchant considered a moment, then nodded.

257

"I will pretend I want more of them. After all, they sell well and I can use as many as I could buy."

"I will not come to your shop every day as I have been doing," Quintus said, "but will seek you out secretly."

"Take care not to be seen," the merchant warned. "If you are, I will be in great danger."

"Caractacus and Commius know where we are," Quintus told Carnu when the merchant had gone. "I am going to rent quarters for you in another part of Londinium until the ship from Rome arrives."

The druid shook his head. "I will not run away when you are in danger. We have a better chance of foiling them if we stay together."

"Then wear a dagger at all times beneath your robe," Quintus counseled. "I will carry one too—and a stout staff."

For another week the search for some trace of Veronica yielded nothing. Then, as Quintus and Carnu were eating a frugal meal of bread, cheese, and wine in their quarters one night, a knock came on the door. His hand on the heavy staff that he now carried always, Quintus opened the door.

A small man in sailor's garb cringed in the corridor. "Are you the Roman seeking a woman who paints on clay?" he asked.

"I am," Quintus said eagerly. "Do you have news of her?"

"A fisherman came from the south coast late today to sell his catch. He spoke of a woman who paints on clay like no one has been known to paint in this land before."

"Where is he?" Quintus asked eagerly.

"On his boat, tied up at the river front." The man extended his hand, palm up. "I was told you would pay well for such information."

"Take me to him," Quintus said quickly. "You will be well paid, I assure you."

"Pay me first," the small man insisted.

Quintus placed a coin in his hand. "Take me there at once then."

From inside the room Carnu said quickly, "I am going with you."

"It is cold outside," Quintus protested. "I can go alone."

"One intending to lead another into a trap would demand payment first," Carnu said in Latin. "But I doubt if any man of Britannia would kill a druid."

It was a sobering thought—and a warning. The small man who'd brought possible word of Veronica wouldn't understand Latin and so could not be warned by the druid's words.

"Come along then," Quintus said in the same language and added grimly: "Keep your hand on your dagger. I trust there is no prohibition in the druidic cult against killing those who seek to kill you."

Few people were abroad in the dark streets of Londinium at night except the criminals who always infested any large seaport. Some distance from the inn their guide took them aboard a fishing boat moored with some others to the river bank. A big man in the garb of a fisherman loomed up in the darkness that half hid the boat.

"Can you tell me anything about a woman who paints on clay?" Quintus asked.

The sword the big man had been holding behind him slashed downward in a vicious cut that would have split Quintus' skull had he not been on his guard. As it was, he just had time to raise the heavy staff he carried and catch the blade upon it. Had the sword been of the Damascus steel which had felled Caractacus, the fight would have ended then and there. But it was fashioned of bronze and so only cut through the staff, giving Quintus time to dodge the blade itself. With the section of the staff remaining in his right hand, Quintus managed to give the big man a whack over the head that put him off balance. Before his opponent could steady himself, Quintus jabbed him in the middle with the staff.

The man's breath went out with a loud "oof." Doubled over with pain, he stumbled backward, catching his foot on the low gunwale of the boat and tumbling into the river with a mighty splash. The water closed over his head and they saw no more of him. When, or if, he came to the surface later, the current had carried him outside their range of vision in the darkness.

Quintus turned to help Carnu but saw that the druid had proved quite able to take care of himself. He was holding the small messenger by the scruff of his tunic, with the point of a dagger at his throat. "Who paid you men to kill the Roman?" he demanded tersely.

The small man gulped, then squealed as the point pricked his skin. "A man who said he came from Prince Caractacus," he babbled. "I was only to bring the Roman here. We meant no harm to you, druid."

"That much is probably true," Carnu said grimly. "What shall we do with him?"

"Let him go," Quintus said. "He cannot harm us, and we know everything he does now."

Safely in their room at the inn once more, Quintus closed the door and turned to face Carnu, a sober look on his face. "That was a near disaster," he said. "But for your happening to think that a man leading another into a trap would demand payment in advance, I might not have been ready."

"Caractacus means to kill you before you can take ship for Rome," Carnu agreed. "He will not let one defeat stop him."

"Then we must leave Londinium."

"And give up the search for your wife?"

"I'll never do that—not until I know for certain she is dead. But I cannot search for her and keep looking behind me at the same time to be certain I will not get a knife in the back."

"Caractacus will have spies watching to make sure you sail on the next Roman ship," Carnu reminded him. "If he does not kill you before then."

"I will sail on it," Quintus said. "And so will you. But somewhere between here and the mouth of the Tamesis I will slip ashore."

"Are you so anxious to be rid of me?"

"You know better," Quintus told him. "But I intend

260

to search the whole island of Britannia if I have to, and it is not fair to make you risk your life."

"You will get nowhere unless you disguise yourself."

"Any shop in Londinium will sell me clothes like those worn by your people."

"No shop can change your speech and your facial appearance. They would betray you instantly."

Quintus had been worrying about that, too, and had not yet come up with a solution.

"As a subject of King Cunobelinus you would be considered an enemy in the country of the Regni on the southern border of the kingdom of the Iceni to the north," Carnu continued. "That is, if you were lucky enough to get out of the kingdom without Caractacus learning you were still here and having you destroyed."

Quintus shrugged. "I will have to take that chance."

Carnu shook his head dourly. "How will you find your wife if you are lying dead under some oak tree?"

"What is the answer then?"

"Only one class in Britannia can go anywhere safely —druids."

Quintus gave him a startled look. What Carnu said was true; the priestly class knew no boundaries. "Would you disguise me as a druid?" he asked.

"It is the only way. Wearing our robes and accompanying me, you can go anywhere—except perhaps in Camulodunum itself, where both of us are known."

"My speech would still betray me."

"Not if you profess to come from Gaul across the Fretum Gallicum," Carnu pointed out. "Naturally you would not speak our tongue well, but a druid is a druid wherever he goes."

Quintus' eager mind had already seized upon the possibilities of Carnu's plan. The greatest danger would be to Carnu; if they were discovered, he would immediately be condemned by his fellow priests.

"I realize the risk you are taking, my friend," Quintus said sincerely. "If we come through this safely, I will not forget it."

"You did not hesitate to fight Caractacus to save me," Carnu reminded him. "I can do no less for you."

A week later Quintus and Carnu stood on the deck of a Roman ship and watched the city of Londinium drop behind them as the slaves at the long oars sent the vessel downstream with the ebbing tide. The vessel had arrived several days after Carnu had outlined the plan by which Quintus would be free to search for Veronica in Britannia disguised as a druid. The garments of the priestly caste, purchased by Carnu in Londinium, were in a package he had brought on board, ostensibly for his own use. The captain of the galley had reluctantly agreed to join in the deception by which Quintus planned to lull Caractacus and Commius into believing he had left Britannia.

Quintus had spent the last few days in Londinium writing a detailed account of everything he had learned about Britannia and addressing it to the Emperor Caligula in Rome. A second account he addressed to Lentulus Gaeticulus in Gaul, telling him the situation here in Britannia. In conclusion he had added the postscript that he was traveling through more of Britannia now in disguise in order to learn as much as he could that would be of value to a Roman invader. In that way he hoped to remove the possibility of being labeled a deserter for not returning to Rome as soon as transport was available.

The letters had been placed in a package entrusted to the care of the captain of the ship. Also included was a letter to Abijah in Jerusalem, telling him of what had happened to Veronica and Joseph. Quintus did not mention his hope that by some miracle they had escaped during the ceremony in which the priests had sacrificed captives in the Grove of the Druids.

With the letters entrusted to the Roman ship captain, Quintus could not help feeling that he had cut himself loose from Rome entirely. The captain brought this home to him again as they stood on the foredeck of the vessel and watched the city fade into the murky fogs that hung over the coast of Britannia for much of the time.

"I wish I could persuade you against going to your death, Tribune Quintus," the burly mariner said.

"Anyone would do the same in my position," Quintus said. "I cannot sail away and leave my wife here."

"I don't want to dampen your hopes, but those vases could have come from Judea by ship."

"The shopkeeper says not. He bought them from a traveling merchant."

"I've seen pottery from the eastern lands in the cities of Gaul. Smugglers among the Veneti land goods from Gaul on the shores of Britannia all the time. We often see their boats in the Fretum Gallicum. The vases could have been bought from smugglers."

Quintus had not considered this possible explanation for the presence of the small vases in Londinium. Looked at now in the light of cold logic, it did seem a more reasonable assumption than that Veronica had survived when all the rest in the wicker cage of the druid's sacrifice had perished.

"But the other scenes," he protested. "Those of the lake and the cottage. The merchant says they are scenes of Britannia itself."

"Wherever people dwell on the shores of lakes," the captain said, "they put their houses on stilts to keep others from attacking them. I have seen such dwellings in many parts of the world. Besides, you cannot be certain they were even painted by the same hand."

"I think they were."

"Why?"

"From the resemblance—and something I feel."

The captain threw up his hands. "If I guided this ship by my feelings, who knows where it would go? Instead I use the sun and the stars and maps drawn by geographers. Be logical, tribune; would you send anyone else on a jaunt such as this, knowing you were probably dooming him at the same time?"

"I suppose not," Quintus agreed.

"Then come with me to Rome. You will be as one returned from the dead and a hero because of what you can tell about the Britanni."

But Quintus shook his head. He couldn't explain it—at least not convincingly enough to satisfy anyone else. But something in his heart told him the small vase with

263

the painting of the blooming thorn was a message Veronica had sent him, a message brought to his attention perhaps by the god in whom she so confidently believed. "I'm going to keep on looking," he said firmly. "At least until I can be sure."

"May Mithras guide you then," said the captain. "I have done all I can do."

Darkness fell before the ship reached the river mouth. Quintus and Carnu stripped and wrapped their clothing in a tight package, together with bread and cold meat enough for several meals. To help them stay afloat when they left the ship they had tied empty wine jugs together, well stoppered so the water could not fill and sink them. Shortly after dark they dropped over the side of the ship at a place where the channel swung close to the northern shore.

The jugs supported them adequately, but the receding tide tended to sweep them seaward in the wake of the Roman ship. Kicking and swimming across the current, however, they soon found themselves in slack water and, after a few moments, touched bottom. Wading ashore, shivering in the cool night air, they scrambled up the bank and sought an open space in the woods. They were naked and their clothes were wet, but Quintus had taken the precaution of bringing flints—such as the Britanni used to start fires—in the package containing their clothing.

Shivering in the darkness, he finally managed to find a dry log from which he peeled a piece of bark. When the inside of this was scraped with his knife—which he also used to strike fire from the flint—a small store of tinder was thus obtained. After a few attempts a spark struck into the dry powder finally glowed into flame, and soon they had a small fire burning briskly. With it they warmed themselves and dried their clothing, while they assuaged their hunger with the food they had brought. When dawn came, two tall druids emerged from the open space in the woods and started across the countryside near the mouth of the river Tamesis.

In a copse near where they had spent the night Carnu found a bush with a peculiar type of brown berry he was seeking. Using the juice, he stained Quintus' face and neck and his hands far enough up the arms so the contrast from white to the darker hue would not be seen within the sleeves of the long gray robe of the druids. By thus changing the color of his skin and letting his beard and mustaches grow, they hoped to avoid any suspicion that he was anything but a druid who had crossed the narrow channel between Gaul and Britannia in order to visit his brother priests in the latter country.

They had decided to begin their search at the Grove of the Druids, where Veronica was said to have met her death in the fire, seeking evidence—however slight —that she might still be alive. Four days of walking across the countryside near the ocean brought them finally to the stream beside which stood the huge oaks that made up the grove. Following the stream inland, they soon came to the place itself.

The grove, now empty, was as Quintus remembered it—the vast towering oaks, the templelike structure to one side with its walls slick with mold, the stone altar in the center with its ring of raised-up stones. He turned away at the sight of a pile of coals and ashes to one side where he remembered the platform and cage had been built, although it was almost certain that other sacrifices had been carried out here since then, for the souls of other Britanni warriors killed in the frequent raids across the Fretum Gallicum.

The keeper of the grove was an old druid who lived in a hut of thatch and wattles back of the temple, which was considered to be the temporal dwelling place of the god who held domain over this part of Britannia. His eyes were rheumy with age and he sniffled as he talked.

"Do you remember when Commius made a sacrifice for the king's son here over a year ago?" Carnu asked the old man.

The druid nodded vigorously. "Adminius lay on the altar there," he said, pointing to it. "When the fires were lighted, the god was appeased and the prince was carried to Camulodunum on a cart."

"Do you remember an old man and a girl among those burned? Their skins were fairer than the Gauls and the girl's hair was like gold."

"I remember," said the old man. "A Gaul with them fought and was killed by the warriors who guarded Prince Adminius."

It was a natural mistake, Quintus thought. The old druid must have seen him bludgeoned by the guards when he'd sought to go to the aid of Veronica and Joseph.

"Did you see the girl and the old man consumed by the flames?" Carnu inquired.

The old man bobbed his head again, like a puppet in the traveling shows Quintus had seen in Rome and other cities.

"All the bodies were burned when I rekindled the fire."

Startled by the old druid's words, Quintus opened his mouth to speak, but Carnu put a restraining hand on his arm.

"Why do you say you rekindled the fire?" Carnu asked. "I saw the flames burning when we were leaving the grove with Prince Adminius upon a cart."

"You were hardly out of the grove when the storm came," the old priest explained. "I remember it well; never have I seen the gods loose so much rain. No doubt they were angry at the Gauls for wounding the son of the king."

"No doubt," Carnu agreed gravely. "What happened then?"

"The fires of the sacrifice were quenched."

"Were the Gauls dead?"

"Some were dead, others lived. The soldiers did not want to guard them in the storm, so they thrust spears through the walls of the cage and killed them all."

"You are sure all were killed? None escaped?"

"None escaped," the old druid said. "I watched the soldiers myself."

"What happened then?"

"In the morning the sun dried the wood and I rekindled the fire. All the bodies were consumed."

266

"You are sure of that?"

Again the old man nodded vigorously. "Only ashes remained."

Quintus had hardly dared hope he would discover anything of value, but the finality of the old man's assurance that Veronica and Joseph had met their deaths here seemed to settle the question once and for all. There was one consolation, however. If Veronica had been killed by the spears of the warriors, as the old druid described, then she had at least been spared the agony of the flames.

Carnu turned a grave face to Quintus. "He told much the same story when I came here to question him after you cured Adminius."

"I suppose it is true then," Quintus admitted resignedly.

"The captain must have been correct about the vases too," Carnu added. "They were no doubt imported into Gaul and smuggled across the Fretum Gallicum by the Veneti."

Leaving the Grove of the Druids, they followed a path along the shores of the stream. Shortly they came to where the mouth of the river began to widen and finally to a place where they could look out across the whitecapped waves of the channel toward Gaul. Here on a piece of high ground the Britanni had built a tower of stones and on top of it a platform where fires could be built.

Quintus thought this might be some sort of an altar, but Carnu explained that it fulfilled a more utilitarian purpose, as a guiding beacon for the seamen who sailed the boats in the attacks against the coast of Gaul to the east. If the boats were caught on the open water at night during one of the raids—or if smugglers were operating in the darkness—those left as keepers of the beacon could build a fire upon the tower to guide the others into the harbor formed by the mouth of the small river.

Quintus and Carnu climbed to the top of the stone tower and stood looking eastward toward Gaul, now only a faint dark shadow on the horizon barely distinguishable from a line of low-lying clouds. Remembering how Veronica had loved Gaul, their small but pleasant cottage in Lugdunum, and even their brief stay at the seaside in the village of Gesoriacum, Quintus could not help feeling a tug at his heart when he saw it again. Now that the probability of Veronica's death seemed settled beyond question, he supposed he was a fool to remain in Britannia where his life was in constant danger. Here on the coast he and Carnu could probably find transport across the narrow body of water. And once in Gaul he had only to reveal his identity as a tribune of the Roman army to be sure of transport to the headquarters of Lentulus Gaeticulus at Lugdunum.

Carnu voiced the same thought as he stood beside Quintus. Pointing southward along the coast to where a number of fishermen's boats were bobbing on the water just outside the line of breaking surf, he said, "Those boats are always smuggling back and forth between here and Gaul. If you are ready to cross over, we can easily hire one of them to set us on the other side."

Quintus could not help feeling a strange reluctance to leave Britannia, for by so doing he would be acknowledging once and for all that Veronica was dead. And yet he knew it was foolish to have any hope now.

"Still," Carnu added, "unless you are sure in your own mind, your soul will only be troubled if you leave Britannia and you will not be able to find happiness."

"I cannot find it anywhere without her."

"From what you have told me," Carnu said gravely, "your wife would not wish that. You say she believes in life after death as we druids do?"

"Yes," Quintus conceded. "That is true."

"And that one person can give his life to save the soul of another?"

"She and Joseph believed the son of their god gave his life for others."

"It is the same thing. Since she is happy wherever she is—expecting to see you after death—why cannot you be the same here on earth?"

"I have never been sure of immortal life," Quintus admitted.

"You carry the memory of her in your own heart, don't you?"

"Of course."

"Then she lives. You need no other assurance."

It was true. Merely by removing the small vase from his robe—where he carried it close to his heart—Quintus could bring back as vividly as on the day he had first seen her the picture of Veronica, serene and beautiful, as she had sat under the tree in the yard of Abijah.

"You do not follow our druidic beliefs," Carnu said almost diffidently, "so I have not spoken of this before. Southwest of here is a city the Romans call Aquae Sulis. Near it is an oracle which is said to give the true answer to any questions asked of it."

Quintus looked at him quickly. "Do you believe in this oracle?"

"I have been there," Carnu said gravely. "And I know that others have learned many strange things from it."

"True things?"

"Yes. Since you are still not certain your wife is dead, let us journey to the oracle and ask the question of it; perhaps then you may finally be at ease."

"But you believe the answer will be the same one the old man gave us—that she is dead?"

Carnu shrugged. "Who can tell what an oracle will reveal?" he said enigmatically.

3

Under other circumstances the weeks that followed would have been pleasant ones for Quintus while he and Carnu trudged the paths linking the towns along the southwest coast of Britannia. Moving across country from the Grove of the Druids, they were at first too close to Camulodunum for complete comfort. But once they had paid a fisherman to ferry them across the broad mouth of the Tamesis at Regulbium, where a bold headland jutted out into the Oceanum Atlanticum, they were in the country of the Cantii. This tribe, although a part of Cunobelinus' kingdom, was largely left to govern itself.

This was the area where Julius Caesar had made his lightning conquest nearly a hundred years before, and evidence of the brief Roman visit was everywhere, in deep ditches surrounding what had been camp sites of the legions, and the decaying walls of temporary Roman forts. At Rutupiae, Dubrae, and Lemanae they paused to show the little vase to fishermen who were also undoubtedly smugglers and ask if any had seen such wares brought over from Gaul. Everywhere, however, the answer was the same, a shake of the head and a disclaimer of ever having seen the small vases.

From Lemanae they followed a path that wound a few miles inland through an open woodland, skirting an area of marshy growth along the shore, and came finally to Anderida, where the remains of a Roman fortress were fairly well preserved. The answer to their query here was the same, but Quintus decided to travel along the coast at least as far as the larger town of Noviomagus, some three or four days' journey to the west. The westward direction of the island's shore line was taking them steadily farther and farther away from the coast of Gaul, thereby lessening the chances that smugglers could have brought in pottery like the vase they carried. If he learned nothing along this stretch of coast line, Quintus was determined to turn inland and consult the oracle.

At Noviomagus they were in the country of the Regni, who did not give allegiance to Cunobelinus, but Quintus and Carnu were adequately protected by their status as druids. The roads were crowded with priests and commoners alike, on the way to visit the oracle and the healing springs at what the Romans had called—because of the health-giving properties of its waters—Aquae Sulis.

At Noviomagus the two travelers struck inland, moving somewhat northwestward along a road that led

270

to Aquae Sulis by way of the small village christened Sorbiodunum by the Romans. Beyond this town they crossed over into the territory of the Belgae and immediately noticed a distinct change in the skills and life of the people. Except for differences in language— and there were remarkable similarities in the tongues— they might have been passing through the fertile central section of Gaul itself. Farming was vigorous; the plows used by farmers bore points tipped with iron whose ore was plentiful in this area. The people were intelligent, and skilled artisans plied many trades, including the smelting and forging of tin, lead, and iron.

The Belgae, Carnu explained, had come from Gaul, having invaded Britannia not much more than a hundred years in advance of the Romans under Julius Caesar. Settling in the eastern area along the seacoast, these energetic people had easily conquered the coastal tribes and penetrated inland to infiltrate the whole southern part of the island where the climate more nearly resembled that of their native Gaul. To the more backward Britanni these Belgae had brought their skills and natural energy. For this reason the southwestern areas of Britannia had developed rapidly ever since, as far as a point somewhat north of King Cunobelinus' capital at Camulodunum and westward along the coast beyond a city called Glevum located at the head of a considerable inlet.

Aquae Sulis was a big town, reminding Quintus in many ways of the Greek centers for the worship of Asklepios at Cos, Cnidus, and Pergamum. The springs bursting from the earth here were bitter and sharp in taste and were said to heal many diseases, although Quintus suspected that whatever action the water possessed came from its purgative qualities.

With so many people going and coming, seeking to cure their ills at the medicinal springs, the danger that Quintus might be recognized by someone from the region of Camulodunum or Londinium was considerably increased. He had let his beard grow while they were tramping through the countryside of Britannia, and his mustache now bristled as fiercely as any warrior of the Britanni. But his speech could still betray him, particularly here where many of the people were familiar with the Roman tongue because of their closer contact with the legions of Caesar.

For that reason—and because he was anxious to learn what, if anything, the oracle could tell him— Quintus urged Carnu to visit the site of the oracle at once. This lay, as seemed to be the custom with all druidic functions, in a grove of massive oaks outside the city of Aquae Sulis. As they were walking toward the oracle, they met many small groups of people returning from it, consulting the oracle being as important an activity in the town as drinking the water and soaking in the tepid baths.

Quintus was busy wording the question he would ask the oracle and so did not notice a small band of men in druidic garb who met them a few yards away as they walked toward the grove. Had he done so he would have seen Carnu stiffen at the sight of a particularly massive figure among the group and turn his head quickly aside before he could be recognized.

The temple where the oracle was located was not particularly impressive, at least not in comparison with the great temples Quintus had seen in Rome, Ephesus, Antioch, and Alexandria. No one could doubt its great antiquity, however. The walls were built of massive graying stone cut in huge blocks, reminding Quintus of the ancient tombs of the Egyptian kings which he had seen on the banks of the Nile. In the damp climate pervading this part of Britannia the stones had long since become covered with moss and lichens, giving the walls a dank and miasmatic appearance that was depressing rather than inspiring, as would be expected of a place from which came the wisest pronouncements of the druidic cult.

In an open square among the great towering oaks that made up the grove was the usual altar built of massive stones. Around it was one of the strange circular rings of hewn stone held up on sturdy pillars. This ring was considerably larger than the one Quintus had seen at the Grove of the Druids near Camulodunum. The construction was identical, however, showing that it fulfilled the same religious function, whatever that could be. Quintus had never asked Carnu to break his vow by revealing the secrets of the druids and had no intention of doing so now in order to satisfy his natural curiosity about the great stone rings.

As they approached the temple, the massive door swung open, moved by no hand that Quintus could see. He was familiar enough with mechanics, however, to realize that a relatively simple device could have accomplished this, while at the same time creating an impression of awe and wonder in the minds of those not familiar with such machines. The outer room into which they entered was wide and high-ceilinged, the roof being supported by great timbers hewn from individual tree trunks so long ago that they had become dark with time. The air inside was cool and pleasant, and there was no sound save the soft rush of water.

The central part of the temple's interior was taken up by a smaller room or compartment whose walls were cut by six doorways. From it came the rushing sound Quintus had heard when he entered the temple itself. As they approached the central room, the sound grew louder.

Carnu had stopped at one of the doors leading into the inner room, and Quintus paused beside him. As yet they had seen no one inside the temple housing the oracle or heard anyone. When Carnu spoke, his voice echoed eerily against the walls in the silence.

"O Keeper of All Knowledge," he said in the lyrical tones used by the druidic priests when they addressed their gods. "We come seeking the answer to a question that gravely perplexes one of us."

"Advance," a voice said from inside the smaller room. The tones were strangely liquid, as if they flowed in a stream like water itself.

The two moved into the smaller enclosure. It was little more than large enough to encompass the fountain that gushed from the center of a giant stone. This appeared to be embedded in the floor of the room itself, but Quintus judged that a spring had actually burst from this rock and the rest of the temple had been built around it. The water from the spring or fountain swirled into a basin, in the center of which was a funnel-shaped opening leading downward. Its walls were of polished obsidian or some similar dark stone, making the depths of the funnel-shaped opening invisible.

Striking the side of the basin, the water was given a swirling motion, pouring down the polished black walls of the funnel-like opening in the form of a whirlpool and disappearing into the dark depths. This rush of water downward caused the sound they had heard when they entered the temple.

"Make your offering to the god who gives life, even after death," the sepulchral voice instructed them. It seemed to come from the fountain itself, but Quintus guessed that it rose actually from the funnel-shaped tube leading downward from the basin. Such a device would be simple enough to make, merely by letting the voice of an unseen priest travel along a tube cut through the rock and thence rise seemingly from the water itself.

Loosening his purse, Quintus tossed in several of the gold coins minted in Camulodunum. They disappeared down the dark maw of the fountain, but by straining his ears he was sure he heard a distinct clink when they struck a solid object somewhere in the room which he was sure now had been excavated below the temple itself. Already he was regretting having come here, for it seemed that the oracle, like similar devices in other temples he had seen, was pure charlatanry, designed to take the gold of those who sought advice from it, gold which no doubt then went into the pockets of the druids operating the oracle.

"Who seeks an answer to a question?" the sepulchral voice boomed.

"My brother here, who comes from Gaul," Carnu said gravely. "The woman he loves—a golden-haired one from the eastern lands—was captured a year ago by the warriors of King Cunobelinus and chosen as a sacrifice by fire in the Grove of the Druids near Camulodunum. He would know whether she still lives—and where."

For a moment there was no answer, then the ghostly voice spoke through the rushing of the waters. "All live forever who follow our teachings," it said.

It was an enigmatic answer, and for a moment Quintus thought the oracle had finished speaking. Then the voice began to flow again.

"Let our brother from Gaul seek the woman above the earth and the water," the deep voice said. "The voice of the god has spoken."

Only the rushing of the water broke the silence in the room now. And it was obvious that the oracle had completed its pronouncement. Carnu took Quintus by the elbow and guided him quickly from the room. Only when they were outside the temple and clear of the open grove itself did he allow Quintus to speak.

"I have been cheated," Quintus said angrily. "Anyone could see that the voice of a priest was piped into that funnel-shaped opening in the stone."

"You and I could see it," Carnu agreed. "But not the ordinary people who come here."

"And he told me nothing! He took my money and told me nothing."

"You are wrong, my friend," Carnu said gravely. "The oracle at least told you your wife is dead."

"How could that be? It spoke only in riddles."

"Oracles usually speak in riddles. This one is easier to understand than most."

"Seek the woman above the earth and the water," Quintus repeated. "The words mean nothing."

"You are angry or you would understand," Carnu said soothingly. "You have often said your wife and the other followers of the man you call Jesus of Nazareth believed they would dwell with him in the heavens after death?"

"What difference does that make?"

"The heavens are above the earth and the water."

Quintus nodded slowly. "You could be right," he admitted reluctantly.

"I hesitated to tell you of the oracle at first, because

I wished to spare you the pain of knowing for sure that your wife no longer lives. Now you need not be afraid of leaving Britannia."

Quintus did not speak; his heart was too heavy for words.

"When the man called Julius Caesar came to Britannia," Carnu said, "he brought death and the sword to those who opposed him. But he left other things, too, and the promise of many more when the Romans returned, things like roads, tools, the plows of the Belgae, and steel from the east whose hardness lets men fashion metals less hard than itself. These things and many others—even physicians like yourself to heal the sick—the Romans will bring when they come again."

"But your people will resist and many will be killed."

"If Caractacus and Commius have their way," Carnu agreed. "But you have traveled over the region where the Roman armies will land. You can draw maps and describe the towns, their strength and their weaknesses. Go to Rome now and take this knowledge with you. The oracle has spoken; your wife is dead. You cannot help her by staying here any longer, but you can save the lives of many who would do otherwise by taking the knowledge you possess back to your friends so their invasion will be swift and thorough when it comes."

Quintus nodded slowly. "I have been selfish in thinking only of myself and my own sorrow. We will rest and drink the water of Aquae Sulis tomorrow. The next day we will return to Noviomagus and seek a boat to take us to Gaul."

"We cannot go back to Aquae Sulis," said Carnu quickly.

"Why?"

"Today, as we were walking toward the oracle, I saw Commius."

"Commius! Why would he come here?"

"It is a shrine. He was with a band of fellow druids

come to take the water and seek answers from the oracle."

This was bad news indeed. Quintus had thought himself rid of the archdruid once and for all. Yet it would be a perfectly natural thing for Commius to visit this central shrine of druidic worship to which came pilgrims from all parts of Britannia.

"Did he see you?" he asked quickly. "Or me?"

"I think not," Carnu said. "Your face was not turned to him, and I looked away as soon as I recognized him. Besides, he would hardly expect to find you in the robes of a druid."

"Then we are probably safe."

"For a little while—unless Commius talks to the priest who is the voice of the oracle. If he learns that two men were asking about a woman with pale hair captured on the shores of Gaul, he will know at once that you are still in Britannia."

"We must leave immediately then," Quintus said. "Surely we can hire a boat at Noviomagus or Anderida to take us across the channel."

"The nearest way back to Camulodunum is by boat along the coast," Carnu pointed out. "Commius probably debarked at Noviomagus and will return there to take a ship again. We might encounter him on the way."

"Then we must travel overland, in a direction Commius would not expect us to take." Quintus' face brightened. "Why not head directly for Londinium? We will be safe there until another ship comes from Rome—at least if we watch our step."

"We could take the road east to Cunerio and thence across the country to strike the river Tamesis west of Londinium," Carnu agreed. "There we could buy a small boat and float down river to Londinium itself."

"It is a good plan," Quintus agreed. "But I would give much to see Commius' face when he learns we have outwitted him."

"Let us defer that pleasure for the moment," Carnu said soberly. "I heard in Aquae Sulis that the Dobuni attacked the Belgae again recently. We will have to cross their borders in order to reach the river Tamesis."

"We are druids," Quintus reminded him. "And as such granted safe conduct anywhere."

"I will feel safe when we are in Londinium again," Carnu said. "Preferably on the deck of one of your Roman ships."

4

Quintus and Carnu headed almost due eastward near the boundary between the Belgae and the warring Dobuni. In this way they could avoid entering any large town while approaching the territory of the Atrebates, who were not at war. Although their status as druids protected them at least theoretically from being molested, they had no wish to become involved even innocently in one of the tribal conflicts which still raged in the area outside that consolidated and made peaceful by King Cunobelinus.

It was winter now and the sun was low on the southern horizon at noonday. Mornings were frosty, and even at midday it was often cold. As traveling priests, they were given beds at most of the farms and estates they passed or allowed to sleep in warm, fragrant hay piled in the barn so they did not suffer from the cold. The people were usually eager to supply their meager needs in return for Carnu's blessing, but this region had been the scene of many border skirmishes recently between the Belgae and the Dobuni, so much of the land was desolate and there was want in nearly every village.

"You can see why this country would be better off under Roman rule," Carnu said as they trudged along. "Then the people would be at peace with each other and would not destroy themselves in petty warfare."

"Your religion may be destroyed too," Quintus reminded him. "Most of the druids have been driven out of Gaul by the Roman authorities."

"Only because they incited the people to resist, as

278

Commius is doing," Carnu said. "Even conquerors cannot erase what a man believes from his mind."

"They can keep him from voicing his convictions."

"Not forever. If you know you are right, others will be led to believe with you—by your action if not by your words."

Quintus smiled. "You should have been a lawyer, Carnu. You turn every statement to fit your arguments."

"We druids are trained to be both lawgivers and judges."

"It is a great power to be wielded by one set of men."

"Surely you have lawgivers in Rome."

"Yes. The senate makes the laws, and we have judges to see that they are enforced fairly—except when the emperor sets himself above all."

"With a wise ruler that should make no difference."

"True, but Caligula is corrupt and greedy. When people have no confidence in their ruler they soon lose confidence in their laws and those who administer them."

"It is the same here. Commius uses his religious power to achieve political control over the king and the people."

"You mean through Prince Caractacus?"

Carnu nodded. "Cunobelinus has always held Commius in check, but the king grows old and his hand is no longer strong on the reins of government. The effects of it can be seen even here between the Belgae and the Dobuni."

"But they are not ruled by Cunobelinus."

"Their lands border with the Catauvellauni," Carnu pointed out. "When Cunobelinus was strong, the neighboring tribes did not dare fight with each other, lest he move against them."

"It is the same with Rome," Quintus admitted. "With a strong emperor, the whole empire is usually at peace. But when a weak one ascends the throne, rebellion soon breaks out."

They were walking through a stretch of dense

woodland near the town of Cunerio when suddenly they heard the sounds of shouts and the clash of metal on metal ahead of them.

Carnu stopped. "It must be a border clash," he said. "We had better not go on."

"The trees will hide us," Quintus pointed out. "We can move closer and see what is happening."

Moving from trunk to trunk, they approached the scene of conflict. Before they could reach it, however, the sounds suddenly died away, as if the fight had moved on.

Carnu breathed a sigh of relief. "It must have been a small clash."

"There may still be wounded. Or dead to be disposed of."

"It is my duty as a priest and yours as a physician to attend any who may need us," Carnu agreed. "Let us go on."

They soon came to a small clearing where the encounter had apparently taken place. The grass and underbrush had been trampled down considerably, and there was blood on some of the bushes. They saw no signs of any of the people who had taken part in the conflict, however, and Quintus and Carnu were about to move on, when a groan came to their ears from the dense underbrush at one side of the clearing. Moving toward the sound, they saw that a rough path had been trampled into the brush and, by following it a few paces, came upon the body of a man. He was obviously grievously wounded, for a pool of blood had accumulated around his left shoulder as he lay on the ground. Apparently the wounded man had dragged himself from the scene of battle in an attempt to save his life, probably during the skirmish Quintus and Carnu had heard.

Quintus made a hurried examination. The wounded man had obviously lost a great deal of blood, but his pulse was strong, though hurried in its beat. He wore the usual tunic and loose breeches of the Britanni but no distinguishing marks to tell what tribe he belonged to.

280

The wound was on the back part of the shoulder, a deep cut in the muscles that was still bleeding freely. From its location Quintus was able to tell approximately what had happened. A sword thrust or dagger cut had evidently been aimed at the man's back and had struck him across the left shoulder blade. This broad bone had stayed the thrust and kept the weapon from penetrating the chest itself and killing him instantly.

"It is a grievous wound," Carnu said. "Surely he will die."

"Not if I can stop the bleeding. Tear a piece of cloth from his tunic; I need it to press against the wound."

While Carnu worked, Quintus drew the edges of the wound together with his left hand. Holding them thus, he pressed hard against the skin with the palm of his right hand. He had been taught to stop bleeding in this way in Alexandria and was pleased to see the flow lessen noticeably.

When Carnu handed him a pad made from the bright-colored fabric of the wounded man's tunic, Quintus released the pressure of his right hand long enough to apply the cloth to the wound. The victim showed no signs of returning consciousness, and Quintus guessed that he had also suffered a blow on the head during the combat, or that the rapid loss of blood and the exertion of crawling into the woods had brought on a deep faint.

When he was sure the bleeding was controlled, Quintus bound the compress of cloth tightly against the wound. This done, he was able to examine the rest of the man's body carefully but could find no other injury except a slight swelling over one temple.

"He has a good chance of living," he told Carnu. "Can you tell what tribe he belongs to?"

The druid shook his head. "He does not look like a warrior, and he carried no weapons that I can discover."

"Perhaps he was a traveler like ourselves."

"Then robbery must have been the motive."

"Who can say? When he regains consciousness we will ask him."

"We had better build a shelter," Carnu said. "It will be getting cold soon, and we might have to remain here overnight."

They busied themselves cutting small branches from the underbrush. These they wove into a sort of thatch against the dampness that was always prevalent here after nightfall. When the shelter was finished, Quintus struck flint to his knife and ignited a bit of tinder, scraped as usual from inside the bark of a dead tree. When a brisk fire was burning, they moved the injured man to the protection of the thatch shelter. He seemed not to have lost any strength but still showed no sign of returning consciousness.

Quintus examined the dressing again. It was stained with blood but not soaked, and he judged that the bleeding had been largely controlled. As he was turning the wounded man back, after adjusting the bandage, he heard a shout from Carnu and looked up to see a tall warrior raising his arm to hurl a spear directly at his unprotected back.

Quintus was on his knees and therefore unable to move quickly enough to throw himself out of the path of the spear. Carnu had been placing a handful of faggots on the fire when he saw the attacker. Dropping these now, he threw himself across Quintus' body in time to receive the point of the spear directly into his back.

Quintus heard the scrape of metal against bone as the heavy spearhead went home in the druid's body. The sound freed him from the momentary paralysis of shock at the sight of the attacker. Even as the warrior who had thrown the spear was drawing his sword to finish them both, Quintus twisted himself from beneath Carnu's body. Seizing one of the faggots Carnu had dropped, he was upon the attacker before the latter could draw either sword or dagger, belaboring him about the head so the man was not able to make any effective defense.

Driven by a murderous rage at the wanton and unnecessary killing of an unarmed man, Quintus hammered the attacker until the latter slumped to the ground. Jerking the bronze sword from his scabbard, he was about to thrust the other through when he realized that the man was unconscious and turned to where Carnu lay with the spear point deep in his chest.

Death was already beginning to glaze the eyes of the druid. The long blade of sharp bronze had been driven almost completely through his slender body, and from the location of the wound Quintus was sure it had penetrated a vital organ.

"Kill the attacker and burn his body," Carnu gasped. "That way my soul will live again." He coughed once, grimaced with pain, and was dead.

Sick with sorrow and anguish, Quintus was quite willing to do as Carnu had begged him. A cursory glance told him the man was already dead, however, his skull crushed by the faggot with which Quintus had struck him. As for the first victim, his condition appeared to be unchanged.

Seen in retrospect, the story of what had happened here seemed clear now. The warrior Quintus had killed must have dealt the first man what he judged to be a fatal wound, during the commotion they had heard shortly before, leaving him for dead. For some reason he had returned later, perhaps having seen the light of their fire through the woods, or again he might have heard their voices. Enraged by the fact that Quintus and Carnu had succored his intended victim, the attacker had tried to kill them. Only Carnu's quick action in sacrificing his own life had saved Quintus from being impaled by the spear.

It took Quintus several hours to gather enough dry faggots and logs to form a pyre. When it was finished, he dragged the dead body of the Britanni over and tossed it upon the pyre but kept all weapons and clothing for his own protection. Next he carried the body of Carnu to a beautiful spot near by beneath a great oak and laboriously scraped out a shallow opening, using the sword and spear which the attacker had carried. Over the body he piled earth and then built a small cairn of the stones such as he had seen erected over the graves of other Britanni. When this sad task was finished, he took a brand from the fire and lit the pyre upon which the murderer was to be sacrificed for the welfare of Carnu's soul, according to the custom of the druids.

Quintus had taken the precaution of removing the dead warrior's clothing. Now he removed his own robes which were somewhat the worse for wear and cast them into the fire. With Carnu beside him he had felt safe in posing as another druid. Alone, however, he knew he would easily give himself away and earn the anger of the priests who would condemn him to death if he were captured alive. While the fire burned, he put on the breeches and tunic of the dead man and laced on the heavy-soled sandals which made up the customary footgear of the Britanni. The round cap of bronze he used as a container to carry water from a nearby brook. The attacker had carried a package of bread and cheese, and these Quintus ate while he watched the fire finish consuming the body.

A groan from the wounded man brought Quintus to his side. His pulse seemed stronger and his face was moist and a little flushed, as if consciousness were returning. His breathing, too, had quickened. Soon he opened his eyes and looked up at Quintus with the blank stare of someone waking to unfamiliar surroundings.

"You have been wounded," Quintus told him in the dialect spoken at Camulodunum. "Someone tried to kill you, but you are safe now."

The wounded man's lips moved, but Quintus had to lean close to hear the words. And even then he was not sure he could believe what he had heard.

" 'Father, forgive them,' " the wounded Britanni said. " 'They know not what they do.' "

Quintus had last heard those words in Antioch, in the synagogue where Joseph of Arimathea had been teaching while they waited for Pontius Pilate to come from Caesarea on his way to Rome. They had been spoken by Jesus on the cross, Joseph had said. Yet here were the selfsame words on the lips of a wounded man in Britannia at the other end of the Roman world, thousands of miles from that hill outside the gates of Jerusalem.

Quintus' heart took a great leap of joy. For in all this part of the world only two people could possibly have known those words and taught them to others.

They were Joseph of Arimathea and Veronica!

5

In the dying light of the funeral pyre Quintus watched beside the injured man who now slept quietly. The moment of consciousness when he'd spoken the words uttered by Jesus on the cross had been brief. Before Quintus could question him further, he had lapsed into a stupor again. Now Quintus had no choice save to wait until he was able to speak again and reveal where he had learned the words of the Galilean healer.

That Joseph or Veronica had taught the words of Jesus to the wounded Britanni, Quintus had not a moment of doubt. The whole pattern of events beginning with his discovery of the small vase with the scene from Jerusalem painted upon it pointed to the fact that Veronica—at least—had somehow escaped the sacrificial pyre in the Grove of the Druids. Just how the man lying unconscious before him had come in contact with her, Quintus had no way of knowing. But he was sure it had been at least long enough to learn the story of Jesus and of his death at Jerusalem. And if he had known Veronica, the man would surely be able to lead him to her.

The knowledge that Veronica was alive—or at least had been alive for a while after her apparent death in the flames—filled Quintus with a vast urgency to find her. Dropping to his knees—as he had seen her do— he spoke a prayer of thanks that he had been led to this spot at just this moment. It did not seem at all out of keeping that his prayer was to the Jewish God, the one Veronica and Joseph had spoken of as the Most High. Or that it should be uttered—as they were accustomed to pray—in the name of Jesus of Nazareth whom they believed to be the Son of God.

While the hours passed, Quintus dozed beneath the shelter, getting up every now and then to pile more faggots on the fire. A damp foggy cold covered much of this country in winter and, although the clothing which he had removed from the dead Britanni was fairly warm, the chill penetrated Quintus' body quickly whenever he had to leave the comfort of the fire to gather more wood. Impatient as he was to learn about Veronica, however, he did not disturb his patient, realizing that sleep would bring back the man's senses more quickly and effectively than anything he could do. Meanwhile, he could only wait for the man to recover consciousness.

Just before dawn Quintus was awakened from an uneasy sleep by the voice of his patient. He tossed a faggot upon the coals which had burned low and in the light of the flames saw that the man's face was much pinker than it had been. His skin was no longer damp either. Instead it was dry with the fires of fever, and when he opened his eyes they, too, burned with the light of delirium. He spoke, but the words tumbled out in a babble of meaningless phrases and sounds. With a sinking heart Quintus realized that the one person in whose mind was locked the knowledge of where Veronica was now lay deep in delirium.

Discouraged as he was by this unexpected turn of events, Quintus had no choice except to make every effort to save the life of his companion. For should the man die from fever caused by the gaping wound in his back, the secret of Veronica's whereabouts would die with him.

Quintus had seen this very picture too many times in severe wounds not to realize how heavily the odds were now weighted against his learning anything more about Veronica. A wound like this, with fever and delirium coming on so quickly, usually resulted in death.

When finally the sun came from behind the fog and clouds, Quintus decided to explore his surroundings. This meant leaving his patient alone, but the man was sleeping again and he did not intend to be gone very long. Besides, the risk of leaving him was small compared with the urgency of finding more adequate protection than the small thatched shelter afforded.

He found nothing in his first venture away from the fire. Returning, he discovered that his patient was still asleep and continued the search. On the third try he found what he was looking for, a shallow cave in a ragged rocky outcrop only a little distance away, deep enough to provide shelter and with a screen of dense underbrush in front to hide the light of the fire. It afforded effective shelter and at the same time a measure of protection. Fortunately a branch leading from a nearby spring passed only a few paces in front of the cave, giving a convenient source of water.

At this time of the year there were only a few hours of sunshine during the day in this region, and Quintus was forced to hurry. First he carried his patient to the cave and then he brought some coals from the original fire to start another. With the fire burning briskly and the underbrush in front of the cave keeping out the cold wind, the new home was almost cozy.

The next problem Quintus faced was that of getting food. It was useless to hunt for berries at this time of year, so he prowled along the bank of the brook where he had seen some fish when he was getting water. Using the spear, he managed, after a number of failures, to spit several fish which he broiled over the coals.

The wounded man was in too deep a delirium to eat, but Quintus was able to give him water carried from the brook in the metal cap. The patient talked almost constantly when he was awake, but the words were for the most part disjointed and unintelligible, save that many of them had to do with the story of Jesus of Nazareth. Once he spoke a name that sounded like Veronica, but Quintus could not be certain.

Several days passed during which Quintus did everything he could to keep up his patient's strength and relieve the inflammation in the wound which had brought on the delirium. Fish supplied most of his diet, but once, returning from the brook, he was able to

287

knock down a hare with his spear as it darted across in front of him. He skinned it and boiled it over the flames in the metal cap, obtaining a nutritious broth which the sick man drank with relish.

And then, four days after they had come to the cave, Quintus returned from an expedition to the brook for fish and found his patient's eyes clear and the fever apparently broken. The man's face showed apprehension when he saw the spear, and Quintus realized that he must have recognized the clothing and thought him the original attacker, come back to finish him off.

"You were gravely wounded," Quintus said in the tongue of the Britanni. "I have tried to make you well."

The sick man looked at him for a long moment. Then, as if reassured by what he saw in Quintus' face, he smiled. "The other—whose clothes you wear?"

"I killed him when he came back to kill you."

"I remember now. He attacked me as I walked through the woods."

"Are you of the Belgae?"

"Yes. My name is Brythar."

"Do you dwell near by?"

Brythar shook his head. "I live on an island named Avalon."

The name meant nothing to Quintus. "Is it in the sea?"

Brythar smiled. "A very beautiful island—in a lake."

Quintus almost hesitated to ask the next question. But he was anxious to know what Brythar could tell him about Veronica—even if the news were bad. "When you were wounded, you said, 'Father, forgive them; for they know not what they do.' Where did you hear these words?"

The man's face lit up, very much as Veronica's and Joseph's faces always had done, Quintus remembered, when they had spoken of Jesus of Nazareth.

"They are the words of the Son of God," Brythar said.

In spite of his pounding heart Quintus held himself in check. "Where did you learn them?"

"In Avalon, from the woman who paints."

From the bosom of his tunic Quintus took the small vase he had purchased at Londinium. "Like this?"

Brythar glanced at the vase. "Yes. She says the thorns bloom like this on the hill where Jesus died to save us all."

"Is her name Veronica?"

Brythar's eyes widened with amazement. "Who are you that speaks our tongue with another voice, yet knows the woman who paints?"

"She is my wife," Quintus said. "I thought her dead, but you have just told me she lives."

"She does live," Brythar said warmly. "She taught us to mold the small vases on the wheel and to bake in the color. Because of her the potters of Avalon have prospered and we have learned of him who came to give us all eternal life—not as the druids promise, where a man can live again as a dog or a pig—but to dwell with the Son of God forever in the high place where he lives until he comes again."

6

The sun was shining brightly, although the air was still cool with the grip of winter, when Quintus at last approached the island of Avalon. To his surprise it lay only a few days' journey from where he had nursed Brythar back to health, at the edge of a great lake. Brythar had improved rapidly, once his fever had broken. In a few days he had been able to walk, but they had traveled slowly, keeping within the limits of his strength.

Twice they had been forced to hide while bands of warriors passed. Brythar identified them as Dobuni and explained that it had been one of the Dobuni who had set upon him in the forest, attacking him before he could explain that the men of Avalon bore no grudge against anyone and always traveled without arms. Quintus was fully armed, but he had no wish to engage in even single combat with anyone. He had searched for

Veronica too long and had come too far now to let anything interfere with the ending of that quest.

And so they came at last—after traveling through some of the loveliest country Quintus had ever seen in this island of Britannia—to a region of green meadows and shallow valleys, rich with trees, grass, and bushes, much of which remained green even here at wintertime. In this beautiful region was the large lake which, Brythar had told him, contained the isle of Avalon.

It was about noon when they came over a little hillock and Brythar pointed down to his town. The village was like nothing Quintus had actually seen before. And yet the houses at least were familiar, for they were exactly like the one painted on the larger vase he had bought in the market place of Londinium. The village spread over an area of considerable size along the edge of the island in a marshy area extending along the shore. Back of it the island was heavily wooded, and in the central portion the ground was considerably higher.

The village, Quintus judged from his first view, included close to a hundred houses or huts. These were circular in shape and built over the marshy area. Some had a solid foundation of logs and brush; others were supported on stiltlike structures made of hewn timbers. The outer border of the village was in the form of a rough semicircle but irregularly shaped. There had apparently been no attempt to make any systematic arrangement of streets, the houses being built almost helter-skelter above the marsh. All were of similar construction, being basically a thatch of wattles—over which mud or clay had been plastered. Upon some the clay had dried in the sun until at this distance it appeared to have almost the consistency of brick. From the fact that a thin pillar of smoke drifted skyward above the covered roof tops of many of the huts, Quintus judged that they contained some sort of an open hearth or fireplace which probably served both for cooking and warming, as did most such fireplaces he had seen in the huts of the farmer people of Britannia.

At one side of the town was a roughly built but

apparently strong landing stage. Moored to this were a number of rafts and canoes, the latter having been hollowed out from logs.

"My people are not warriors," Brythar said with a note of pride in his voice. "We are potters and artisans, as our fathers were before us. Because we do not make war, we can sell our wares to everyone."

"A satisfactory arrangement," Quintus commented. "As long as others respect your status."

"They always have," Brythar said. "If I had been near our village, the Dobuni warrior would not have attacked me. But I was searching for pigments to use in painting our pottery and had to go into the territory of some Dobuni who do not know us."

Quintus did not argue the point; he was too anxious to find Veronica. His experience had been that as men indulged in warfare more extensively, the lust to kill usually grew in them until they lost all respect for the rights of others.

The area of water separating the isle of Avalon from the shore of the lake was narrow here. When they came to the shore Brythar loosed one of the hollowed-out canoes from its moorings and held it steady while Quintus stepped in and took a seat in the bow. Brythar then shoved off and quickly paddled to the landing of the village.

They disembarked and Quintus waited while Brythar moored the craft with some others to the landing. There seemed to be no particular question of property rights here, for no names or other means of identification that Quintus could see showed on the boats or the rafts.

"Where will Veronica be?" he asked.

Brythar pointed to a large building that stood to one side of the village itself on some higher ground. "She lives and works there and we meet near by to worship," he said. "Leave your weapons here; you will have no need for them on the isle of Avalon."

Quintus dropped the weapons into the canoe. Something about the whole appearance of this village—in addition to what he had learned in his talk with Brythar

—spoke of peace and love for one another, rather than of competition and bloody combat.

"You will want to go to her alone," said Brythar understandingly. "I will seek out my family and tell them I am still alive."

A narrow platform built above the water connected the village with the higher ground where the larger building Brythar had pointed out was located. Quintus' heart was beating rapidly as he hurried along the platform. Now that he was nearing the end of his quest, the whole thing seemed almost a dream. And then he felt the small vase in his tunic pressing against his body and knew that it was not.

The building he was approaching stood to one side on higher and more solid ground. From the hum of voices and the whir of potters' wheels he judged that it was the pottery shop for the entire village. This was corroborated by the sight of a large chimney at one side which probably served the oven used for baking the wares. Not wanting to meet Veronica where others were, he walked around the building to see if he could find her.

Another structure stood just behind the pottery house, he saw now, hidden by the larger building. A wooden cross hewn from saplings stood above the door of the smaller building, just such a cross as often identified the places of worship used by those who followed Jesus of Nazareth.

Moving around the pottery shed, Quintus came to an open space on the protected southern side of the building where the sun shone brightly. A slender figure sat here, her gaze intent upon the delicate scenes she was painting upon a small vase. It was a familiar scene to Quintus, as was the golden aureole of her hair and the graceful slender body, the skilled fingers holding the brush. He'd last seen her in the midst of the flames at the Grove of the Druids many days' journey across the breadth of Britannia, but she had not changed. She still had the same delicate beauty, the same serenity, and the aura of goodness and loveliness which he remembered from that day in Jerusalem so long ago when he had seen her for the first time.

For a moment he did not speak her name, content to stand there and drink in her loveliness, just as he had seen it in his dreams so often since he'd lost her. Busy at her work, she had not yet realized she was being observed.

"Beloved." He spoke finally in her own tongue, using the word she had taught him. At the sound her body went rigid and the brush dropped from suddenly nerveless fingers.

Slowly Veronica turned her head. When her eyes met his, the light he wanted to see more than anything else suddenly sprang into being there. Then, dropping her paints and the tray of vases she had been holding upon her knees, she ran to throw herself into his arms and lift her lips blindly, her eyes filled with tears of happiness.

7

When they were able to speak again—the joy of their reunion had removed any need for words—Veronica led Quintus to a bench beneath a large tree that gave shade to the area in summer. "How did you find me?" she asked.

"The little vases, with the thornbushes blooming on the hillside. I found one of them in a shop in Londinium."

"I painted that scene because I knew you would recognize it if you saw it," she said, her eyes shining. "I must have painted hundreds during the past six months."

"I saw several of them in Londinium, but I hardly dared believe even then that you were still alive. When the old druid at the grove insisted you had been killed by the soldiers that day, I was almost ready to give up hope."

"I wanted to die when I saw them bludgeon you down," she confessed. "They carried you away, but I could not be sure you were alive. Then the rain came and put out the flames. The guards thrust their spears into the cage to kill us, but I was carrying the veil and it protected me."

"You were not harmed?"

"No, but one spear went into Uncle Joseph's back. I managed to crawl out from beneath the pile of bodies while the storm was raging. The rain had driven the guards away, and I was able to pull him out without anyone knowing we had escaped. We crawled through the woods in the rain until I found an empty hut where I could bind up Uncle Joseph's wound. We stayed there a few days, living on fruits and berries, and then moved on."

"Surely you didn't cross Britannia by foot."

"Jesus guided us," she said simply. "We had no idea where we were going, but at every step I could almost feel his touch, showing me the way."

"How did you come here?"

"We were exhausted and could go no further when we reached the lake. I found an old raft and somehow we managed to crawl upon it. The wind blew us to Avalon. The people were peaceful and did not harm us."

"And you have been here ever since?"

"Yes. They are good people, Quintus, potters like my family. I taught them what I know, and in gratitude they listened when Uncle Joseph and I spoke to them of God and his Son. Many have been brought to Jesus."

"I know. Brythar told me."

"He is the leader of the church here, the first in all of Britannia. You did a great service to Avalon in saving his life."

"I am beginning to think I have done nothing save follow the dictates of a power greater than any of us," he admitted soberly.

Veronica's eyes shone as she took his hand and pressed it against her cheek. "Uncle Joseph always said you would come to see the truth, once God's purpose for you was revealed."

"But what could that be?"

"He brought you to Britannia—and I came with you. Here we can teach others about Jesus."

"Even the oracle at Aquae Sulis must have been part of the plan then," Quintus said wonderingly.

"What do you mean?"

"When I consulted the oracle, it said I should seek you above the land and the water. I thought it meant you had died and gone to live with your god, but the oracle was really telling me you were here on the isle of Avalon. These houses—the ones you painted on the vases—are above the land and the water."

"Jesus said not a sparrow is lost from the sight of God," Veronica said. "Why shouldn't he speak through the voice of a druid, just as he guided you to the spot where Brythar lay wounded so you could save him from death."

"Carnu did that," Quintus told her. "One day I will tell you about him and everything that has happened since we came to Britannia. Now let us go and find Joseph."

"The wound made by the spear of the warriors at the Grove of the Druids never did heal," she told him. "Uncle Joseph grew steadily weaker, and when the veil did not heal him, we knew Jesus had called him to heaven. He lived only two months after we came to Avalon."

"Then his death is my fault, in a way."

"Don't say that," Veronica protested. "It isn't true."

"But it is. Had I made him remain in Rome, or even in Lugdunum, he would be alive today."

"Uncle Joseph never once doubted that he was obeying God's will in all of this," Veronica assured him. "He died happy, Quintus. Not only was he going to live with Jesus, but he knew the seed he had planted in Gaul and here in Britannia would multiply and expand—as it is doing. He was so sure you would find me that he left a message for you."

"A message?"

"As he was dying he made me promise to plant a thornbush on his resting place."

"But why a thorn?"

295

Her smile was enigmatic. "There are many here, and they are very beautiful. Come with me and I will show you."

She led him to the small church the people of Avalon had erected back of the pottery shed. There, on the south side of the building where the sun shone bright and warm as it did in Joseph's garden at Jerusalem where the body of Jesus had lain, Veronica showed Quintus the place where the people of Avalon had lovingly buried Joseph of Arimathea.

A thornbush stood in the center of the grave. And although it was the winter season, the bush was covered with gloriously beautiful white blossoms.

" 'Tell Quintus to watch the bush when the winter comes,' was his message to you," Veronica said softly. "Now you can see why."

Looking at the flowering thorn, Quintus knew at last that he understood all the things Joseph of Arimathea —and Veronica—had wanted him to know. As surely as the thorn of Avalon bloomed here in midwinter, so surely did he know that the gentle old man he'd come to love was not really dead. Instead Joseph of Arimathea was with him he served, Jesus of Nazareth —the man Quintus could not hold back from serving any more. Like Jesus and all who served him, Joseph, too, had triumphed over death.

"It is a miracle," he whispered, but Veronica shook her head.

"No, darling," she said. "We—Uncle Joseph and I —saw Jesus himself. We felt him ever afterward in our hearts and were content. Some—like Jonas the hunchback and you—needed a sign before you could really come to know him. There is the sign by which everyone can know death is not the end—the winter thorn of Avalon."

Keep Up With The BESTSELLERS!

Keep Up With The
BESTSELLERS!